Early Praise for *Til...*

"*Till There Was You* explores what happens when an aspiring chef meets a musician on the edge of fame and becomes his inspiration for a hit single—in other words, it's a complete delight! Lindsay Hameroff's debut is witty, warm, and charming with a healthy dose of hilarious one-liners and clever dialogue. Fans of Emily Henry and Robinne Lee's *The Idea of You* are going to go crazy for this one!"
—Jennifer Close, author of *Marrying the Ketchups*

"Falling for a talented musician who writes dreamy songs about you is pure wish fulfillment, and that's exactly what Lindsay Hameroff delivers in *Till There Was You*! Fans of Holly James and Amanda Elliot won't want to miss this one!"
—Alicia Thompson, bestselling author of
With Love, from Cold World

"Lindsay Hameroff blends beloved romance tropes to create a modern-day fairy tale that is both delightful and satisfying. A tasty treat, *Till There Was You* hits all the right notes."
—Jean Meltzer, international bestselling
author of *Kissing Kosher*

"Laugh-out-loud funny, delicious with desire, and heartbreakingly romantic. *Till There Was You* will make you believe in true love and make you hungry on the same page."
—Taylor Hahn, author of *The Lifestyle*

"I tore through *Till There Was You* laughing and crying in equal measure. Lindsay Hameroff's debut rom-com is equal parts sweet, sexy, and funny, with surprising vulnerable depths."
—Meredith Schorr, author of *As Seen on TV*

"With *Till There Was You*, Lindsay Hameroff delivers a deeply satisfying star-crossed celebrity romance, skillfully balancing butterfly-inducing fantasy and heart-squeezing emotional honesty."

—Ava Wilder, author of *How to Fake It in Hollywood*
and *Will They or Won't They*

"*Till There Was You* is the best kind of love story—the kind where big, serious emotions live side by side with laugh-out-loud wit and glamorous escapism. Hameroff has written a celebrity romance that feels achingly real: a delicious, whirlwind tale of courtship amid rising fame (with one hell of a hot musician) that's still somehow grounded with a tender, thoughtful heart. I loved this assured debut and know it's destined for readers' favorites shelf."

—Ashley Winstead, author of *The Boyfriend Candidate*

"Lindsay Hameroff's *Till There Was You* is a swoon-worthy debut! Lexi is a delightfully relatable heroine, a young chef searching for authenticity in Manhattan . . . while accidentally falling for an overnight sensation, musician Jake Taylor. Hameroff does a stellar job exploring the emotional ups and downs of a hot-and-heavy romance between a normie and a celebrity. Both Lexi and the reader are pulled into a swirl of glittery lights and intense scrutiny—a world turned upside down thanks to the fragility of first love and the wow factor of dating music's newest heartthrob. This book was impossible to put down, with a rom-com grand gesture that'll leave you grinning from ear to ear."

—Alison Rose Greenberg, author of *Bad Luck Bridesmaid*

"With prose as delicious and savory as a home-cooked meal, Hameroff delivers a warm, swoony, laugh-out-loud love story between a chef and a rock star that twists well-loved tropes into something utterly fresh."
—Livy Hart, author of *Talk Flirty to Me*

Till There Was You

A Novel

LINDSAY HAMEROFF

ST. MARTIN'S GRIFFIN
NEW YORK

First published in the United States by St. Martin's Griffin, an imprint of St. Martin's Publishing Group

TILL THERE WAS YOU. Copyright © 2024 by Lindsay Hameroff. All rights reserved. Printed in the United States of America. For information, address St. Martin's Publishing Group, 120 Broadway, New York, NY 10271.

www.stmartins.com

Designed by Gabriel Guma

The Library of Congress Cataloging-in-Publication Data is available upon request.

ISBN 978-1-250-90291-7 (trade paperback)
ISBN 978-1-250-90292-4 (ebook)

Our books may be purchased in bulk for promotional, educational, or business use. Please contact your local bookseller or the Macmillan Corporate and Premium Sales Department at 1-800-221-7945, extension 5442, or by email at MacmillanSpecialMarkets@macmillan.com.

First Edition: 2024

10 9 8 7 6 5 4 3 2 1

For Avi, who made it all possible

If music be the food of love, play on.

—WILLIAM SHAKESPEARE

I met her once and wrote a song about her.

—HARRY STYLES, "CAROLINA"

1

MISE EN PLACE. A place for everything, and everything in its place. It's a French expression based on the idea that a good meal can only come from an organized kitchen. It's also the first lesson every student learns in culinary school.

In the kitchen, a chef must anticipate everything before the process of cooking begins. There are pans to prepare, stations to sanitize, and vegetables to cut, peel, slice, and grate. Proper *mise* is all about planning, time management, and foresight. For most of my classmates, it is the worst type of drudgery. For me, it is a symphony.

A symphony that, at the moment, has me in the Institute of Culinary Education's kitchen at 6 A.M., a full hour before my first class. It's my turn to prep Chef's *mise* for today's demonstration, so I've been here since dawn, peeling head after head of garlic like we're expecting a visit from the Volturi.

Truthfully, I don't mind the early hour. There's something magical about this time of morning, when the kitchen is quiet, and I can lose myself in the soothing rhythms of food preparation. Potatoes, peeled. Onions, diced. Fat, trimmed. And every prep bowl laid out with military precision.

I pause to inventory my work, basking in its orderliness before glancing up at the clock. *Shit.* How is it already 6:45? I throw on my toque, grab my coffee and purse, and head down to my classroom.

Though I'm one of the first to arrive, I'm happy to see my friend Ali is already in our usual spot. I slide into the seat next to her, take out my notebook, and start copying the day's menu.

Sautéed lamb chops with herbes de Provence. Radish, asparagus, and burrata salad with chives and lemon. Creamy watercress, pea, and mint soup. I'm salivating at the thought of sampling it all at lunchtime.

"So?" I whisper, as I neatly write down each item. "Don't leave me in suspense. How did it go last night with Bobble Boy?"

I've known Ali less than a year, but in that time, she's managed to go on a truly mind-blowing number of bad dates. First there was Tony, the brilliant chef behind a buzzy fusion place in the West Village. Unfortunately, his passion for the culinary arts was rivaled only by his love for cocaine.

After that came Ted, a Wall Street broker with a great sense of humor and McDreamy-level hair. He was perfect—or at least he'd seemed that way, right up until the wife he'd never mentioned crashed their date at Gallaghers and started rage-hurling hunks of filet mignon around the dining room. Ted got a faceful of Worcestershire sauce. His wife got a restraining order. And Ali got a to-go box.

And who could forget the gaslighter; the embezzler; the guy who called his mom for forty-five minutes in the middle of their first date; or the one with an Instagram account that featured photos of him sleeping in human-sized bird nests? Naturally, my anticipation was high for her date last night: the long-awaited meetup with a guy we've been exclusively referring to as "Bobble Boy," due to the fact that his Tinder profile claims he owns more than four hundred bobbleheads.

"Lexi, the evening exceeded even my wildest expectations." Ali grins at me, her brown eyes sparkling. "Not only did he have *exactly* as many bobbleheads as he claimed, but they're all displayed on shelves facing his bed. Like, *watching* him. Do you have any idea how hard it is to orgasm when you're being stared down by the bobblehead version of Sheldon from *The Big Bang Theory?*"

I try and fail to suppress a snicker. Ali leans into my shoulder as we collapse into a fit of giggles, earning a glare from John, the ever-serious forty-year-old career changer. I adore Ali, but every time she recaps one of her disastrous escapades, I silently renew my vow to avoid dating for the duration of culinary school.

Before I can say anything else, Chef Jean-Pierre takes his place at the front of the room and clears his throat, signaling the start of demonstration. We spend the next hour and a half in rapt attention as he expertly sears lamb chops, cooks asparagus to tender perfection, and elegantly arranges it all on a platter.

And now, it's our turn. Chef makes it look effortless and intuitive, but replicating his recipes is never easy. He assigns us each a dish, and I'm tasked with the pea soup.

Time never moves faster than in the minutes before service, and before I know it, it's time to plate. My hands tremble as I ladle the thick green soup into a ceramic bowl and gingerly place the carrot garnish on top. Then I carry my dish to the metal flat top in the center of the kitchen. My classmates follow suit, and the air grows thick with savory aromas.

Chef circles the room silently, his expression unreadable as he takes a small taste of every dish. I hold my breath as he approaches my soup. Subconsciously, I raise my fingers to my mouth to chew on my nails, forgetting they're covered in Band-Aids from yesterday's ill-fated attempt at grating lemons. I shudder when my lips brush against the sticky adhesive, and the lingering smell of garlic fills my nostrils.

Chef raises a spoon to his lips. He sips, then pauses. His eyebrows furrow. His forehead wrinkles. I'm not sure what face he's making, but it doesn't seem good.

"Tell me something, Miss Berman." He levels a stern gaze at me. "What did you think when you tasted this soup?"

The taste test. How could I have forgotten? I suppress my mounting panic as I figure out what to say next.

"Um, actually, I didn't," I confess, shifting my weight from one foot to the other. "I sort of . . . ran out of time."

Chef's mouth hardens into a line. "That makes sense." He holds out a fresh spoon and gestures toward the bowl. "Go ahead and try a bite."

A fat bead of sweat rolls down my spine. Heart pounding, I dip the spoon into the bowl, filling it with steamy soup before raising it to my lips. Disappointment floods through me—it's bland as rainwater.

"It seems we've forgotten an important step, haven't we?" Chef asks. The entire class seems to have tapped into my humiliation now, as they busy themselves staring out the window or fussing with their own dishes. I try to imagine how this could have gone so wrong, but my mind is drawing a blank.

Think, Lexi. What could you have forgotten? I lift the spoon again for another small taste. The flavors are all there—cool, crisp mint, tart crème fraîche. But Chef is right: something is missing.

"Miss Berman," Chef's accented voice cuts through my internal monologue, "I'm afraid you've failed to properly season your base."

I feel the heat rising to my cheeks. *Of course.* I'd been so focused on following the recipe exactly that I completely forgot to season between ingredients. I can't believe I've made such a basic mistake. After all, I'm already six months into the two-year program; it's not like this is my very first day of classes.

For his part, Chef seems to soften when he notices my humiliation.

"Look," he says quietly. "Cooking is more than just following a recipe. It's also about instinct and intuition. It needs to come from here." He gestures toward my stomach. "In your gut."

I nod quickly, blinking back hot tears. Chef moves down the line to taste Ali's salad, humming in approval as he takes a bite.

The rest of the day passes in a blur, and when classes end, I can hardly get out the door fast enough.

"Hey, Lexi, wait up!" Ali hurries toward me, her sneakers squeaking against the linoleum floor. Even after a blistering day over a stovetop, she looks fresh in a tie-dye hoodie and ripped jeans, her dark ringlets brushing her shoulder blades. She links her arm through mine as we push through the kitchen doors into the hallway.

"Listen, don't worry about the soup thing, okay? So it was a bit bland. Big deal! Trust me, Jean-Pierre does not need any more sodium. He's basically a pillar of salt as it is." When I'm unable to hold back a snort, she grins and tosses an arm around my shoulders.

"There, that's more like it." She beams. "Now, on to more important things: Will you make it to happy hour this afternoon?"

I groan. It's finally Friday, and there's nothing I'd enjoy more than ending the week with Food Network and Chinese takeout. But it's not so much an invitation as a demand. If I know Ali, she'll lovingly hound me until I give in. It's the price I pay for keeping the company of extroverts. "Sure," I reply, hoping my smile covers the flatness of my voice. "I just need to run home and change."

"Great!" she chirps. "Chloe's meeting us, too. I'll text you the deets."

THE AFTERNOON AIR IS unseasonably warm for March, and after shoving through the school's double doors I slip off my denim jacket, tucking it under the strap of my tote.

Despite the sunny skies, the Financial District skyscrapers cast long, gloomy shadows across the sidewalk, mirroring my mood. I sigh as my mind runs back through the day. Ali's right—one lackluster dish isn't *that* big a deal. Not in isolation, at least. It's just that everything seems harder in the classroom than it does at home. In my own kitchen the process feels smooth, natural. But at school, under the pressures of time and demands for perfection, I never seem to get it right. There's something about the performative aspect of being in class, of doing what I love most under the critical eye of instructors, that rattles me. It's probably why I love prep so much. It's the only time of day when I feel in control, instead of bulldozed by the stress of endless, fast-paced demands.

I wish I could blame my struggles on being the youngest, but at twenty-three, I'm one of the oldest students in my class. Almost everyone else is eighteen or nineteen, straight out of high school. And while my parents didn't force me to get a college education first, it was clear from the dozens of college admission pamphlets left on my nightstand and the SAT prep course they enrolled me in that they viewed it as an essential step. Ultimately, I agreed, and accepted a spot at NYU. Unfortunately, four years of beer pong and British literature did little to improve my culinary savvy. At this rate, it will be a miracle if I even land a decent externship, let alone a position in a credible restaurant.

I sigh as I head down the cement stairs to wait for the 4 train, lost in thought. I used to enjoy cooking. No, not just enjoy—relish, delight in, enthuse over. Nothing filled me with joy quite like popping into Eli's Market on my way home from school and letting the seasonal produce inspire my next creation. Plump scarlet tomatoes for gazpacho. Shiny golden peppers for a frittata. Lush emerald spring greens for a simple salad. A kaleidoscope of color to fuel my creativity.

Mom was always my biggest and most enthusiastic fan. I can still picture her hunched over her laptop at our dining room table, tortoiseshell glasses perched on the edge of her nose. No matter how busy she was, she'd happily set aside her legal brief to sample anything I created.

"When you're a Michelin-star chef, I'll be eating in your restaurant every night," she declared the night I served her a plate of sage and brown butter gnocchi, my first successful attempt at home-made pasta. I still remember the way she squeezed my hand, her skin nearly translucent from the chemo.

If she'd known then how unlikely a dream it is, that only 1 percent of Michelin-star restaurants are led by women, I wonder if she would have reconsidered. Not that she'll ever get the chance. She died before I finished high school. It's her faith in me that pushes me to succeed, no matter how badly my day goes. I can't bear the thought of letting her down, of allowing her confidence to be misplaced.

A twinge of guilt weaves through my stomach when I get off at my stop and take in the familiar sights. Immaculate prewar build-ings. Glossy department store windows. Nannies pushing strollers that cost more than a car payment. I always feel a bit uneasy when I come home at the end of the school day. Most of my classmates live in cramped student housing; Ali's the only one who knows I live alone in a two-bedroom, doorman-guarded apartment on the Upper East Side that I've called home my entire life.

After a scalding shower, I pull on a white top with ruffled sleeves and a pair of jeans. Standing in front of the mirror, I ap-praise my reflection.

When I was growing up, people swore I was the spitting im-age of either my mother or my father, depending on which one of them I was with. But the truth is, I'm a combination of the two. My clear blue eyes and thick, dark brows are all my dad, but I inherited my mom's full lips and straight, dark blond hair.

I dot on some concealer and add a few swipes of mascara. An improvement for sure, but there's no covering the telltale dark circles beneath my eyes from a week of predawn wake-up calls for school.

My phone vibrates and a notification pops up on the screen. Call Dad. I sigh and switch off the weekly reminder. Without my dad and his monthly stipend, I couldn't afford school or even happy hour drinks in the city. But tonight, I don't have it in me to feign interest in his latest adventure with my stepmom at their Boca Raton country club. It's Friday afternoon, my friends are waiting, and, most importantly, drinks are half-price until seven.

2

TODAY'S HAPPY HOUR DESTINATION is Paddington's, an East Village dive bar with a faded red awning and wooden sign reading "Bar and Grill." Pushing open the wooden door, I step inside and scan the room for my friends.

The small space is dim, its scuffed floors cluttered with mismatched chairs. A string of Christmas lights casts a red glow against the back wall, every inch of which is covered in eclectic decor. It only takes a moment to find Ali and Chloe at a table in the corner.

Even from a distance, Ali's laugh cuts through the hum of the crowd. Though barely five feet one, the girl's got more than enough personality to make up for it. It's no wonder she's already become so close with Chloe, even though I'm the one who's known Chloe for a decade. Ali's eyes light up as she catches my gaze and waves me over.

I head over to their table, leaning in to give them both hugs. Chloe throws me a quick smile before turning her attention back to her phone.

"Everything okay?" I ask as I slide into the rickety chair across from her. She blows out a long exhale without bothering to look up.

"It's fine. I just need to change Chad's social media passwords before he gets himself involved in a scandal even I can't save him from." Chloe's PR job consists of putting out fires for D-list celebrities, including Chad, a former *Bachelor* contestant whose daily misadventures put him in constant danger of being canceled. Last week, he posted photos of his new tattoo, a rose surrounded by Japanese text. Chad thought it meant "deflowerer of beautiful maidens." Twitter detectives discovered it actually meant "gardener of sensual beef jerky."

Sighing, she flips her phone over and shoves it away with a look of disgust, as if she isn't going to pick it up again in exactly three minutes. She finally looks up, flashing me a smile as she tucks a perfectly styled blond wave behind her ear. My eyes linger on her glossy red manicure, a stark contrast to my own stubby, bitten-down nails.

A server materializes, setting down a pitcher of margaritas and three salt-rimmed glasses. He leans forward, his square jaw melting into a grin as his emerald eyes sparkle.

"Can I get you ladies anything else?" His Australian accent is thick and, admittedly, dead sexy. I shake my head as he walks off with a wink.

"God, I love a man with Hemsworth energy," Ali whispers the moment he's out of earshot. She grabs the pitcher to pour us each a glass. "What do you think, Lex?"

"An unparalleled Adonis," I reply. "And not for me. Because, like I've told you both on multiple occasions, I'm not interested in dating right now. I need to stay focused on school if I'm ever going to—"

Ali holds out a hand, cutting me off.

"Yes, yes, we are all well aware of your intended career trajectory. I still don't understand what that has to do with getting your needs met. Honestly, you're wound too tightly for your own good." She takes a long sip of her margarita. "Just imagine how much better you'd perform in the kitchen if you had someone to"—she wiggles her eyebrows—"loosen you up a bit." She leans back in her chair and grins. "Speaking of which, I've got a date tonight with a guy I met on Hinge. An ob-gyn teaching fellow. For once, I'll be with someone who doesn't need a map to find his way around my vagina."

I roll my eyes. "Maybe he can teach your vagina to have better taste in men."

Chloe snorts, then picks up her phone again. "You two make me grateful I'm gay. I don't know what I'd do without these weekly reminders of what I'm not missing."

I kick her underneath the table, swinging my legs out to the side before she can reciprocate. The two of us have been inseparable since the day Mrs. Stoker paired us as lab partners in ninth-grade biology. So many of my friendships fell apart when Mom died, but Chloe never left my side. We've been through everything together over the past decade: boyfriends and breakups, bad grades and first jobs. In many ways, she's like the sister I never had. Sometimes it feels like she's the only family I have left.

"So, how are classes going?" Chloe asks, typing furiously.

"They're going . . . fine," Ali answers, doing her best not to meet my eyes. I appreciate her discretion, but frankly, I'm in the mood to vent.

"Yeah, they're going fine for Ali, because unlike me, she's mastered the oh-so-difficult technique of adding salt to her food," I grumble.

"Uh-oh," Chloe says. "Did your teacher go all Gordon Ramsay on you or what?"

"Something like that." I grab the pitcher, refilling my glass. "But he does have a point. Maybe I'm not meant to be a chef after all."

"Not with an attitude like that!" Ali sniffs. "Now cheer up. I can't have you killing my vibe. My friend Jackie from barre was here last weekend and said the new musical act is fine as hell. And some of us have not taken self-imposed vows of celibacy, thank you very much."

We order a second pitcher and a side of mozzarella sticks as we wait for the show to begin. But an hour and a half later, the stage is still vacant, and Ali, having realized she has no idea when the show actually starts, has lost interest. She stands, announcing she needs to get ready for her date. Chloe gets up to leave, too. She's got dinner reservations with a client turned friend at a new fusion place downtown. She invites me to join, but I decline. It's been a long day and my social battery is drained.

Still, I could use another drink, an excuse to linger and forget about school for a little while longer. So when Chloe and Ali walk out, I hang back, slide onto a barstool, and order my favorite cocktail, a whiskey sour. *Just one more,* I tell myself. Then I'll call it a night.

But what appears in front of me moments later is a brutal disappointment. A quick sip confirms it's got all the key ingredients: bright, biting lemon juice; warm, fragrant bourbon; and a hint of simple syrup. Yet it's missing its jewelry, the pièce de résistance: the Maraschino cherry.

As usual, I'd requested not one, but two cherries. I like to slide them off the wooden spear with my teeth, rolling them over my tongue to release their tart juices before taking my first sip. But like the rest of the week, this cocktail falls short of expectations. Even the napkin, soggy with condensation from the frosted glass, seems disappointed.

I press my elbows against the sticky, mahogany countertop and lean forward to get the bartender's attention. "Excuse me?"

It's no use. He's deep in conversation with two guys at the other end of the bar, and the Lizzo song on the overhead speakers is drowning out my voice.

Somewhere behind me a woman cackles, and wooden chair

legs scrape noisily against the floor. My face grows hot with irritation, and a dull headache begins to form just around my temples. I should have called it a night when my friends did. I could be wallowing on my sofa right now, remote in one hand and a glass of Chardonnay in the other. At home, I could have as many goddamn cherries as I want. Turning back to the bar, I make one last attempt at getting the bartender's attention.

"Excuse me?" I say it louder this time, so loud that I'm practically shouting. But it's no use. Frustrated, I sulk back against my barstool. I'm just about to grab my purse and slap a few bills on the counter when I hear a voice: "Rough day?"

I look up. There's a guy sitting a few stools down, a faded white baseball cap emblazoned with a large "G" slung low on his brow. Beneath the brim, his full lips stretch into an amused smile.

"You could say that." I flash a perfunctory smile, hoping he'll take the hint.

He doesn't. "Wanna talk about it?"

"Just a long week at culinary school." I sigh. "Turns out soup tastes better when you season it."

White-cap guy chuckles. It's a warm, melodic sound that cuts right through the background noise. Normally, this is the point where I'd cut off a conversation with a stranger. But there's something about him that makes me continue.

"And to add insult to injury, I'm trying to drown my sorrows in a whiskey sour, and the bartender forgot my cherries." I cringe internally as I hear myself ramble. *Why am I telling him all of this?*

He studies me, dark eyes flitting over my face. Then he leans over, reaches an arm over the bar, scoops up an entire handful of cherries with a napkin, and hands them to me.

"Hey! You can't just take those!" I glance around nervously, wondering if the bartender saw.

"You said you wanted cherries." He shrugs. "I think the words you're looking for are 'thank you.'"

My face flushes. "Yeah, thanks." I turn away, burying my face in my drink. Great. Now I've offended a well-intentioned stranger. Bang-up day all around, Lexi.

He laughs again. I pivot to face him. He's moved to the stool next to mine, and luckily, he looks more amused than offended. Angling his body toward me, he dips his head closer. My head swims with the scent of fresh laundry and Dove soap.

"Culinary school, huh?" Up close, I notice his eyes are the color of milk chocolate. His skin is lightly tanned, and a few tufts of glossy brown hair have slipped out beneath his hat. *Wow*. He has got to be the most attractive human I've ever seen up close. I'm full-on, creep-mode staring now, but I can't tear my eyes away.

"That's impressive. I can barely make ramen." His vowels spill out languidly, and I wonder fleetingly where he's from. Definitely not New York. His knee grazes my leg and I intake a sharp breath, attempting to ignore what feels like a troupe of acrobats performing backflips in my stomach.

"Taylor! This one's on me, man. Good luck tonight!" White-cap guy breaks our eye contact to glance backward. A burly, red-faced man is holding out a glass of bourbon.

"Thank you, good sir." His face splits into a wide smile and I see he's got a dimple on his right cheek. Because of course he does. He accepts the glass and sets it on the bar, tracing his finger absentmindedly around the rim. I notice there's another, barely touched drink at his elbow.

"Looks like you had a rough day too." I raise one eyebrow. "Taylor, is it?"

"Jake, actually. Jake Taylor." His smile broadens as he extends a hand, and we shake. "And no, my day's been fine. Everyone here just enjoys liquoring me up. Feels rude to decline, but I prefer not to drink when I'm working. You want it?"

I shake my head no. "You work here?" I ask. That explains the cherry swiping. But why is he in front of the bar?

"Uh, not exactly." He laughs softly. Before I can ask what he means, a burst of feedback screeches through the speakers. A staff member in a flannel shirt and black beanie is fumbling with a microphone stand in the center of the stage.

I roll my eyes. "Guess the musician finally decided to show up."

Jake raises one eyebrow. "Don't sound too excited there. You hate music or something?"

"More like apathy than hate." I twirl my stirrer, emboldened by the heady combination of liquor and flirtation. "The last concert I attended was a Kelly Clarkson show in 2012. With my parents, I might add. So, I can't say I really keep up with the latest hits."

He grins. "Okay. Beyond *The Best of American Idol,* what selections might I find on your playlists?"

"Oh, only the finest stuff." I take another long sip of my cocktail. "Vintage Britney. The soundtrack to *Bridgerton.* And, of course, the best genre of music known to man: Broadway showtunes."

Jake bursts into laughter. "Showtunes, huh? What's your favorite?"

"All of them. I mean, *Newsies* is great. And I love *The Sound of Music.* I always wished I had six brothers and sisters," I confess. If I'd had siblings, things would have been so different after Mom died. But I don't need to trauma-dump that on a stranger. Especially not such a cute one.

Jake purses his lips and nods in agreement. "*The Sound of Music* is indeed a classic. Though personally, I'm a loyal *Les Mis* fan."

"Yes, the best!" I groan, throwing my head back. "The opening number alone! A perfect example of a prologue in musical form!"

"Hey, if cooking doesn't work out, you should consider teaching English. Can't say I've ever heard anyone describe Broadway shows with literary devices."

"I was an English major," I admit. "Although you may be hanging out with the wrong people if no amount of your recreational time is devoted to the literary analysis of Broadway musicals."

"Well, maybe I need some new people to hang out with." My heart thunders against my chest as Jake's eyes bore into mine. He leans forward, lips parting. And then—

"Ladies and gentlemen, the man you've all been waiting for." A voice at the microphone interrupts the moment. "Please welcome to the stage, the one and only Jake Taylor!"

My mouth drops open. Jake takes off his cap and runs his fingers through his thick chestnut hair, then plops it back on his head and twists it backward.

"If you'll excuse me for just a few minutes." He stands up and reaches under the bar, grabbing a guitar case. *Has that been there the whole time?* Mouth gaping, I stare as he makes his way to the stage.

"Good evenin', everyone." He takes a seat on the stool, props up one knee, and balances the guitar on it. His drawl seems heavier now, and his grin widens as the crowd claps and hoots. A few chords fill the room as he tunes the strings.

"It has come to my attention that we have a Broadway fan in the house tonight." He winks at me, and my cheeks turn hot. Someone in the back whoops loudly.

A familiar melody floats through the air, and my breath catches. Jake leans in, pressing his lips to the microphone, and starts to sing.

I recognize the lyrics immediately. It's my favorite song from *The Music Man*, the one Marian sings to Harold Hill in the second act. I've heard "Till There Was You" a hundred times before, but never like this. Jake's rendition is slower, pared down. And the words sound infinitely better in his honey-smooth voice.

His eyes stay locked on mine as he sings, one corner of his mouth inching up in a crooked grin. I can feel the other patrons' heads turn toward me, but I can't tear my gaze away. I'm transfixed as he closes his eyes over a long, breathy note.

My own eyes flutter shut as his lips curl over the words. I've never had this type of reaction to music before. My heart simultaneously slows and quickens as an unfamiliar feeling of tranquility washes over me. The rest of the room fades to a blur, and when I open my eyes again, all I can see is him.

He finishes the song, his dimple popping as the crowd breaks into applause. He pauses, acknowledges the audience with a nod, then bends over the guitar again.

This next song is different, with a faster beat and a rock and roll rhythm. I don't recognize it, but it's catchy, whatever it is. I feel the thrum of the crowd and scan the room.

Everyone is leaning toward the stage, tapping their feet and bobbing their heads as if they're all vibrating on the same wavelength as Jake. I get it: the guy has charisma. The crowd's almost doubled since I arrived at the bar two hours ago. A few people are holding up cell phones to record, and I wonder how many came just to see him.

Jake plays three more songs before wrapping up his performance with a quick bow.

"Thank y'all for being here tonight," he says slowly into the microphone, beaming as the crowd applauds again. A small group of fans jumps to their feet, cheering and whistling. And for the first time in a long time, I regret my ban on dating.

3

"SO, WHAT'S THE VERDICT? Can I even hold a candle to Miss Kelly Clarkson?" Jake strolls back to the bar. It takes every ounce of self-control to keep my expression neutral.

"You could say that," I reply, with what I very much hope comes off as a casual shrug.

He grins at me, a slow, devastatingly handsome smile that sends a ripple through my belly. "Wanna get out of here?"

I take a deep breath. *Okay, Lexi, be rational here.* This man is a stranger. A gorgeous stranger, yes. But for all I know, he's a serial killer. Didn't Charles Manson play guitar?

Even so, my plan to spend the night binge-watching *Top Chef* sounds a lot less appealing than it did before Jake's set. And the truth is, I'm not ready to let him go just yet.

"Sure," I reply. "Let's do it."

Jake grabs a leather jacket from the back of his barstool and takes me by the hand. I toss a few dollars on the bar and let him lead me out the front door.

"So, where are we headed?" I ask, reluctantly letting go of Jake's hand as he readjusts the guitar strap on his shoulder and feeling a rush of excitement when he takes it again.

"It's a surprise." He bites back a smile when I pull a face. "Though I'm sensing you're not exactly the impulsive type?"

"Being impulsive is one thing. It's the whole 'allowing a stranger to take me to an unknown destination thing' that's giving me pause." Jake laughs softly, and I take a minute to study his profile.

He really is insanely handsome, broad-shouldered, and taller than I originally thought, his boyish face juxtaposed by a light smattering of stubble along his jawline. Dark lashes frame his animated brown eyes.

"Not to worry," he says. "My demon sex cult only meets on Thursdays, so you're in the clear."

"Well, that's a relief."

"We're headed to the F train," he continues, "which gives us at least ten minutes to get fully acquainted." He pronounces "get" like "git," a trait I find inexplicably charming.

"Okay. Let's start with the basics." I narrow my eyes and put on my best bad cop face. "What's your full name? Where are you from? And how many arrests do you have on your criminal record?"

"Excellent questions." Jake swings our hands lightly. "I'm Jacob Aaron Taylor, but everyone except my mother calls me Jake. Born and raised in Marietta, Georgia. And I'm proud to say I have never been arrested. Though I was once detained by security at the Coca-Cola factory for attempting to sneak into the 3-D theater without a ticket."

"You hooligan," I say, shaking my head.

Jake smirks again. "Your turn. Same questions, and please say you are wanted by authorities in at least three different states."

"Let's see. Alexa Danielle Berman, but everyone calls me Lexi. Native New Yorker. And alas, I've never so much as cheated on a math test."

"Figures," Jake says with a snort. "You've got 'good girl with a thing for rebellious musicians' written all over you."

We reach the platform just as the train arrives and scramble into the closest car. I steal another look at Jake—*Am I seriously about to go through with this?*—when an automated voice rings out. "Stand clear of the closing doors, please."

Welp, I guess this is happening.

T WENTY MINUTES LATER, WE'RE standing outside (Le) Poisson Rouge in the heart of Greenwich Village. I raise a questioning eyebrow at Jake, who tips his chin toward the poster in the window. Four musicians are pictured in over-the-top '80s attire with the words "Living on a Prayer" written beneath them in sparkly bubble letters.

"You'll never see a better eighties cover band," he says as he pulls the door open. "Predates your beloved Y2K pop by a few years, but I promise you'll love it anyway."

We step through the double doors, and I take in the scene before me. Rows of glossy black tables and chairs fill the cavernous room, illuminated by dozens of pink and blue overhead lights. The bass is so loud it vibrates through me, pulsating in my chest like a heartbeat.

After depositing his guitar at coat check, Jake slips his hand through mine again, and we squeeze through the crowd, making our way to the neon-pink bar. He leans over the counter, holding up two fingers. When the bartender returns a moment later, Jake turns around and hands me a shot glass. "A toast!"

I raise my eyebrows. "And what are we toasting, exactly?"

"To the weekend officially starting." He lifts his own glass, the corner of his mouth hiking upward. "And the future analysis of many Broadway musicals."

His eyes lock on mine, and my breath catches in my throat as the air around us stills. I think he's about to say something more, but then he clinks his glass against mine and swallows it back.

I grimace as I take my own shot, and Jake hands me a lime slice he's nicked from the bar behind us.

"Seriously? You can't just keep taking stuff," I protest. "There are rules, you know, in modern society."

Jake shakes his head. "Are you always such a rule follower?"

"Always."

He laughs, then tips his head toward the dance floor. "Shall we?"

"Fine," I huff. "But I'm definitely going to need another shot."

"Atta girl!" His dimple pops, and I feel a ripple through my stomach.

He places another shot in my right hand, then takes my left and molds it into a fist. Keeping his eyes locked on mine, he slowly draws my hand to his mouth and licks it, then sprinkles a bit of salt on top.

My heart thumps against my rib cage as I will myself to breathe. *Just keep it together, Lexi.*

"Lick the salt off your hand before you take the shot," he explains. "It—"

"—helps ameliorate the burning taste of the tequila. Yeah, I know."

I run my tongue over the salty skin before bringing the shot glass to my lips. Jake's eyes bore into mine, the heat in my belly growing.

"Better?"

I nod, and he grins before swallowing the contents of his own glass. Just then, magenta rays of light flash across the room, and the band begins playing. The opening notes to Whitney Houston's "I Wanna Dance with Somebody" blast through the speakers.

"Shall we?" he asks, gesturing toward the dance floor. When I follow him out to the center, he laces his fingers through mine, pressing our palms together. He lowers his face toward me, and then, when his lips are inches from mine, he throws his head back, belting out the refrain in an impeccable falsetto.

I can't help but laugh, and Jake's eyes are bright as he loops my arms around his neck. I curl my fingers into his shoulders, feeling his muscles work beneath the soft cotton of his shirt. His hand slips down to the small of my back, drawing me closer.

My heart is hammering against my rib cage, trying to keep up with the music and the surge of adrenaline coursing through my veins as Jake's hands find their way to my hips. I can't even remember the last time I had this much fun. For once, the nagging voices in my head are silent, the cautionary warnings drowned out by chocolate-brown eyes, tequila, and Whitney Houston.

TWO HOURS AND MANY sweaty dances later, Jake's arm is draped around my shoulders as we stroll up Sixty-Third Street. Before I know it, we've reached the entrance to my apartment, a fourteen-story prewar building with a limestone facade.

"Well, this is me."

"I'll make sure you get inside safely," he insists. He pulls the door open, and I duck under his arm to step through. I wave hello to Lionel, the doorman. He takes one look at Jake and grins, then makes a show of burying his head in his newspaper.

The alcohol is still enveloping me like a fuzzy coat, and I jab the elevator button a few times before it lights up. Rocking back on my heels, I study the lobby's familiar marble paneling, trying my hardest to ignore the electricity emanating from Jake's body beside me.

Finally, the elevator chimes. The doors slide open, and I step inside, tapping the "6" button. Jake presses one hand against the door frame, then dips his head to brush his lips against my cheek. When he pulls back, his eyes have darkened.

"Good night, Lexi."

"Good night, Jake." I flash a smile and try to ignore the disappointment flooding through me as the doors clang shut.

I slump against the metal wall, taking a deep breath to slow my racing heart. The evening's events flash before my eyes like scenes from someone else's life. Someone bolder and more spontaneous, who does impulsive things like drinking too much and going out dancing with complete strangers. Someone whose daily life isn't dictated by a five-year plan. But if I were really that person, I'd never have let Jake go so easily.

Finally, the elevator reaches my floor. My apartment is only two doors down, and I've just extracted the key from my purse when the heavy thud of footsteps echoes up the emergency staircase. I whip my head around, my heart catching in my throat as a breathless figure bursts through the door.

"Jake? Did you forget something?"

He nods wordlessly as he steps closer. His eyes run over my face, the muscles in his jaw twitching. I'm just about to ask if he wants to come inside, but before the words leave my mouth, his lips crash down on mine.

Instantly, my body is on fire. Jake takes my face in his hands, cupping my cheeks and lifting me toward him. I twist my fingers in his hair, tugging gently as he walks us backward until we stumble into the doorframe.

His hips pin me to the wall as our kisses grow frenzied, his hands working their way through my hair before sliding down to my waist, pulling me closer. I gasp when he drags his lips away from mine, but before I can complain, he's planting a trail of kisses down the tender skin of my throat.

I'm not exactly sure how long we stay like this, our bodies a tangle of fingers and hot breath, before I'm able to come up for air.

"Do you want to come in?" I finally manage. My voice is ragged, and I can feel his heartbeat hammering through his shirt as erratically as my own. Jake's eyes burn into mine as he nods, and I fumble with the lock before we stumble into the dark apartment.

Suddenly unable to recall the location of my light switch, I trip through my pitch-black entryway and the back of my head collides against the wall with a soft thud. We erupt into giggles before his mouth finds mine again in the dark and swallows the sound entirely.

His hands grip the back of my thighs as he lifts me up, and my fingers curl around the soft cotton of his shirt. "Bedroom," I rasp, pointing toward the room at the end of the hall. I wrap my legs tightly around his waist as he walks us toward the doorway, using one foot to kick the door open.

When Jake's legs collide with the edge of my bed, he sinks onto it and pulls me into his lap to straddle him. My hands find their way under the hem of his shirt, rolling over the hard ridges of his abs. *Damn, you could wash laundry on these things.*

I lift my shirt over my head and drop it behind me, grateful to have worn the nicest lingerie I own tonight. Jake bites down on his lower lip, his eyes darkening as they roam over my exposed skin. Then he dips his head to suck gently along the underside of my jaw. One hand presses into the small of my back, gently holding me in place, as the other trails up my spine to the hook of my bra. I intake a breath as it releases, and his calloused fingertips slip beneath the loosened fabric. He palms my breast, swirling a thumb around my nipple, and heat pools between my legs.

"God, you feel so good," he murmurs against my skin.

I yank my fingers through his hair and pull his face upward to kiss me. With a groan, he flips us over so I'm lying on my back. He unbuttons my jeans and tugs them off, tossing them over the side of the bed. Hooking one of my legs over his shoulder, he presses his mouth against the inside of my thigh, his tongue tracing small circles against my skin as he descends closer and closer to where I want him most. By the time he slides one hand into my underwear, stroking his fingers over me, I can hardly breathe.

He pauses to meet my eyes. "Is this okay?" he asks, his voice low and raspy. Pulse skittering, I nod wordlessly. It's more than okay, actually. I can't remember the last time I wanted anyone, or anything, this much. I keep waiting for a sense of self-preservation to kick in, for my body to remind me that this is absolutely not something I do with a man I've just met. Instead, it does the opposite, arching toward Jake like it's being pulled by some magnetic force. And yet somehow, I still want more. I *need* more.

"Jake," I whisper, reaching for the waistband of his jeans. He inhales sharply as I slide a hand inside.

"Do you have a condom?" I ask. His brow furrows and he shakes his head.

"No, I don't carry . . . I mean, I didn't expect . . ."

"Wait, hang on," I say. I yank open my night table drawer and reach inside, groping around blindly until my fingertips brush the edges of a foil package. *Thank god for Ali.* A few months back, she had extracted a handful of Trojans from her purse and shoved them inside the drawer so that I would be prepared "on the off chance that I ever tire of the Virgin Mary routine."

Jake covers his body with mine and kisses me again. His tongue parts my lips, and I gasp as he eases himself inside of me.

"Lexi," he breathes, and something stirs in my chest as he begins to move. We find our rhythm together, and I'm vaguely aware that I'm calling his name as the waves of pleasure build higher and higher. Then they crash down over me, erasing every thought entirely.

4

T HE FIRST RAYS OF early morning light rouse me from sleep. Rubbing my eyes, I take in Jake's lightly snoring form on the other side of the bed. He's lying on his side, facing me. I drink in the sight of him; his cheek is pressed into the pillow, pink lips pursed, brown hair falling messily over his forehead. And I can't help but grapple with the strangest feeling of familiarity. Like somehow, I've known him my entire life.

Ridiculous, I chide myself. Jake is a musician, and a flirty, charismatic one at that. This feeling is nothing more than the by-product of his magnetic presence. He probably charms his way into a different girl's bed every weekend.

Rolling over, I check the clock on my nightstand: 7:08 A.M. Time to start the day.

I slide out of bed, grabbing a sweatshirt and a pair of yoga pants from my drawer. Tiptoeing down the hallway, I make my way into the kitchen. A rush of excitement snakes through my belly at the prospect of cooking breakfast for someone, an opportunity I haven't enjoyed in ages. What should I make? Eggs Benedict with homemade hollandaise? Crème brûlée French toast? I scroll through my mental Rolodex before landing on my favorite recipe.

I open a cabinet, taking a moment to admire my baking supplies. The rest of my life might be a hot mess, but these? These are pristine. Neatly stacked, neatly labeled, and neatly stored in matching OXO containers. I grab the flour, sugar, and baking powder, and have just pulled a carton of eggs from the fridge when the bedroom door creaks open.

Jake pads into the kitchen, wearing nothing but his boxer shorts. One wayward lock of hair sticks straight up as he rubs sleep from his eyes. Good lord, he is adorable.

"Damn, you get up early. Do you moonlight as a farmer?"

I smile as I rinse a handful of blueberries.

"I've always been an early riser," I admit. "Though that particular side gig might be worth it for the fresh eggs. Speaking of which, are you hungry?"

"Starved," Jake murmurs, as he comes up behind me to kiss my neck. "So, what are you making us, Madame Chef? Scones? Brioche? A casual breakfast croquembouche?"

"Sorry to disappoint, but I'm afraid it's just good, old-fashioned blueberry pancakes this morning," I reply. "Also known as The First Dish I Ever Mastered."

"Really?" Jake slides into a barstool across from me, taking an apple from the fruit basket and passing it from one hand to the other. "Family recipe?"

"Hardly. My parents were lawyers, and I'm pretty sure neither ever cooked a meal in their lives."

"So, how'd you get into cooking?" Jake takes a large bite of the apple as he leans back to study me contemplatively.

"Well, this recipe was stolen from a magazine in a nail salon."

"Aha! You *are* a criminal. I knew it." Jake beams with satisfaction. I can't help but giggle as I move through the kitchen, grabbing the tools I'll need and lining everything up neatly on the island. Jake rests his chin on his fist as he watches with amusement.

"Are you always like this?" he asks.

I frown. "What do you mean?"

"Just so . . . precise. I mean, everything is so orderly. Doesn't it get exhausting?"

"I like order," I reply as I whisk the milk into my dry ingredients. "It makes me feel . . . I don't know, calm, I guess."

Jake nods. "I wish I were more like you sometimes. I've got a small following on TikTok, but I'm not organized enough to really grow my social media presence. Maybe I'd be a bit further in my career by now if I had your level of discipline."

"But you've got talent. I mean, you're an absolutely amazing performer." My cheeks heat with my unintentional confession. *Way to play it cool, Lex.*

At my praise, Jake's face lights up. "Well, let's hope the music industry shares your sentiments. I'm off to LA on Monday to record my demo album."

I'm so shocked I nearly drop my whisk.

"Seriously?" I cringe slightly at the shrillness of my own voice. I recalibrate, attempting to make it sound as normal as possible. "That's amazing!" Jake's face splits into a grin, dimple smirking, and my stomach does a tiny flip. "So, how does that work, exactly? Are your songs already written?"

"Mostly. Just need one or two more. Most demos only have about four or five songs anyway. After that, I'll start sending it out to record labels and agents, maybe even try to score some radio time." The last sentence comes out in a rush, his voice laced with both excitement and apprehension.

"Why LA?" I ask. "Aren't there recording studios in New York?"

"My college buddy Elliot works in a recording studio out there. He's able to get me in for practically nothing." The corner of his mouth twitches. "Dive-bar gigs don't exactly pay big bucks, after all."

He leans back in his seat and shrugs, as if to suggest the process is no big deal. But I can see the fire in his eyes, can hear the desire in his tone. He wants to be successful, and he wants it bad. It strikes me how similar we are in that way.

"You'll be great," I say. Grabbing a lemon from the bowl on my counter, I slice it in half and squeeze the juice into my batter. The dash of acidity will make the flavor of the berries pop.

A few minutes later, breakfast is ready. Ten fluffy pancakes, precisely uniform in height and circumference, are stacked neatly on a plate. Grabbing a couple of forks, a stick of butter, and a bottle of syrup, I walk around the island to take a seat on the barstool next to Jake. He loads a few pancakes onto his plate, dousing them with syrup before taking an enormous bite. His eyes flutter shut as he hums in appreciation, and warm pleasure rushes through me. Watching someone enjoy the food I've made is hands down my favorite thing about cooking.

"I'm sorry, Alexa Danielle Berman, but your instructor has no idea what he's talking about. You are a phenomenal cook."

"Why, thank you, Jacob Aaron Taylor." I pour some syrup into the center of my pancake before cutting it into four even pieces.

"Who knew there was lemon in blueberry pancakes?" he muses, before stuffing another bite in his mouth.

"Their complementary flavors make the perfect pairing," I explain. "They're made for each other." Jake turns toward me and his eyes lock with mine. A long moment passes. Then, mercifully, he breaks the spell, twisting in his chair to survey the living room.

"This is quite a place you've got here." I follow his gaze as his eyes drift around the room. He's too polite to say it out loud, but I know what he's really thinking: *How can you, a full-time student in her early twenties, afford to live alone in a classic six on Park Avenue?*

I keep my eyes on my plate as I mumble an answer to his unspoken question. "I can only afford it because there isn't any rent. The apartment is paid off. It belonged to my parents. My family, really. I grew up here."

Out of the corner of my eye, I see Jake freeze. He turns his head slowly, his gaze burning right through me. Heart thumping, I shove a bite of pancake into my mouth, but I barely taste it.

"Belonged to your parents?" he asks tentatively. "Where are they now?"

Tears well as I clench my fists together and take a deep breath. *Calm down, Lexi.* There is no way I'm going to let myself fall apart in front of some guy I barely know.

"My mom died when I was sixteen," I explain. "Uterine cancer. She and my dad had been together since their first semester of law school. So, you can imagine my surprise when my dad got a new girlfriend four months after my mom passed, married her five months after that, and proceeded to move to Florida the minute I left for college."

As soon as the words leave my mouth, I regret them immediately. Throughout the years, I've learned this is a story others prefer not to hear. They never know quite what to say or how to respond, so they inevitably stand there, looking uncomfortable as they waffle between asking polite follow-up questions or offering a segue to lighter topics of conversation.

To his credit, Jake does neither. He leans forward, placing his hand over mine. A flicker of electricity passes through his warm skin.

"That must have been really hard," he says softly. "I'm sorry you had to go through that."

My stomach knots with discomfort at my uncharacteristic oversharing. *What is it about this guy that makes me spill my guts?* "Sorry, I don't know why I'm telling you all of this. We barely know each other, and you didn't order breakfast with a side of melodrama."

Jake's gaze is unflinching. "Don't apologize. I want to get to know you."

Shifting my body to avoid his eyes, I stand up and push in my stool.

"Anyway, it's ancient history. And living here rent-free means I can afford to attend school full-time and get started on my career plans as quickly as possible."

Before moving to Florida, Dad transferred the deed for the apartment to my name. He insisted it was for my financial protection, but I've always wondered how much of it was motivated by guilt. Like he knew he was abandoning me, so he saved my childhood home as a proxy for his presence. He covered my college tuition, but I insisted on taking out loans to pay for culinary school myself so that I'd be indebted to him as little as possible. He mails me a small check each month to help with groceries and utilities. I genuinely appreciate all his help. Monetarily, he's given me so much, and I know how fortunate I am. But it's impossible to ignore the fact that my circumstances have come at the expense of so much heartache. I'd trade it in a heartbeat to have my family back.

Jake nods solemnly. "Makes sense. Plus, you get to keep living with that sexy mallard." He tilts his chin toward the green ceramic duck perched on the living room bookshelf, a gift my dad received from a client in the mid-1990s. Despite myself, I burst into laughter, the knot in my chest immediately dissolving.

"Yeah . . . I've never really gotten around to redecorating."

Picking up our breakfast plates, I carry them over to the sink for a quick rinse. Then, I turn to face Jake expectantly. I imagine this is the point where we'll say our goodbyes. To be honest, I'm a little surprised he's stayed this long.

"So, what are you up to today?" he asks.

Oh. This is an unexpected turn.

"Big plans, actually. Hulu just started streaming *Golden Girls*."

"*Golden Girls*? My mom loves that show!" Jake's chest ripples with laughter. "We used to watch reruns together all the time."

"My mom and I did too." Watching old episodes while digging into cartons of Chinese takeout was a Friday-night ritual. Even now, the show makes me feel close to her. Judging by the wistful look in Jake's eyes, I realize he feels the same way.

Jake shoots me a bashful look. "Man, I haven't watched it in ages. Mind if I join you?"

"Um, sure." I rearrange my face to hide my embarrassing level of excitement. "You don't have anything else to do today?"

He shakes his head. "Not really." He collapses onto the sofa and grabs the remote, then swivels his head to grin at me.

"Ready to travel down a road and back again?"

TWENTY MINUTES LATER, WE'RE curled up beneath the fluffy white blanket on my crinkled leather sofa. Jake's arm is around me, my head resting on his shoulder. On screen, Blanche is criticizing Dorothy's lack of grace. Dorothy shoots her a signature eye roll and quips that Blanche does her best work in back alleyways.

"Has anyone ever told you you're a total Dorothy?" Jake asks.

"You think I'm Dorothy? That's so mean!" I gasp with feigned horror.

"Not at all! Dorothy is the best character. She's smart, down-to-earth, and she calls people on their bullshit."

"True." I nod. "But you're definitely a Blanche. A highly promiscuous southern belle if I've ever met one."

"Oh, that's it." Jake's long fingers slip beneath my armpits, tickling as he pins me to the sofa, and I shriek as I half-heartedly attempt to shove him off. He stops after a minute, his brown eyes locking intensely on mine.

"I have a confession," he says softly. My chest is still rising and falling rapidly, and I suspect I won't be catching my breath anytime soon.

"You have a side gig selling your hair to make wigs for aging debutantes?"

"Well, that." Jake dips his head close enough that our noses brush. "And I've been dying to kiss you all morning."

"Then by all means, don't let me stop you."

I grin as he pulls me onto his lap to straddle him, using one hand to tuck a strand of hair behind my ear. His eyes move thoroughly across my face, as though he's trying to memorize my features. Then he leans forward and presses his mouth to mine. A sound escapes my throat when his tongue parts my lips, sliding between them to taste me.

I've been kissed before, but not the way Jake kisses, which feels urgent and all-consuming. His hands slide down my body to grip my hips before he drags his mouth along my jawline and nips lightly at my throat. I let out a shaky cry as one hand dips lower.

"Jake," I moan, and his eyes lock on mine as I rock against his lap, my breath growing labored until he leans forward to meet my lips again, and the world around me goes hazy.

THE DULL ACHE IN my neck slowly drags me back into consciousness. I lift my head, rolling it to relieve the pain, then blink in the darkness. Jake's silhouette slowly materializes into view. He's sitting upright, but his head has fallen back against the couch cushion, his chest rising and falling gently.

I lean over to grab my phone: 2:57 A.M. I can't believe we spent the entire day on this sofa. I blink the darkness into focus, wincing as my eyes drift over our empty wineglasses and the Vietnamese takeout containers littering the coffee table. I never let a mess sit for so long.

"Jake," I whisper, nudging him lightly in the side. He groans softly but doesn't move. I reach up to grab the blanket that's pooled around his ankles and wrap it around his slumbering form. He exhales softly, and a hint of a smile plays on his lips. Without thinking, I brush back a dark lock of hair from his forehead.

I'm slipping into dangerous territory here, and I know it. Jake is traveling across the country next week, and who knows if I'll even hear from him again when he gets back. Getting attached to him will only lead to heartbreak.

Sighing, I scan the apartment, attempting to see it through his eyes. It was a beautiful space once. Any realtor would salivate over its hardwood floors and original crown moulding. But over the years, it's steadily fallen into a state of disrepair. The dark, heavy furniture has been out of style for at least a decade, and the floral-print chairs, the height of fashion during the shabby-chic era, now look like they belong at a yard sale. One kitchen cabinet is dangling sadly from a loose hinge, a repair I've been meaning to tackle for months but have never gotten around to.

Truthfully, the entire apartment is in desperate need of updates. It's been sorely neglected ever since my mom got sick. Even so, I can't bring myself to change a thing. She designed every room herself, each lovingly curated detail still retaining her essence. How could I possibly erase her from it?

When I moved into my parents' bedroom two years ago, I promised myself I'd donate some of her things, but I've always found excuses not to do it. It's my room now, but at the same time, it's still hers. The comforter on the sleigh bed no longer smells like her, but it's still comforting to crawl underneath each night. Only now there's a new scent, one that's soapy and clean. I'm surprised how much I like the change.

"Jake," I whisper again, shaking his arm lightly. "Wake up." He groans as one corner of his mouth rises in a sleepy half smile, his eyes still shut tightly. "Let me sleep, you insatiable woman. I need to regain my strength."

I shake my head as I slip my fingers through his, ignoring his protests as I drag him up to a sitting position. "Come on, let's go to bed."

5

WHEN I AWAKE AGAIN, a stream of sunlight is pouring through my bedroom window. Dragging one eye open, I roll over to check my clock. It's quarter to ten in the morning. I never sleep this late, and I feel like I'm on the bottom of the ocean. Propping myself up in a sitting position, I see Jake at the foot of my bed, slurping cereal out of a soup bowl.

"Hey, Edward Cullen, you always watch girls while they sleep?"

Jake pulls the spoon from his mouth and points in my direction, his eyes narrowed. "Only the ones I'm planning to murder."

"Don't you have an apartment to go home to?"

Jake shrugs. "Sure. But I'd rather stay here and hang out with you."

I yawn, pulling back the covers. "Where do you live, anyway?"

"Brooklyn. South Slope. With three dudes who all think they're the next John Mayer." Jake tilts the bowl upward, slurping down the rest of the milk in one long gulp. He looks more adorable than ever first thing in the morning, white T-shirt rumpled, chestnut hair sticking up in every direction.

"How're those Cheerios?"

He shrugs. "Incomparable to your blueberry pancakes, of

course. But I was starving, and I couldn't bear to wake you. You looked too peaceful. Not to mention beautiful."

Beautiful. My heart flutters at the sentiment, especially coming from the hottest man to ever grace my bedsheets.

"I think I can be persuaded to make another batch. But it's going to cost you."

Jake's face breaks into a mischievous grin.

"Oh, Dorothy," he moans, wiggling his eyebrows suggestively as he leans forward to brace his hands against the pillows behind me. I grab him by the neck of his T-shirt, tugging his body downward as he silences my laughter with kisses.

AN HOUR LATER, I finally cajole Jake out of bed with the promise of pancakes and a shower, followed by pasta and slow-cooked tomato sauce that simmers for the better part of the afternoon.

By the time it's ready it's nearly 6 P.M., and the setting sun has cast long, tangerine-colored shadows that spill through the living room windows and across the wooden floors. Grabbing a pair of tongs, I remove the onion halves, carrots, and basil stems from the pot and toss them into the trash can. The air is potent with the warm smell of spices, making the apartment feel comforting and cozy. It's been ages since I've done so much home cooking, and my heart swells with contentment.

Jake is propped up against the wall in the living room, wearing only his wrinkled undershirt and a pair of my sweatpants. His head is bent over the guitar, white baseball cap twisted backward, brow furrowed in concentration as his fingers run over the strings. He mutters something to himself, and the apartment fills with a few chords before he stops, readjusts, and begins again. I reach for my salt and pepper shakers, adding a few twists of each spice into the sauce to season it. I'll be damned if I ever forget to season a dish again.

Dipping a wooden spoon into the pot, I scoop a bit of sauce and bring it to my lips. It's perfect. I scoop up a bit more and, carrying a dish cloth beneath it, walk it carefully over to Jake for him to sample. He wraps his lips gratefully around the spoon and emits an approving moan.

"Heaven," he sighs, a small smile playing across his lips. He keeps his eyes locked on mine as his fingers move over the guitar strings once more, bobbing his head along to a melody I don't recognize.

"She's got a certain way about her, an alchemy that's all her own, something that makes me feel at home."

Confused, I tilt my head to the side. I don't recognize this song.

"Did you write this?" I ask. He responds with a sheepish smile, dipping his head before he continues.

"Found the key to my heart and what does she find? I've got the taste of blueberries on my mind."

I snort and toss the dishrag at him. Jake holds his elbow out in front of his face to block it.

"Hey! Is that any way to treat a man who's trying to write a song for you?" he protests. "Honestly, a million girls would die for this honor."

"Talented and humble," I muse as I return to the stovetop. "Besides, that song is less about me and more about your mounting obsession with my blueberry pancakes."

"Touché," he replies, propping the guitar against the wall. He strides into the kitchen, and I feel the heat of his body as he moves to stand behind me. When he wraps his arms around my waist, tucking my head under his chin, I instinctively run my fingertips over his forearms. It feels so right, being together like this. Too right.

"Ready to eat?" I ask. I turn around to face him, hoping my voice sounds more nonchalant than I feel.

Jake, however, does not seem convinced. His unsmiling eyes

run over my face, studying me carefully, and I feel myself blush under his gaze.

"What is it?" he asks softly after a moment. "Did I do something wrong?"

"No, of course not," I assure him. "You've been wonderful. Better than wonderful, really. But you're also leaving."

Jake's frown deepens. "Yeah, I know. But it's not like I'll be gone forever. It'll be two, three weeks, tops."

"It's just . . . maybe we shouldn't ruin this." *What are you doing?* my inner monologue shrieks, but I press it down as I continue.

"This thing between us. It's been perfect. And maybe that's all it was ever meant to be. One brief, perfect affair that we'll remember fondly when we're old and gray."

Jake is quiet for a long moment. His eyes search my face as he runs a hand through his tousled hair. "Is that really what you want?"

I nod, staring down at the floor. There's no way I'll be able to hold it together if I look at him right now.

"Listen, Lexi," he says. "I know we just met, and we barely know each other, but I feel like we have something here. A connection. And I'm pretty sure you feel it too." Sighing, I finally look up at him. He reaches a hand up to rest his palm against my cheek.

My face burns and I'm sure he can feel the heat against his skin. I take a deep breath, swallowing the jumble of emotion that catches in my throat. How have I managed to get so attached to this man in one weekend?

Jake pulls me into his chest. To my horror, a few tears escape, spreading in warm, wet splotches across his shirt. Tears for him leaving, but also for the unfairness of something new wilting away before it even had the chance to fully blossom. A confusing feeling, since I wasn't looking for a commitment to begin with. School needs my full attention right now, and the last thing I need is a distraction. So why do I even care?

"Hey, now, let's have none of that," Jake says softly. "Seriously, there's no crying in meatballs."

I let out a half laugh, half sob, burying my face deeper in Jake's shirt. "That's not the expression!" I protest into the fabric.

Jake chuckles as he pulls my hands away from my face. "How about we eat this absolutely insane-smelling dinner, and afterwards, we take a walk?"

FORTY MINUTES LATER, WE'RE strolling down the sidewalk, Jake's fingers interlaced with mine as the lights of the city glisten behind us. We've just about reached the subway when we spot a playground on the street corner.

Jake turns, a mischievous grin spreading across his face.

"Shall we?"

I'm about to tell him that public parks are closed at night and it's illegal to go inside after hours, but before I get the chance, he releases my hand and races ahead of me. Reluctantly, I chase after him, and by the time we reach the swings I'm panting with laughter.

Moments later we're swinging side by side, pumping our legs and staring up at the night sky.

"How about a contest?" he asks, his breath slightly ragged. "To see who can jump the farthest."

"Hmm. What are the terms?"

"If I beat you, I get to stay over again tonight."

"Oh yeah? And if I win?"

"Name your wager."

"When you're famous, I want you to take me to see a Broadway show. And I want to sit in the very first row."

"Deal," he agrees. "Okay, here we go: one . . . two . . . three!" We launch ourselves into the air, laughing as we tumble onto the rubberized surface below. Jake lands several inches behind me, arms spread above his head, wheezing dramatically. I roll over and place my hands on his chest.

"Are you okay?" I ask. "And I mean, are you okay emotionally, since you were just dominated and effectively committed to seeing *Mean Girls: The Musical*."

"Ugh, you win," he groans, bringing a hand to cover his face. "How could I say no? You're impossible to resist." He reaches out his other hand to tickle me, and I squeal as I roll over and onto my back.

Jake leans his body over mine, propping himself up on his elbows so he's staring down on me. His chocolate eyes darken as he skates a thumb across my cheek. Slowly, he leans down to brush his lips against mine. Pleasure spreads through my body as my fingers twist into his hair, pulling him closer and deepening our kiss.

I inhale slowly as I commit every detail to memory—the pressure of his hand against my cheek, the rubbery smell of the recycled tires beneath our backs, the low rumble of traffic in the distance—because I want to remember this moment for the rest of my life.

I groan when he finally breaks our connection, rolling onto his side and studying the clouds above us. Then he turns his head and grins.

"Any chance I can still get that sleepover?"

I smile back. "I think something can be arranged."

J AKE LEAVES AROUND SIX the next morning so he can have time to pack before his 2 P.M. flight.

He's lingering in the doorway, balancing his guitar on one shoulder, when I press a foiled-wrapped package of leftover pancakes into his hand.

"Something to remember me by," I say.

Lifting my chin, Jake raises my face toward him. His eyes are piercing as he gazes down at me. When he speaks, his voice is resolute.

"This isn't goodbye. It's just 'see you later.' Besides, I could never, in a million years, forget you, Alexa Berman."

I take a breath to quell the butterflies in my stomach.

"I'll call you when I'm back in town." He leans forward, giving me a long, languid kiss before he finally tears himself away. As he heads down the hallway, I feel myself deflate.

I smile weakly, waving as the elevator doors clang shut behind him. Luckily, it's already time to leave for class, which means there's no time to overanalyze the nagging sense of unease rising in my chest.

6

WHEN I GET DOWN to the lobby, Lionel is seated at the front desk. His pencil-thin mustache twitches in amusement when he sees me.

"Well, look who it is. Imagine my surprise when I was signing in this morning and saw a young man exiting the elevator from the sixth floor."

"Presumptuous of you to assume he was my guest. Mrs. Ackerman is back on the market, you know. She ended things with her boyfriend after he moved into assisted living on the West Side. Said he was, and I directly quote, 'not worth the cab fare.'"

Lionel is undeterred. "Handsome fellow. Is it serious?"

I scoff. "Hardly."

"You say it like it would be the worst thing in the world."

"Well, it wouldn't be the best thing! You know how busy I am with school right now."

Lionel's cheerful expression fades. "I do. I just worry about you. Living in that apartment alone."

"Lionel, I appreciate how invested you are in my love life, but I promise, I'm fine. Anyway, I have to leave before I'm late for class."

"Ah, that reminds me." He smiles. "Your toll." Grinning, I reach into my shoulder bag and pull out a Tupperware of leftover meat sauce and pasta. Lionel lifts the lid, sighing as he takes a whiff.

"How early is too early for lunch?" he asks dreamily.

Tossing him a wave over my shoulder, I head out through the lobby doors.

A FTER GRABBING THE LARGEST coffee available at the bodega, I make it to class just as demonstration is getting ready to start. Chef spends the morning explaining how to prepare venison tenderloin and aspic, a meat-infused Jell-O that looks like one of Jim Halpert's pranks from *The Office*. For once, I am not the least bit interested in having leftovers for lunch. Thankfully, the apple tart we'll be preparing for dessert looks delicious.

We head into the kitchen as soon as he finishes, and it isn't until I'm done marinating the bones that Ali and I finally get a chance to chat.

"So," she says, setting the sauce on the stove to reduce. "How was the rest of your night on Friday? I didn't hear from you all weekend."

I take a deep breath, choosing my words carefully. It's hard to think straight while battling through the fog of exhaustion. I've been up since 3 A.M., when I woke to Jake's hand slipping between my legs.

"Actually, I ended up going out after you guys left. Have you ever seen the eighties cover band at (Le) Poisson Rouge?"

Ali's eyes narrow with suspicion. "Can't say that I have. How did you end up there?"

"Um . . . I met a guy at the bar after you left, and he invited me." I avoid her curious look as I busy myself preparing the molds for the aspic, carefully picking one up and encasing it in plastic wrap.

Undeterred, Ali yanks the mold out of my hand and slides it

out of my reach. "Excuse me?" she squeals. "You met a boy, and you're just now telling me?"

"Hey, give that back! We need to get those into the freezer so they have enough time to chill." Snaking my arm around her, I grab the molds and head to the cold side of the kitchen. Ali is waiting for me when I return, her chin propped on her fist as she stares at me expectantly.

"You will spill this tea immediately."

"There's not much to tell," I say. "He was . . . cute. We had a few drinks, danced a little bit, and he walked me home. I had fun." I brush my hands on the dish towel I've tucked into the band of my apron, even though they are already dry.

"He walked you home?" Ali raises her eyebrows as she regards me skeptically. "Did you kiss him?"

The same butterflies from Friday night erupt through my belly as images flash through my mind. Jake's hips pressing my body against the doorframe. Jake's fingers sliding beneath the hem of my shirt. Jake's hot breath against my ear.

"Uh, yeah. We kissed." My body betrays my attempts at nonchalance as a hot flush snakes its way up my neck and spills onto my cheeks.

Making no effort to hide her mounting excitement, Ali taps her fingertips together gleefully. "I can't believe this! Tell me every detail!"

Her eyes bore into me, as though she can see right through my scalp to the filthy images burned into my brain. The palms of my hands grow clammy under her gaze. She studies me for a second before clapping a hand over her mouth, her eyes widening to the size of saucers.

"Ohmigod!" she squeals through her fingers. She drops her hand, staring at me in disbelief. "You *slept* with him?"

I bite my bottom lip, staring back in silent confirmation.

"Incredible," she says, shaking her head. "In the six months

I've known you, there's been zero dick in your life, and the one night I leave you to your own devices, you opt not to take 'Netflix and chill' literally."

I've gotten so close with Ali since the start of school that I sometimes forget she's only ever known the version of me that currently exists. The truth is, I was a boy-crazy preteen, the type who wallpapered her bedroom with photos of floppy-haired pop stars and spent hours daydreaming about cute boys at school.

But love in all its forms lost its luster after Mom died. I stopped being a child the day she left me, and suddenly boys and silly crushes seemed a lot less appealing. Sure, there had been a few men in my life since then, but none were particularly noteworthy. Until now, of course.

"Geez, Ali, can you keep it down? Some of us are trying to work." John, the career changer, glares at us from his station.

"Oh, fuck a tree, John," Ali hisses. "I promise, the day you finally get laid, I'll throw you a goddamn parade in celebration." John's face turns the same shade as his bright red hair. He grumbles under his breath before returning to his *mise*.

"I can't believe you boned a dude you just met," she continues, shifting her attention back to me as she bumps her tiny shoulder against mine.

"I know," I sigh. "It's so unlike me."

Ali tips her head back and laughs. "Now there's the understatement of the century. I think I might be rubbing off on you."

"I wouldn't go that far," I say. Ali's easily the most impulsive person I've ever met. She once got matching tattoos with a stranger she met in a bar after losing a bet. Prior to this weekend, the craziest thing I'd ever done was ignore the dry-clean-only labels on my laundry.

She's right, though: this is a very out-of-character move for me. Sure, I dated a few guys in college, but it took weeks before I was willing to have sex with any of them. But there is something about

Jake that's different from other men. The prerequisites seem to matter less somehow. I can't decide if it makes me excited, anxious, or a combination of the two.

"So, tell me everything. How was it?"

"It was—" Jake's handsome face materializes before me. His square jaw twitches as he steps through the stairwell doors and heads toward me, closing the space between us. My stomach flip-flops at the memory. "It was everything."

Ali's still smiling as she leans back against the counter. "Dude, I'm so proud of you. You finally got to experience the joy of engaging in casual sex while still sleeping alone in your bed."

"I wasn't alone. Jake stayed for the weekend. I made him my blueberry pancakes."

"I'm sorry . . . he spent the entire *weekend*?" Ali's voice squeaks at the end. She crosses her arms and regards me closely. "Lexi, I know one-night stands aren't your area of expertise, but trust me, that's not how you do it. In fact, you might actually be married now."

Desperate to change the subject, I pick up the plastic-wrapped dough we prepared earlier and pass it back and forth between my hands.

"We really need to get started on this apple tart," I remind Ali. "Which would you rather do: Roll out the pastry dough or slice the apples?"

"I'll take the dough." She smirks. "You've already gotten a good pounding."

Groaning, I grab a Jonagold apple from the basket at our station and start peeling it. We work quietly for a few minutes, and I'm just starting to think the conversation has ended when Ali re-opens the subject. "So, are you going to see him again?"

"Um, I doubt it. He's in LA for a few weeks for work. Honestly, this was probably just a one-off. Best-case scenario for everyone."

Ali opens her mouth and then shuts it again, like she's thought better of it. Narrowing her eyes, she shakes her head. "We'll talk about this later."

Breathing a sigh of relief, I get back to my *mise*. Despite her excessive interest in my love life, for once, Ali doesn't push. Besides, there's little opportunity to discuss it further, because just then, Chef pokes his head into the kitchen to remind us that we only have an hour left. We frantically return to our tasks, and blessedly, I'm too busy to entertain any more thoughts about Jake Taylor for the rest of the morning.

The afternoon passes in a blur. By the time I leave the building and head to the train, every limb in my body aches with exhaustion.

After getting off at my stop, I lumber up the sidewalk, half-heartedly staring at the buildings as I pass. My heart sinks a bit as I pass a familiar pink nail salon at the corner of Fifty-Seventh and Lex. I haven't been able to bring myself to go there since the last time I went with my mom.

I was fourteen years old the day I decided to become a professional chef. It happened by the dryers at Diva Darlings, my mom's favorite nail salon. She'd recently started dragging me along to her Saturday-morning manicures—she insisted keeping my nails polished was the only way to stop me from biting them—and I was trying to keep myself occupied without smudging my nails before the polish had fully dried.

Bored, I'd grabbed an old copy of *People* magazine from the rack by the coat stand and started gingerly thumbing through the worn pages. After flipping past photos of stars who were "just like us," and bypassing a profile on Jennifer Aniston, who once again insisted she was absolutely fine as a single woman, I landed on a page at the very back of the magazine featuring a recipe for the "Best Ever Blueberry Pancakes."

I read through the article once, and then twice more, drinking in every rich detail of the featured photograph. I studied the flow of the syrup as it dripped sensually down the sides of the golden stack, the way the juicy blueberries burst through the top and sides of the pancakes. Growing up in New York, I'd enjoyed plenty of killer brunches, but there was something thrilling about the idea of making my own version. My parents loved pancakes; how much fun would it be to serve them something I created?

When my mom announced her nails were finally dry and it was time to go home, I tore out the page as covertly as possible and stuffed it into my pocket. I kept my head down as we left the shop, making sure to avoid eye contact with the other patrons just in case one should have caught my thievery.

On the walk home, I begged Mom to stop off at the market so I could pick up all the ingredients I needed to make my pancakes. Though somewhat bemused by my sudden interest in cooking, she agreed to make the trip. I remember exactly the way I felt as we made our way through the aisles. It was the first time I felt that thrill, that magic that comes with choosing fresh ingredients for a new recipe.

Cooking became my passion, and when Mom got her diagnosis, it also became my escape. The more I learned and the harder I worked to hone my skills, the less powerless I felt. Mom was deteriorating before my eyes. Her body was shrinking, her complexion growing paler by the day. Worst of all, she was depressed; she hated feeling like she was letting me down, like she had nothing left to give me. But I still had something to give her. Food was a gift I could give my family, something warm and whole and substantial that could keep us going when we felt like giving up. A way to help during a time when I felt helpless. I loved seeing the joy on my parents' faces when I presented a new dish I'd made just for them, even when Mom started having trouble keeping it down.

Amid the chaos of her decline, I had purpose, something to focus on that filled me with a sense of satisfaction. Cooking had always been the one thing that made me feel good about myself . . . that is, of course, until I started culinary school.

ALI AND I HAVE visited the Union Square farmers market every Saturday morning since we first met at ICE this past fall. When I step out of the train station a little before noon, I'm so joyful that I'm practically skipping. It's one of those perfect spring days, the kind that makes people want to pack up a wheel of brie and a bottle of white wine so they can dine alfresco in Central Park.

After scanning the crowd for a minute, I locate Ali by an artisanal honey stand on the corner of Sixteenth Street. She's dressed in black leggings, pink high-tops, and a long-sleeved T-shirt decorated in all of Justin Bieber's tattoos.

"Nice shirt," I quip as I approach her, wrapping one arm around her in a quick hug.

"It's the closest I'll ever be to Justin's naked torso," she sighs wistfully. She holds up a glass mason jar wrapped in checkered blue cloth. "Speaking of hot, what do you think: Do I need to know what hot honey tastes like?"

"Absolutely. Think about how great it would be drizzled over a sourdough waffle." I grin at her. Coming up with new combinations is one of my favorite parts of cooking, something I thought I'd do more of in culinary school. But our classes are all about set recipes and mastering skills, not making up your own dishes. I can't wait for the day I'll get to make my own menu, changing it seasonally to come up with new creations using the freshest produce.

"Ooh, I love the way your mind works. Always so creative." Ali drops the jar into her tote bag and hands a couple of bills to the cashier. Hooking her arm through mine, she leads us farther into the market.

"So, have you heard from your new boyfriend yet?" she asks as we stop in front of a fresh produce stand.

"He is not my boyfriend," I correct her. "But yeah, he has texted a few times." The truth is, I've kept my cell phone beside me at all times since Jake left on Monday morning. I practically had a heart attack when it vibrated against my sheets at 2 A.M. last night, only to discover it was a Grubhub spam survey.

As if on cue, my phone buzzes in my hand. Butterflies erupt through my stomach when I see Jake's name flash across the screen. Clicking the message open, I see a photo of a half-eaten, soggy stack of pancakes.

> Had a hankering for blueberry pancakes but these amateur efforts are a B- at best. Missing the lemon juice, no doubt.

I grin as I type back a response.

> Well, if you want the good stuff, you know where to find me.

Ali grabs my elbow, turning my body toward her.

"Oh my god," she says slowly. "Lexi Berman, as I live and breathe. You do not merely like this boy. You *love* him!"

"I do not!" I object, shrugging to free my arm from her grasp. "Honestly, I barely know him."

"You've already started planning your wedding," she continues, ignoring me. "The Pierre. A June wedding, naturally. Classic, chic. You'll wear white, and I, your maid of honor, will wear tasteful champagne."

I groan as I pay for my peaches and drag Ali toward the next stand. The market is brimming with luscious March greens: artichokes, broccoli, brussels sprouts. I do my best to push Jake out of my mind and focus on all the possibilities in front of me.

"What about stuffed artichokes?" I lift one up and gently

finger its pointed petals. "I could roast them with some melted butter, then fill them with breadcrumbs and a bit of pecorino? Or should I just play it safe and get a pound of tomatoes?"

To her credit, Ali refuses to be distracted. "Tell me the truth. Are you getting his name tattooed on your ass?"

I rib her in the side before stopping in my tracks and squinting into the distance. "Wait. Is that . . . Shawn Mendes?"

Ali whips around so fast she nearly drops her basket. I attempt to bite back a giggle, but after taking one look at her face, burst into loud laughter.

"Sorry, I couldn't help myself."

Ali's nose wrinkles in playful anger.

"You're going to pay for that one!"

"How about an iced coffee to make amends? After I pay for these tomatoes."

"Sure," she says. "If you do me one favor. Admit, out loud, that you like this boy."

I roll my eyes. "Fine! I like him, okay? I really, really like him. Which makes no rational sense, because we just met, and we barely know each other. But there's something about him that's . . . I don't know. Special. And I can *maybe* see it going somewhere. There, are you satisfied?"

"Supremely so," she says, grinning as she links her arm through mine.

IT'S A LITTLE AFTER 1 A.M. that night when the buzzing of my cell phone slowly rouses me from the depths of sleep. Bleary-eyed, I grab the phone, rubbing my eyes with the heel of my hand. My body jolts awake at the sight of Jake's name on the screen. We've been texting all week, but this is the first time he's called since he left on Monday morning.

"Hey!"

"Lexi! You're never going to believe what's happened!" Jake sounds breathless, his excitement palpable even through the phone.

Before I can answer, he hurries on.

"So, Eddie and I were out at the bar tonight, and I decided to go up onstage and play a few songs, right? Afterwards, a few people came up to congratulate me and guess who one of them was? Seriously, you'll never guess."

"Who?" I ask, my stomach fluttering with excitement.

"Tommy Russo! Tommy *freakin'* Russo!"

I'm silent for a moment. "Sorry, who?"

"Oh, right. Sorry. He's this hot-shit music exec with El Sol Records. He was at the bar scouting out new talent, and he said he liked *my* music. But that's not even the wildest part. He wants me to come down to the studio tomorrow and audition for the head of the label. If all goes well, they might even sign me."

"No way!" I squeal, flopping down on my back and staring up at the ceiling. I grin as I imagine Jake onstage, guitar on one knee, his dimple popping as he smiles at adoring fans.

"I know. This is just so surreal," Jake sighs. "Listen, I gotta go. But I'll call tomorrow, okay? I promise."

"Sure," I reply. "Sounds great."

"And Lexi?"

"Yeah?"

"Better go ahead and pick out those Broadway tickets."

Grinning, I hang up the phone and plug it back into my charger. My heart is still pounding with shock and excitement. This could be it for Jake, his big break. Closing my eyes, I drift off to sleep, oblivious to the reality that awaits.

That this will be the first and last phone call I receive from Jake Taylor.

7

FOR AS LONG AS I live, I'll never forget the first time I heard "Blueberry" on the radio. I was in the school kitchen, cleaning up after a long morning of service. It was early September, the start of my final year of culinary school, six months since I'd last heard from Jake.

One of my classmates flipped open her laptop and connected to Spotify for some background music. As a familiar melody wafted through the speakers, I felt the hairs rise on the back of my neck.

"She's got a certain way about her, an alchemy that's all her own, something that makes me feel at home."

"Oh my god, I freakin' love this song! Turn it up!" Ali squealed. The music grew louder, and as his voice came through the speakers, the plate in my hand slipped through my fingers, crashing to the floor and shattering into a million pieces.

With a murmured apology, I knelt to the floor to pick up the shards. Trancelike, I listened to the lyrics as though hearing them for the first time.

"I met her once, but she's gotten to me. Slipped inside me, made me feel so woozy. Found the key to my heart and what does she find? The taste of blueberries on my mind."

No, it couldn't be. It wasn't possible. Was it?

My eyelids fluttered shut as I was transported back to the first time I heard this song. The smell of meat sauce wafting through the kitchen. Long fingers sliding elegantly over guitar strings. A pair of chocolate eyes warming as they met my own.

"My newest imaginary boyfriend," Ali sighed, interrupting my thoughts as she knelt beside me, dustpan in hand. "His name is Jake Taylor. You ever heard of him?"

I DON'T KNOW WHY I'VE never told anyone the truth about my relationship with Jake. Maybe because it would make it less real, cheapen it somehow. The secrecy preserves what we had: the memories are mine alone, locked away in my heart, like Rose De-Witt Bukater's romance with Jack Dawson.

I waited all day to hear from Jake the morning he went to meet with the El Sol executive. By 10 P.M., I gave in and called him, my heart thumping as the phone rang in my ear. And rang. And rang. Until finally, it clicked over to voicemail. I sent him a text, since only psychos leave voicemails. Hey, it's me! Call me when you get this. A moment later, three dots appeared on the screen. Then nothing.

Two days and another unanswered text later, I was starting to get worried. When I tried him again, a robotic female voice informed me that the voicemail box was full. A day after that, he sent me a quick text: Sorry, I've been swamped! I'll call tomorrow. But he didn't.

The rest of the week passed in a fog. I spent most of it staring forlornly at my phone, willing it to produce a message from Jake. The phone stared back at me blankly, showing nothing but the hours passing.

By the time our weekly happy hour rolled around, I was a sullen mess. Ali was also in rare form that afternoon. Still white-hot with rage after yet another disastrous date, she'd mounted one of her soapboxes to deliver a TED Talk on "How All Men Are the Worst."

"You can't conflate every bad experience you've had into a blanket statement about men," Chloe argued. "Besides, they're hardly the only offenders. Do you not remember Jo from Macy's PR department? The one I brought home for Christmas after they told me they wanted to be exclusive, only to ghost me the minute we got back to the city?"

"Point taken," Ali relented. "I'm just so over dating in New York. All anyone here wants is a fuck and to fuck off. I'm seriously considering joining a convent. You know, if they made one for Jews." By that point, she'd already refilled her margarita glass three times, and her words were beginning to slur. She tipped her chin toward me to punctuate her point. "I mean, just look at what joining the dating pool has done to our little Lexi."

They both turned to stare at me then, the pity in their eyes impossible to miss. In fairness, it wasn't unmerited. I knew how I looked, with my unwashed hair and eyes that had gone red after too many late nights spent staring at my phone, willing it to ring.

"My thing is not like your thing," I protested. "Jake's going to call. He's just . . . busy." Ali and Chloe exchanged a look, and I felt my cheeks grow hot. Even to my own ears, it sounded pathetic.

"They're all 'busy,'" Ali retorted. "They're all 'busy' and 'tired' and 'overworked,' and whatever other line they feed us. We've got to stop making excuses for these dismissive assholes! Are we seriously going to spend the best years of our lives chasing fuckboy finance bros who send us one-word text messages at two A.M., or are we going to stand up for ourselves and demand better?" I considered pointing out she was the one chasing finance bros, not me. But before I got the chance, she grabbed the phone from my hand and began scrolling through my messages.

"Your last text from this clown was three days ago, when he said he was going to call you the next day. Did he?"

"No," I admitted, my voice small.

"And did he provide any reason as to *why* he didn't call?"

"Well, he—"

"Yes or no?" she pressed on.

"No," I conceded sulkily.

"And aren't you better than this? Don't you *deserve* better than this?"

After a pause, I nodded at her wordlessly. She was right. After years of coming in second place to my dad's new life in Boca, I'd somehow managed to fall right back into the same pattern with Jake. I did deserve better.

I watched her mouth settle into a determined line, and then she began typing furiously. When she handed it back a minute later, my entire message history with Jake had been erased.

"What did you do?" I asked, though I wasn't quite sure I wanted to hear the answer.

"What you don't have the balls to do yourself." I stared at her in silent disbelief until she relented and said, "I simply reminded him that you are a majestic unicorn who deserves to be treated with respect. And then I deleted him from your contacts, because you don't need to spend another minute reading back over your messages, obsessing over what you said to each other and trying to figure out where it all went wrong."

When I started to protest, Ali put out a hand to stop me. "Don't bother trying to deny it. Believe me, I'm doing you a favor by freeing you of the temptation. Jake is a grown man. The ball is in his court. If he wants to talk, he knows where to find you."

But he didn't find me. He didn't text me back for the rest of the evening, or the day after, or the one after that. The silence continued for another week until the truth finally hit me. I wasn't going to hear from Jake. Not now, or ever again.

After the initial sting of rejection wore off, I told myself it was all for the best. Those two excruciating weeks of thirsting for texts from Jake like they were droplets of water in the desert had wreaked havoc on my performance in the classroom. Which was ridiculous, considering male-induced distractions were the whole reason I avoided dating in the first place. It was good that things between us had fizzled out before he became an even bigger diversion.

I couldn't help feeling like an idiot, though. How could I have misread the situation so badly? Yet, as my mother would have said, the facts of the matter were irrefutable: Jake was no longer interested in talking to me, and I had only made a fool of myself by continuing to reach out to him. Clearly, I'd romanticized the whole thing from the get-go, and this was the punishment for breaking my no-dating rule. It was time to move on and forget the whole thing had ever happened.

The thing is, it's nearly impossible to stop thinking about a guy you slept with when his face is plastered on every bus in Manhattan.

8

"DO YOU EVER WONDER what Jake Taylor is like in bed?" I blink twice as I stare at Ali's reflection in the mirror, wondering if I've heard her correctly.

"Excuse me?"

It's the first week of May, just two weeks shy of graduation. Ali and I are standing in my bathroom, getting ready for the graduation party we're co-hosting at my apartment.

She grins as she slides a hoop through her earlobe. "I've had 'Blueberry' stuck in my head all day. That song is so freakin' *sexy*. Wait, let me put it on."

Ali strides into the living room and clicks on the TV, scrolling to a music channel. She types in Jake's name and the now all-too-familiar opening chords fill the air. For the past eight months, I've avoided reading anything about Jake, averting my eyes when I see his face splashed across the covers of grocery store tabloids and fan accounts on TikTok. I flat-out refused to join Ali when she invited me to his show at UBS Arena last month on the grounds that "concerts aren't really my thing." But it's impossible to escape the popularity of the hit single that skyrocketed Jake to fame. The song is everywhere: blasting through the overhead speakers at the grocery store, pouring out cab windows, and playing faintly in the background of Instagram reels.

"I mean"—Ali's voice cuts through my daydream—"that *voice*. There's no way a man who sings like that isn't sexually gifted. He just has that energy about him, you know?" A series of memories flashes across my brain. Jake's fingers twisting in my hair. His teeth scraping against my throat. His brown eyes, heavy-lidded, as he lowered himself between my legs. My thighs clench as I remember *exactly* how gifted he is.

"Um, I guess," I reply noncommittally.

"God, imagine being the girl he writes songs about. Have you heard his latest single, 'Dorothy'? I'd literally kill for a man to be that in love with me. And you know what he means when he refers to blueberries." She wiggles her eyebrows at me.

I shake my head. "Has it ever occurred to you that maybe the song really *is* about blueberries?"

Ali rolls her eyes. "Yeah, right. And 'Watermelon Sugar' is about Harry Styles's passion for fruit salad." She glances around the kitchen. "Do you think we have enough to drink, or should I run down to the bodega?" Her eyes slide over the display of alcohol and mixers I've arranged neatly on my island countertop.

"We have plenty. People will bring stuff, too." My stomach rumbles loudly. "And hopefully also some food."

"Dev said he's going to bring his famous five-layer bean dip." Ali's eyes practically turn into emoji hearts as she says his name. She's been dating him for a few weeks now, and I've never seen her so excited about a guy. "He's literally the nicest person I've ever met," she told me and Chloe over happy hour margs a week after their first date. "He's a first-grade teacher, owns a three-legged rescue dog, and there isn't a single photo of him holding a fish on his Hinge profile. I think he might be The One."

"Just stay off my bed," I groan. "Seriously, I just washed the sheets."

Ali shrugs. "Let's get this party started, shall we?" She pulls two shot glasses off the counter and fills them practically to the brim with vodka.

"To finding true love."

She places one glass in my hand and raises hers in the air.

"To our culinary futures," I correct her. We clink and knock back our shots, wincing as we bang the empty glasses down on the counter.

"You'd better hook us up with something classier than Smirnoff when you're at The Carlyle," I croak, washing the shot down with a long sip of lemon seltzer. Even though we still have a couple of weeks left of classes, Ali has already secured her post-graduation job at The Carlyle hotel's acclaimed restaurant, the same place where she did her externship. I'm thrilled for her—she's so talented, and this is an incredible opportunity—and she is thrilled about the possibility of potentially serving celebrities.

"It's a deal," she agrees, filling up our glasses for a second round. "But for now, we drink this shoe polish like the peasants we are."

We throw back another and I wipe my hand across my mouth, shuddering.

"Okay, I'm ready," I say. "Let's close out the school year like champions."

BEFORE I KNOW IT, June has arrived. After submitting my résumé to a few different places, I end up interviewing at Olive & Pomegranate, an upscale Mediterranean restaurant in Midtown. Three days after my interview, I'm invited back for a *stage*, a sort of trial-run to assess my skills in the kitchen and how well I interact with other staff. I spend the evening beforehand reading every article I can find about successful *staging*, and by the time I arrive the next morning, I'm feeling confident.

I'm just about to head inside when the pocket of my jacket vibrates with an incoming text. When I pull out my phone, I see Dad's name, and I close my eyes for a moment before reading his message. Good luck on your first day, Loo! My heart swells at his use of my childhood nickname, yet my fingers hover over the keyboard, unsure how to respond. I appreciate that he wants to support me—he always has, even when I've resisted his efforts (and Fran's, for that matter)—but it feels wrong to have one of his pep talks delivered via text. He should be here, wishing me luck in person while we linger over everything bagels and lox at Ess-a-Bagel. Not down in Florida, living a replacement life with a replacement wife.

It's not that Fran is a bad person. It's just that she was too soon. My dad met her in an online support group—she'd lost her spouse too, in a biking accident—and after that, everything happened so fast. My parents had been together for over twenty years; they'd built an entire life together. When she died, my world crumbled, and I expected that my dad's would too. But he didn't even seem to mourn her. He packed up and moved down to Florida to be with Fran before we even celebrated my mom's *Yahrzeit*. No matter how hard she tries, I can't forgive Fran for taking my dad away from me. My mom was my best friend, and losing her was hard enough. But thanks to Fran, both of my parents were taken from me in one fell swoop.

Call me later and let me know how it goes, he texts now, but I shove the phone back into my pocket without responding before pulling open Olive & Pomegranate's double doors.

Though the restaurant is closed, a young brunette hostess who introduces herself as Hannah leads me back to the kitchen. It's early, and without the hum of appliances, the space feels peaceful. As soon as we step through the doors, I spot Oren, the sous chef who interviewed me. His hazel eyes crinkle in the corners as they connect with mine. He takes a step toward me, extending a hand.

"Alexa, welcome back!" His voice is kind but booming, a perfect match to his round, rosy cheeks and salt-and-pepper scruff. "Let me quickly introduce you to the rest of the team."

He motions for me to follow him. The tour starts with a walk-through of the line, the cornerstone of the kitchen. It's T-shaped and split into two sides: hot and cold. A fifteen-foot stove serves as the centerpiece. Directly across from the T is the pass: a stainless-steel table where cooks deliver their food to Chef for plating, and Chef passes it to waiters for serving. Oren leads me to the hot side first, pointing out the designated areas for cooking meat, roasting fish, and boiling pasta.

"Lexi, this is Juan, our *rotisseur*." He gestures to a balding man with meaty forearms, who jerks his head in greeting as he carves away at a thick slab of red meat. A gold wedding band gleams on his knife-wielding left hand, flecks of blood splattered across his thick fingers.

"And this is Corbin, our *poissonnier*." Corbin is much younger than Juan, mid-twenties at most with a mop of curly blond hair. When he says "hello" with a wide, toothy grin, I notice his voice is tinged with an accent. French, maybe? I make a mental note to ask later.

Next, Oren introduces me to Stefan and Hank, the *entreme-tiers*. Stefan is scooping handfuls of diced vegetables into a blender, while Hank is working on a wine reduction.

"These are our vegetable cooks. If hired, you'll be doing a lot of garnish work alongside these guys," Oren explains. "For every steak Juan prepares, you'll need to make at least half a dozen garnishes to go with it. Any part of a dish that needs to be wilted, roasted, pressed, grated, dressed—that's where these guys come in."

I nod, doing my best to take it all in and remember as many names as possible. We cross the room, walking around to the other side of the T.

"This is the cold side of our kitchen, where you'll primarily be working," Oren explains. I take a quick look around the bare-bones setup, a gleaming metal countertop with two induction burners and a convection oven. A roll-in freezer and a pair of lowboys flank either side of the small workstation. Goosebumps creep up my flesh, and I rub a hand over my arm absentmindedly. "Cold side" is a fitting description for this section of the kitchen; with an emphasis on refrigeration, there's little by way of heat.

"Don't worry, by the time service begins, you'll be sweating," Oren adds, as though he's read my mind. Then he gestures to a sandy-haired man rolling out dough a few feet away.

"And this guy"—he walks over, throwing his arm around the other man's shoulders—"is Ethan, our esteemed pastry chef."

A flutter rolls through my chest as Ethan lifts his head. His eyes, a dazzling shade of cerulean, run over my face appraisingly. He's not especially tall but he's in great shape, with broad, muscular shoulders that fill out his chef's coat. He brushes his hand on his apron before extending it toward me, raising one corner of his mouth in a half smile. "Welcome to the madhouse."

Oren snorts as he rolls his eyes. "Don't listen to a word he says, Lexi. He's just salty because he's about to lose a bet and be out twenty bucks." He claps a hand against Ethan's back. "Don't worry, buddy. You can pay me back with drinks at Freddie's later."

"Yeah, yeah." Ethan shakes his head before returning his attention to his dough.

Oren flashes me a quick grin. "Freddie's is the bar across the street where we hang out after work. You're welcome to join us this evening."

"Sure, I'd love to." I'll go to any bar he wants me to if it means I'll be getting the job.

Oren rolls his shoulders in a stretch, cracking both sides of his neck. "Come on, let me show you to our garde-manger station. That's where you'll be working tonight." We move down to the other end of the cold station, where a woman is prepping greens and separating them into metal bowls. Her dark hair is cropped in an undercut pixie that highlights her prominent cheekbones. The muscles of her strong, tattooed arms flex as she works.

"Hey, Mia. This is Lexi Berman. She'll be helping you out

tonight." Mia's brow lowers as she runs her eyes up and down my body, her mouth twisting into a smirk. She looks like she's about my age, maybe a year or two younger, but the second her eyes meet mine, I have a sinking feeling we won't be making friendship bracelets together anytime soon. I gulp when my gaze snags on the chef's-knife tattoo behind her ear.

"If you're here, who's minding the counter at Ann Taylor?" Mia deadpans. I glance down at my clothes, running a hand self-consciously over my blue button-up blouse. All the websites I checked told me to dress professionally. What have I done wrong?

Oren makes a noise beside me, and when I look over at him I can tell he's biting back a smile. "Yeah, you'll need to borrow some whites. I'll grab you a spare set when we go back to the office to meet Chef." *Oh, right.* My stomach drops as a wave of humiliation washes over me. Why didn't it occur to me that I would need chef whites tonight?

"Speaking of which, ready to meet the big guy?" I nod silently, following him as he leads us to an office in the corner. We've no sooner approached the doorway when a tall man with a head of thick, dark curls and a scruffy beard emerges from within, his face bent over a thick pad of paper.

"Speak of the devil! Lexi, this is Amir, our executive chef." Chef flicks his eyes upward, giving me a cursory nod before walking off. Oren shoots me a conciliatory smile. "Yeah, Chef's not much of a talker. But his food is incredible."

He steps into the back office, reappearing moments later with a white poly-blend chef's coat and black pants in hand. I take a deep breath and try not to dwell on my faux pas. At least I had the sense to wear my work clogs.

Oren's smile is warm and reassuring. "Don't sweat it. A lot of people make this mistake on their first day." He gestures to a bathroom beside the service exit. "You can get changed there. When you finish, I'll get you set up for *mise.*"

By the time 4 P.M. rolls around, the kitchen is buzzing with energy. The air fills with the *whoosh* of ignited burner flames, the sizzle of fat in frying pans, and the clatter of steel pans on metal countertops.

Oren gives me a quick run-through of my tasks for the evening. Tonight's special is a hanger steak served with carrot puree and a potato galette. I'll be responsible for making the galettes, as well as helping anywhere else I'm needed. Oren grabs a Yukon gold from my station, using a chef's knife to model how thinly each potato should be sliced.

"If you need any help, Mia's your girl," he says. I glance over at my cooking companion who has been steadfastly ignoring me ever since our introduction. Somehow, I doubt she's going to be any help this evening.

"Where the hell are my pans?" A torrent of Spanish explodes across the kitchen before Corbin hands Juan a pair of stainless-steel saucepans. Juan snatches them, shaking his head in frustration.

Exhaling, I return my attention to my own station, taking a few deep breaths to quell the feeling of anxiety rising in my chest.

Concentrate, I remind myself. *Now's the moment to show everyone what you've got. Just stay calm and pretend you're at home, in your own kitchen. Imagine you're cooking for Mom.* I bristle at the intrusive thought, worried it will throw me off my game entirely, but I feel pleasantly surprised when the thought instead sends a spark of joyful confidence through my veins.

I begin chopping the potatoes as quickly as possible, tossing them into a bowl of cold water to remove the excess starch. Oren comes by to chat with Mia about the carrots, modeling how to pass them through a sieve to achieve the ideal texture. "Not too soupy—we're not making baby food here," he instructs. She mutters a reply under her breath but resumes the task, returning the carrots to the blender so she can finish the puree.

Within minutes I'm out of potatoes, so I head to the back

storage room to grab another basketful. When I return to my station, the first thing I notice is that my knife has vanished. A quick glance across the flat top confirms my fear: Mia's hand is firmly wrapped around the base of the eight-inch blade.

"Hey, I, uh . . . that's my knife."

"I'm sure you have another." She smirks. "I'm sure your parents bought you a fancy set when you graduated from your fancy culinary school." Her words slice through me like the Japanese blade in her hand. Cold. Sharp. Precise. I bite the inside of my cheek, blinking back hot, threatening tears. There's no way I'm going to cry in front of this girl. Not here.

"Actually, my parents weren't at my graduation," I say quietly. "My mom died when I was fifteen and my dad was . . . otherwise engaged." What I neglect to mention is that my dad wasn't at graduation because I didn't invite him. He would have brought Fran, and I couldn't bear the thought of seeing her there beside him, bleached teeth gleaming as she snapped photos on her iPhone. She didn't belong there; it was my mom's dream to see me become a chef, not hers, and I had no interest in an inadequate substitute. I could hear the hurt in my dad's voice when I told him not to bother coming, that I probably wouldn't even walk. But he didn't argue. He never does. I appreciate that he respects my boundaries, but his acquiescence always stings a bit. Part of me wishes he would push back, that he would fight harder for me.

Mia stiffens slightly beside me, but keeps her mouth set in a firm line. Nevertheless, she slides the knife back to me, grumbling under her breath as she grabs another. I take a deep, steadying breath and get back to work.

A few minutes later, I'm ready to begin my galettes. Starting in the center of a skillet, I arrange the potatoes and shallots in a circular pattern, slightly overlapping the slices until the six-inch pan is completely covered. I press down with a spatula, letting the galette sizzle for a few minutes before sliding it onto a cutting board. Pinching off the edge, I pop a bite into my mouth. It's hot but delicious.

Soon, I've gotten myself into a nice rhythm. Slice, circle, sprinkle, fry. My confidence grows in synchrony with the mounting stack of galettes at my station. Before I know it, an hour has passed, and Chef has begun circling the kitchen to taste-test each dish. He makes his way slowly down the line, nodding his approval as he samples Corbin's sauce and Mia's carrot puree. By the time he arrives at my station, my heart is thundering against my rib cage.

He takes a small bite of galette, chewing contemplatively before shaking his head. My stomach bottoms out, an unpleasant sensation of déjà vu snaking its way through my body.

"Too soggy," he says quietly. "They need to be crispier. Again."

"Again?" My eyes flit over to the stack of galettes I've been making for over an hour. "Like . . . all of them?"

Chef raises a single dark eyebrow. "Yes. All of them."

Hot panic surges through my veins. Just like that, I'm back in the classroom, nerves fraying under the pressure. How am I going to be able to remake all these galettes in so little time? But before I can freak out any further, Mia grabs a bowl of potatoes and a peeler.

"What are you doing?"

"Helping you, of course." The peeler in her hand flies over the potato, flaying off its golden skin with expert speed. "Customers are still going to want their galettes, regardless of how hopeless the new kitchen staff is."

"Oh, um. Thanks."

She rolls her kohl-rimmed eyes. "It's not, like, a personal favor. That's just how things operate around here. Culinary school may be all about mastering technique, but working in a kitchen is about teamwork."

Miraculously, we manage to remake the entire stack in a little under thirty minutes, and when Chef rotates through again, he smiles in approval.

"I really do appreciate your help," I say again, throwing Mia a grateful smile. She grunts, shrugging off the compliment.

"Well, buckle up. Second seating is gonna start any minute now."

As if on cue, the kitchen fills with the buzz of the ticket printers. The first dinner orders have started rolling in. A moment later, Oren strides over to our station.

"You ready, Berman?" he asks. I nod, lifting my chin resolutely. "Good. Because it's showtime."

From there, things move quickly. Within minutes, we're swamped with salad orders, and I begin grabbing the dishes as quickly as Mia plates them, swinging them over to the pass.

"Service!"

Oren jogs over. "What table?"

"Um . . ."

Panicked, I turn to Mia. "Nine," she responds coolly, glancing at the ticket. Thank goodness each station has its own printer.

"Nine," I repeat. "And the hummus bowl is on twenty-two."

Oren smiles approvingly but there's no time to revel in my success. A flurry of white dishes soars past me, landing on the pass for plating. Timers ring out.

"Service!" Chef calls.

"To the pass!"

The buzzing of the printers is faster now, barely a moment of silence between each order. Two hours whirl by before they finally slow down again, and the entire atmosphere of the kitchen seems to exhale. Breathless, I take a glance around: the team is red-faced and sweaty, slowly bringing their messy stations back to order. Slumping against the metal counter, I take a long sip of water from my thermos. Just then, a plate of hummus and pita slides across the counter toward me.

"You should eat something. New cooks always forget to eat on their first night." Ethan, the pastry chef, is standing in front of me, a small smile playing on his lips. He nudges the plate forward. My stomach growls and I realize he's right—I'd been too nervous to partake in family meal, and now I'm starving.

"Wow, thank you," I say gratefully. I pick up a piece of bread, dip it in the hummus, and pop it into my mouth. Ethan opens his mouth to say something further just as Oren lumbers over.

"Hey, nice job tonight," he says.

"Thanks!" I manage, swallowing quickly. "I had a lot of fun."

Oren leans over, grabbing a piece of pita off my plate and stuffing it into his mouth.

"So . . . can you start on Friday?"

My face splits into a wide smile. "Really?" A rush of excitement pumps through my chest. All my hard work, the struggles, the disappointment that led to this moment were worth it. *I did it.* I've finally gotten my first restaurant job.

He grins. "Yep. And service is rounding to a close, so we should be able to head out of here in an hour, once we finish *mise* and clean-down. Join us at the bar?"

T HE FIRST THING I do when I step out of the service entrance is take long, greedy gulps of the cool night air. I can't believe how fresh it feels in my lungs after spending the last twelve hours straight in the kitchen.

Crossing the street, I follow Oren and Ethan to Freddie's, a wood-paneled pub that seems to be entirely filled with members of the food service industry.

Even though it's well after eleven, and we've all been working for hours, the crowd inside is buzzing with energy. We make our way to the back, where Oren exchanges high fives with the bartender, a curly-haired man in his mid-forties.

The bartender retrieves a glass from beneath the bar and pours a glass of whiskey for Oren, which I find strange considering I hadn't heard him order anything. I guess the staff really does come here nightly; the bartender seems to have memorized their orders.

"The team comes here almost every night after work. The closers will meet us a little bit later," Ethan says, as though he's read my mind. He slides onto a stool next to me, resting his elbows on the bar. Now that he's changed out of his chef whites and into a light blue T-shirt that makes his blue eyes pop, he looks at least five years younger.

"Seriously?" I ask incredulously. "Aren't you guys exhausted?"

He shrugs, running a hand through honey-colored curls. "When you work the kind of hours we do, there isn't a lot of downtime. You need a place to blow off steam, you know?"

A sense of displeasure creeps through my body. Now that I'm staff, will I be expected to go out every night as well? The thought is wholly unappealing.

"What can I get you?" The bartender is standing in front of me, eyebrows raised expectedly.

"A whiskey sour, please. Two cherries."

When he places the glass down in front of me a moment later, I drain half of it in an eager swallow. It burns my throat on the way down, reminding me just how dehydrated I am, and I make a mental note to do a better job drinking water during my next shift.

The bells chime over the doorway as Mia steps inside, flanked on either side by Juan and Corbin. Hank trails behind them.

Mia saunters over to the jukebox, then makes her way over to us, wiggling her hips to the Lana Del Rey song she's selected. She's changed into dark jeans and a black leather jacket that make her look even more intimidating than she did in the kitchen.

"Sup, Mia." The bartender flashes her a grin. "Gin and tonic?"

"You know it."

She looks over at me, carefully eyeing me up and down.

"Well . . . you did okay tonight," she admits after a pause. "Even if you did come dressed as a receptionist."

"Really? Thanks." I get the feeling that for Mia, this is practically a compliment.

She turns to Hank.

"Pool?"

The two of them head off to the table in the back corner.

"Wow, praise from Mia," Ethan remarks once they're safely out of earshot. "That's no small feat, you know."

I shrug my shoulders. "I'm just grateful I got the job. To tell you the truth, I was pretty nervous I'd blow it."

He smiles. "I know what you mean. My first night on the job, I threw up in the bathroom."

"No!"

"It's true." He gives a frank shake of his head. "I've been working in kitchens for five years now, and I still get nervous. Everyone does. We all have bad nights here and there. The secret is, when you need to cry—and trust me, at some point, you will—you do it in the walk-in. Get in there, let it out, and then get back to work."

I raise an eyebrow at him. "People really cry in the walk-in fridge?"

"Lexi, everyone cries in the walk-in." He tips his chin toward Oren. "Especially that guy."

I glance over at Oren, his hulking frame bent over the bar as he chats loudly at the bartender. Try as I might, I can't picture it.

"Trust me, you'll see," Ethan says, as though he's read my mind again. "Dude's like a molten lava cake. Hard on the outside, soft and weepy on the inside."

As if on cue, Oren strides over to us, clapping Ethan on his shoulder. "It's time to settle up, kid. A bet's a bet, after all. And I won this one."

Ethan reaches into his back pocket, extracting his wallet. He pulls out a twenty-dollar bill and slips it to Oren, who salutes him before lumbering back to the bar.

Confused, I turn to Ethan. His ears are tipped in red.

"So, what was this bet, exactly?"

Ethan glances up at me, his expression flushed with mortification.

"I bet Oren that Mia would scare you off before you finished your *stage*. He said you could hold your own, that you were tougher than you look." He runs a hand through his hair sheepishly. "He was right, of course. You did great tonight. I'm sorry, Lexi. Really, I feel like a jerk."

"It's fine," I assure him. "But just so you know, you're buying me another drink."

Ethan's face splits into a relieved grin. "You've got yourself a deal."

I'M NOT SURE IF it's the exhaustion, the adrenaline, or the two whiskey sours pumping through my bloodstream, but by the time I get home around 1:30 A.M., my whole body is buzzing. I take a quick shower, hoping it will settle me down, but when I crawl beneath the bed sheets, I'm still cold brew–level twitchy. I pick up my phone, intending to relax by scrolling through videos of my favorite internet Yorkie. But when I open Instagram, my fingers seem to operate of their own accord, and the next thing I know, I'm typing the words "Jake Taylor" into the search bar.

I never followed Jake on social media, and in an effort to preserve my sanity, haven't looked him up once since his career took off. But there's something about landing my first restaurant job that makes me think of him, and to my chagrin, I realize I'm longing to tell him about it.

Pulling up his page, I mindlessly thumb through the grid, scrolling past a mixture of onstage snapshots and airbrushed photos from magazine shoots. I pause when I reach a black-and-white photo of him. He's seated with his back against a wall, head bent over the guitar in his lap. I linger over the image, my eyes drinking in every detail: the sharp line of his jawbone, the fullness of his lips, the dark lock of hair that spills lazily across his forehead. Just as I've convinced myself to get a grip and close the app, my gaze snags on the caption. As I read it, my mouth goes dry.

> About 12,500 women a year die from cancers of the uterine body. This disease steals away friends, daughters, and mothers, leaving behind a void that can never be filled. But we can help. I've partnered with the American Cancer Society and have donated a portion of proceeds from my first album to support research for endometrial cancer. I urge you all to do the same. Click the link in my bio to donate now.

I read the caption again and again, pulse hammering erratically. It has to be a coincidence. There's no way that Jake could have remembered my mother died of uterine cancer. Yet despite the logic in my reasoning, I can't quite convince myself that it's true.

Squinting at the photo, I pinch it with two fingers in an attempt to zoom in, but accidentally double-tap instead to "like" it.

"*Shiiiit,*" I hiss, staring in horror at the red heart beneath the image. I did not mean to do that. What if Jake sees it and realizes I've been stalking him online?

I stare at the screen helplessly, wondering what to do next. Should I unlike it? Will he still get a notification if I do?

Calm down. He's not going to see it, a voice in my head argues. *This post has over ten thousand likes. He won't notice one more.* At the thought, my body relaxes. I'm definitely overreacting. I doubt Jake checks his social media at all; he probably has someone who handles it for him.

I stare at the photo again for a long moment, a different emotion slowly replacing my panic. When my mom passed away, it felt like no one could say the right thing. A few of my friends stopped by the apartment the week we sat shiva, but their attempts at comforting platitudes always fell short. My blood boiled every time I heard the words "I'm sorry." "Sorry" was what you said when you stepped on a teammate's foot in gym class, not when someone loses the most important person in her life. "It's going to be okay" was just as bad, because things were never going to be okay again. The only person I could tolerate was Chloe, who sat quietly beside me on a stiff metal folding chair for the entire week. Somehow she knew that I didn't need empty words, just the simple gesture of staying beside me, never leaving. But Jake's gesture is on another level entirely. If the little voice inside me is right—and I'm increasingly sure it is—this is the most meaningful response to her death I've ever received. And I'm not quite sure what to do with that.

Exhaustion finally crashing over me, I plug my phone into the charger and drift off into a dreamless sleep.

9

I'S JUST BEFORE 9 A.M. when I arrive for my first Saturday morning shift. Running a hand over my double-pressed white coat, I step through the service doors and into the kitchen, pausing to appreciate the soothing orderliness around me. Kitchens are always at their best in the morning. The stainless-steel appliances glimmering, the pots and pans freshly scrubbed, and the white china stacked in tidy columns on shelves. I feel like an artist admiring a fresh ream of white paper, itching to release a new project from my fingertips.

I've just finished prepping my station when a small rectangular plate with a sliver of apple tart slides in front of me.

"Mind trying this and letting me know what you think? I'm testing out a new crust." Ethan smiles at me from across the island. I dig my fork into the flaky crust. Instantly, my mouth waters from the divine taste.

"Wow, this is amazing," I gush, brushing a crumb from the corner of my lip. "You just came up with this?"

Ethan jams his hands into his apron pockets and rocks back on his heels. "Technically, it's pretty similar to the one I normally make. But everything tastes better when you add extra butter."

"You got that right," I say with a grin.

"Do you like baking?" he asks.

I wrinkle my nose. "Honestly," I admit, "I hate it."

Ethan leans back against the counter, crossing his arms across his chest. "Really? And why is that?"

"There's just so much room for error," I explain. "I'll spend so much time working on a dessert, and then the entire thing will end up being a disaster because I made one small mistake that set off a mysterious chain of chemical reactions that I don't really understand."

Ethan laughs. "Fair enough. Baking requires so much precision."

"Trust me, I appreciate precision. What I don't enjoy is the lack of control. With cooking, if you make a mistake, you can still fix it. You can always add more stock or more salt. If you mess up when you bake, you're done for."

Ethan shakes his head. "That's not necessarily true. Things might not always turn out the way you planned, but that doesn't always mean they're ruined."

Turning away, I stare down at my empty plate, twirling the fork around the crumbs.

"True, but you're forgetting about the flour. I hate being covered in flour. Why does it always get everywhere?"

Ethan tips back his head and laughs again. The scent of vanilla fills my nostrils as it wafts off his skin.

"You're right," he admits. "Flour is the worst."

We grin at each other, and it strikes me how easy it would be to date someone like him. A person who has my same schedule and career goals. I imagine our relationship would be sweet and uncomplicated, devoid of all those irritating butterflies. Most importantly, I wouldn't be in danger of falling again, of losing control the way I did with Jake. This time, my heart would be safe. But before we can continue our conversation any further, the kitchen fills with commotion, a sure sign that the lunch rush is starting. Ethan swings a dish towel over his shoulder.

"Here we go," he says with a smile.

I'VE JUST FINISHED CLEANING up my station around 10 P.M. when Ethan sidles up beside me.

"Any big plans for the weekend?"

"Not really." I shrug.

"Well, I noticed that we're both off tomorrow night, and I was wondering if you would want to go see a movie or something."

Color rises to my cheeks as I stare down at my knives. "Oh . . . um. I don't know."

Ethan frowns. "Sorry, that was way too forward of me. You probably have a boyfriend."

"No, I don't. The complete opposite, actually."

"Sorry to hear that. Recent breakup?"

"Not exactly." How would I even begin to explain Jake? *Well, I met this guy who I thought might be my soul mate, but then he became a rock star and never spoke to me again. Oh, and did I neglect to mention he wrote a hit song about me?*

"I was seeing someone a while ago. It . . . didn't end well," I say.

Ethan nods. "I get that. My girlfriend and I broke up two months ago. Completely broke my heart. We'd been together since our first semester at Le Cordon Bleu."

"Yikes. That sucks."

He shrugs. "After school, she took a job as a private chef for some ex–boy bander with a bunch of tattoos and a suspiciously uneven British accent. Last I heard, they're sleeping together and he's hired a new chef. I can hardly blame her. It isn't easy to date someone with our work hours. Plus, how could she resist? The man's got great hair."

I smile. Despite how hard I've resisted dating, I can't deny that

I enjoy Ethan's company. Besides, it's been over a year since Jake. It's time for me to get back on the horse.

"You know what? Let's go see a movie," I say. "There's a new one out that I think you'll enjoy. A love triangle, where a British bad boy steals someone's girlfriend."

I throw my hands up to protect my face as Ethan flings a dish towel at me, and I laugh—really laugh, for the first time in months.

THE FIRST THING I do when I open my locker is check my phone. Panic rushes through me when I see it's flooded with messages from Ali. Not bothering to read them, I call her immediately. She picks up on the first ring, crying so hard that I can't quite make out what she's saying at first.

"Dev broke up with me," she finally musters through muffled sobs. My heart twists at the misery in her voice.

"I'll be home in thirty minutes," I assure her, whipping off my jacket and clogs as quickly as possible. "Come over, okay?"

MEN ARE TRASH," ALI says, launching herself into my arms the moment I open my front door. I squeeze her tightly, breathing in the familiar smell of her Moroccanoil shampoo.

"It's going to be okay," I murmur, rubbing small circles in her back. "I promise, you're going to get through this." Ali sniffles, wiping her nose with the back of her hands.

"I thought this was it," she says softly. "I thought he was the one." I've never seen Ali in this state. Her small frame, usually full of larger-than-life energy, is deflated. I lead her to the sofa and wrap a blanket around her shoulders.

"What can I get you? How about a Johannsson Special?" Ali nods, wiping a hand across her tear-streaked face.

I head into the kitchen, switch on the Keurig, and pull two

mugs out of the cabinet for hot chocolate. Then I gather ingredients for the sandwich Ali and I invented the semester we took Contemporary Desserts. Our instructor, Chef Johannsson, had an inexplicable hatred of Nutella. After class, Ali and I would head to my place where we'd slather bread with hazelnut spread, bananas, and strawberries, just so we could rave about our creation within Chef's earshot the next morning. It's been one of our go-to snacks ever since. I might not be able to fix her broken heart, but I can offer my best friend the next best thing: comfort food.

When I return, Ali accepts the plate gratefully and shoves a huge bite of Johannsson in her mouth.

"Tell me everything," I say, placing her mug on the coffee table and taking her hand.

"He left me a voicemail." She sniffles. "What kind of person dumps someone over voicemail? I don't even check mine half the time."

She picks up her mug and peers inside, as if the Keurig dregs hold the answers to life's great injustices. She lets out a heavy sigh as the steam curls around her face. "Do you have anything stronger than cocoa?"

I nod, heading back to the kitchen and returning with a bottle of amaretto.

"Apparently, it's 'too hard with my schedule,'" she continues, making sarcastic air quotes with her fingers. "Because I'm 'always working' and 'never around.' Which is completely unfair. He knew what my hours were like when we started dating. But now, all of a sudden, being unavailable for happy hour trivia with his work friends is a dealbreaker." She accepts the bottle and fills her mug to the brim before taking a long gulp.

"I love my job. Becoming a chef is the only thing I've ever wanted to do. And yes, the hours are brutal. But does that mean I should have to choose between my career and having a relationship? Are these my only options?"

I reach an arm around her, pulling her into a side hug. As much as I hate to admit it, I can understand where Dev is coming from. Chef hours are merciless. It's impossible to maintain a relationship when you work so many nights and weekends.

"I know I've given you a lot of shit about not dating, but I think you've actually been doing it right all along. At the end of the day, even the nice guys turn out to be assholes," Ali declares with a small hiccup. Then she looks up at me, glassy-eyed. "There's only one good man left in this world, Lex. And I need him tonight."

A few minutes later, we're curled beneath my fuzzy white throw blanket, watching reruns of *The Price is Right* on YouTube. For reasons I will never quite understand, Ali has nursed a lifelong crush on Bob Barker. Every time she's down, she binges his show.

"Just look at him in his pinstriped suit," she sighs, taking another swig from her mug. "I mean, the way he commands that stage with such loving compassion."

A model comes out to showcase the latest item up for bid: an eighteen-carat white gold necklace interspersed with pearls. The first contestant, a breathless blonde named Kristina, starts the bidding at $900.

"Nine hundred? Honey, this necklace isn't from Costco!" Ali yells at the TV. A petite woman named Pamela gets the closest bid, and she races to the stage, throwing her arms around Bob and planting a kiss on his cheek.

"God, she's the luckiest girl in the world," Ali sighs. "What I wouldn't do right now for a Bob Barker hug and a round of Plinko."

I lift her empty mug. "Want some more hot chocolate to go with your liquor?"

She nods, and I head back into the kitchen. It takes me a few minutes to prepare a fresh cup, but by the time I bring it over to Ali, she's fast asleep, drooling lightly on one of my throw pillows.

I pick up the blanket, draping it lightly over her shoulders and switching off the light. Exhausted, I do the fastest, laziest washup of my life. It's well after 1 A.M., and I feel like I've been hit by a bus.

I'm just crawling into bed when my phone buzzes with a text. It's Ethan.

Looking forward to our movie date tomorrow :-)

I smile, plug my phone into the charger, and finally, finally crawl into bed. The comforter is soft and warm, wrapped tightly around my chest. I click off the light, falling asleep almost instantly.

I WAKE TO A RINGING sound. *Is that Plinko? Dice Game? Am I the next contestant on* The Price is Right? With a groan, I roll over to check my alarm clock: 2:43 A.M. Who on earth could be here at this hour? Then I realize: Dev. He's come for Ali.

Without turning on the light, I grab my robe and step into the hallway. My eyes dart to the sofa. It takes a few seconds to adjust to the darkness, but after a moment, I realize it's empty. The white blanket has become an abandoned heap on the floor. Ali must have woken up and gone to sleep in the guest bedroom.

The buzzer rings again, and I groan under my breath as I lumber through the living room, wiping sleep from my eyes with the heel of my hand.

"Hang on, I'm coming!" Anger simmers inside me. It's been a long day, and the last thing I want to do right now is listen to his pathetic excuses for hurting my friend. I should be passed out in bed, exchanging witty banter with my dream version of Bob Barker.

I push the "call" button, and groan sleepily into the intercom. "Yeah?"

"Miss Berman?" The deep baritone of James, the weekend doorman, drifts through the intercom. "There's a young man here to see you."

"Let him up," I mumble. I glance toward the closed door of the guest room, wondering if I should wake Ali and ultimately deciding against it. Dealing with her wrath after waking her mid-slumber is a fitting punishment for this clown.

When I hear footsteps approaching, I yank open the door, my lips already parted to give Dev the lecture of the century. But the words catch in my throat when a set of chocolate-brown eyes melts into mine.

10

MY HEART IS POUNDING with adrenaline, but my body is frozen, as if it's been turned to stone. It's been fifteen months since I last saw him, yet somehow, it seems like no time has passed at all. I've imagined this moment so many times, rehearsing what I'd say if I ever came face-to-face with him again. But now that he's here, standing right in front of me, I'm too shocked to get a single word past my lips.

"Lexi." My head spins as a flood of emotions crashes over me.

His mouth sets in a hard line as his eyes run cautiously over my face. Even in the dark, I can see the swollen bags beneath them.

"Jake," I finally muster. His lips hitch upward at the sound of his name, and something like relief flickers in his eyes. He exhales, and I catch a whiff of bourbon.

He rakes a hand through his messy hair. It's longer than it was the last time I saw him, falling in soft waves that brush the nape of his neck. "Can I come in?" His words are ever so slightly slurred, his bloodshot eyes pleading.

Despite my better judgment, I open the door a bit wider and motion for him to come inside. It's not until he's through the doorway that I notice he's not only carrying his guitar but also a small duffel bag. My eyebrows shoot up in surprise when he places them by my hallway closet, as though it never occurred to him that I wouldn't invite him to stay.

He turns to face me. "Listen, Lexi—"

"What are you doing here?" I've finally found my voice and its harsh edge is shocking, even to my own ears.

Jake recoils. "I know I should have called first, but—"

"I haven't heard from you in over a year. And now suddenly, you're showing up at my door at two in the morning?"

Jake shuffles over to the sofa, collapsing onto it. Beneath the moonlight streaming through the windows, I notice his forehead is creased with exhaustion. He sighs as he stares down at the floor.

"I'm so sorry, Lexi. Really. I don't even know what to say. I just . . . I screwed everything up."

My body battles against conflicting emotions. On the one hand, I want to yank open my door, shove him through it, and tell him never to show his face here again. But there's another feeling too. A tiny flutter of something long dormant stirring inside my stomach. Unable to decide what to do, I just stand there, gaping at him.

Jake is still staring at his feet, shoulders slumped. When he speaks again, his voice is strained.

"I had a fight with my manager tonight. I told him I was done, through with this whole thing. I can't do this anymore. I can't be this . . . this *puppet,* just performing at will. So, I packed a bag, grabbed my guitar, and left. I didn't even know where I was going; I just knew I couldn't be there anymore. I went to the bar, had a few drinks. And I started asking myself: When was the last time you were happy? Like, really happy?"

Jakes drags his gaze upward to meet mine. "And the next thing I knew, I was standing outside your apartment building."

My heart is hammering so loudly in my chest that I wonder if he can hear it. It's everything I've wanted to hear for so long, and now that he's saying the words, I have no idea how to feel. I look at

Jake—his expression so earnest, so full of longing. But I just can't bring myself to give in.

A thought presses its way to the forefront of my brain, and I hear myself asking the one question that's been haunting me for the past year.

"Why didn't you call me?"

Jake is quiet for a long moment.

"Everything just happened so quickly. I was completely overwhelmed. I meant to call you; I really did. But I wanted to respect your wishes, and then after so much time had gone by, I didn't even know what to say."

There's more to the story, something he's not telling me. It's evident in his restless hands, the way he's furiously twisting the leather bracelets around his wrist. And I'm not sure what he means by "respect my wishes." I'm not the one who stopped returning phone calls. But it's late, and I'm too stunned by his arrival to unpack this any further right now.

I sink into the floral chair across from him, the one my mom always sat in after a long day of work. With any luck, it will help me absorb some of her wisdom. Mom would know just what to do. I, on the other hand, haven't the slightest clue what to do next.

I dig my fingernails into my thigh and take a deep breath. "You hurt me."

He nods, his brown eyes swimming with remorse. "I know."

"What you did was shitty, Jake. I had no idea what happened to you until I saw you on the side of a fucking bus."

Jake lets out a shaky exhale, burying his face in his hands.

"I know. I screwed up, and you have every right to hate me. I'm probably the last person you want to see right now. I'm so sorry. This was a mistake." He puts his hand on his knees, starting to rise. And in that moment, I realize, despite the voices in my head warning me to be practical, and despite the fact that my chest positively aches at the sight of him, and despite the logic that dictates there's no way this reunion can possibly end well, I am not ready to let Jake Taylor walk out of my life again.

I cross the room to stand in front of him.

"Don't go. You've been drinking and it's the middle of the night."

Jake looks up at me, his expression guarded. "Are you sure?"

"Yes. You can crash here tonight. We can talk more in the morning." I don't even know what I'm thinking at this point. All I know is what I'm feeling. My eyes roam over him, my heart squeezing as I take in his sad, exhausted face. Who is this person, and what happened to the boy who had fire in his eyes when he waved goodbye to me a year and a half ago?

"Thank you, Lexi." Jake glances at the closed door of my guest room. "I'll just pass out if that's all right." He lifts his duffel bag, tossing it over his shoulder as he starts walking toward the door. It's only then that I remember Ali.

"Wait!" I whisper-hiss. He turns around, surprised. "I forgot . . . my friend is here. In the guest room."

"Oh." He turns and looks back toward the sofa. "No worries. I'll just sleep out here then."

I stare at him, taking in his slumped shoulders and swollen eyes. *You can sleep with me,* a small voice whispers in the back of my mind, but I push it away quickly.

"Okay," I say instead. "I'll get you a pillow and a blanket."

I slip into my bedroom, grabbing a spare pillow and an extra set of sheets from my closet. But when I return a few minutes later, Jake is already fast asleep on the sofa. He's taken off his shirt, and I can see his bare chest rising and falling slowly beneath the throw blanket he's wrapped around himself.

I stand there for a minute, studying his silhouette in the darkness.

"Goodnight, Jake," I whisper.

Heavy with fatigue, I tiptoe back to my bedroom and slide back into bed. A trickle of cool night air drifts through the window, and I bring the comforter up to my chin. But try as I might, it's impossible to fall asleep knowing Jake is just outside my door. A million thoughts race through my brain, competing for my attention.

Am I making a huge mistake? Why did I let him stay here? I'm not usually such a pushover, and frankly, I'm annoyed that Jake has brought out this side of me. But there was something about his wide, sorrowful eyes and trembling hands that got under my skin.

At first, I thought I wanted him here so we could talk in the morning. I wanted to make him explain himself. But now, I'm not sure I'm prepared to hear what he has to say. Or if he even deserves the opportunity.

I need a distraction. Climbing out of bed, I grab the bag of clean laundry that was delivered two days ago. I've been too busy to put it away, and the clothes have gotten wrinkled from so many days stuffed in the corner. The rhythm of folding my T-shirts and stacking them in a tidy pile soothes me, and I feel myself begin to relax as I sort through my thoughts one at a time.

I'm still so angry at Jake for not calling me. I might not have been able to reach him, but he had my number. Would it really have been so hard to take five minutes to let me know what was going on?

When I finish with the T-shirts, I move on to my underwear, folding them evenly into thirds. And why did he come back now? He's had plenty of time to reach out. What changed?

A nasty voice in the back of my head answers for me. *You inspired the song that catapulted him to stardom. He's back for more material.*

Yet one thought keeps echoing in my head, louder than all the others. Jake's sad, defeated voice: *I started asking myself: When was the last time you were happy? And the next thing I knew, I was standing outside your apartment building.* I hate the way my heart flutters at the sentiment, the way his words make me want to forget every other nagging feeling. For so long, I've wondered if Jake was thinking about me too. Now I know for sure. I'm not the only one who has wondered what might have been.

It's a comforting thought, one that finally relaxes me. After placing each pile of laundry into my dresser, I crawl back into bed and sink into a deep, dreamless sleep.

WHEN MY ALARM GOES off at 7 A.M., my body feels like it's filled with sand. I sit up with a groan, rubbing sleep from my eyes. All at once, the events of last night come flooding back to me. *Jake.*

Suddenly wide awake, I leap out of bed and throw on a pair of sweats. Then I step into the hallway, gently pulling the door shut behind me. The first thing I hear is the sound of the shower. My eyes dart to the sofa. It's empty.

I head toward the bathroom and nearly collide with Ali. She's wearing the pajama pants and fuzzy socks she keeps in my guest room, and worst of all, a concert tee with Jake's face sprawled across it. *Shit.* I totally forgot she was here.

"Well, well, well," she says smugly, drawing out each word. "I do believe someone had a gentleman caller in the wee hours of the night. One who is currently hogging the bathroom, no less. Care to explain yourself, young lady?"

My pulse quickens. What should I say? Ali scans my face, then her eyes widen. Her mouth drops open into a perfect O. Her face is sparkling with excitement.

"Oh my god. It's that guy from the bar, isn't it?" When my silence confirms it, she claps a hand over her mouth.

"You little minx! I can't believe you are giving him another chance. Seriously, I cannot wait to meet the person who corrupted my straitlaced little Lexi." She twists her body, trying to elbow her way past me, and I thrust out a hand to stop her.

"Wait, Ali, you don't understand—"

Before I can finish my thought, the bathroom door creaks

open, and Jake's figure fills the doorway. My mouth instantly goes dry at the sight of him. His long, toned chest is flecked with tiny droplets of water, the lower half of his hip bones disappearing under the towel wrapped loosely around his waist.

A guttural noise behind me snaps me out of my reverie, and I twist my head to look at Ali. Her jaw is hanging open, her eyes bulging. Turning back at Jake, I see the faintest hint of a smile playing in the corners of his lips.

"Cool shirt," he says, lifting one eyebrow. Ali says nothing, her mouth still gaping as the color drains from her face.

Jake redirects his attention to me, jerking his thumb toward my bedroom. "Is it okay if I get dressed in there?" I nod as he slides past me. The door shuts behind him, and I hear his muffled footsteps across the wooden floor.

Ali stares at the closed door for a full minute before turning to face me. She opens her mouth, then closes it again. After a moment, she pivots on her heel and returns to the guest room. I groan as she shuts the door behind her. So far, this is going splendidly.

I've just finished brewing coffee when Jake pads into the kitchen dressed in a navy hoodie and a pair of gray cotton pants he must have pulled from his duffel. His hair is damp against his forehead, and I can smell the scent of soap on his skin from across the room.

"Hey," he says, eyeing me tentatively.

"Morning." I shoot him a half smile, and he visibly relaxes. He slides onto the island stool across from me, and I hand him a warm mug. Half coffee, half milk. Just the way he likes it.

"I was just getting ready to make pancakes for Ali," I say. "You hungry?" Jake's face splits into a grin, his dimple popping. "Always."

I do my best to ignore his eyes burning into me as I sift through my fridge and cabinets to gather ingredients. Cooking will keep me busy, which is a relief since it's jarring to see Jake sitting on one of my barstools. His elbows are casually splayed on my marble countertop, as though there's nothing unusual about the current situation. As though he never left.

I'm flipping over the pancakes when Ali comes out of her room, blessedly no longer wearing Jake's silkscreened face across her chest.

She jolts to a stop as she walks into the kitchen. Her eyes zero in on the pint of blueberries splayed open on the counter. She looks at Jake, then back to me as understanding dawns on her face.

"Oh. My. God. That song really *is* about fruit," she says softly. Jake's eyes travel to mine, and we stare at each other for a moment before bursting into laughter. The tension between us instantly dissolves.

"Guess I'll just see myself out." Ali jerks her thumb toward the door, but doesn't make any move to leave, her eyes still fixed unbelievingly on Jake.

"Hey, if you could just keep this between us—" I start.

Ali holds up her hand. "I swear, my lips are sealed." She chuckles ruefully. "Not that anyone would believe me anyway."

"Are you sure you don't want to stay for breakfast? I'm making your favorite."

She shakes her head. "I'm sure you guys have a lot of catching up to do. Besides, I've got plans. I need to go home and set myself on fire."

Jake snorts, and I can't help but smile at him, my heart fluttering when he grins back. So much for keeping my distance.

Ali shoots me a look as she passes through the doorway, holding two fingers against her face to mime a phone and mouthing *Call me!* before pulling the door shut behind her.

Shaking my head, I stack a plate with three pancakes and slide it across the counter. Jake hums appreciatively as he takes a bite. "Even better than I remember." His face brightens as a thought occurs to him. "Wait, you've graduated, right?"

I nod. "Yup, a few months ago. I'm working at Olive & Pomegranate in Midtown. I'm usually on brunch service, but I was off today."

Jake's grin stretches to his eyes. "I'm so happy to hear that. Everything worked out for you. I knew that it would."

I arch an eyebrow. "Seems like things worked out pretty well for you too." Jake's face flushes and he stares down at his plate. "Yeah. About that. I know I haven't exactly handled things the right way. Writing that song and never saying anything about it to you."

"I think we can agree it was a dick move." I shoot him my best attempt at a wry smile and he offers me a weak one in return. I fix myself a plate but stay in my spot on the other side of the island. Keeping some distance is going to be imperative if I want to stay levelheaded this morning.

"So, what happened?" I ask softly.

Jake blows out a sigh and slumps back against the stool. He looks better this morning than he did last night—the purple circles beneath his eyes have lightened a shade or two—but his forehead is still creased in fatigue.

"It was a complete whirlwind. One minute I was standing in the El Sol office, expecting the CEO to laugh in my face. And then next thing I knew, he was on the phone, asking for a contract to be drawn up."

He gives his head a slight shake, as if the reality is still inconceivable. "He actually told me the only way I was leaving his office was out the window or through the door with a signed contract in my hand."

"That's amazing," I say, and I mean it. "You made it, Jake. You're famous."

Jake huffs out a bitter laugh. "Trust me, fame isn't all it's cracked up to be. I feel like I don't even know who to trust half the time. Everyone just wants something from me." He straightens and scoops up a bite of pancake into his mouth, chewing it contemplatively.

"The worst part is how guilty I feel. I mean, you're right: all my dreams have come true. I got lucky, and I'm grateful, I really am. But it's not at all what I thought it would be. So much of what you see from the outside—it's not real. I'm tired of pretending to be someone I'm not. And it's like, are these my only options? Go along with a lie, or give up everything I've worked for?"

He looks so crestfallen that it takes everything in me not to walk over and wrap my arms around him. I grip the countertop tightly as I resist the urge, digging my nails into the hard surface.

"When I signed with El Sol, my new management warned me that my life was about to change. They even offered to swap out my phone number, insisting people would come out of the woodwork the minute they heard I got a record deal. At first, I thought they were crazy. People wouldn't really do that, right? But then the text messages and DMs started pouring in. I felt like I was drowning. I just couldn't keep up with it all."

He shifts his gaze toward me, his eyes swimming with remorse.

"But I should have tried harder, Lex. I can only imagine how you must have felt. You had every right to say what you did in that text, but—"

"Wait, what?" I interrupt. "What text?"

Jake's brow furrows. "The text you sent me, a couple weeks after I got to LA." He reaches into his pocket for his phone, but before he withdraws it, I'm suddenly hit with the full force of the flashback. That night at the bar when Ali swiped my phone, deleted our texts, and reassured me that she'd taken care of the problem. *How did I not realize?*

Jake opens our message history and I read my last text over his shoulder with barely restrained mortification: I, Lexi Berman, am an exquisite goddess who deserves better than you.

"Oh, lord," I groan, covering my face with my hands. "I didn't write that. My friend Ali did. She thought she was helping but . . .

she deleted all our texts before I saw what she typed. I had no idea it was . . . *that.*"

An amused smile plays in the corners of Jake's lips as he tucks his phone back into his pocket. "The fact that it was written in third person was kind of a tip-off. But I figured at the very least you'd signed off on it. That you wanted nothing to do with me. And in the moment, I agreed. You did deserve better. So I left you alone. Once the dust settled, though, I realized how badly I'd handled it all. I should have apologized, tried to explain. At the very least, I should have reached out to you when the song was released. But by then so much time had passed, and I had no idea if you even wanted to hear from me."

He scrubs a hand across the back of his neck before continuing. "You're lucky, you know. To have friends who care that much about you. People you know you can trust, who have your best interests at heart."

Jake's gaze travels to mine again and his voice softens.

"I screwed up, Lexi. Trust me, I would do anything to take it back. And I know we only spent that one weekend together. But the truth is, I think about you all the time."

My fingers drift toward my lips and I nibble the edge of my thumbnail as I weigh his confession. There's a part of me that wants nothing more than to forgive Jake. But even if I could, it's not like we can just pick up where we left off. Whether we like it or not, we live completely different lives now.

"I know I don't deserve another chance," he continues. "But if we could just—"

His words are cut off by the buzzing of my phone. We glance down simultaneously to see Ethan's name flash across the screen. Jake's brow furrows, and I can practically hear the wheels in his head turning.

"Right," he says under his breath. "Of course."

I realize what he must be thinking. But he's only been back in my life for a few hours, so I feel no obligation to tell him Ethan and I have yet to go on a single date.

Jake glances down at his own phone. "I suppose I should call Vinny, my manager, and let him know where I am before he has an aneurysm."

"Is he still in LA?"

"No, we both arrived in New York last night. I'm going to be here for the next two months or so, laying down tracks for my second album." *Oh.* So that's why he suddenly reappeared in my life. This isn't about me. It's just a matter of geography. I wonder how many other times he's been in the city and not bothered to reach out.

Jake's eyes flick back to mine. "I was actually hoping we could hang out while I'm here. If that's something you want."

"I'd like that." I smile. Jake smiles back, pulling his cell phone from his pocket as he wanders into my bedroom. Gathering the breakfast plates, I carry them over to the sink.

When Jake returns twenty minutes later, the color has drained from his face. I carefully rearrange my own features in an attempt to keep my expression neutral.

"I think I talked Vinny off the ledge, but I told him I still need a few days off to get my head together before I'm willing to go back to work. He got me set up in a suite at The Pierre, so I guess I'll head over there now." His eyes shift reluctantly to the door.

"You should come over for dinner tomorrow night." The words escape before I have a chance to think about their implication. *Lexi!* my brain shouts. *What! Are! You! Doing?* "I mean, I'm sure it's been ages since you've had a home-cooked meal."

Jake's face lights up, the tension in his shoulders dissolving. "I would love that," he admits. "If it isn't too much of an imposition."

"It's nothing. I'm off on Mondays, and I was planning to cook anyway." It's a boldfaced lie. I can't even remember the last time I bothered to make myself anything beyond scrambled eggs on my day off. But I'm thrilled by the idea of having someone to cook for. It's been ages since I've done a full meal for someone, and I'm already mentally flipping through my recipe file. And if I'm really being honest, I'm not ready to let Jake go again just yet.

He grins as he pulls the door open. "I'll see you tomorrow, then."

"See ya." As soon as he's gone, I collapse onto the sofa, blowing out a long breath.

11

"WHAT, AND I CANNOT stress this enough, the actual fuck?" Ali's eyes are as wide as saucers when she yanks open the door of her Murray Hill apartment. "Get in here and tell us everything."

I still had a few hours to kill until my date with Ethan, so after cleaning up breakfast and hopping into the shower, I headed over to Ali's. It's a decision I'm already regretting.

"Us?" I ask wearily. Peering over her shoulder, I spot Chloe sitting cross-legged on Ali's mustard-yellow sofa, sipping a pamplemousse La Croix through a metal straw.

"Ah . . . I see you've called in the cavalry."

Ali grabs my wrist and drags me inside, collapsing down next to Chloe. I slip off my shoes before sinking onto the chair across from them and glance around the room. Since the last time I was over, Ali's hung a new piece of art on the wall across from me, a Warhol-style portrait of Ruth Bader Ginsburg. I turn my head to avoid her piercing gaze. *Don't judge me, RBG. We can't all be as iron-willed as you.*

"So." Ali locks eyes with me, twisting a finger through one of her dark curls. "At what point were you planning to tell us that 'Jake from the bar' was not just any run-of-the-mill douchebag, but in fact *the* Jake Taylor? As in, has-a-number-one-hit-single Jake Taylor? As in, just-did-'Carpool-Karaoke'-with-James-Corden Jake Taylor? As in, *Jake Taylor* Jake Taylor?"

"As in, the Jake Taylor you told I was an exquisite goddess who deserves better? And what's with the one-eighty? Didn't you tell me just last night that there is no such thing as a good guy, that all men are flaming bags of garbage?"

"Admittedly, that does ring a bell. However, we are not talking about me. Or mortal men. We are talking about *the* Jake Taylor."

I slump back into the chair. I'm not in the mood for this—I'm still processing Jake's return myself—but judging by the looks on my friends' faces, there's not a chance in hell I'm getting out of this conversation. Chloe isn't even on her phone for once. She's staring at me with the same intensity she'd give a client after learning they'd retweeted J. K. Rowling.

"Well . . . he wasn't *the* Jake Taylor when I met him. He was just Jake. And we only spent that one weekend together, before he was famous. I'm not even sure why he came over last night, to be honest."

"Nice try." Ali's not buying it. "But I remember how swoony you were over him. And the way you guys were looking at each other this morning? It took hours to tame my subsequent lady wood. Now spill."

I groan, burying my face in the satin throw pillow Ali picked up during our last thrift-store expedition. I've got to hand it to her—the girl has a remarkable talent for treasure hunting. The only treasure I ever found while vintage shopping was a used condom in a cookie jar.

"Lexi." Chloe's voice is slow and deliberate. She levels a serious gaze at me as she sets her drink on the coffee table. "Is 'Blueberry' about you?"

"I plead the fifth!" I protest, my voice muffled beneath the fabric. Chloe drags the pillow off my face, one eyebrow raised in a way that says, *I know you slept with a stuffed bunny until you left for college, so don't try to bullshit me.*

"Okay, *fine*, it's about me," I admit. "I mean, technically, it's about my blueberry pancakes. I'm just tangential to the recipe."

Chloe tilts her head. "And his other songs?"

I bring my hand to my mouth, biting my thumbnail. If I have anything resembling cuticles left after this conversation, it'll be a miracle. "It's . . . possible that I inspired a few others on the album. Have you ever heard the song 'Dorothy'?"

"Holy *fuckballs*!" Ali squeals. "So, you mean to tell me that for the past year and a half, while I've been playing his songs on repeat, and watching reels, and reading his Wattpad fan fiction, you've just been sitting on the fact that you're Jake Taylor's secret muse and soul mate? Does our friendship mean *nothing* to you?!"

"I'm sorry!" I say pleadingly. "I just didn't have any idea how to tell you the truth. And honestly, I never expected to see him again, so I figured there wasn't any point."

Ali frowns. "I just wish you would have told us what was really going on in your life. We would have—"

"I know," I say, cutting her off. I swallow. "It was all just really . . . I don't know. Surreal."

Chloe lets out a measured sigh. "So, when you told us Jake ghosted you—?"

"He went to LA to record a demo. I didn't expect it to go anywhere. Honestly, I don't think he did either. Neither of us expected him to become an overnight sensation."

Everything else spills out, from the night I met Jake to our last phone call. This is the first time I've told the full story out loud, and my relief is palpable. The night we met and all the craziness since has been playing on a continuous loop in my brain for the past year, and it feels amazing to finally process it all with my friends.

When I finish, Chloe twists her lips contemplatively. "What are you going to do?"

I shake my head. "I have no idea. He wants another chance. But I need some time to think about it."

"Let me get this straight." Ali leans in, her dark eyebrows raised. "Jake Taylor, as in *People* magazine's pick for 'sexiest chart topper,' knocks on your door and begs for another chance to ravage your mortal body, and you have to *think* about it?"

"Of course she does!" Chloe protests. "He really hurt her, and she's supposed to forgive him, just like that?"

"Listen, if she doesn't want him, I'm more than happy to fill in."

"Ali!"

"I'm kidding! I would never get in the way of true love." She pauses to look at me. "Unless, like, you were one hundred percent over him and wanted to let him know you have this friend who's super cool, possesses above-average dexterity, and makes an A-plus brisket."

"I do not love Jake Taylor," I mutter, crossing my arms sulkily. "I mean, sure, we had this, like, instant, inexplicable connection, and mind-blowing sex, and a mutual appreciation for *The Golden Girls. . . .*"

"I'm sorry, you found another human being under the age of eighty-five who appreciates the cheesecake queens of Miami?" Chloe's eyes are wide. "I'm reconsidering my position. You may need to marry this man."

"I'll never forget my first love," Ali says dreamily. "Josh Berkowitz. I lost my virginity to him after his AEPi date party. The sex only lasted for ninety seconds, but afterwards, he took me to the dining hall for all-you-can-eat chicken fingers. It was literally one of the best nights of my life."

"The things you'll do for fried food." Chloe shakes her head incredulously.

Ali nudges her. "You ever been in love?"

Chloe shrugs, swirling her straw around the can. "The closest I've ever come to love was New Year's Eve 2015 with Nancy Wu. That girl had magic fingers." She drifts off, smiling wistfully.

I groan. "You two are no help at all."

"In all seriousness, Lexi." Ali fixes her gaze on me again. "I remember the way you practically levitated through the farmers market the week after you met. You like him. Like, *really* like him.

And based on the songs he's written about you, it's pretty clear he feels the same way. So do something about it."

"Yeah, I don't know. Things are finally starting to go right for me. I've just started a new job, I'm earning a paycheck so my dad no longer has to help me out. And I have a date tonight with Ethan, my very nice, handsome coworker."

Chloe tilts her head and gives me a quizzical look. "Ethan, huh? I've never once heard you mention this person."

"No? Well, he's great. We work together, we have a lot in common, and he's really . . . really nice."

"You said that already," Chloe observes with a wry smile.

"Hmm, who should you choose?" Ali muses. "A dead-sexy rock star who's written multiple love songs about you, or a coworker who's exceptionally *pleasant*? Wow, what a nail-biter."

Chloe reaches out to take my hand.

"I know you're worried about getting hurt. I get it. I'm not so sure about this either. I don't like the way Jake disappeared on you, and after what happened with your dad, I can definitely see how that would be triggering." I let out a shaky breath and twist my body away from her, studying an invisible spot on the wall. Hot tears prick my eyes as she continues, undeterred.

"But ever since you lost your mom, I've watched you play it safe and avoid any situation where things aren't completely within your control. I know routine makes you feel safe, Lex, but maybe it's time to go off script for once. Take a risk and see where it leads."

I bite my bottom lip, forcing myself to stay collected. Deep down, I know she's right. And besides, it's not like Jake and I need to figure everything out right this second. The guy is asking for a few hours of my time, not my hand in marriage.

"Well," I say after a minute. "I did invite him over for dinner tomorrow night."

Ali claps her hands together and squeals. "Oh my god, *yes*. You should recreate that scene from *Sex and the City*, the one where

Samantha makes all of that sushi and lays across the kitchen table with it spread across her naked body."

"And on that note"—I stand up, grabbing my tote from the floor—"I have a date to get ready for."

"Hope you're going out to eat," Chloe quips. "The next man you cook for might write a Pulitzer Prize–winning novel about the experience."

Lifting a hand over my head, I flip her the bird as the door closes behind me.

*E*VEN THOUGH I ARRIVE ten minutes early, Ethan is already waiting for me outside the theater. He looks as handsome as ever in a blue button-down that highlights his broad shoulders and a pressed pair of khakis. When he sees me, his eyes light up, and I immediately feel a confusing pang of guilt. I haven't done anything wrong—Jake and I are not together—so why do I feel so traitorous?

"It's not often I meet someone who arrives earlier than I do," I observe wryly.

"Punctuality is important," he says, pressing a kiss against my cheek. "My dad always says you can't respect someone if you disrespect their time."

"Your dad sounds like a wise man."

Ethan smiles, brushing a hand through his blond curls. "You look beautiful, by the way."

"Thanks. You don't look so bad yourself."

He beams in response. "You ready?"

*D*ESPITE MY TEASING ABOUT British love triangles, we end up seeing an action flick and sharing a bucket of popcorn. We're still hungry afterward, so Ethan suggests stopping for frozen yogurt. As we head out of the theater, he slips a hand around my waist, and I flinch involuntarily. *He's not Jake,* a voice whispers. I'm shocked by my body's response. What is going on with me today? Would I feel this way if Jake hadn't reappeared less than twenty-four hours ago?

Ethan notices my reaction. He pulls his hand away. "Sorry, I didn't mean to—"

"No, it's fine! I don't know why I'm so jumpy." But my voice rings false, even to my own ears. It's too bright and entirely unconvincing. I clear my throat and try again, as I take his arm and motion him to keep walking.

"Actually, I had sort of a weird night last night. I didn't get enough sleep. Also, I, um . . . ran into my ex. The one I was telling you about."

"Oh." Ethan slows his pace, his frown deepening. "So, are you two, like . . . seeing each other again?"

"No, no. Definitely not." My declaration doesn't feel entirely accurate, given that I've invited Jake over for dinner tomorrow night. But Ethan seems happy enough with this answer, his expression brightening.

"Well, I'm glad to hear that. And I'm fine taking things slow if that's what you need. I like hanging out with you, at whatever pace makes you feel comfortable."

I smile at him. "I like hanging out with you too." And I mean it. Ethan is such a sweet guy and exactly the type of person I should be dating. If only I could convince the Jake-shaped hole that's currently eating away at my heart.

After we finish our yogurt, Ethan walks me to the train station. At the steps, he pauses, then takes a small step toward me. My heart races with panic—*Is he going to kiss me?*—but I exhale with relief when his lips brush my cheek instead. *Thank the great ghost of Betty White in the sky.* When he pulls back, the kind look in his eyes hits me with a fresh wave of guilt.

"See you at work Tuesday."

12

B Y THE TIME JAKE arrives the next evening, I've already been to the market, torn through my collection of cookbooks, showered, and changed my outfit four times. I finally settled on black leggings, a long white tee, a half-up top knot, and some delicate gold jewelry. The perfect "I didn't put in effort, I just happen to be this cute" look.

When I open the door, Jake is standing there holding a bottle of Chardonnay. My pulse trips over itself at the sight of him, the blood in my veins throbbing violently against my skin. He's dressed in a gray knit with a pocket across the front. It looks so soft it takes every ounce of self-control to keep myself from leaping across the threshold and burying my face in it. His glossy brown hair flips out beneath a tan beanie, and it's then that I notice the absence of his signature white cap.

"Hey," he says, leaning forward to brush his lips against my cheek. I smile and gesture for him to come inside, taking a deep yoga breath to steady myself. I hate that after all this time, my attraction to him hasn't faded in the slightest.

"What happened to your hat?" I ask. The corners of his mouth droop slightly. "Oh, uh. My stylist sort of banned it. She said it didn't go with the image my label is trying to project. Something about 'the end of my Cracker Barrel era.'" He shrugs as he steps into the kitchen, and it's clear he wants to drop the subject.

"It smells great in here," he says by way of transition.

"Really? I've barely done anything yet," I laugh.

"Must be the anticipation." Jake grins as he slides onto a bar-stool. "Should I open the wine?" I nod, grabbing two glasses from a kitchen cabinet. He fills each one generously, and I pause to take a long, appreciative sip. Then I walk over to the fridge, pulling out the ingredients I'll need. I want to cook something that would make Jake feel at home, relaxed, and at peace. After much deliber-ation, I've settled on the most comforting recipe I could think of: roast chicken. My grandparents have been gone for years, but it's what my bubbie always made when we visited them in Westches-ter for the High Holidays. The smell of it is transporting, reminis-cent of home. And family.

"Tell me more about your new job," Jake says. His eyes study my hands closely as I begin spatchcocking the chicken, my knife slid-ing with perfected skill into the just-right spot between its joints. A wave of confidence rolls through me as I consider how much stron-ger my culinary skills have gotten since we last saw each other.

"Well," I sigh. "It's a lot of work."

Jake nods. "But do you enjoy it?"

I shrug. "I mean, it's not exactly a dream job, but it's a neces-sary step in my career plan. Now that I've gotten a position at a restaurant, I just need to work my way up the ranks from line cook to sous chef and then executive chef." And then, I'll finally be able to do the things I love most about cooking. To be creative and cre-ate dishes that bring people joy. To see the impact food can have.

Jake nods. "Seems like you've got things all figured out."

"My mom is the voice in my head that keeps me going. She was always so supportive of my cooking career."

I blink back the hot tears prickling behind my eyes. "I can still remember this one night, about two weeks before she passed away.

By then, she could hardly keep anything down, so I decided to make her some matzah ball soup. It was just a box mix, but at the time, I was so proud of myself." I take a deep breath before continuing.

"It must have been so hard for her to even force that much down, but she ate every bite like it was the best thing she'd ever tasted. And when she finished, she took my hands in hers, and said, 'When you open your restaurant, remember that I was your first and proudest fan.'" I smile at the well-worn memory, the image of her hands in mine burned into my retinas. Her nails, left unpolished for the first time, looked so foreign to me, but her touch was warm as ever.

Jake tilts his head slightly as though he's trying to work something out. "So, working in a restaurant," he says softly, his voice tinged with sympathy. "Is this your dream, or your mom's?"

His question jolts me back to reality. For a moment, I'm frozen. Then I busy my hands, lining the baking sheet with thyme sprigs. I carefully arrange the chicken on top before finally turning to face Jake.

"It's my dream. Cooking has been my passion since I was a teenager." I take a deep breath, attempting to loosen the tightness in my chest. "It's fulfilling to make something that brings strength and comfort to someone else. Food is love, you know?" And it's true. But there's also more to it than that, something I'm less willing to admit out loud. Cooking feels like a way to preserve my mother's memory, to continuously feel like I am making her proud, just like I did when she was alive. When I cook, I remember exactly how it felt when we were all together as a family. When we were happy.

"Hmm." Jake nods again but doesn't say anything else. But a look of understanding is etched into his handsome face, and somehow, I know he gets it. That he recognizes how deeply my goals for the future are intertwined with my memories of the past.

"Well, good for you for not letting anything stop you." He holds my gaze, his eyes boring into mine. We stare at each other for a long moment before I clear my throat to break the spell. I grab a bag of baby potatoes from the countertop.

"Here, help me slice these," I say, anxious to change the subject. I hand him a knife and a cutting board. He cocks his head slightly as he stares in confusion at the supplies, and I can't help but laugh.

"I'm embarrassed to say I've eaten many of my mom's potatoes, but never bothered paying attention to how she made them," he admits sheepishly.

"You just cut them in half, like this," I explain, sliding a knife lengthwise through the skin of a small red potato. He moves to stand next to me, and my shoulder buzzes with electricity in the spot where his arm brushed alongside it. That old current is still there, crackling in the air between us.

"Ah, of course." Furrowing his brow, he holds the knife tightly before making the slowest, most deliberate cut I've ever seen. He lifts his head to look at me, waiting for approval.

"Well done," I comment with a nod. "Though at that rate, we'll be eating this for breakfast."

Jake chuckles, the dimple in his right cheek popping, and my stomach does a traitorous flip.

"Okay, okay, I'll pick up the pace."

Once he finishes, I arrange the sliced potatoes around the chicken, then add seasoning and lemon slices before sliding the pan into the oven.

"It'll take about an hour and a half for the chicken to roast," I tell Jake. He glances toward the TV.

"Guess that leaves us with plenty of time for a *Golden Girls* binge." He turns back to me with an impish grin. "Dorothy."

AFTER A MINI GOLDA-THON and a roast chicken dinner that Jake insists Ina Garten would envy, we're sitting a respectable distance apart on the sofa, each of us nursing a third glass of wine and a mild food coma. Jake drums his long fingers against his thigh, and I'm reminded of the sensual way he dragged them across his guitar strings that first night we met. For a second, I forget to breathe.

"That dinner was amazing," he says softly.

"Thanks," I reply, nuzzling back into the couch cushions. "I'm happy with how it came out." A shadow passes over Jake's face, his expression suddenly serious. He opens his mouth, then closes it again, like he's working out exactly what he wants to say.

"I was trying to remember the last time I had a home-cooked meal," he says. He's staring down at his shoes, jaw flexing, and I can tell he's working up the nerve to continue. "When things first started taking off for me, it was exhilarating. All my dreams were finally coming true. It wasn't until the shine wore off a few months in that I realized how lonely I was. Tonight's the first time in ages I've felt . . . home."

He drags his gaze upward and studies me, as if to gauge my reaction to his confession. Goosebumps rise on my arms. I've lived in this apartment my entire life, but it hasn't felt like a home in years. But tonight, chatting and having dinner with Jake like it's the most natural thing in the world, something has shifted. It terrifies me to acknowledge that I feel the same way.

Desperate to move to a lighter topic of conversation, I slide closer to him on the sofa and lean my head back against the cushion. "Tell me more about your year. What's the best thing you've gotten to do?"

Jake's eyes light up. "Easy. Being on *Sesame Street*." He scrunches up his face and affects a Grover voice. "*B* is for blueberries."

I choke on my wine, spraying a bit of Chardonnay. "Okay, okay," I say, wiping my lips with the back of my hand. "Favorite place you've visited?"

"Hmm." He presses his fingers to his lips as he contemplates his answer. "Probably Austin. Or maybe New Orleans." He grins at me. "You would love the food scene there. Have you ever been?"

"Nope. We didn't travel that much when I was growing up."

"Really? Why not?"

"Well, my parents were lawyers and they worked all the time. There were a few summers when we rented a house in the Hamptons, but we never managed to go anywhere else. We'd always try to make plans, but then a big case or something would come up. Their schedules never meshed well."

My eyes flit over Mom's favorite chair, the same one I sat in two nights ago. It's where she sat when she told me she was unexpectedly being sent to London for a case, and our upcoming Disney World trip would have to be postponed. We never did go, in the end. Then she got sick, and we never traveled anywhere.

Jake presses his palms into his knees. "Guess I'll get out of your hair and head back to the hotel."

"I bet you have the most gorgeous suite," I say a bit wistfully. The Pierre has always been one of my favorite spots in Manhattan. I've never rented a room, but my parents took me to their afternoon tea service for my tenth birthday, and it's held a special place in my heart ever since.

Jake nods. "It's beautiful. Just a bit . . . I dunno, sterile. But that's hotel life for you." He offers me a weak smile that's entirely unconvincing, and my heart twists. "I know, it's a real champagne problem."

"Don't you have anywhere else to stay? Somewhere homier? What about the guys you lived with in Brooklyn?"

Jake's expression darkens. "Yeah, that's not gonna happen."

"What does that mean?" I ask.

He blows out a sigh and drags a hand through his hair.

"After I signed with Vinny, one of my old roommates, Luke, asked me to get him a meeting. I tried, but Vinny wasn't interested. I told Luke I'd done my best and even offered to help him with his demo so he could start approaching other agents. But he was convinced I'd deliberately screwed him over. He started calling me nonstop, at all hours, until I began avoiding my phone altogether. Eventually, I had to change my number. Just like my management predicted."

He shakes his head. "I always told myself that if I ever made it, I wouldn't change, that I wouldn't be one of those celebrities who ditches all of his old friends. But I hadn't accounted for the fact that other people would change. Turns out, there's nothing like fame to make you realize who really has your back. It's been the worst part of this whole thing. Learning who you can and can't trust."

A beat passes as I contemplate his words. "How do you know you can trust me?" I ask.

Jake's eyes drop to his lap. "The truth is, I didn't at first. The way I ghosted you . . . I know it was beyond shitty. But after what happened with Luke, I was scared. I mean, you inspired a hit song. You would have gotten paid a fortune to sell the story. Getting betrayed by a friend sucked, but if the same thing happened with you? Honestly, I didn't know if I could handle it."

He fiddles with his cord bracelets, still avoiding my gaze. "Of course, you never said a word, and I realized pretty quickly I'd made a huge mistake. But by then, it was too late. I knew I'd blown it."

When Jake lifts his head, his brown eyes are wide and glassy. We stare at each other as I process his confession, a flame of indignation slowly building inside me.

"Come on, Jake. That's bullshit, and you know it. You were famous for, what, twelve seconds and you thought I'd go running to TMZ? To, what, tell them about our favorite episodes of *Golden Girls*? Do you really think that little of me?"

Jake's face pales. "No, of course not. I—"

"Just because your roommate went all *Single White Female* on you, that doesn't mean I would have done the same. But you never gave me a chance to prove otherwise. And what about before all of that happened? You completely dropped off the face of the earth. Like, who does that?"

Jake looks absolutely miserable. "I fucked up. I got wrapped up in the thrill of it all, and then I was so rattled by what happened with Luke that I let it completely cloud my vision. It's a shit excuse, but it's the truth. I know I hurt you, Lex, and that's what kills me the most. Trust me, I'd do anything to take it back." We sit in painful silence for a few more moments, until finally Jake pushes himself up to a standing position.

"It's late. I should really get going." He heads toward the front door and I trail wordlessly behind him. He pulls the door open, then turns to face me.

"Thank you, again, for everything. For dinner, and for giving me a chance to explain myself. I'm so happy to hear about your new job. I wish you nothing but the best. You deserve nothing but the best." He leans forward, pressing a kiss to my forehead. My eyelids flutter shut as I savor the feeling of his lips against my skin, the heat of his body so close to mine. Then he steps through the threshold and into the hallway. I'm just about to close the door behind him when I hear his voice again, low and strangled.

"I came back here once."

I freeze, my fingers tightening around the doorframe. "What?"

He turns back to me, his expression tortured. "I did a concert in Elmont, but I had a meeting in the city the day before. I walked over afterwards and stood outside your building. I was dying to see you, but I couldn't bring myself to ring the bell. I guess I was afraid of how you'd react, that you would hate me for what I did. I know I would."

He bites on his bottom lip and shrugs. "I never forgot about you, Lexi. And I never will. I know that what I did was inexcusable.

I just hope that one day, you'll be able to forgive me anyway." He turns to leave again, and something tightens inside me. Maybe it's the earnestness of his apology, or how right it felt to be with him again tonight. All I know is, I'm tired of being angry.

I'm well aware that for most people, this is where the story would end. If Ali were in my shoes, she'd slam the door in Jake's face, open a pint of ice cream, and never think about him again. But I'm not Ali. Yes, Jake made a mistake, but it didn't come from a place of malice. And the fact is, he's been burned too. Even though the rational side of my brain tells me I should close the door, both literally and metaphorically, and put this chapter of my life behind me, I just can't bear the thought of letting another person I care about walk out of my life. Not this time.

"Don't go." The words slip out before my brain has a chance to stop them. "Stay here. With me."

Jake's jaw falls open, and I'm not sure which one of us is more shocked by the invitation. But my mouth, now operating entirely of its own accord, continues its rambling.

"Look, I don't see how we can be together again. But I'm willing to try and be your friend. I think you could use one right now. And yeah, it's not exactly The Pierre, but I've got the spare bedroom and all. I know you're tired of bouncing from one hotel room to another, and honestly, I wouldn't hate the company."

Jake runs a hand through his already tousled brown hair, tugging at the roots as he considers my invitation.

"You sure? It wouldn't be an imposition?"

"Not at all." I can't believe what I'm saying right now. It's so impulsive, so unwise. So incredibly unlike me. But when I'm around Jake, I feel like a completely different person. Someone unrestricted by rules and consequences. I wonder how far I'll let myself go. How far I'll swim out into the deep end, untethered by a life jacket, before the tide pulls me under. And the truth is, this new revelation has shifted something within me. Despite the cautionary voices in my head, I'm dying to find out what will happen next.

Jake offers me a small smile. "In that case, I'm in."

W HEN I STEP OUT of my bedroom the next morning, the first thing I see is Jake sprawled out on the living room floor, doing crunches. My eyes zero in on the sweat glistening across his bare chest, his muscles rippling beneath his tan skin. It takes tremendous effort to tear my eyes away and walk into the kitchen.

"Good morning. Hope I didn't wake you up, but I couldn't sleep. Still getting over the jet lag."

"No worries," I reply, not daring to glance back in his direction as I head into the kitchen to switch on the coffee maker. It's then that I notice a tin-foil-covered plate on the island.

"What's this?" I ask. Jake stands up and rests his hands on his waist.

"I, uh . . . made you some breakfast." I lift the edge of the aluminum to see some half-burnt scrambled eggs and a piece of buttered toast. When I turn back to him, the tips of his ears go pink.

"It's not much," he admits sheepishly. "I definitely don't have your skills. But I don't want you to feel like you have to do all the cooking while I stay here. Plus, I wanted to do something for you, as a thank-you for letting me crash."

I press my hands into the counter, gripping the edge tightly to slow my racing heart. *Chill out, Lexi. It's breakfast, not a marriage proposal.*

"That's really sweet," I tell him. "Seriously, I don't remember the last time someone made breakfast for me."

Jake's look of apprehension melts into a relieved smile. "It was my pleasure, really."

I take a bite of the eggs. They're slightly cold but I hum appreciatively as I chew. "What time are you going to the studio today?"

"Probably around ten. We've already written two tracks, so

we'll lay those down first, and then I'll probably spend some more time writing in the afternoon." He pads into the kitchen and slides onto a barstool. He looks up at me, brown eyes warming. "Luckily, I can hang around there as long as I want, since I no longer have to worry about hourly studio fees. Success does have its perks."

I pour the coffee into two mugs, handing one to Jake and leaning back against the countertop as I sip my own. So much has changed for Jake since I last saw him, and I feel a small surge of pride that I knew him before the rest of the world did.

"Speaking of which, I was wondering if you'd want to come in with me some time," Jake says, shaking me out of my thoughts. I freeze mid-sip, studying him over the rim of my mug.

"To the studio?"

"Yeah, why not? I mean, that's where I'm going to be spending most of my time over the next two months anyway, and it would be fun to show you what I do all day. Besides, I'd love to introduce you to everyone. Are you free tomorrow?"

I am curious how, exactly, Jake would introduce me. I mull it over for a second, my heart sinking when I remember tomorrow is Tuesday.

"I'm working tomorrow," I reply, full of more regret than I care to admit.

"Oh, right. Of course." He stares down into his mug.

"But I'm off on Thursday."

Jake looks up and an exuberant grin stretches across his face. "All right. Thursday it is."

We finish our coffee quickly, and when I leave the apartment fifteen minutes later, he's back on the floor, this time in a push-up position.

Thankfully, Tuesday morning prep is busy enough to keep me from replaying the image of a shirtless Jake on my living room floor. It also means I'm able to avoid Ethan, which is ideal since I have no idea what to say to him.

When the kitchen finally slows around three, I slip out the service doors and meet Ali and Chloe at a park a few blocks away with a brown paper bag filled with lunch-service leftovers.

"Please tell me you brought burrata," Chloe says, as she sits down beside me at the picnic table. "I'm having the sort of day that can only be rehabilitated by cheese."

"Of course. I brought your favorite kind, the one with the pesto." I reach into the paper bag and hand her a takeout container. She pops open the lid and lets out a contented sigh before digging a fork inside.

"What's the matter, Chlo?" Ali asks between mouthfuls of pita and hummus. She's seated across from us, her work clogs discarded beneath the park's picnic table. "Chad still angling to get his DJ career off the ground?"

"I've squashed that one for now," Chloe says, taking a sip of water. "Though I must say, he was a little too amenable to your suggested stage name of 'DJ Douchebag.'"

Ali punches a victorious fist through the air as Chloe continues. "If anything, my efforts have backfired. My firm is so impressed with how well I handle that fuckboy they've assigned me another Bachelor Nation client." She blows out a frustrated sigh. "I'll never understand why anyone wants to date these people."

"You are a poster child for performance punishment," I remark.

"Speaking of dating." Ali turns to me. "How was your date with the Pleasant Pâtissier?"

"Oh, um. It was . . . really nice."

"Girl, rein it in! I can't take the heat!" She shakes her head. "Seriously, how is it fair that you, a person who has relentlessly sworn off dating, is currently juggling two boyfriends, while I, a person who is extremely interested in finding love, remain painfully alone?"

"You are not alone!" I protest, grabbing her hand and giving it a squeeze. "Besides, Ethan isn't my boyfriend. And Jake . . ." I trail off, unsure how to finish the thought. What are Jake and I, exactly? "Friends" just doesn't feel like the right word.

Chloe turns to me. "Yes, what about Jake?" she asks. "Are you going to see him again?"

At the mention of his name, I avert my eyes to hide my burning cheeks. I can feel Chloe's eyes boring into me, and I wonder why I'm even bothering to play it cool. For as long as I've known her, Chloe's been a human bullshit detector. It's one of the reasons she's so good at her job.

"Actually . . . I saw him this morning. I figured he could use a break from all the hotels and traveling and stuff, so I invited him to stay with me for a little while."

Ali practically chokes on her water, sending a spray of droplets across the grass. She wipes her mouth with the back of her hand and then stares at me, wide-eyed.

"I'm sorry. Jake Taylor, as in Grammy-nominated Best New Artist Jake Taylor, is currently *living* with you?"

"Is it necessary to use a superlative *every* time you mention him?"

"Oh, Lexi." Chloe tilts her head, regarding me closely. "Are you sure that's a good idea?"

I shrug, avoiding her eyes. The fact is, it's a horrible idea and we both know it. But no matter how hard common sense tries to wiggle its way into my brain, my heart is not ready to say goodbye. Not yet. I can't even remember the last time I had as much fun as I did last night. Jake always brings out that side of me, the fun, flirty parts of myself that I usually keep buried.

"Okay, let me make sure I have this right," Ali interjects. "You let a rock star with the body of a Marvel hero move into your apartment, and then you casually go to work this morning and leave him on your couch to write another ballad about his undying love for you, as if it were just a regular old Tuesday?"

"He is not writing ballads about me! He was actually, um . . .

doing sit-ups." My pulse jackhammers at the memory of Jake's slick, taut abs. Still, that nagging voice in my mind is back, the same one I heard the night he returned. Is that why he's back, so I can help inspire more hit songs? Am I nothing more than a muse to him?

Ali reaches out a hand and grabs my wrist. "Lexi. As your best friend, I am begging you: install a nanny cam."

I groan, shaking her off. "Come on, he's had a hard time. He can't trust many people these days, and he just wants to feel like a regular person." I shoot her a meaningful look. "And normal people do *not* like to be recorded on nanny cams."

Ali purses her lips. "I've been with a few men who would negate that claim, but your point is taken. So, what does this mean? Are you getting back together now that things are over between him and Madison?"

"Madison?" I ask. Ali and Chloe exchange a look.

"You know, Madison St. James," Ali says slowly. "It was all over the tabloids."

"Madison St. James, the pop star?"

Ali raises her eyebrows, like she's stunned by my ignorance, and I shake my head. "I kind of made a point to not read anything about Jake."

"Oh, it was a huge scandal!" she rushes on, her voice almost gleeful. "Madison, like, discovered him. They were recording in the same studio when she heard his stuff, so she decided to take him under her wing or whatever. At the time, she was engaged to Oliver Cortes. You know, the new Batman? And then these pictures came out of Madison and Jake hanging together in LA, and the next thing you know, the engagement was off! Everyone was saying it was because Madison had an affair with Jake. And, like, who could blame her? You've seen the guy. He could melt panties off a nun." The grin evaporates from her face the second she notices my horrified expression.

Chloe bumps her shoulder against mine. "Don't listen to a

word she says. The whole relationship reeked of a PR stunt. No one in my office believed it for a second. Though Madison certainly helped Jake get his career off the ground. I mean, his music is great and all, but no one achieves that level of overnight fame without being attached to an A-lister like Madison. She's basically the Usher to his Justin Bieber."

"You think Jake faked his relationship with Madison for fame?" It's true that I barely know Jake, but still, I can't imagine him doing something like that. Yet his words from earlier are already echoing back: *So much of what you see from the outside—it's not real.*

Chloe shrugs. "Who knows? The photos might have gotten leaked by someone on his team. You'd be shocked by how often celebrities are manipulated by their management." She narrows her eyes and gives me a searching look. "Listen, I don't know Jake, but I do know you. You still have feelings for him, don't you?"

"It doesn't really matter," I say, averting my eyes. "Because it's not going to happen. I've been working too hard for the past few years to lose sight of my goals now. The last thing I need is to get distracted by some boy." Especially when that boy is a celebrity who's liable to disappear again the second I get attached to him. That's how life goes, after all. The people you love don't stick around forever. Sooner or later, everyone moves on, and then you're left to put the pieces of your broken heart back together like the shards of a shattered vase. It can be reassembled, sure, but it will never be exactly the same. Even when it's whole again, there will always be cracks.

I pretend not to notice the way Chloe's staring at me, her eyes tinged with sadness, as I toss my trash into the bin and brush off my pants. "I'd better get back to work. Chloe, I hope Chad contracts a penile infection that puts him out of commission for a few days. And Ali, stop getting all your information from trashy tabloids."

"Sure thing, Mom." Ali grins at me. "Say hi to your boyfriends for me."

13

 O, WHAT'S THE PLAN for today? Recording more songs about break-fast foods?" I ask. Jake and I are seated side by side in the back of the town car that pulled up in front of my building fifteen minutes ago. The driver is currently jerking his way through early-morning traffic as we make our way to the Times Square recording studio.

Jake smirks at me. "I don't know. I thought your blueberry pan-cakes had my heart, but now that I've had that roast chicken, I'm realizing there might be even more to fall in love with."

We stare at each other. Something seeking and unspoken passes between us. Sweat pools in the palms of my hands, and my shallow breaths are so loud I wonder if he can hear them. Jake opens his mouth, on the verge of saying something more, but then the car pulls to a stop, and we abruptly break eye contact.

"Here we are," the driver announces. He opens my door, ges-turing toward the pavement. I step out onto the curb of an unas-suming red brick building.

Jake comes up alongside me and places his hand on the small of my back. "You ready?" I nod, his warm touch rendering me speechless.

Just then, a series of flashes ignites from the sidewalk, and a loud clambering of voices overtakes us.

"Jake! Look here, Jake! Are you working on your new album? Will any of your new songs be about Madison?" I hadn't even seen the paparazzi, but suddenly they are surrounding us. They must camp out here, waiting to spot musicians coming in and out of the studio.

Jake twists his body to create a protective barrier between me and the cameras. Wordlessly, he pushes me through the doors and into the lobby. I can feel his body tense up beside me.

"Holy crap! That was insane! Does that happen every time you go places?" A flurry of panicky thoughts races through my brain. *Did the cameras catch me? Is my photo going to show up online? What would Ethan think if he saw the pictures? Or worse, Oren?*

A dark cloud passes over Jake's face, his mouth tightening into a hard line. "That was nothing," he says under his breath. He inhales deeply and lets it out slowly. "Sorry there's no back entrance I could sneak you in through. But we're safe here. You ready for a tour?"

The studio is four stories tall, with three recording studios and two offices on the ground floor. When we reach the third floor, Jake pulls a door open and gestures for me to go inside. My eyes widen as I glance around the room, taking it all in.

The interior is split into two smaller rooms, a studio space, and a control room. We step into the control room, which contains a long black sofa pushed against the wall, flanked by two leather chairs. In the center of the room, two large computer screens hang above an enormous mixing console. A few men are seated in folding chairs in front of it, chatting and fiddling with the dials and levers.

"Let me introduce you to everyone," Jake says. He seems a bit lighter since we've stepped inside the studio, no longer enveloped in the cloud of anxiety that shrouded him outside. He leads me over to the group, giving out high fives and clapping a guy wearing a headset on the back.

A tall man with dark, wavy hair and a scruffy five-o'clock shadow slowly unfolds himself from a chair. He carefully buttons his suit jacket as he strides toward us, frowning as he stares at me like I'm some sort of interloper. As he approaches, I feel Jake stiffen beside me.

"Lexi, this is my manager, Vinny."

Vinny nods politely but doesn't quite smile. His dark eyes run over my face, studying me closely.

"The famous Lexi. We meet at last." At last? Jake's manager knows about me?

Confused, I turn to look at Jake. Color creeps up his neck as he jams his hands into his pockets and rocks back on his heels. "Yeah, I may have mentioned you once or twice."

A jumble of emotion catches in my throat. "Really?" Jake's mouth twitches.

"Of course," he admits shyly. "I mean, I think we both know you inspired a track or two."

I clasp my hands to my chest and gasp in mock surprise. "You wrote songs about me?"

Jake groans and elbows me gently. The tension leaves his body as he grins sheepishly at me, infamous dimple popping, and I can't help but grin right back.

The moment is interrupted as Vinny clears his throat. "Right. Let's get started, shall we? We only have Studio J booked for the morning."

"Of course." Jake turns his attention back to me. "Can I get you anything? A soda? Water?"

"Water's fine," I reply. Jake hands me a bottle of water from a mini fridge and gestures for me to take a seat on the sofa. He heads into the adjoining room visible through a large glass window and greets the small crowd of people hanging out inside. As they take their seats at various instruments, I realize they're his backing band.

Vinny pulls up a chair across from me.

"So, I take it you two have worked things out?"

"Um . . . I guess? We agreed to try and be friends."

Vinny nods approvingly. "A wise decision."

I raise an eyebrow. "What does that mean?"

Vinny leans back in his chair, pursing his lips as though he's trying to figure out exactly how to put what he's thinking into words.

"You must know how difficult a relationship with Jake would be. His schedule is packed, dictated by appearances and concerts and tour schedules. There are promotional events to attend, contractual obligations to fulfill. His career takes precedence over everything. Especially his personal relationships."

My mood darkens as I take in his words. Now I understand what Jake meant when he said he felt too overwhelmed to even look at his phone. Working in kitchens is hardly a cakewalk, but if I had this many demands placed on me all day, I'd probably hide in bed with the blankets pulled over my head. A feeling of protectiveness washes over me. Jake needs someone in his corner, someone who isn't just interested in what he can do for them.

Vinny takes a long swig of water from his bottle before continuing. "Trust me, becoming romantically involved with Jake would be a mistake. The lifestyle can be tough for someone who isn't in the industry. I've seen more than my fair share of relationships fall apart when a celebrity client tries to date a . . . well, for lack of a better term, a *normal*."

"Yeah, but I knew Jake before he was famous. When he was still, uh . . . a 'normal.'"

Vinny's gaze is piercing, his mouth set in a hard line. "You need to understand something," he says, his voice low. "Jake isn't the same person he was when you met. Things are different now. He's on a path to become a superstar, and there are a lot of people whose jobs depend on his success. The last thing he needs is to get off track."

I stare into the glass booth at Jake, who is wearing a pair of headphones and glancing suspiciously back and forth between us with his arms crossed. When he catches my eye, he pulls out both hands, pressing his fingers and thumb together to mimic a talking mouth. Rolling his eyes, he mouths the words *Blah blah blah.*

I subtly run my index finger across my throat to signal for him to cut it out. In response, he grabs his neck, contorts his face as though his throat's been slit, and collapses to the floor with a loud thud.

Vinny turns, leaping to his feet when he no longer sees Jake standing in the booth. Unable to suppress my laughter, I bury my face in my shirt sleeve and do my best to disguise the noises coming out of me as coughs. Jake slaps one hand onto the ledge, and then the other, dragging himself up. He grins at me and winks. Swiveling his head to follow Jake's gaze, Vinny studies me, his eyes narrowing in suspicion.

"Christ, it's worse than I thought." He pulls out his cell phone and punches a few numbers.

"Lydia, it's me," he barks into the receiver. "Schedule a meeting with the entire PR team." He throws me a look over his shoulder before continuing. "We have a situation."

A ROUND 1 p.m., WE break for lunch. Jake suggests we walk to Bubby's, an American eatery a few blocks away, where he insists we can eat without causing too much of a scene. Apparently, the restaurant is used to accommodating local diners, many of whom happen to be tabloid regulars.

The interior of Bubby's is brightly lit, with a full back wall of windows and plenty of green accents. I'm pretty sure I see SJP seated at the bar, but before I can get a good look, our waitress escorts us to a booth in the back. We spend a few minutes poring over the menu before I decide on a smoked salmon bagel plate. Jake opts for the fried chicken biscuit.

The waitress returns with our drinks a few minutes later, placing an iced tea in front of Jake and handing me a glass of water. I watch with mounting horror as he pours one packet of Splenda after another into his glass. He takes a sip after the fourth one, frowns slightly, and adds one more.

"What in the world are you doing?" I ask.

"Making sweet tea, of course." He raises the drink to his lips again, then pulls a face. "Eh. Not as good as my mom's. You just can't get quality sweet tea in New York."

"You must get pretty homesick. Have you been back to Marietta recently?"

Jake shakes his head with a grimace. "I've only visited twice in the past year. I haven't had much time with my schedule. Not that I should complain too much about that. I just hope I'll get to see my family more this next year. That things will normalize, if that's possible."

He leans back in his chair, folding his arms across his chest. One corner of his mouth ticks upward as he stares at me unapologetically from across the table, as if I'm the only person in the room. It makes me feel both self-conscious and strangely exhilarated.

"So, what do you think so far?" he asks.

"Of what?"

"All of it. The chaos. The studio. Me."

I pause for a moment, contemplating my answer. "Well, I don't think Vinny is going to be my number-one fan."

The smile on Jake's face immediately fades. His shoulders sag as he picks his sunglasses up off the table, turning them over in his hands. "I couldn't care less what Vinny thinks," he mutters.

"What does that mean?" I ask.

A wrinkle forms between Jake's brows, and I can tell he's contemplating exactly how much he wants to tell me. Then he scrubs a hand through his hair with a resigned sigh.

"A few weeks before my album debuted, a story broke about me and Madison St. James. I was out in LA, having dinner with Vinny and one of my producers at Craig's. Madison was there too, and she came over to introduce herself. She'd been recording at the same studio as me, and apparently, she heard some of my stuff and really liked it. She's from the South too—Louisiana, actually—and she offered to take me under her wing, mentor me and whatnot. We walked out together, still talking about it, and the paparazzi got a photo of us.

"I know the way it must have looked, the way I was smiling at her. But it wasn't because anything was going on between us. I was just . . . kind of starstruck. I mean, she's Madison St. James, you know? And she liked *my* music."

Jake's lips curl into a sheepish smile. But a second later, his expression changes again, and his eyes steel. "Anyway, apparently Madison and her boyfriend, Oliver, had just broken up, and it didn't take long for TMZ to run a story about how the relationship ended because she'd cheated on him with me. Especially when she was posting about me and my album release so much. The truth was she was just a supportive friend. But it got twisted in the media."

A muscle twitches in his jaw. "I hated it. The idea of my name being dragged through the mud like that, of people thinking I'd ever . . ." He trails off for a moment, then shakes his head as if to clear it. "I'm not an idiot. I get that stuff like this happens when you're in the public eye. You can't really control the crap that runs in the tabloids." He pauses for a moment, and his shoulders stiffen.

"But the night I came to your place, I'd just found out that Vinny was the 'anonymous source' who'd spread the rumors about us to the tabloids. And Lexi, I completely lost it. When I confronted him, he tried to justify it by saying 'all press is good press,' that he and my publicity team have a planned trajectory for my career, and after all, hasn't it paid off so far? But it just felt like a slap in the face. Like he didn't believe in me enough to think I could be successful based on my music alone, like I had to be part of some celebrity scandal in order to get my career off the ground."

My heart twists in my chest at the emotion in his voice. I can't even imagine what Jake must be going through. To feel like you'll never be good enough, no matter how successful you are. And worse, that you can't even trust the people who are supposed to believe in you. I reach across the table to grab his hand.

"You know it's not true, right?" When Jake lifts his head to look at me, his eyes are glassy. "You are incredibly talented, Jake. You always have been. There's no way you would have gotten as far as you have if you weren't." I lower my voice conspiratorially. "I mean, you didn't need any amount of fame to get me into bed. You did that with your voice alone."

Jake chokes out a reluctant laugh, and I grin at him. The tension in the air immediately dissolves, and I give his hand a squeeze.

The waiter arrives a moment later, setting our plates down in front of us.

"How's the chicken?" I ask once Jake's taken a few bites.

He lifts one shoulder in a half shrug. "Fine, I guess. Also nowhere near as good as my mom's, of course. Or yours."

"I bet. I'll have to get her recipe some time." I take a sip of my water. "What's your mom like?"

At the mention of her, Jake's eyes light up. "Amazing. Always smiling, always trying to feed people. The perfect Southern hostess. You'd love her, actually."

"And your dad?"

Jake's smile fades a decimal. He tears off the edge of his buttermilk biscuit, popping it into his mouth. "He's a hard worker. Very serious, driven to succeed. He's the kind of dad who never coached Little League, but always had plenty of notes after each game on how I could improve." He takes another bite of his biscuit and chews thoughtfully. "He's never really understood the whole music thing. Pretty sure he still thinks this is just a phase, and in a few more years, I'll come around to the idea of joining the family business." Before I can ask what type of business his family does, he shifts in his seat and his leg brushes against my knee, and I immediately lose my train of thought.

"Let's just say he's not like my mom." His eyes go soft around the edges as he chews. "She loves it when I sing and play guitar for her. The feeling I get when I'm performing, knowing that people are enjoying music I've made . . . it's such an adrenaline rush. I got completely hooked on it."

I nod because I know exactly what he means. Not because I've ever enjoyed performing in front of a crowd. I can still remember the way my stomach knotted when I stood in front of my third-grade class to deliver a presentation on Martha Washington. But I can relate to the high of creation, of knowing that something you made brings joy to others. It's addictive.

Jake smiles. "Tell me more about your parents."

"Growing up as an only child, my parents were my best friends. They were complete workaholics, but no matter how busy they were, they always made time for me. We were like the Three Musketeers."

Jake eyes me carefully. I can tell he's doing his best to tread lightly, to not push too hard on a wound that's still so raw.

"Is it hard living in the apartment by yourself now?"

Yes, my heart replies. "Sometimes. But unlike my dad, I'm not willing to just pack up and move on." My stomach twists as I wonder how long it will be before Jake takes off again. After all, he's a musician; traveling is an inevitable part of the gig.

When the waitress brings the bill to our table, she leans forward slightly to speak to Jake quietly.

"I'm so sorry, but there are a few paparazzi out front." She frowns as she tilts her head toward the glass windows. Sure enough, half a dozen men dressed in various shades of black are lingering outside, cameras hanging from thick black straps around their necks.

"Just want to let you know, in case you want to stagger your exit."

Jake grimaces. "Thank you," he says, handing her a credit card. When he faces me again, his eyes are remorseful.

"I hate that I put you in this position," he sighs. "I thought we'd be safe from the paparazzi here."

"What does she mean by 'stagger our exit'?" I ask.

"It means that unless you want to be featured on TMZ tomorrow morning, we should probably leave the restaurant separately."

"Does it really matter if the press spot us together? I mean, I'm a nobody. They aren't going to care about me."

Jake clenches his jaw, and a line deepens on his forehead. "Trust me, Lexi, it would become a big deal."

I open my mouth to respond, but before I can say anything, my phone buzzes with an incoming text. Ethan's name pops up on the screen.

"Is that your boyfriend?"

I flick my eyes upward, taken aback by the change in Jake's tone, and I notice his shoulders have tensed.

"No, I'm not . . . he's a coworker. The pastry chef at my restaurant." I shove the phone into my purse, but I can feel Jake's eyes trained on me. "Listen, I need to run to the market. This was great, though. Thanks for showing me around."

"No, thank *you*," he says, and the lines in his face mercifully soften. "For coming today. For letting me show you a little piece of my world."

"Of course. I'll see you back at the apartment later?"

Jake nods. I walk around to his side of the table, pulling him in for a quick hug. His familiar smell, clean and warm as ever, comforts me as it fills my nostrils. I feel his eyes on my back as I make my way to the front of the restaurant, and I can't wipe the smile off my face as I push my way through the glass doors and step out into the street. I'm still grinning as I walk past the unsuspecting paparazzi.

14

DINNER SERVICE BEGINS AT 5 P.M. the following evening. Most customers who arrive at this hour come for an after-work drink with friends or a quick bite to eat before heading off to the theater, so the first hour of my shift is light. We send out two orders of spicy feta and chickpea crostini, three orders of our signature fig and olive tapenade, and half a dozen olive oil and crostini samplers.

But an hour and a half later, the dining room has started to get loud. The kitchen pulses with heat, and my body feels slick beneath my white jacket. I take a quick slug of water from my canteen and push back a sticky strand of hair that's slipped out from beneath my toque. Across the room, printers buzz with a fresh flurry of order tickets.

"Hey, how's it going?" Ethan's suddenly at my elbow, smiling at me earnestly. "Just wanted to tell you I had a great time the other night."

"Me too!" I respond a little too brightly. "It was a lot of fun."

"I'm actually off this Thursday too," he continues. "I was thinking we could go to Eataly and walk around the bakery. Maybe do a little wine tasting."

It sounds like an incredible way to spend the day; Eataly is one of my favorite spots in the city. But I can't ignore the hesitation pulling at my thoughts.

"Listen, Ethan," I hedge. "I think you're a really great guy, and I enjoyed our date—"

"But," he supplies. The corner of his mouth rises in a half smile. "Sorry, I was sensing a 'but.'"

"But," I say, trying to keep my voice light. "I've seen my, um, ex again. We're not getting back together, but . . . it's complicated right now. And it wouldn't be fair to you." Ethan's expression falls, but he collects himself quickly.

"Sure, I get it," he says, his eyes landing on every spot in the kitchen but me. "I should get back to my prep. But see you at Freddie's later?"

"Definitely," I say, letting out a relieved breath I didn't realize I was holding. Fortunately, the conversation doesn't go any further, because just then, Chef's voice cuts through the kitchen.

"It's showtime, people!" he calls out. "Here we go. Ordering: two halibut, one salmon, one tagine, no olives. Followed by one campanelle and a hanger steak, MR."

"*Oui*, Chef!"

"And," he continues, "picking up on twelve, six, nine, thirty-one, forty-two."

"*Oui*, Chef!"

"Six!" calls Mia.

"Six!"

Timers tick, pans clatter, oil sizzles. The air swells with the fragrance of melted butter, roasting fish, and sweat.

"Plates!" Oren bellows. I reach under the pass and grab a fresh stack of white china. Oren swings past me, grabbing them off the countertop without even pausing to make eye contact.

Across the kitchen, an enormous pot of water bubbles. Our timer indicates there are only three minutes left until the pasta finishes, and a quick glance at the countertop confirms there won't be space for all the dishes. I grab a handful of trivets and start looking for places to stash the hot plates.

Chef rotates through the kitchen, quietly sampling each dish. The campanelle with mushroom and asparagus sauce gets his approval, as does the halibut, but he stops abruptly in his tracks when he samples the steak's chimichurri. He thrusts the pan back at Corbin, instructing him to add more seasoning.

Meanwhile, Mia and I are swamped with appetizer orders. We take turns, alternating between salad and hummus platters. I'm at it for less than five minutes before Oren calls my name from across the room.

"Lexi! I need a hand with plating!" I shoot Mia an apologetic look as I dash over to meet him at the pasta station. I quickly scoop pasta into shallow porcelain bowls, then ladle the mushroom sauce on top. My presentation isn't nearly as pleasing as Oren's, but in a hurry, it's the best we can do.

"Service!" Chef yells. A parade of waiters hurries into the kitchen. They pluck up the plates, hoist them two at a time on their arms, and usher them out to the waiting guests.

A second timer goes off. More dishes sail over to the pass. Another round of waiters comes through the kitchen, grabs them, and dashes through the kitchen doors.

An hour passes before the ticket printer finally stills. I'm just leaning against the metal countertop trying to catch my breath when Mia slides up beside me. Her dark eyes sparkle with amusement as she crosses her tattooed arms and leans back against the countertop.

"So. You and Ethan, huh?"

"Is that bad?" I ask, a knot of panic forming in my chest. "I didn't think there were any rules against dating coworkers here. I mean, you always hear about kitchens and—"

"Chill, Ann Taylor! You're cool. Practically everyone in this joint has hooked up at some point." She bites back a smile. "I'm just a little surprised you'd go for the human embodiment of vanilla extract." We both glance over at Ethan, who's wiping a dab of sweat from his halo of blond curls. His biceps flex as he sweeps crumbs from his station. Mia has a point: the guy's a walking stock photo.

"Don't get me wrong, you're about as basic as they come," she continues. "But I suspect there's more to you than meets the eye. Underneath all that pumpkin spice and neurosis, I think there's a fierce-ass bitch with green M&M energy just dying to get out." She grins at me, and I can't help but smile back.

Just then, Hannah, the hostess, bursts into the kitchen. Her dark eyes are wide, and her cheeks are flushed pink.

"Oren!" she hisses as she hurries over to our station. "We have a situation."

"Christ," he mutters under his breath. "Another re-fire? It'll be the third one tonight." We call anything that returns to the kitchen a "re-fire," because it usually means the dish will be returning to the oven for one reason or another: it isn't cooked to the correct level of doneness, or the customer didn't find it warm enough. Re-fires usually fall under Oren's jurisdiction, and honestly, I'm not sure he has it in him to handle another one tonight.

Hannah shakes her head, her dark curls bouncing back and forth. "Not a re-fire, Oren. There's a *celebrity* here, and he wants to come back to thank the staff personally."

My stomach drops. No . . . he wouldn't. *Would he?* Oren's face lights up. "Well, by all means, bring him back!" he instructs.

Hannah beams with excitement and practically bounces through the swinging doors. A minute later, she returns, Jake in tow. He gives the staff a little wave as he showcases his dimple. Hannah practically dissolves into a puddle.

"Sorry to interrupt y'all," he says. "I just wanted to say thanks for the incredible meal."

He turns to look at me with a sheepish smile. "Hey, Lex."

"Jake, what are you doing here?"

For the first time all night, the kitchen goes silent. The entire staff turn their heads to gape at us, including Hannah, whose wide-open mouth bears a striking resemblance to our signature branzino. Her eyes ping-pong back and forth between us as she tries to puzzle out the connection.

Jake rocks back on his heels as he tugs a hand through his already tousled hair. "Sorry, I hope this is all right. I thought it would be fun to stop by and see where you work. Since you got to spend yesterday at the studio with me and all."

"Uh, sure. I just wish you would have let me know in advance. We're a little busy right now," I reply, doing my best to keep my voice controlled. *What the hell is he thinking, showing up here in the middle of service?* Twenty-four hours ago, he was stressing about the paparazzi seeing us together, and now he's casually announcing our relationship to every one of my colleagues?

Oren, who has recovered himself, reaches out a hand toward Jake.

"It's a pleasure to meet you, Mr. Taylor," he says. "I'm Oren, the sous chef. Huge fan of your music. We are so honored that you chose to dine here at Olive & Pomegranate. This is Amir Hussein, our head chef." He gestures toward Chef, who stares back stoically for a moment before returning to his meal preparations.

Oren shifts as he clears his throat. "Anyway, I hope your dining experience was to your satisfaction."

"Everything was great, really. Who do I have to thank for the delicious apple tart?"

And just like that, I know exactly what he's doing here.

Oren, still oblivious, beams as he claps Ethan on the back.

"That would be the work of this guy right here! Best pastry chef in the city." Jake extends a hand to Ethan, who stares at him for a long minute before shaking it begrudgingly.

Jake returns his attention to me, his triumphant smile faltering slightly as I glare at him.

"Well, I guess I'll just see you at home?" he offers. A hot flash of annoyance sparks through me; did he really just announce to my entire team that we're shacking up together? Is he for real right now? Too angry to speak, I simply nod, biting the inside of my cheek as I pretend not to feel the weight of a dozen sets of eyes boring into me.

After Jake and Hannah disappear through the kitchen doors, I turn back to the sauce I was prepping, only to notice a thin film has now developed on the top. *Terrific.* I've just grabbed a fresh spoon to stir it when Ethan materializes at my elbow.

"So. You neglected to mention that the ex-boyfriend who suddenly reappeared in your life is Jake Taylor," he says tightly. "And that he's *living* with you." I turn my head to meet his aquamarine eyes. They're narrowed to slits and full of hurt.

"Well . . . it's not the sort of thing that really comes up in conversation." I offer him a conciliatory smile, which he does not return.

"Yeah, well, I think you should have tried a little harder." Before I can say another word, he turns on his heels and shuffles away. My heart sinks in my chest. *Great.*

The moment he's out of earshot, Mia comes up behind me, clapping me on the shoulder.

"Now *that's* what I'm talking about," she whispers. "I haven't had this much fun at work since Hannah yakked on Corbin's shoes during last year's Christmas party."

Finally, it's closing time. Mia and I set to work labeling our leftover *mise* and packing it into Cambros. The rest of the staff is busy with cleanup; the lemony scent of dish detergent wafts through the air as stations are doused with soapy water.

After I finish tidying my station, I quickly change out of my uniform. I'm just about to exit through the service doors, secretly thankful no one besides Ethan has mentioned going to Freddie's, when Chef's voice rings out from his office.

"Lexi? A word?"

Rounding the corner, I poke my head through the doorway. Chef is seated at his desk, a pile of inventory sheets in front of him. He gestures for me to come in and I step through the door tentatively. Chef never addresses me personally; our interactions are generally restricted to conversations about kitchen prep and food orders. A rush of panic bubbles in my chest.

Chef looks up from his desk. His dark eyes regard me carefully over a pair of reading glasses.

"As a policy, we don't invite our friends into the kitchen," he says slowly.

"Yes, I know that, and I'm so sorry. I had no idea he was coming."

Chef's mouth straightens into a hard line. "Yes, well . . . I think it would be best to make these expectations clear to your friends from now on."

I bob my head, swallowing back the hot, humiliating tears that have begun to threaten. If I had known Jake was going to show up here, I would have made plenty of things clear to him.

"Absolutely, sir. It won't happen again."

Chef gives me a quick nod, satisfied. "Nice work today."

"Thanks, Chef."

I HEAD TO THE TRAIN, growing angrier and angrier with each step. Who the hell does Jake Taylor think he is, waltzing into my place of work like that? Being a celebrity does not give him the right to barge into places anytime he chooses.

The train arrives, its seats sparsely populated this late on a weeknight. Exhausted, I collapse into one, closing my eyes as I attempt to organize the threads of my furious inner monologue.

What if this had affected my job? Despite his calm tone, I could tell that Chef was pissed. I don't know if anyone has ever been fired for having kitchen visitors, but I am not interested in finding out. Things are finally going the way I want them to, and the last thing I need is for Jake to barge in and mess everything up.

This is exactly why I didn't want to get involved with anyone to begin with. Relationships are just too complicated, too messy. There are far too many opportunities for emotions to jeopardize everything I've worked so hard for.

I'm still seething when I turn the key in the lock and step into the dark living room. I expected to find Jake awake, but he's sprawled across my sofa, fast asleep beneath my white throw blanket. Two untouched glasses of wine are sweating on the coffee table. It's a little after midnight, and I realize I never told Jake what time I'd be home. I wonder how long he waited up.

He stirs as I shut the door behind me, pushing himself up into a sitting position.

"Hey." His voice is thick with sleep as he brushes a messy lock of hair off his face. "I tried to stay awake, but I guess I dozed off. How was work?"

"How was *work*?" I ask incredulously, my voice rising an octave on the last word. "Hmm, let me think. There was the customer who had me remake her salad three times because she wasn't satisfied with her 'dressing-to-arugula ratio.' Oh, and then this guy I spent one weekend with a year ago barged in and tried to mark his territory like some sort of caveman."

"Lexi, I . . ." Jake starts.

"Do you actually think that just because you wrote a hit song about me that it means you've staked some sort of claim? I'm not yours, Jake. You left, remember?"

Two bright splotches of color blossom on his cheeks. "I know that. I didn't mean . . ."

"Just forget it," I say curtly as I slip off my shoes and place them neatly on the rack by my front door. "It's been a long day and I'm going to hop in the shower. Go back to sleep."

I take two steps toward the kitchen when something catches my eye. The cabinet beneath the sink, that one that used to dangle from its hinges, is now repaired, its door sitting straight and uniform with the rest of the kitchen cabinetry. Something stirs in the pit of my stomach.

"Yeah. I fixed that for you," Jake's voice comes from behind me. "I hope that's okay."

"It's . . . it's great," I say, my heart twisting with an emotion I can't quite place. Hurrying to the bathroom, I shut the door behind me, exhaling slowly as I lean against the wood. I close my eyes and take a few steadying breaths before turning on the shower.

The hot water does wonders to soothe my aching muscles, and I linger in the shower for a good fifteen minutes, letting the steady stream wash over me. By the time I get out, wrap myself in a fluffy white towel, and brush my teeth, I feel like a human again. But every ounce of calm is erased from my body when I return to my bedroom and see Jake sitting on the edge of my bed.

"Um, hello."

"Sorry. I didn't mean to startle you. Or, uh, intrude. I just wanted to apologize for today. I was trying to be supportive. I really am proud of you, Lexi. And I'm trying to make up for all the time that I wasn't around. But it was wrong of me to come into the kitchen unannounced. I realized my mistake the second I saw your face. In my world, it's all about people showing up, coming to performances or whatever. I didn't think about how, for you, that'd be an intrusion."

I raise one eyebrow skeptically. "So you're telling me that jealousy played no part whatsoever in this little visit of yours."

Groaning, Jake drags a hand across his face. "Okay, okay. It's possible that a *modicum* of jealousy factored into my decision." He stares at me, and his expression is remorseful. "Look, I know that we're not together. I blew any likelihood of that happening a long time ago. I just thought . . ." He trails off, then shakes his head once as if to clear whatever thought is plaguing him. "I truly am sorry for any trouble I might have caused tonight."

The air goes thick with unspoken words, until I finally gather the courage to ask the question that's been on my mind since the moment he stepped through my doorway a week ago.

"Why did you come back, Jake?"

Jake's head snaps to attention and blinks at me. "What do you mean? I told you the other day, I—"

"But why *now,* after all this time? You said you came here once before, but didn't have the guts to ring my bell. So what's changed?"

His Adam's apple wobbles as he swallows hard, and a splotch of red creeps up his neck.

"I saw that you liked my Instagram post," he admits quietly. "After the way I behaved, I figured you wouldn't want anything to do with me. Then I saw that, and I thought . . . I don't know, that maybe I still had a chance. It was stupid and arrogant of me, and I can see now that you've moved on. But I've missed you, Lexi. And I'd really like to be a part of your life, in any way that you'll let me."

His confession steals the breath from my lungs. Leaning against the doorframe, I grasp the handle for support. A long beat passes before I speak again.

"I've missed you too," I admit. "But I meant what I said. Getting involved again . . . I just don't think it's a good idea."

Jake nods quickly, as though this was the answer he was expecting. "Yeah, I get it."

"And if you're going to stay here, you need to be more considerate," I continue. "This is my life, and you can't be so reckless with it. You have to understand what the stakes are for me. I've worked hard to get where I am, and I can't let anything mess me up." *Or anyone,* my heart whispers.

Jake nods, his expression remorseful. "I know. Trust me, I feel terrible. You've been nothing but supportive of my career, and I want to be the same for you. I'm going to do better."

I pause, taking a moment to mull it over. "Your apology is accepted," I tell him after a beat. Then I walk over to my dresser and pull out an old T-shirt and a pair of sweatpants. "Now, do you mind giving me a little privacy?"

"Oh, right. Of course." He swivels to face the wall, and I let the towel fall to the floor as I slip into my pajamas. I pick it up to towel-dry my hair as I sink onto the bed beside him.

"Well, I'll let you get some rest," he says, pushing himself into a standing position. Without thinking, I reach out and grab one of his hands. *Shit.* What am I doing?

"No, stay. We can watch a movie or something until I fall asleep."

He looks surprised but doesn't protest as he slides back onto the bed, and I notice with bemusement that he's left a generous, *friendly* gap of space between us. As if there's enough space in the world to erase the memory of what happened last time we were in this bed together.

I hand him the remote and he starts flipping through Netflix, stopping when he gets to 10 *Things I Hate About You*.

"Jackpot," he whispers.

I snort, twisting to face him. "Seriously?"

"Who doesn't like to kick back with a nice rom-com at the end of a long day?"

"Um, lots of people? They're so contrived."

"Well, not me. If anything, I hate the way I don't hate them. Not even close. Not even a little bit. Not even at all." His mouth curls into a lopsided smirk at his own joke.

"Do you think your fans have any idea that you're such a massive dork?"

"Not a chance. Though I think they're beginning to suspect it in Europe."

I reach out to shove him playfully, and he grabs me by the wrist. Our faces are so close together that I can feel his warm exhale as his chest rises and falls. Electricity crackles between us, and the air grows thick with possibility about what might happen if he were to lean an inch closer.

Jake's eyes drop to my mouth, and I know that despite what I said earlier, if he reaches forward to try and kiss me right now there's not a chance in the world I would stop him.

"Lexi," he says, his voice a low scrape. He dips his head, his lips a whisper from my own. My eyes have just fluttered shut when the sudden blare of a car horn outside my window causes me to jump back.

"Jesus, what is *wrong* with New York City?" I groan. Jake laughs softly, wrapping one arm around me.

"Come here," he says as we lay back against the headboard. I rest my cheek on his chest and he draws me closer. I feel my entire body relax as his fingers drift gently through my hair, and sleep overtakes me before I find out what Bianca loves more than her Prada backpack.

A STREAM OF LIGHT POURING in through my window wakes me before my alarm. My comforter feels hot, much hotter than usual. I try to push it off before realizing it isn't a comforter at all, but Jake's body sprawled across mine. His head is cradled against my chest, and his left arm is wrapped around my waist. I close my eyes again, reveling in the feeling of our bodies intertwined. It's warm and comforting and just so incredibly right. Too right. I need to get out of bed before I can overthink this.

I give Jake a gentle push so that I can free my arm. He rolls onto his stomach and murmurs softly but doesn't wake. Grabbing a sweatshirt and a pair of yoga pants, I dress quickly, then tiptoe over to the door. Unable to help myself, I steal a look back over my shoulder at Jake's sleeping form.

His messy brown hair is sprawled in a halo around him, his cheek pressed against the mattress, his full lips soft and pursed. He looks so peaceful, so incredibly young. A completely different person from the fragile man who rang my doorbell a week ago. He's already taking up a lot of space, in more ways than one, and I'm not sure what bothers me more: the fact that Jake has torpedoed his way back into my life, or that I don't hate it nearly as much as I wish I did. Shaking the thought from my mind, I carefully pull the door shut behind me.

15

WHEN I RETURN HOME from brunch shift the following Sunday, the first thing I see is Lionel pacing back and forth in the lobby, his expression strained as he stares at his cell phone.

"Hey, is everything okay?" I ask, taking a few steps toward him.

Lionel's brow furrows. "Audrey's got the flu. I'm trying to order her some soup, but I can't figure out this damn app." I put my hand over Lionel's fist, still wrapped tightly around his phone.

"Don't order anything. I'm going to head upstairs and make her some matzah ball soup. Trust me, there's no better cure for the flu than Jewish penicillin."

Lionel looks up at me, his expression flooded with relief. "Oh, that would be wonderful. You're not too tired from work?"

I wave a dismissive hand. "Absolutely not. It would be my pleasure."

As soon as I get into my apartment, I pull an old composition notebook from the bookshelf and begin thumbing through handwritten recipes. I haven't cooked matzah ball soup since the night I made it for my mom, and when the words appear in front of me, memories burst through my consciousness like a tsunami. My first attempt had been a disaster, to say the least, the dense orbs sinking to the bottom of the pot like cannon balls.

"Just use the boxed stuff." My mom laughed, though it sounded more like a soft wheeze. "There are some things science has perfected, and matzah ball soup mix is one of them."

She'd been right, of course. The next batch came out perfectly. But that was a decade ago, and I'm a classically trained chef now. Closing my eyes, I conjure up Chef Jean-Pierre's face, that vein in his forehead popping as he watches me tear open a box of Streit's. At least I wouldn't have to worry about seasoning my base.

No, I'm thinking about this all wrong. Making this soup isn't about impressing Lionel's wife with my culinary skill. It's about offering relief with comfort food. I've just begun typing the ingredients I'll need into my Notes app when the front door opens.

"Hey, hey." His skin is still glistening with sweat from the session he just had with his trainer. With a rush of pleasure, I notice that his old, white cap is twisted backward on his head, a few damp strands poking out the sides. The old Jake is slowly returning, and I couldn't be happier to see him.

"What are you up to?" he asks, shaking me out of my thoughts.

"Lionel's wife is sick. I'm going to make her some soup."

"Oh, no! Not Audrey!"

I bite back a smile. "You know Audrey?"

"Of course. She brings Lionel a bologna sandwich for lunch every Wednesday. It's her day off at the beauty shop." He grins triumphantly.

I shake my head. Of course he's already charmed both my doorman and his normally reticent wife. "Listen, I need to run to the store to pick up some ingredients. You need anything?"

"I'll come with you," Jake offers.

"Are you sure?" I ask. "Aren't you worried about getting recognized?"

Jake shrugs. "Some people are worth the risk." He shoots me one of his dimpled grins. "Let's make Audrey some soup."

A N HOUR LATER, WE'RE back in the kitchen. The heady scent of roasted carrots and celery perfume the air, and I pause to inhale the familiar scents of childhood as I pull the sheet pan from the oven.

The box instructed me to add a quarter cup of vegetable oil to the matzah ball mix, but by way of compromise, I replaced half of it with schmaltz I picked up at the grocery store, as well as some chopped fresh dill for extra flavor. Jake is standing at the stove, and I hand him the vegetables, which he scoops into the pot to simmer with the matzah balls. The soundtrack to *Six* is blasting through my laptop speakers and Jake wiggles his shoulders as he shimmies into my line of vision.

"Be honest: How much does my dancing elevate your experience in the kitchen? And before you answer that, keep in mind that I've worked with professional choreographers."

"You give J.Lo a run for her money," I say as I place the lid on the pot and turn down the heat. Jake grins at me as he shoves his hands in his back pockets.

"This is nice," he says. "Cooking with you." My heart tugs at the sentiment. It feels more than nice. It feels . . . right. There's something magical about getting to share the joy of making food with Jake, of letting him be a part of my world. And I can't help but notice the way he keeps tidying his prep area, like he's doing his best to impress me. His gaze snags on mine, a ghost of a smile twitching in the corner of his mouth, and I consider how badly I want to taste those lips.

"You're really something, you know that?" he says. "It takes a special person to come home after a twelve-hour workday and immediately start making soup for someone else."

I shrug off the compliment. "Lionel is like family. I've known him since I was a little girl."

"I get that. But I don't think you have any clue how amazing you are. You're not like anyone else I know."

I look away, both embarrassed and touched by his words. "I'd better get this packaged up for Lionel," I say, crouching down to open the Tupperware cabinet.

"I'll take care of it," Jake insists, shooing me away. "But I'm saving a bowl for you. And when I get back from the lobby, I'm running you a bath. You need some R&R. I've got a surprise planned for you tomorrow evening, and I need you to rest up."

"A surprise? I hate surprises."

Jake's eyes gleam. "Trust me, you won't hate this one."

THE FOLLOWING AFTERNOON, JAKE asks me to meet him in his suite at The Pierre, since Vinny's scheduled him for a midday interview with a *Rolling Stone* reporter.

Jake told me to swing by around 4:30 P.M., but I left the apartment early just to be safe, and it's only a few minutes past four when I step into the hotel's elegantly appointed lobby, a jaw-droppingly glamorous affair that looks like it's been plucked straight from Kris Jenner's wet dreams. The black-and-white checkered floors are gleaming beneath a couple of crystal chandeliers, and the ceilings are trimmed in gold. An oversized, polished round table is covered in several stunning, pink floral arrangements.

A security guard named Tony is waiting for me by the front desk. He greets me with a curt nod before escorting me to the thirty-fourth floor. I follow him down the hall until we finally reach the last door on the left. There, he withdraws a room key from his wallet to unlock the door to Jake's suite. I take a deep breath and run a smoothing hand over the bottom of my skirt. Jake still hasn't told me where we're going tonight, but he cryptically instructed me to "dress nicely" for the occasion. Whatever that means. Figuring an LBD is always a safe bet, I selected a tiered black poplin mini dress from Zara and black flats. I take a deep breath as Tony opens the door and gestures for me to step inside.

The minute I cross the threshold, I'm thrust into chaos, and I immediately understand why Jake has avoided the hotel. There are half a dozen people scattered throughout the suite, every surface of which is cluttered with food trays, bottled water, and tech equipment. Vinny is staring out the window, growling intensely into his phone, and two girls who look to be in their mid-twenties are perched on the love seat, long, manicured fingers flying furiously over their phone screens. A woman who I assume is a stylist, judging by the pink measuring tape draped around her neck, is barking directions at an assistant holding up two different black suits. And in the center of it all, dressed in black leather pants and a white shirt with huge, billowing sleeves, is Jake.

His face lights up when he sees me, his dimple flashing.

"It's epic," the stylist declares, as she adjusts the scalloped collar across Jake's neck. "It absolutely screams, 'Look at me, I am a rock star.'" The assistant cups her fingers around her chin, nodding in approval.

"Well," he asks, turning toward me and stretching his arms out to his sides. "What do you think, Lex?"

"I think it screams, 'Look at me, I'm Captain Jack Sparrow.'" The room goes silent. Every head swivels toward me. My face flushes. *Whoops, did not mean to say that out loud.*

Jake bursts out laughing. His stylist, on the other hand, is less amused.

"I'm sorry, who are you?" she asks, running a hand over her messy top knot.

"Guys, this is my friend Lexi. Lexi, this is everybody," Jake announces, sweeping out one arm to gesture toward the other occupants in the room. I bristle at the word "friend," bothered by the label for reasons I can't quite put my finger on. That's what we are, right?

The women on the sofa raise their heads and flash curt smiles before returning their attention to their phones. The assistant stylist appears slightly more interested; she cocks her head to one side, sliding her eyes up and down my outfit as she indiscreetly sizes me up. The only person besides Jake who looks remotely pleased to see me is a balding man in rumpled slacks sitting on a straight-backed chair. Based on the laminated press pass around his neck, I assume he is the *Rolling Stone* reporter. He rises from his seat, gripping a recorder in one hand and extending the other toward me.

"Nice to meet you. What did you say your last name was?" I open my mouth to reply, but before I can say a word, Vinny steps between us. He leans down, dipping his head toward my ear.

"You're early," he says, his voice a low growl. "Jake's day is meticulously scheduled for a reason. I told you before, he doesn't need distractions." Then he turns to the reporter, his face transforming into a broad smile. The effect is deeply unsettling; up until this moment, I didn't know Vinny's face had the capacity to display pleasure.

"Thank you so much for coming out today," he says, patting the reporter lightly on the shoulder as he guides him firmly toward the door. "We look forward to reading the article. And of course, don't be afraid to reach out if you have any further questions."

Vinny follows the reporter into the hallway. Once the door closes behind them, I glance at Jake, wondering if he witnessed our exchange. But he's already turned his attention back to his stylist.

"Well, Adena, should we try another option?"

Adena mutters under her breath. She shoots me a dirty look but nevertheless walks over to the portable clothing rack where she and the assistant whisper to one another as they flip through garment bags.

Jake strides over to me, gripping my elbows lightly and kissing my cheek.

"You look beautiful."

"Well, I did the best I could, given your cryptic instructions."

Adena reappears at his side, holding up a black garment bag. "Here, try this," she instructs.

He unbuttons the white blouse, slipping it off and handing it to the assistant. For a long moment he stands there, shirtless, and I find myself powerless to look away. Somehow, he's even more stunning than I remember: sculpted shoulders, taut abs, a small circle of hair that rings his belly button and tantalizingly disappears into his pants. He tugs a T-shirt over his head before Adena hands him a brown leather moto jacket. He slips it on, and she takes a moment to fuss with it, straightening the collar and smoothing out the sleeves.

"Better?" he asks, glancing over at me, and I nod. He looks like Jake again.

"Much."

"I'll have an assistant drop off a pair of jeans at the front desk this evening," Adena informs him, not even bothering to glance in my direction this time.

"No need. I've got jeans here."

Adena rolls her eyes. "Like I said, they'll be here this evening."

Jake grins. "Yes, ma'am."

She shakes her head but doesn't say another word to either of us as she and the assistant pack up. A few minutes later, the entire team has headed out, and Jake and I are finally alone. He excuses himself to take a quick shower, and I plop down on the plush, rose-colored sofa. The glass coffee table in front of me contains a tidy pile of photography books and a potted white orchid.

There's also a stack of tabloid magazines tabulated with Post-it flags, likely left behind by the PR team. I flip one open to see a paparazzi photo of Jake walking down the street wearing his white cap and sipping an iced coffee. The headline above him reads "Stars: They're Just Like Us." I smile and turn the page, revealing a feature story about Madison St. James and her newest charity project, Paws with a Cause. *Ugh.*

Flipping the magazine shut, I toss it back on the table. It's not that I'm jealous of Madison, per se. I mean, it's not like she and Jake are together. It's not like Jake and I are together, for that matter. And yet, I can't help but notice a gnawing in my stomach every time I see her face.

Jake emerges from the bedroom, devastatingly handsome in a gray button-down with cuffed sleeves and black jeans. He runs a towel through his hair as he heads over to the mini fridge and pulls out two small bottles of Pellegrino.

"Excited for tonight?" he asks, handing me one.

"Excited as one can be for an evening so shrouded in mystery."

He smirks. "Well, the first part isn't quite so mysterious. We're just going downstairs to grab a quick bite in the restaurant. The main event doesn't start until eight."

I tip my chin toward the magazine. "I, uh . . . read an article about Madison's charity," I say carefully. "As your mentor, does she help you decide what organizations you support?"

Amusement crosses Jake's face. "Are you asking if I support cancer research because of Madison?"

I shrug, suddenly mortified by my decision to bring it up at all. Jake squats so that our gazes are level, his brown eyes warming as they lock with mine.

"No, I didn't do it because of Madison. I did it because of you. I knew it was too late to reach out, to make things right. But I still thought about you. All the time. And I wanted to do something to honor that, something just for you."

THE DINING ROOM AT The Pierre is as stunning as the rest of the hotel, with striped carpeting in neutral shades and chic white light fixtures. Still, from the moment we step through the doors,

Jake's celebrity status is impossible to ignore. Heads turn, and excited whispers fill the room as we pass through. Jake's shoulders stiffen almost imperceptibly, but otherwise, he ignores the commotion he's caused.

Once we're settled, we order a bottle of Malbec, which the waitress returns with almost immediately. I wonder fleetingly if the service is always this great, or if Jake's celebrity status has afforded us extra-special treatment.

"Listen, I'm sorry about the pirate comment earlier," I say after taking a long sip of my wine. "That was completely rude. I really don't know what came over me."

He waves a hand dismissively. "Please do not apologize. Seriously. I can't tell you how refreshing it is to be around you, to have someone be honest with me, for once." He lifts his wineglass off the table but doesn't drink it, staring at its contents contemplatively as he swirls the maroon liquid. "I don't always know who I can trust, who's there for the right reasons."

I run a cloth napkin through my fingers as I mull over his words. "Why do you think that is?"

Jake sighs, his eyes trained on his menu. "When everyone around you is worried about staying on payroll, getting invited to great parties, and becoming famous themselves, it's hard to find someone who's willing to take a break from the rat race and just be a friend. People forget I'm still a regular person and not just a cog in a machine. All they're worried about is clogging the motor."

He drains his glass in one swig, and then meets my eye across the table. His expression softens as he drinks me in, holding my gaze meaningfully. "People who are genuinely concerned about your well-being are hard to come by, so when you find them, you never want to let them go."

Our conversation soon transitions to Jake's interview, and then I tell him about the crazy night we had in the kitchen two days ago, when a food critic popped in unexpectedly. We're just finishing up our dinners—chestnut cappelletti for me, a burger for him—when Jake clicks on his phone to check the time.

"Ah, we'd better be heading out." He dabs his mouth with a cloth napkin, his eyes dancing over the top of the white fabric. The excitement he's radiating is contagious, and my insides flutter.

By the time Jake's driver slows to a stop in front of the Imperial Theater on West Forty-Fifth Street, my heart is threatening to beat out of my chest. I practically fly out of the car and onto the sidewalk, my knees trembling with elation as I look up at the dangling French flag and familiar letters stamped onto the marquee: *Les Misérables.*

I whip my head around to beam at Jake, who's leaning against the car, arms crossed, an enormous grin stretched across his face.

"Seriously?!"

"I made you a promise, didn't I?"

I'm too overcome with emotion to formulate words, so I merely nod. A small crowd has begun to form near Jake. He pauses to sign autographs and take a couple of selfies, and then we make our way into the theater, where our usher shows us to our seats in the center of the fifth row. Jake's lips brush against my ear as we settle into our spots.

"I know you wanted to sit in the first row, but then you'd have to arch your neck. These are definitely the best seats in the house."

"It's perfect," I whisper back. And I mean it. My mom loved Broadway, and as a kid, my parents used to take me to see shows all the time. I can still remember the burst of excitement I felt when we saw *Guys and Dolls* in 2009. I loved the energy that radiated off the stage, the way my dad sang "Sit Down, You're Rockin' the Boat" in the shower for an entire week after. But I've never had seats like this. A rag-clad member of the ensemble peeks through the wings. I wave at him and he grins, waving back before disappearing again from view.

A few minutes later the lights dim, and the overture begins.

Jake slips his hand through mine, and I squeeze it tightly. When the lights go back on after the second act, the skin on the back of his hand is stained with tears and black mascara.

"That was amazing," I say, dabbing my eyes. "Seriously. Thank you so much."

Jake beams. "Well, it's not over yet. Ready to go backstage and meet the cast?"

I blink at him uncomprehendingly. "Are you serious?"

His grin widens as his eyes run over my tear-soaked face. "Hey, there have to be some perks to bunking with a celebrity, right?"

Taking me by the hand, Jake guides me over to the stage doors. He pulls a laminated pass from his back pocket and shows it to the guard, who nods and pushes the doors open so we can step inside.

The crowded backstage area is tighter than I expected and filled to the brim with props. There's a black bookshelf shoved against one brick wall packed tightly with woven baskets and leather-bound books. Beside it sits a blue rubber tub filled with glass liquor bottles and a baby doll wrapped in a tattered swaddle. Cosette's mopping bucket rests beside it. Glancing upward, I notice the fronts of Parisian buildings dangling above our heads. Suddenly, a scream rattles through the air.

"Oh my god, you guys! It's Jake Taylor!" The young actress who plays Éponine rushes toward us. She's still in costume, a filthy trench coat draped loosely around her shoulders and a leather belt cinching her waist. She twists her head over one shoulder and calls out to her castmates. "Dustin! Tammy! Get over here!" There's a flurry of movement, as the actors who play Marius and Cosette, as well as several members of the crew, make their way over to us.

"Wonderful show," Jake tells them. "Congrats to all of you. I wanted to introduce you all to Lexi Berman."

Éponine stretches out a hand. "Great to meet you, Lexi," she says warmly. Then she turns back to Jake, her eyes wide with excitement. "Any chance we can get a picture with you, Jake?"

He returns her smile, his dimple popping. "Only if Lexi can be in it too."

I raise my eyebrows. "You sure you're okay being in a photo with me?"

He grins widely. "Trust me, it's worth it for the look on your face right now."

Moments later, we're huddled together, and I'm handing my phone to a stagehand. My body is still buzzing with excitement fifteen minutes later when we slip into the back of a yellow cab.

"This was the most amazing night," I sigh happily.

"It was," Jake agrees. "Nights like this remind me why it's worth it. I see the cast up there, pouring their hearts into their performances, giving up nights with their families and friends. I recognize their love for the art, the commitment. Getting to share that passion with the world is the best part of this whole crazy ride."

I lean toward him, so close our foreheads are almost touching.

"Can I tell you a secret? When I was little, I used to fantasize about playing Éponine on Broadway. I had this suede newsboy cap that I bought from a street vendor, and I would wear it with my dad's trench coat and stand in front of my bathroom mirror singing 'On My Own.'"

Jake's mouth quirks. "Can I tell *you* a secret? I had the same fantasy."

I raise my eyebrows. "I hate to break it to you, but I'm not sure you have the range for it."

He chuckles. "Not Éponine . . . Marius. I've always wanted to play him onstage. I even sang 'Empty Chairs at Empty Tables' at my sixth-grade talent show."

"No, you didn't!"

"It's true. I was going through puberty and my voice kept cracking. Everyone was laughing at me, but I didn't even care, because they were sort of laughing with me, you know?" He leans his head back against the seat, smiling at the memory. "Man, I loved every second of it. The way the audience responded to me, the way I felt like I could absorb their energy. I just knew I wanted to chase that high for the rest of my life."

His accent grows thicker as he talks, in that stupidly adorable way it always does when he gets excited. I study his profile, the way his dimple is faintly visible through his stubble.

"You could still do it, you know. Try your hand at Broadway."

Jake's cheerful expression fades and he shakes his head. "I appreciate how much faith you have in me, but I'm not sure Vinny would be on board with that plan. My team has a fully developed trajectory for my career, and Broadway is definitely not any part of it."

NOW THAT OUR SCHEDULES no longer lend themselves to Friday afternoon happy hours, Ali, Chloe, and I have rescheduled our weekly catch-up sessions as Monday morning breakfasts. When I arrive at Manhattan Bagel at 9 A.M., Chloe is already seated at a table in the corner, half of a scooped-out bagel on a plate in front of her. As usual, she's bent over her phone, furrowed brow pinned firmly in place.

"Which do you want first: The good news or the bad news?" she asks when I slide into the seat across from her.

"Good morning to you, too."

Chloe looks up at me and smiles. "Sorry. Good morning to you and your stunningly beautiful face, which I do not see nearly enough. Now, which will it be?"

"I'll take good news for two hundred."

"The good news is that today marks the one-week anniversary of the last time I left a prank voicemail on Dev's phone," Ali's voice comes up from behind me. Pulling out the chair next to me, she sits, plopping a brown paper bag and an iced coffee down on the table in front of her. "My therapist has deemed me 'slightly less unhinged than usual.'"

"Mazel tov! Chloe, does this trump your good news?"

"Debatable," she replies, eyeing me with uncertainty. "You need to look at this. Apparently, you're a blind item on DeuxMoi this morning."

"Deux what?"

"See for yourself."

She slides the phone across the table so that I can read the Instagram screenshot.

Sent via form submission from *DeuxMoi*
Pseudonyms, Please: Mademoiselle Anon
Email: Valjean24601@gmail.com
Subject: A Rock Star No Longer on His Own?
Message: A certain breakfast-loving Billboard darling was spotted at Broadway's Les Misérables revival last night with an unknown blonde on his arm. Is she just a friend or is this fan favorite cooking up a new romance?

I stare at it a moment, trying to wrap my mind around the words. "Sorry, how is this good news?"

"Well, there's no picture of you. Not yet at least. The bad news is that it doesn't take a genius to figure out they're talking about Jake, and it's only a matter of time before someone identifies you. And when they do, the paparazzi are going to be all over you like a Republican senator on abortion rights."

"Shit. How many people do you think have seen this?"

"How many people read DeuxMoi?!" Ali asks. "Do the words 'Armie Hammer' and 'toes' mean anything to you?"

"*Shit*," I say again. "Okay, what should I do?"

Chloe straightens her shoulders, and I can see her shifting into business mode. "Okay, step one: start keeping a low profile. Set all your social media to private and avoid being seen in public with Jake. The press will lose interest if you don't give them anything to write about."

I take a minute to consider her words. "Don't you think that's a bit of an overreaction? It's not like we're together."

She gives me one of her patented, no-nonsense looks. "Keep telling yourself that."

"I'm serious! We're just friends!" I protest. But as soon as the words leave my mouth, I wonder if they're even true. Something has shifted between us recently. We aren't together, but it doesn't feel like we're just friends either. To be honest, I'm not quite sure where we stand.

"Just admit it," Ali says. "You want to bone him."

"I will admit no such thing."

Chloe kicks me under the table. "Lexi, you can pretend not to be in love with him all you want, but at least have the decency not to lie about *that*."

"Meanwhile," Ali interjects. "While you're shacking up with a rock star, I'm fielding DMs from strangers on Instagram requesting photos of my feet."

She turns her phone around to show me her screen. "Check it out. This one guy is offering fifty bucks per photo."

My jaw drops open. "You're not going to actually do it, are you?"

She shrugs. "Might be the easiest money I'll ever make. It's not like I'm rolling in dough as a line cook in a hotel restaurant." She takes a sip of her iced coffee. "I hate being poor. Chef life sure isn't what I thought it would be."

"Tell me about it," I sigh. "I thought my job would be so much more creative. I always imagined myself inventing new recipes and making someone's night with a hot meal. But what I actually do is chop salad greens for sixteen hours a day."

"We have made a terrible mistake. We should have gone into waitressing. At least then we'd make tips."

She's joking, but I can't shake the impact her words have on me. *Have I made a mistake?* Ali can joke all she wants, but we both know that she feeds off the fast-paced energy of the kitchen like some sort of emotional vampire. But try as I might, it's getting harder and harder to ignore my lack of excitement when I head into work each morning. I love cooking, but I've never enjoyed it as much at work as I do at home. Making that matzah ball soup for Audrey was the most exciting thing I've done in the kitchen in weeks.

I'm still mulling it over as I head over to the counter to order my usual, a sesame bagel with vegetable cream cheese and a coffee. But when I get back to the table, both of my friends are waiting, their arms crossed. I even have Chloe's full attention, and frankly, it's kind of disarming.

"We're serious about Jake," Ali says quietly. "We know you don't want to acknowledge the way you feel, but as your best friends, we can't let you continue to pretend like nothing is going on between you two."

"The way I feel"—I pull off a piece of my bagel and chew it thoughtfully—"is highly wronged, because you have been working at The Carlyle for months, and I have yet to benefit from its sophisticated wine list. What is the point of you working glorious hotel hours if I can't occasionally enjoy some free Sancerre?"

Ali brushes crumbs into her paper wrapper and pitches it into the trash can across from our table. "We aren't finished with this conversation," she says. "But you are getting off the hook for now because I have to go to work." I know she's right—it's getting harder and harder to pretend that Jake and I are just friends—but for now, I'm not ready to explore my feelings for Jake. Maybe it's because I know that once I venture down that thorny path, there's not a chance in hell of finding my way back.

I expect Chloe to follow Ali out the door, but once she's gone, Chloe opens her navy Goyard tote and extracts a laptop.

"You take meetings at the bagel shop now?" I ask with amusement.

Chloe groans. "I've scheduled an appointment with Chad. He got banned from the office after the day he pushed every button in the elevator."

Right on cue, the door to Manhattan Bagel swings open, and a tall man with spiky blond hair and the most punchable face I've ever seen steps inside. He's wearing a tight gray V-neck that shows off his considerable muscles and a pair of basketball shorts. Even from a ten-foot distance, the smell of his AXE body spray is overwhelming. When he spots us, his face splits into a grin, showcasing a matching set of dimples.

"Chlo-money!" he yells from the doorway.

"I've asked you repeatedly not to call me that," she says through gritted teeth. "Now come here so we can get this over with." Chad shrugs and sidles over to us. As he approaches, I notice his sneakers are on the wrong feet.

Chad stops in front of me and flicks up his Ray-Bans, allowing his hazel eyes to roam over me.

"Don't believe we've met," he says, offering me a meaty hand and a megawatt smile. "I'm Chad."

"Don't speak to her," Chloe says. She snaps her fingers in front of his face to get his attention and then points to a chair, indicating that he should sit. Obediently, he does. Draping an arm over the back of his chair, he twists his body to face me. His eyes lock on the bagel in my hand, and his body starts trembling as he attempts to hold back laughter.

"I'm afraid to ask what's funny," Chloe says wearily.

He points to my bagel, his face flushed with glee. "She's got . . . so much cream . . . in her hole."

Chloe's eyes squeeze shut as she presses a closed fist to her forehead. "Serious question, Chad: Are your parents related?" Chad stops laughing and his mouth sets in a hard line. His eyes glaze over as he considers it.

Chloe puffs out a sigh and straightens her shoulders, resigned. "Moving on," she says, flicking open her laptop. "You know why I asked you to meet me here, right?"

Chad interlocks his hands behind his head, flexing the tendons in his enormous biceps. "Is this about the videos?"

"Of course it's about the videos." She turns the screen to face him, and I see she's opened the browser to a page full of Chad photos. In most of them, he's completely naked, save for a single red rose covering his genitals.

"We've talked about this. You'll never get on *Bachelor in Paradise* if you don't delete your OnlyFans account. You've already gotten a cease and desist letter from ABC."

"But chicks *dig* it!" he says emphatically. "How can I deny my fans what they want?"

"No one wants this, Chad," Chloe replies tersely. "Seriously. There's a change.org petition floating around calling for you to get a vasectomy. It already has twelve thousand signatures."

"What I hear you saying"—Chad smirks—"is that America is obsessed with my pork sword."

"And that's my cue." I stand up, pushing in my chair. "Chad, it was a pleasure to meet you. Chloe . . . good luck."

16

I CAN HEAR JAKE'S HUSKY voice through the walls of my apartment before I even slip the key into the door. My chest warms as I step through the entryway to see him perched on the sofa, head bent over his guitar, and my heart flutters the way it always does when I hear him sing. Thank goodness my next-door neighbor, Mrs. Tannenbaum, is over eighty and can barely hear, and the Ackermans, who live two doors down, have been in Philly with their grandkids for the past month. It's a small miracle that no one else in the building seems to notice I'm harboring a celebrity.

"Hey!" His face brightens when he lifts his head up in greeting, and I'm struck by how natural it feels to see him in my home. He seems as much a part of the fabric here as the floral-print chairs. A vision of our future in this shared space flashes before me. Him on the sofa, brows knit in concentration as he works out lyrics to a new song. Me in the kitchen, surrounded by pots and pans, the air thick with spice as I work out a new recipe. The idea is so dreamy that I have to shake my head to dispel it before I can get lost any further. Jake is a rock star, and I am a chef; even if we were together in some alternative universe, we'd never have a future as two homebodies. Forgetting that is only going to lead to heartache.

"New song?" I ask as I hang up my jacket. Jake's cheeks go rosy.

"What can I say? I've been feeling inspired lately." He nods toward the kitchen. "By the way, there was a package waiting for you in the lobby." My smile fades as I follow his gaze. Sure enough, there's a large brown box waiting for me on the counter. I knew it would arrive this week, but I didn't expect it this soon.

Grabbing a pair of kitchen scissors, I slide the blade under the packing tape, popping the lid open. My stomach clenches as I inventory the familiar contents. It's the same thing every year.

"Get anything interesting?"

Before I can answer, Jake strolls over and begins rummaging through the box. "Twizzlers, balloons, candles . . . Funfetti cake mix?" He lifts his head as understanding registers on his face. "Wait, is it your birthday?"

I nod. "On Friday. My dad sends me a care package every year after I turn down his offer to come to Florida and celebrate. This year, I told him I'm going out for a girls' night."

"Oh. With Ali and Chloe?"

"Yes. Well, no. I mean, I'm not really doing anything. I don't like making a big deal out of my birthday."

Jake's brow wrinkles. "I don't get it. It seems like your dad wants to spend time with you. Why are you avoiding him?"

"Because I'm mad at him, that's why! He abandoned me to move down to Florida, and he's never come back since. If he wanted to see me so badly, he could visit me here." I scowl bitterly at the box, like it's to blame for my father's shortcomings.

Jake's quiet for a moment before he shifts his attention back to the box. "Why Funfetti?" he asks softly.

I can feel the pressure rising in my chest. "Because that's the type of cake my mom made me every year." Heat burns the back of my eyes, and I blink rapidly before the tears can spill over. "I guess he thinks he's keeping the tradition alive. But that's the thing about birthday cakes. The whole point is that you're not supposed to make them for yourself."

"Come here." Jake advances toward me. I bury my face in my chest and his arms encircle me tightly, folding me into a hug. We stand there for a few minutes, my tears dampening his chest. His nose brushes against my hair as he rubs small circles on my back.

"It's okay," he whispers, pressing his lips against my forehead. Inhaling his familiar scent, I feel the tension in my chest loosening, replaced by a crushing sense of comfort I definitely don't care to read into.

"I'm fine," I say, clearing my throat. "Really." Jake doesn't answer. His eyes bore into me, and the silence stretches thin between us before he cuts it.

"You know, I've been planning to visit my parents in Marietta. Why don't we go together this weekend? I know you don't want to make a big fuss, but no one should be alone on their birthday."

I bite my lip contemplatively. The offer is enticing. Plus, it would alleviate some guilt, since I wouldn't be lying to my dad about having plans.

"Well, I don't work on Thursday. I guess I could take Friday off, as long as we're back in time for my shift on Saturday?"

Jake's face lights up. "Yes! You'll love it out there. You can meet my family and get away from the city for a little while. It will be great!"

My earlier trepidation is already melting into excitement.

"Okay," I say, offering him a smile. "Let's do it."

IT'S A FORTY-FIVE-MINUTE DRIVE from the Atlanta airport to Jake's childhood home in Marietta. As soon as Jake pulls out of the parking lot in the black Jeep he's rented, I plug my phone into the aux cable, turn on the stereo, and scroll through my playlist. Moments later, the first track of *Red* blasts through the speakers.

"Taylor Swift? Seriously?"

"What? We're in the South! I need to get in the mood," I reply defensively when he pulls a face.

"Taylor Swift is from Pennsylvania."

"That *is* the South."

He shoots me a sideways glance and shakes his head, but I notice one corner of his mouth rising in a tiny smile.

"Only according to New Yorkers."

When we finally pull into the driveway, my breath catches in my throat. Jake's childhood home is positively stunning, with a facade constructed entirely out of dark stone that stretches across a well-manicured lawn.

I'm not sure exactly what I'm expecting when we knock on the dark-wood-paneled front door, but when it swings open, I immediately recognize the petite woman standing there as Jake's mom. She has the same chocolate-brown eyes and chestnut hair, though hers is styled in a half ponytail. Her face instantly breaks into a warm smile.

"My baby!" she cries, throwing her arms around Jake and pulling him into her chest. He wraps his arms around her, placing his chin on her forehead as he pulls her closer.

"I've missed you, Mom," he whispers into her hair. They stay like that for a moment, and when Mrs. Taylor finally pulls back, she wipes a tear from her eye with the back of her knuckle.

She turns her head to look over at me. "You'll have to excuse me, blubbering on like that." Her accent is a tad more pronounced than Jake's, and her apple cheeks are rosy as she beams at me. "I am so glad to finally meet you, Lexi. You're even more beautiful in person than Jacob said you were."

"Mom," he groans with the exasperation of an embarrassed teenager. But she ignores him, stepping forward and folding herself around me. Her touch sends a spark through my core. It's been years since I've felt arms wrap around me in a warm, maternal embrace, and I hadn't realized how much I missed it.

"I am just so thrilled that you both are here."

"Thank you so much for having us, Mrs. Taylor."

"Please, call me Trish," she says, waving a dismissive hand.

"Well, there's no need to stand out here on the porch all day. Let's go inside."

As I take in the elegantly appointed home, with its high, vaulted ceilings, white paneled walls, and clusters of wrought-iron chandeliers, I'm grateful for my outfit of choice: a pair of black knit pants and a pale pink, ruffled pullover. It's a more formal look than I'd normally choose for a flight, but it was my first time flying first class, and I'd wanted to look the part.

Mrs. Taylor hangs our coats in the hallway closet, and then leads us into the kitchen. I gasp audibly at the sight.

The farthest end of the kitchen is wall-to-wall windows, which flood the kitchen with natural light and overlook a lush, green backyard. An enormous island with a black-and-white marbled countertop sits in the center, surrounded by half a dozen black leather barstools. A heaping bouquet of flowers in a blue-and-white chinoiserie vase sits on top, alongside an oversized wooden charcuterie board filled to the brim with prosciutto, cheese, fig jam, and breadsticks. An enormous ivory chandelier hangs from the ceiling, casting a soft light over the entire space. It's official: I have died and gone to heaven.

"This . . . is the kitchen of my dreams," I declare before I can censor myself, and Mrs. Taylor breaks into an easy laugh.

"One of the many benefits of being married to an architect," she admits. I throw a questioning look at Jake—why hasn't he ever mentioned his dad is an architect?—but he's already helping himself to the charcuterie board. It's only then I realize I never did ask him about the family business.

"Your home is absolutely stunning, Mrs. Taylor," I gush.

"Trish," she reminds me. "And don't think I'm going to let you get away with not teaching me a thing or two while you're here. It's not every day I get to have a professional chef in my kitchen."

"It'd be my pleasure," I say. Trish grins at me. Unlike her son, she has not one but two dimples that form deep indentations on either side of her mouth. Jake presses his hands against the kitchen counter, hoisting himself up to sit on the marble.

"Now, what can I fix y'all to drink?" Trish asks. "How 'bout a sweet tea?"

Jake claps a hand over his heart.

"Thought you'd never ask."

A FEW MINUTES LATER, WE'RE all happily settled in on the enclosed back porch. I tuck my feet under myself as I take a hearty sip from my glass.

"God, I've missed this," Jake confesses, draining his tea in a single gulp and then grabbing the pitcher to pour himself a refill.

Trish beams. "Good to know that no matter how famous you get, you'll never get tired of your mama's sweet tea." She grins at me. "I know it's only August, but since Jacob's schedule is so busy, I decided to make a small-scale Thanksgiving dinner tonight. Just in case he's not around in November." She flips her wrist over to glance at her watch. "Speaking of which, it's nearly two. We'd better get started on that turkey."

"You haven't started it yet?" I clamp my hand over my mouth the second the words leave my lips, startled by my own bluntness. "I'm so sorry. I didn't mean to be so rude. It's just . . . it takes half a day to roast a turkey."

Jake and his mother exchange a look and then burst into laughter. His eyes travel to mine, amusement dancing across his handsome face.

"Welcome to Georgia," he says. "Down here, we deep fry our turkeys. It'll only take an hour."

When we finish our teas, Jake leads me down the porch steps and into the backyard to set up the deep fryer. He places a burner onto a bed of rocks and connects it to a propane tank, while explaining how he uses a level to make sure it's straight. He dries the pot before adding oil and positioning it on top.

"I thought you said you didn't know how to cook," I say as I watch him submerge the turkey.

"This ain't cooking . . . it's deep frying." His accent has deepened since we've gotten here, but it's not the only thing that's changed. His entire body has visibly relaxed, like he's more comfortable, more himself than I've seen him in a long time. I suppose at home, he gets to take a break from being Jake Taylor, rock star, and just be Jake. He grins at me, and for the first time in a long time, I see the boy who smiled at me in the bar all those months ago.

"Jacob! Daddy is home."

Jake's back stiffens for a moment, and he lets out a breath. Flipping the fryer off, he grabs me by the hand, and leads me up the staircase of the deck and into the living room.

Stepping inside, I notice the room is warm and tastefully decorated, the walls painted a soothing shade of silvery blue that's paired with a coordinating rug and overstuffed beige furniture. A middle-aged man with salt-and-pepper hair is pacing in front of the brick-lined fireplace, brows knit together as he studies the cell phone in his hand.

"Hi, Dad," Jake says as he steps into the room. He walks over to his father, giving him an awkward, one-armed hug. I notice with a frown that the embrace seems strained, distant somehow.

"Play us a song, Jacob?" Trish has materialized at my side. She rests a hand lightly on my elbow, but her eyes are fixed on her only child.

Jake lets out a groan. "Even at home, there's no rest for the weary." But the contented expression on his face belies the sentiment, and he strolls over to the piano in the far-right corner of the room. Tucking himself onto the bench, he flexes his hands and then brushes his long fingers across the keys. Lifting his head, he meets my eyes. "I know just the one," he says softly.

He drops his chin, brow creasing in concentration, and the air whooshes from my lungs as the opening notes of "Edelweiss" drift into the air. *He remembered.*

I'm frozen in place, hot, unexpected tears prickling the back of my eyes at the familiar melody, and a knot forms in the center of my chest. There's so much that I want to say, but when I finally manage to form words, the only thing that comes out is, "I didn't know Jake plays piano."

Trish nods. "Oh, yes. Jacob plays many instruments. The guitar, the piano, the tuba."

"The tuba?" I let out a tiny breath of laughter and the pressure in my chest loosens a fraction. Trish shakes her head ruefully, a smirk playing on her lips. "Yep. Of all the instruments to pick for the high school band, that's what he went with."

Jake's deep, gravelly voice lilts through the air, and his eyes squeeze shut as he drops his head back. Powerless to look away, I relinquish myself to the pull of his orbit, my eyes drinking in every detail of him. The silky brown hair that curls lazily around one ear. The square line of his jaw. The flutter of his pulse beneath the tender skin of his neck. The shifting of his back muscles beneath his shirt. The tendons in his forearms that ripple as his long fingers dance gracefully across the ivory keys. I feel my own limbs grow heavy, the world around me becoming hazy as everything but Jake melts away.

Through my dreamlike state, it occurs to me that I'm witnessing something rare and special, something that most people never get to see. Jake's fans worship him; they may even think they love him. But the truth is, you can't love someone you've never met. They'll never get to see what I see, all the little pieces that compose the incomparable magic of the man in front of me. The real Jake. Because he is so much more than a celebrity. He is everything.

By the time he finishes playing, glancing up at me with a sheepish grin, I can't even speak.

"That was . . . beautiful," I muster through dry lips, aware that I am sinking into the chocolate depth of Jake's eyes as they bore into mine. I'm not sure how long we stand there, staring at each other, before Jake's father clears his throat.

"Well, are we having Fake Thanksgiving or not? I don't know about y'all, but I'm absolutely starved."

THE FEAST SPREAD ACROSS the table before us is nothing short of spectacular. Whiskey-glazed carrots. Skillet cornbread. Macaroni and cheese. Sweet potato pie piled high with marshmallow meringue. And of course, the deep-fried turkey.

I take a huge bite of crispy dark meat, eyes fluttering shut as I savor it.

"Oh my god . . . this is incredible. I'm never eating oven-roasted turkey again." Trish's face lights up, her eyes sparkling with pleasure, and I remember Jake's words about how much his mother enjoys feeding others.

"There's nothing like comfort food," she says warmly. "And I'm so glad you're enjoying it. I'm sure it's a nice change of pace to not have to be the one cooking." She's right. Truth be told, I was a little worried that's exactly what I'd end up doing today. I've heard horror stories from classmates about showing up to holiday dinners and being expected, as "the chef of the family," to prepare the entire meal. It really is a pleasure to be taken care of for once.

Mr. Taylor clears his throat behind the napkin he's dabbing over his mouth.

"Alexa, Trish tells me that you're a chef," he ventures.

"Yes, sir. I'm currently working at a restaurant in Manhattan."

"And how's that?"

"Exhausting," I say with a laugh. "The hours are pretty brutal."

Trish offers a sympathetic smile. "I bet. But do you enjoy it?"

I twist my lips, contemplating the best way to answer. "It's kind of monotonous," I admit. "What I really enjoy is coming up with my own recipes. But you have to start somewhere. I'm planning to work my way up the ladder and become an executive chef someday. Then I can open my own restaurant and cook the sort of food I want to."

Trish winks at me from across the table, and I feel a surge of pleasure. Even though she isn't my mother, the maternal pride she exudes feels like a warm hug.

Mr. Taylor purses his lips in approval as he tucks into his sweet potatoes. "Very smart to have a steady, well-planned career path like that."

Jake stiffens beside me, and I can feel a palpable shift in the atmosphere. I'm not quite sure what's going on, but I attempt to change the subject. Unfortunately, it turns out to be the wrong subject.

"So, Mr. Taylor—you're an architect? Did you build this house?"

Jake's father straightens in his seat, chest puffing. "Yes, as a matter of fact, I did. This one and most of the others on this street. I'm the CEO of Taylor & Son, the top architecture firm in Marietta for the past twenty-five years. I inherited the business from my own father. Of course, in my case, the 'son' part has never actually come to fruition."

"Jeffrey." There's a warning tone in Trish's voice, but her husband ignores her as he presses on.

"Did Jacob ever tell you that he graduated top of his class from the B.Arch program at LSU? He would have been such an asset to the company. But instead, he fooled around in New York for a few years, and hasn't been home much since. He's never quite let go of this music hobby of his."

Jake's voice is strained. "My first single held the number-one spot on the Billboard Hot One Hundred chart for eight consecutive weeks. I think it's safe to say my music career is more than just a 'hobby.'"

"Yes, it's all very exciting. For now. Until your fifteen minutes of fame are over, and you're left with no job and no prospects. Fame doesn't last forever, Jacob. You need a long-term plan."

Jake's jaw tightens, and I feel my heart deflate in a way I know I'm not entitled to. I've never been in this position; my parents always threw their full support behind everything I set out to do, convinced I'd succeed at anything I put my mind to. If anything, I've suffered from the opposite affliction. Sometimes I felt exhausted from trying to live up to their expectations of my projected greatness.

"Well, I don't think my fifteen minutes are ending anytime soon," he says tersely. "And as a matter of fact, my team and I do have a plan. I've also been in the studio almost every day in New York, working on my second album. It will be finished by the end of next month."

As I contemplate the implication of his statement, a wave of panic washes over me. I had nearly forgotten that the only reason Jake has spent the past two months in New York was to lay down his album. And that can only mean one thing.

"Wait," I hear myself ask before anyone else can respond. "Does that mean you're leaving again?"

Jake's attention flies back to my face. His mouth drops open, hanging there for a moment as he searches for the right words.

"Well . . . yeah. But, I mean, it's not like I'll be gone forever. I'll still be around New York fairly often, doing press and stuff."

I stare down at my plate, dragging my fork across my food without picking anything up. My appetite has vanished. "Yeah, I've heard that before."

Jake's father lifts his glass of sweet tea with a triumphant smirk. "I guess that's just the cost of your bohemian lifestyle, eh, Jacob?"

Jake's shoulders sag, and I immediately feel a surge of guilt for bringing this up in front of his family.

"Well, I think it's just amazing. I'm so proud of my boy," Trish says, beaming at Jake from across the table.

"Me too," I add, attempting to backpedal from my earlier outburst. "Seriously, that's incredible." Jake's features flood with relief, and I feel his hand brush mine underneath the table. I thread our fingers together and he smiles, his brown eyes warm as he squeezes my hand.

"Thanks."

Trish stands, pushing back her chair.

"Well, I think we're ready for dessert." She looks at me, her eyes bright. "And in lieu of pie, I've got something in the kitchen for the birthday girl."

She disappears through the doorway, and I turn to face Jake. "You didn't," I whisper.

"How could I deny her the pleasure?" he whispers back. "Besides, it *is* your birthday, and you deserve to be celebrated."

Trish returns a moment later, placing an expertly decorated cake with vanilla frosting and a single lit candle in front of me.

"Jake said you don't like to make a big deal of your birthday, so we won't embarrass you by singing," she says, placing a hand on my shoulder. "But go ahead and make a wish." As I glance around the room at Jake, his mom, and even his less-than-stellar dad, I realize the wish I've been making for years has already come true. But then Trish slices the cake and I spot the tiny dots of color inside. She places a piece in front of me, and my heart leaps into my mouth.

"A little birdie told me Funfetti is your favorite." Speechless, my gaze travels to Jake's. Something silent but powerful passes between us. And in that moment, I know that Jake Taylor and I will never be just friends.

Jake leans forward and presses his lips against my forehead.

"Happy Birthday, Lexi," he whispers.

WHEN WE FINISH EATING, everyone carries their plates into the kitchen, and I offer to help Trish with the dishes.

"Thanks again for dinner. Everything was delicious," I gush, setting a few glasses beside the sink. "I can't even remember the last time someone cooked for me."

Trish squeezes my hand before reaching around me to pick up one of the glasses. She gives it a quick rinse under the faucet before placing it carefully into the dishwasher. "Well, if there's one thing I've learned from Nora Ephron, it's that food is love."

My stomach flutters at the familiar words. "My mom used to say the same thing." Trish tilts her head to look at me. Her eyes, which are far too like Jake's for comfort, regard me carefully.

"Jacob told me about your mother," she says sympathetically. "It must be really hard for you, especially around the holidays. But I want you to know that you are always welcome here. Consider this an open invitation to come over anytime."

I nod, attempting to smile. I'm touched by the sentiment, by the prospect of having a new, adoptive family to replace the one I lost. Yet I can't help but feel simultaneously heartbroken. What if her offer never comes to fruition? What if history repeats itself and Jake and I lose touch again? The thought is almost too much to bear.

"I also want to thank you for taking such good care of Jacob," she continues. "You don't know what it means to see him so happy again. And I know it's all because of you."

I struggle to formulate a response.

"He's been doing great, with his career and all," I finally manage.

Trish shakes her head softly. "It's not the music career," she muses. "I've been married so long that I forget what it's like sometimes, to be young and in love."

"Oh, we're not . . . I mean . . . we're not even together." My face betrays my mortification as I stammer over the words. Despite my efforts, it's getting harder and harder to bury my feelings for her son.

"Your generation has such an aversion to labels." Her voice is laced with an unmistakable trace of amusement, and she shakes her head again. "Doesn't change what's clear as day to everyone else. I know my son, and I've never seen him look at anyone the way he looks at you."

I open my mouth to respond, but the words get stuck in my throat. Instead, I turn my attention to drying. When we finish a few minutes later, we head back into the living room, where Jake is seated at the piano again. Jeffrey's lounging in an easy chair, a newspaper in one hand and a tumbler of bourbon in the other.

Curiously, I approach the wall-to-wall white bookcases on the other end of the room, which are filled with books, trinkets, and, most interesting, a handful of framed photographs. My eyes drift over each image. Jake as a toddler in a soapy bathtub. Jake seated at the top of a red plastic slide, a sunhat clipped under his chubby chin. Jake in his soccer uniform, several teeth missing. And then—

"Um . . . is this a photo of you tap-dancing?"

Jake's head whips around, his panicked eyes locked on me as Trish laughs softly from the sofa.

"Ah yes, Jake's tap-dancing days," she reminisces. "I could never figure out what to do with him when he was that age. So much energy—he was always bouncing around, showing off to anyone who gave him the slightest bit of attention. The worst was when it was my turn to host book club. We'd all be gathered in the living room, and here comes Jake, wearing my sunglasses and leaping off the furniture, singing Elvis Presley to all the ladies." She appears wistful at the memory. "I had to do something to help him get his energy out, and let's face it, the boy belonged on the stage."

Jake rises from the piano bench and walks purposefully toward me, his hand outstretched. "Give me the photograph, Lexi."

"Absolutely not. This belongs to me now." I clutch the frame tightly to my chest. "I'm going to turn it into wallpaper and cover my room with it. It will be the last thing I see when I close my eyes at night, and the first thing I will see when I wake up in the morning."

Jake narrows his eyes, staring me down for a long moment.

Then he launches toward me in an attempted surprise attack. I dodge his arms, leap over the sofa, and scamper through the doorway.

"You already have wealth, success, and international fame. Just let me have this one thing!" I yelp over my shoulder, yanking the back door open as I sprint outside. I jump down the metal stairs, racing to safety on the grassy backyard.

Jake thunders after me, easily closing the distance. The lawn is soft as he tackles me to the ground. His fingers find my armpits, and I explode into giggles as he tickles me into submission. My death grip on the frame releases. He snaps it up and falls backward, holding the photo triumphantly above his head.

"You're too late!" I shout, falling onto my back beside him as I gasp for breath. "I already called *Us Weekly*!" Stretching out, I stare up at the night sky.

"Stars," I muse. "They're just like us."

The grass is damp and prickly against my neck and hands. I can't remember the last time I laid on the ground like this, without even a blanket underneath me. It feels liberating.

Jake collapses beside me, his arm brushing against mine. I breathe in his smell, soapy and comforting. His mother's voice echoes in my brain: *Doesn't change what's clear as day to everyone else.*

He rolls over, his face so close to mine that our noses are practically touching. His warm breath tickles my cheek. "Speaking of stars . . . how about we go for a drive?"

"ARE WE THERE YET?" I ask again, my patience waning. We've already been driving for half an hour, and the farther we get from Jake's house, the more remote the view from outside my window.

"Patience, young grasshopper," Jake jokes. "Just a few more minutes."

"And where are we going, exactly?"

"To one of my favorite spots. I want to show you something you can't find in New York City."

I study Jake's handsome profile in the moonlight. His glossy hair, neatly combed at the start of the evening, is now smothered by his white cap, and his square jaw is set in concentration as he stares at the long stretch of road ahead of us.

I finally tear my eyes away from him and turn toward the windshield, studying the glow of the headlights illuminating the winding road ahead. Dark silhouettes of trees dusted with moonlight whip past my window as he picks up speed.

A few minutes later, he slows down, pulling off the gravel road and onto a dirt path. We crawl slowly up a hill, the Jeep jerking over the rocky surface beneath the tires. I grip the door handle nervously, and Jake chuckles under his breath.

"Don't worry," he says, reaching out to take my hand in his. "I've driven over this path a thousand times."

We pass through a clearing, and the car comes to a stop on a grassy plane. Jake turns off the ignition but leaves on the headlights. I open my door, pressing my shoes into the green grass and taking a breath of fresh air.

Jake walks around to my side of the car. He slips his hand in mine.

"What are we doing here?" I ask. Jake turns his head to look up at the night sky.

"I wanted to show you the one thing you can't find in New York City. The *real* stars."

I tilt my chin upward to follow his gaze. Away from the pollution of the city, the inky blue sky above me is impossibly clear and speckled with hundreds of tiny white stars. It takes my breath away.

Jake brings his chin down and studies me intensely. "What do you think?"

"It's beautiful," I whisper.

"What do you say we stay for a while?"

Turning on his heel, he walks around to the back of the truck, popping open the bed and pulling out a woolly plaid blanket. He gestures for me to take the opposite end, and we open it together, smoothing it out across the grassy bank. I sit down gingerly on the blanket, and Jake collapses beside me. Stretching our hands out behind us, we tip our heads back and stare at the mesmerizing sight. Half a moon peeks down at us, flanked by dozens of twinkling lights.

"Your dad's an interesting guy," I venture after a moment, as I pluck a few blades of grass from the ground. Jake lets out a snort.

"Jeffrey Taylor lives a life of disappointment. Gives up a football scholarship to follow in his own father's footsteps and take over the family business, never anticipating that his son might not do the same." He lets the words hang there in the air, neither one of us caring to say anything further about it. A few more minutes of comfortable silence stretch out before I ask the one question that's been on my mind all day.

"Why didn't you ever tell me about him?"

Jake's shoulders sag. "Because I'm afraid if I acknowledge the way he feels about my career, it might become real," he admits. "My dad doesn't take what I do seriously. He's just waiting for me to fail. And what if he's right? I mean, look what happened with Vinny. My own management didn't believe I could succeed."

He sits up a little, sliding his forearms beneath him to prop himself on his elbows and squint at the night sky. I can't help but stare at him, his biceps flexing beneath the weight of his body, square jaw twitching, full lips pulling downward in a pouty grimace. It's no wonder the world has fallen in love with him.

As though he's read my mind, Jake continues.

"In the beginning, I went along with whatever Vinny said, booking every talk show he wanted, refraining from addressing the rumors around me and Madison. I trusted him, even when it made me uncomfortable, because he was the 'expert' or whatever, and I wanted to make it so badly. I was willing to do anything to show my dad I could become a successful musician, because I couldn't bear the thought of letting him be right about me." He flicks his gaze toward me, and his eyes are swimming with remorse.

"I'm not an idiot. I figured something else was going on, but I never asked questions. Maybe it's the way I was brought up. My parents taught me to respect authority figures, not contradict them. Or maybe I was just willing to accept whatever he told me because I was desperate to succeed in this industry. He always used to say, 'Your wins are my wins.' Even when it felt wrong, I trusted that Vinny would steer me in the right direction. So I handed over the reins, and he made me a star."

He pushes the heels of his hand into his eyes. "But I regret it, Lexi. I regret it every day. I sold myself to be successful, and now I barely recognize the person I've become. And the worst thing of all is that it cost me you."

My heart aches at the sadness of his tone, and all the things he must worry about constantly: who he can trust, if his manager really has his best interests at heart, if he truly has what it takes, and whether his father's doubts will come to fruition. I reach my left hand out and grab his right one, gently running my thumb across his palm.

"They're idiots," I say quietly. Jake turns toward me, his eyes wide and his face full of emotion.

"What?"

"They're idiots. They'd have to be, if they can't see what I see. Because you're not like anyone else I've ever met, Jake. You're kind, and thoughtful, and funny, and insanely talented. You've never needed to change yourself or lie about who you're dating to be successful; you're gifted enough on your own, and you always have been. If Vinny and your dad can't see it, then that's their loss."

The words hang in the air between us, pulsating with energy. Jake's eyes are pinned on mine as he stares at me, his face half shadowed by moonlight.

"Thank you," he says hoarsely. "For always being my ally. You don't know what it means to me, having you in my life. You probably think I only brought you to Georgia to cheer you up. And it's true. But honestly, I was doing it for me too. I couldn't bear the thought of coming here without you. You never make me feel like I have to prove myself. When I'm with you, I feel like who I am is enough."

I realize at that moment I feel the same way. That my world has completely changed since he walked back into it. That for the first time in years, I don't have that hollow feeling in my chest when I wake up in the morning. That I no longer feel enslaved by a desire to control everything. That for the first time since I lost my mom, I feel truly happy again. That maybe, just maybe, I need him as much as he needs me.

But instead of saying it out loud, I bring my hands up and place them on either side of his face. His stubble tickles the skin of my palms, and his chest constricts as he intakes a sharp breath. Before I have a chance to overthink it, I bring my face forward to press my lips against his.

The kiss is slow and steadying, evoking a sense of rightness. It's softer than the ones we've shared before, raw and tender. I reach up and run my fingers through his hair as he exhales softly into my mouth, wrapping an arm around my waist to bring me closer.

When I pull away a moment later, Jake's eyes are hooded. His gaze burns into mine as he searches my face.

"What was that for?"

"Just for being you."

I lean back against the blanket, folding my hands behind my head as I stare up at the night sky. After a moment, Jake does the same. His arm brushes mine as he lays down beside me, and a shiver runs down my spine.

"Tell me something no one else knows," he whispers. I stare intently at the night sky, trying to think of something to share.

"When I was little, I loved the Mary Martin version of *Peter Pan*. My mom was obsessed with all those classic Broadway shows; we had every one of them on VHS. I watched that tape so many times I became convinced that I could learn to fly like Wendy. I used to stand on the edge of my parents' bed and jump off, certain that if I just jumped high enough, if I just believed with all of my heart, that I could learn to fly too."

Just like that, I'm back in my parents' bedroom, bare feet curled on the edge of their bed. My face is scrunched up in concentration as I tell myself that this time, at last, I'm going to make it happen.

"A young Lexi Berman," Jake's voice cuts through my memory. "Even then, you were so driven."

I roll over to face him. "Your turn. Tell me something no one else knows."

Jake's brow lowers as he stares at the inky sky. He's quiet for a long moment before he finally speaks again. "I secretly loved those tap-dancing classes."

My burst of laughter cuts through the night air. Jake wraps his arm around me as I settle onto his chest. It feels so right to be back in his arms, and I find myself wishing that this moment could last forever, that it could always be just the two of us, far away from the rest of the world.

17

THE NEXT EVENING, JAKE insists on taking me out to see his home-town. I've only just finished slipping into a pair of lace-up san-dals when I hear a knock on the guest bedroom door. When I pull it open, he's leaning against the doorframe, dressed in a gray T-shirt and black jeans, his white cap twisted backward on his head. He stands frozen in the doorway for a moment, his eyes drinking me in. His expression of blatant tenderness sends a shiver down my spine. Then he clears his throat, adjusting the collar of his shirt.

"Wow," he says softly. "You look amazing."

I look down at my navy, off-the-shoulder prairie dress—something Ali pulled out from the back of my closet, insisting it complemented my hair, and that I favor because it doesn't require heels. My hair hangs in loose waves around my shoulders, and I've accessorized with a thin gold bangle that belonged to my mom.

"Thanks," I say, feeling shy. "You don't look so bad yourself." Which, of course, is the understatement of the century. He's so im-possibly handsome that it takes genuine effort not to stare at him.

"You ready?"

A SHORT JEEP RIDE LATER, we're standing inside Annie's, a small, dimly lit dive bar in Atlanta.

Glancing around, I take in the glossy black walls lined with red leather couches and matching ottomans. A handful of wooden tables and chairs are scattered across the floor and two oversized chandeliers hang from the ceiling.

"Oh, Lexi. This is going to be a night to remember," Jake says, drawing out each word carefully.

"Yeah? And why is that?"

Jake looks at me devilishly, barely able to contain his excitement. "Because tonight is the night you make your musical debut."

I follow his gaze over my shoulder and notice there's a makeshift stage and mounted television screen in the center of the room. And that's when it hits me: Jake Taylor has dragged me to a karaoke bar.

"Nope. Absolutely not." My face must be a mask of horror because Jake takes one look at me and laughs.

"Aw, come on, it's only fair! You get to hear me sing all the time, but I have yet to hear your Britney impression."

His brown eyes are dancing, and I realize with mounting dread there isn't a chance in the world that I'm about to turn him down.

"Fine," I huff after a minute. "But I'm definitely going to need a cocktail."

"One order of karaoke punch, coming right up!" A moment later he returns, carefully balancing two red plastic cups.

"Do I even want to know what's in karaoke punch?" I ask as I peer inside the rim. It's filled to the top with red juice, cherries, and a single lime for garnish.

Jake ticks the ingredients off on his fingers. "Hawaiian, punch, liquid courage." He clinks my cup in a toast, and I raise it to my lips. The drink is way too sweet and tastes nothing like alcohol, a sure sign that it's incredibly dangerous.

"So, what vibe are we going for tonight? 'Not a Girl, Not Yet a Woman'? Or are we going fully 'Toxic'?"

After adding our names to the sign-up, we slide into one of the leather couches facing the stage. My head is already fuzzy from the alcohol (*Seriously, what is in this?*) and I slide closer to Jake, my thigh brushing against his. He wraps a lazy arm around my shoulder, running his fingers through the bottom of my hair, and I lean into him, breathing in his clean, comforting scent.

From behind us I hear muffled voices, and I peer over my shoulder to see two women, their heads bent close together as they whisper excitedly. They're staring right at Jake and one of them is covertly trying to snap a picture on her phone.

I swivel my head back toward Jake. "I think you've been spotted," I whisper as I press against him. "Should we get out of here?"

Jake offers me a half smile and shakes his head. "No. This is still my city, and for once, I don't want to hide. Tonight I just want to be Jake. Let's have fun, okay?"

When our names are called, Jake grabs my hand, leading me up to the stage. We've only provided our first names, but as soon as we're standing up there beneath the lights, a faint murmur ripples through the crowd and several audience members begin hooting with appreciation. I look over at Jake to gauge his reaction, but he's busy flipping through a binder full of laminated song sheets, unbothered by the attention.

After settling on "Oops! . . . I Did It Again," Jake grabs me by the hand, a microphone clenched tightly in the other. The music cues and the lyrics pop up on the screen across from us. By the time the chorus begins, the liquid courage is pumping through my veins, and I grab the mic from his hand, gyrating as I do my best Britney choreography. From the corner of my eye, I see Jake doubling over, his arms wrapped around his stomach.

He's panting beneath the hot lights as we hit the last note together, his chest rising and falling as the crowd explodes with applause. He's never looked more beautiful to me than he does at this moment, and I can't tear my eyes away from him as I study the brightness of his eyes and the way his cheeks have grown pink with excitement. He may not love everything about fame, but the joy he derives from being onstage is undeniable. I wonder how much happier he'd be if he could do this every night, to just sing and entertain without all the pressures of being a celebrity.

I'm so lost in him that I fail to register the exploding flash of a camera in the crowd.

T HAT WAS QUITE A debut you made this evening," Jake observes as we stumble into the back of our waiting Uber. "It's a shame you forgot to pack your red pleather jumpsuit, though."

"Who said anything about it being my debut?" I retort, and Jake squeezes my hand while laughing softly.

"You hungry?"

"Starved. And I want McDonalds."

"McDonalds?" He snorts. "Aren't you a classically trained chef?"

"I contain multitudes, Jacob. And right now, my spirit demands a Quarter Pounder with Cheese."

Jake asks the driver if he'd be willing to take us to a drive-thru, and fifteen minutes later, I'm clutching a grease-soaked paper bag.

"Happy?" Jake asks after the driver drops us off in front of his house.

I beam up at him, popping a french fry into my mouth. "The happiest. You?"

He stares at me, his eyes serious as he takes my hand, lacing his fingers through mine.

"You have no idea how happy."

Just then, a clap of thunder rolls through the air. The trees in his front yard begin to shiver as a gust of wind whips through them. Seconds later, the sky opens, and a torrent of rain crashes down on us. I throw my head back as I stare up at the inky blankness. Rain washes over me, instantly soaking my hair and clothes.

"What in the hell is this?"

"A Georgia thunderstorm," Jake yells over another clap of thunder. "Come on, let's get inside."

He curls a warm, heavy arm around my shoulders, pulling me close to him as we sprint across the yard to the safety of his covered porch. Bringing a finger over his lips, he signals for me to be quiet as we step into the unlit foyer, tugging off our shoes and leaving them in the darkened doorway.

"Wait here," he whispers, disappearing into the blackness before returning a moment later with a towel in hand. He pulls it around my shoulders, running his hands up and down my arms to warm my shivering frame. My breath catches as his hands move over my body.

"Better?" His voice is husky as his eyes lock on mine, and I nod once, suddenly unable to speak. He draws a breath and steps back, clearing his throat as he drags a hand through his wet hair. "It's getting late. We'd better get to bed."

Wordlessly, I follow him upstairs, reluctantly lingering in the doorway when we reach the guest room.

"Goodnight, Lexi," he says softly. His eyes soften around the edges as he reaches forward to tuck a wet strand of hair behind my ear. I gasp at his touch, my lips parting instinctively. Jake's eyes grow heavy-lidded as he leans closer, and I can see him wrestling with something inside himself. When he speaks again, his voice is low.

"What we had last year. It was real, wasn't it? It was just one weekend, but fuck, Lexi. It was the best weekend of my life."

It feels as though all the oxygen has been sucked out of the room. The air between us grows thick and silent, save for the warning thump of my heart as it slams against my rib cage. I feel that familiar longing, my body pulling toward him as though guided by an invisible string. Jake strokes his thumb against my cheek, and I let out a soft whimper when his fingers graze my burning skin.

I want to tell him everything. That I ached for him when he

left. That I felt like a shell of myself when he was gone. And that I finally feel alive again now that he's back. But fear refuses to release its tight hold on my heart. Things that seem too good to be true usually are. Letting out a slow exhale, I take one step back.

"Goodnight, Jake," I whisper. Turning, I walk into the spare bedroom, shutting the door behind me.

Breathless, I slide down against the wood and sink to the floor. I wrap my arms around my knees, attempting to calm myself, but it's no use. My skin feels like it's on fire, a lustful, burning sense of need sneaking its way up my belly.

What am I doing? For the past month, I've tried to convince myself that Jake and I could just be friends, that I could ignore the attraction, the chemistry, the way my chest contracts every time he brushes against me. But I can't deny the way I feel about him anymore. Not to him, and most of all, not to myself.

I pull myself up and yank the door open, stepping back out into the hallway at the exact moment Jake opens the bedroom door across from me. His rain-soaked hair is slicked across his forehead, his shirt stretched tightly across his chest.

"Hey."

"Hey."

Our gazes lock, and I see Jake's jaw twitch. He takes a small step forward, and then I'm racing toward him, closing the space between us. Grabbing me by the waist, he lifts me effortlessly, and I wrap my legs around his body as his lips mold against mine.

He tastes like karaoke punch and greasy french fries, and I cannot get enough of him. My fingers twist in his hair as he pulls me closer, his hands sliding down my back. He walks us backward into his bedroom, stumbling blindly until we crash against his bookcase, its contents rattling precariously on the shelves. I try to shush him, but the sound gets swallowed by his mouth as he pushes me against the wall, our kisses growing deeper and more desperate.

His hands slide down to the hem of my dress, his fingers

knotting themselves around the fabric. Then he takes a small step back, his eyes never leaving mine as he lifts it slowly over my head and discards it on the floor behind him. His eyes glimmer in the darkness as they run over me.

"Lexi." His voice is deep, gravelly.

"Jake."

Calloused fingertips brush against my cheekbones as he leans forward to kiss me gently. Then he drags his mouth down to my jawline, my neck, my stomach, his tongue exploring every inch of exposed skin. Lowering himself to his knees, he gently tugs my underwear down to my ankles. His hands grasp the back of my thighs, and I gasp when he presses his mouth between my legs, my fingers knotting themselves in his hair.

"Jake, please," I pant, as I arch into him.

Taking my hand, he leads me over to his bed, sinking down into it and pulling me onto his lap.

"Nice twin bed," I whisper as I pull his shirt over his head and toss it to the floor. "Do you bring all the girls up here?"

A devilish glint forms in his eyes as he traces a finger down the base of my spine.

"I'm actually not allowed to have girls in my room, so I'd appreciate it if you didn't mention this to my mom."

I giggle as he pulls me toward him. His lips move across me, planting kisses on my lips, my nose, my cheeks, before moving down to the crook of my neck. He weaves one hand through my hair and uses the other to cup my breast, gently catching my nipple between two fingers. With a soft moan, I roll my hips against him, and he pulls back to grab his waistband and slide out of his bottoms.

My breath grows shaky as I move to lie back on his bed. Jake sits on the edge of the bed, lips parted as his eyes run over every inch of me.

"What is it?" I ask, reaching for his hand. He takes it, rolling his thumb in small circles against my palm.

"Nothing," he breathes. "I just want to look at you for a second."

It's intoxicating, the way he's staring at me with such pure desire, and I feel myself arching toward him, ready and needing. He bends to retrieve his wallet, extracting a condom before returning to cover his body with mine. When he slides into me, I gasp, my fingertips pressing into his bare shoulders.

"Oh god." His voice is ragged as he buries his face against my skin. "You have no idea how long I have wanted this. How long I have wanted you."

"Me too," I gasp, pulling him closer as he moves in and out of me. "Me too." We find our rhythm together, the need slowly building inside of me. He moans my name, his voice raspy as he pulls me down deeper, deeper into the waves, until they take me over completely, and I am gone.

Afterward, I rest my head on his chest, sighing as his fingers trace a lazy, featherlight trail back and forth around my arm. We lay there, listening to the steady patter against the roof and breathing the cool scent of rain that drifts through the window. Jake leans his head down to kiss the top of my head gently, and even in my state of bliss, a shiver runs through me. A few minutes later, his breathing grows heavier, and I know he's fallen asleep.

I lie awake for a few minutes, wondering what chain of events we have set into motion, what it will mean for the future, and what will come next. But eventually, I succumb to exhaustion and bliss and the steady rhythm of Jake's heartbeat against my cheek and slip into a deep and dreamless slumber.

WHEN I WAKE UP, the first rays of dawn are seeping in through the plantation shutters. Jake's facing me, eyelashes brushing the pillowcase, and I lay there, drinking in his sleeping form as I watch the flicker of movement behind his eyelids. There'd been so many nights over the past year when I'd wondered what it would be like to touch him again, to kiss him, to feel the weight of his body against mine. After a while, I wondered if I'd simply built him up in my memories, creating an impossible standard that no one, not even he, could ever live up to. But being with him last night was somehow even better than I imagined. Our bodies remembered each other instantly, uniting in perfect synchrony, as though no time had passed. And in a way, it was better than it had ever been. Because things are different now. The time we've spent together, eating and cooking, learning about each other's worlds. It's made everything between us deeper.

I lift my head up, rolling my neck before repositioning my head on the pillow a few inches over. Jake stirs beside me, one arm reaching out to encircle my waist and pull me closer.

"Where do you think you're going?" he murmurs sleepily against my hair. I lean into him, resting my cheek against his shoulder. It feels surreal, impossible, to be beside him again, but at the same time, nothing has ever felt so natural.

"We need to get up. Our flight leaves in ninety minutes."

He groans, throwing one arm over his eyes, his fingertips brushing lazily down my spine.

"Fine. But only because we need to get out of here before my mother finds out you spent the night in my room and grounds me." Jake leans in for a final, languid kiss before rolling out of his bed. Snatching his pants from the floor, he pulls his phone out of his pocket. The smile melts off his face as he stares at it, the line behind his brow deepening.

"What is it?" I ask, as I pull my dress over my head. "Did she already find out? Has she sent you a series of stern texts because she's too polite to barge in and scold us in our scandalous state of undress?" I turn to Jake, expecting a witty retort, but freeze when I see the tension in his expression. "Jake?"

"I thought one night out in my hometown would be no big deal, that even if people got some photos on their phones, it wouldn't be big news. I can't believe I was so naïve. I know better than that." He tosses the phone onto his desk and collapses back into the matching blue rolling chair, pressing the heels of his hands into his eyes.

"What are you talking about?" I rise from the bed and walk over to stand behind him, wrapping my arms around his shoulders.

"One of the girls who spotted us in the bar last night posted her photos to Twitter and they went viral. Lydia just texted me."

He shoves the phone toward me, and my eyes widen. The images are grainy, but clear enough: Jake and me at the bar, tossing back glasses full of karaoke punch. The two of us giggling on the stage, a microphone pressed to my lips. A darker photo of us sitting at a table, his arm slung casually over my shoulder. My heart aches for Jake; I know he was desperate for some sense of normalcy on his trip back home. Yet there's another emotion competing for my attention: the faintest flicker of happiness. These are the first photos I've ever seen of Jake and me together, and I can't help but savor them. Besides, there are hundreds of candid photos of Jake floating around the internet. What difference can a few more make?

He stands and walks over to the window. "I'm sorry," he says softly. "This is all my fault. I should have done a better job of protecting you." He crosses the room, putting his hands on either side of my face. My eyes flutter shut as he leans forward to brush his lips against mine. Then he folds his arms around me, holding me tightly. "I just can't lose you. Not again."

A wave of confusion washes over me. "Why would you lose me?"

Jake bites his bottom lip. "There's something more." He eyes me carefully.

More? What else could there be?

"I don't know how, exactly, but once the tweet started getting attention, the press was able to ID you. Apparently they received an anonymous tip, and it didn't take long for them to put two and two together and realize 'Blueberry' is about you."

Letting out a shaky breath, he takes my hands in his.

"Lexi Berman, the whole world is about to know your name."

18

OUR PLANE WAS SUPPOSED to touch down in New York at 9:15 A.M., but a series of last-minute delays put us two hours behind schedule. By the time I arrive at Olive & Pomegranate, it's nearly noon, and my clothes are damp with stress sweat.

The first thing I notice when I approach the restaurant is the small group of paparazzi lurking outside the front doors. They're talking among themselves, cameras dangling from their necks as they sip coffee from paper cups. One of them flicks the tip of his cigarette into a potted plant. Quickly, I slip in through the service entrance, miraculously managing to escape their notice.

"You're late." Oren's voice is terse when I step into the kitchen. I yank my fingers through my hair, twisting it back in a messy knot. Then I pull on my toque and send a silent prayer into the universe that no one has noticed the cameramen lurking outside the restaurant.

"I know."

"You can't do this, Lexi. You missed half your *mise* time."

"I know, I know. I promise, I'm going to catch up."

But my words are futile. Lunch service is already starting, and within minutes, I'm in the weeds, helpless to resist the pull of my own downward spiral. No matter what I do, I can't seem to catch up, and my head pounds against the pressure of a never-ending to-do list.

I try to reassure myself that I can prep during service if my station isn't hit too hard, but it's no use. Salad orders are at their heaviest during the lunch hour, and between trying to prep and plate, I'm drowning.

Mia does her best to bail me out, taking on as much of my workload as she can, but there's only so much she can do. It isn't long before Oren is forced to set up his own station beside us, his expression clouded with annoyance. He directs me to finish my *mise* while he takes over my salad orders.

Head spinning, I begin dicing vegetables as quickly as possible. This day is already a complete disaster, and I have no one to blame but myself. I never should have agreed to go to Georgia with Jake in the first place. What on earth was I thinking, taking that kind of gamble with time? I've never been late to anything in my life, and after one weekend with Jake, I'm showing up two hours late to work. I'm lucky Oren didn't fire me on the spot.

But there's more to my panic than just time management. So much has changed within the past twenty-four hours, and I'm still trying to sort through what is happening with Jake. On the one hand, it feels incredible to finally stop fighting my feelings for him. But on the other, I can't escape the mounting sense of anxiety about being outed by the press. I've spent the last three years avoiding the drama of romantic entanglements, and now, in a particularly cruel twist of irony, I've fallen headfirst into a relationship so conspicuous that a gang of paparazzi are lingering outside my workplace. How long will it be before someone here notices? What if the photographers try to come into the restaurant? Or worse, the kitchen?

I'm so caught up in my inner monologue that I barely notice the flash of pain shooting through my knuckles until a pool of crimson spreads across the cutting board. Within seconds, my diced onions are coated in warm, sticky blood.

"Ow!" It's a delayed reaction, though now that it's caught my attention, it hurts like hell. Oren snaps his head around, face paling as he takes in the mess I've made.

"Jesus, Berman. First aid, my office. *Now*." Muttering a series of curses under his breath, Oren grabs my bloodied cutting board, flinging its contents into the trash before tossing it into the sink.

Mortified, I wrap my hand in the bottom of my jacket and hurry into Oren's office. I find the first aid kit in his top desk drawer, half buried between a collection of notepads and phone chargers, and head to the bathroom. After rinsing my hand in the sink, I dab on some antibacterial ointment and wrap Band-Aids around my three injured fingers. I'm too shaken to head back into the kitchen—I can already feel the threatening sting behind my eyes—so I head to the walk-in fridge instead, slumping to the floor as hot tears spill out of me.

I bury my face in my palms as a million thoughts race across my brain. How could I have been so careless? I've worked so hard to get where I am now, and for what? To fuck it all up for some boy? And not just any boy, but a megastar, who will be leaving me imminently. Then what will I do? Abandon all my goals and give up my career to follow him around the globe? There isn't a chance in hell.

That's if I can even hold on to my job. It was disruptive enough the night Jake visited the kitchen. What's going to happen now that the world knows I'm the mystery woman behind the song that catapulted him to stardom?

I'm crouched there for an entire minute, shivering against the cold and doing my best to ignore the offensive fish smell wafting through the air, when I hear Mom's voice in the back of my head. *Get up, honey. You are strong. You are not a quitter.* I sniffle, her voice ringing in my ears so clearly, it's as if she's right next to me. She was so strong, always preaching the importance of tenacity like the living embodiment of a "Keep Calm and Carry On" poster. There's no way I'm going to let her down now, not after everything I've accomplished, just because things are tough.

Pulling myself up, I take a deep breath, hold it for five seconds, and release it slowly. Then, I leave the fridge and head to the bathroom to wash my face.

When I return to my workstation a few minutes later, wearing the clean chef whites I grabbed from Oren's office, Mia looks genuinely surprised to see me.

"You're still here?"

"Of course I'm still here. You think I would just abandon you in the middle of a shift?" I shoot her a wry smile. "I seem to remember someone telling me that working in a restaurant is all about teamwork."

Her shocked expression melts into bemusement. "Well. That person sounds like a bad-ass bitch."

B ERMAN?"
I'm getting ready to head out the service door around eleven when Oren's voice calls my name. I linger in the doorway of his office, too nervous to step all the way through. After my crying jag in the fridge, I managed to make it through the rest of my shift without incident, but I've been avoiding him as much as possible, paranoid that he's going to hand me a pink slip the moment he spots me.

"I need you to cover an extra shift on Thursday night. To make up for the day you missed yesterday." He holds up the clipboard with the call-sheet schedule, and relief floods through me as I realize that's all he's after.

"No problem, Oren. I'll see you tomorrow?" I'm about to turn toward the hallway when his voice calls me back.

"By the way"—he raises his eyebrows at me as he leans back in his chair—"there were a few men with cameras asking for you this afternoon. Trevor got rid of them. Told 'em we've never heard of any Alexa Berman." Oren attempts a reassuring smile, but it does little to improve the sinking feeling in my stomach. *Shit.* I'd really hoped the paparazzi had given up after failing to catch me coming in this morning, and that the team would never have been the wiser.

"Thank you, Oren. I'm so sorry again, really." I'm about to continue my groveling when a thought hits me.

"Wait, Trevor? Isn't Hannah on today?"

"Hannah doesn't work here anymore." He pauses, throwing me a meaningful look. "Who do you think tipped the paparazzi off in the first place?"

My mind flashes back to that day Jake visited the kitchen, the glazed look on the hostess's face as she stared up at Jake. *Of course.*

"Geez, Oren, I'm so sorry. I didn't mean—"

"It's fine," he says, waving me off. "It was a long time coming. Especially after the second time I caught her doing a line of coke in the walk-in with one of the busboys. You know how strict Chef has been with the new zero-tolerance policy."

"Oh, right." Come to think of it, I do remember thinking it was strange to see her in dry storage a few weeks ago when I'd gone downstairs to refill the salt bin.

"So." Oren's tone has softened. "Things are getting pretty serious with this kid, huh?" I open my mouth, intending to deny it, but there's no use. I can't deny it anymore, not even to myself. Resigned, I simply nod.

He tugs his beard. "Look, I'm hardly qualified to give anyone relationship advice. I mean, I'm divorced, for Christ's sake. But I've been in the restaurant game for seventeen years and I'll tell you what I do know. Being a chef and being in a relationship—the two just don't mix."

"Oren, I—"

"Just let me finish," he says, holding up a hand. "I know you want to rise through the ranks, become a sous chef, and one day, maybe even be an executive chef. And you have every right to dream that big. You're bright, hardworking, dedicated. You have what it takes.

"But I want you to be realistic about exactly what that path will entail. The hours aren't going to get any better. The commitment it takes to get to the top . . . it's inhumane. The sacrifices you're expected to make, the things you're expected to give up. You need to surrender every night, every weekend, and I can tell you from experience, there are very few partners, nevertheless celebrities with jam-packed schedules, who are going to be okay with that sort of lifestyle. It cost me my marriage, and I can guarantee you, it's going to cost you your relationship."

He takes a deep breath, giving me a long, meaningful stare.

"If you're not willing to give it everything you have, if you're not willing to sacrifice your personal life for your professional one, then I can tell you right now, it's not worth it. You need to ask yourself if this is really what you want."

Oren's words are still rolling around my brain when I push through the service doors and head outside toward the subway. Of course working in a restaurant is what I want. How could he even ask me that? It's a goal I've spent years of my life working toward, and I'm not going to just give it up now.

Then again, why shouldn't I get to have it all? Why should pursuing my career goals mean I can't also have a relationship? Just because Oren's marriage failed doesn't mean that things can't work out for me and Jake. After all this time, Jake and I have finally found our way back to each other, and I'm not about to let him slip through my fingers again. We're going to find a way to make it work. We have to.

I T'S A LITTLE AFTER 5 P.M. when I arrive back at my apartment after my Sunday shift, bleary-eyed and full-body exhausted, palms burning beneath the weight of the three overstuffed bags of Trader Joe's groceries I picked up on my way home. Balancing the paper bags between my knees, I start digging through my purse. I've just retrieved my keys when I hear a voice call out from behind me.

"Lexi!"

Without thinking, I turn around, shocked to discover I'm surrounded by half a dozen photographers. Flashes erupt all around, and I throw an arm across my forehead to shield my eyes. *What in the holy—*

"Lexi! How long have you and Jake been an item?"

"Lexi! How does it feel to have inspired a song? Have you ever been an artist's muse before?"

"Lexi! Are you getting a cut of Jake's profits?"

I stand there, frozen like a deer in headlights. I'm not sure how much time passes—three seconds? Three hours?—when a set of fingers presses into my arm and a familiar voice cuts through the noise.

"Get out of here, all of you, before I call the police and have them slap you with harassment charges!" Lionel's face is contorted with anger. My limbs are leaden as he picks up my bags and leads me into the lobby. The door slams shut behind us, drowning out the commotion on the street.

"Are you okay?" Lionel's eyes are wide with concern.

"Yeah, I think so." But my heart is thumping against my rib cage. And I can't help but wonder if I'll ever really be fine again.

B E STRAIGHT WITH ME. How bad will things be now that we've gone public?"

An hour later, I'm sitting in my living room across from Chloe and Ali, whom I summoned for an emergency meeting. After promising to take me on as a pro bono client to help me navigate all PR issues, Chloe has been firing off emails left and right. Ali's contribution thus far has been taking stealthful sips from the bottle of tequila she swiped from work and scrolling through TMZ "for purposes of research."

Chloe exchanges a look with Ali.

"I'm not going to lie to you, sweetie. It's not going to be great."

I raise my thumb to my mouth, tearing off the edge of the nail with my teeth.

"That's it? You don't have anything more profound to share?"

Chloe attempts to offer me a reassuring smile, but it doesn't quite reach her eyes.

"Look, a lot of people fantasize about dating a celebrity. But the reality is that non-famous partners get the short end of the stick. The press is going to say things about you; most of it will be untrue, and almost all of it will be hurtful. Not to mention the social media trolls. You're going to have to develop a thick skin. And you're definitely going to have to go private on Instagram. People can be the worst."

"Who's the worst?" I ask sullenly. "Oren's been pretty understanding."

"Girl, have you not checked Twitter lately?" Ali is sitting cross-legged on my couch, a bag of hazelnut Oreos balanced carefully on her lap.

"I don't have Twitter," I say. "Why?"

"The hashtag '#LexiLeggings' has been trending all week. It has come to the attention of the online world that you wear an exorbitant amount of black leggings."

"What's wrong with leggings? They're comfortable!"

"Nothing." Ali flicks a crumb from the corner of her mouth. "Except that they aren't real pants and every pair you own has a hole in the vaj."

A quick peek confirms she's right and I cross my legs. It's one thing to flip through "Who Wore It Best" articles about celebrities you don't know, and quite another to be the subject of it. Am I going to need a whole new wardrobe now that I'm with Jake? My stomach rolls as I contemplate how much work that will take and worse, how much it will cost. Even with a culinary degree, I'm only earning minimum wage at Olive & Pomegranate, and I still have student loans to pay back.

Chloe takes a deep breath before continuing.

"The best thing you can do is give them as little information as possible. Never speak to the press. Never post pictures of you and Jake on Instagram. And whatever you do, never, *ever* read the comments."

I gulp, trying my best to take it all in. I trust Chloe—this is her profession, after all, and her advice makes sense. She's right: I just need to be as boring as possible and hope the public will lose interest soon.

To this end, Jake moved back to his suite at The Pierre this morning, anticipating that the press would be dissuaded once they realized they wouldn't get any more shots of us coming or going. But the apartment feels empty without him, and suddenly way too big. Considering how long I've lived here on my own, I'm stunned by how lonely I feel. The silence is louder than the noise, somehow.

Chloe tilts her head sympathetically. "Listen, Jake seems like a good guy, and honestly, I'm thrilled to see you so happy. So do your best to ignore the noise and try to focus on what matters: you and Jake. You deserve this."

I can't help but smile, my earlier tension dissolving.

"You guys are the best." I rise to my feet and head to the kitchen to refill my wineglass. "Any chance you want to spend the night? I can make us some brownies." By "make us some brownies," I am of course referring to adding an egg and some oil to a boxed mix, the extent of my willingness to bake.

Chloe slips her MZ Wallace tote bag over her shoulder, her attention already returned to her phone.

Till There Was You 199

"Wish I could, babe, but I've got an early meeting tomorrow. We're doing an intervention for Chad to convince him to go to rehab."

"Oh. I didn't realize he's an addict."

"He's not. Unless you count an addiction to being an asshole."

"I've actually dated several men who suffered from that affliction," Ali quips from the sofa.

Chloe sighs, shaking her head as she types. "Anyway, the public loves a good recovery story, and sending him off with an apology and a plan to 'do better' is a great way to repair his image." She smirks. "Plus, there's no internet access at the Betty Ford Center."

I turn to Ali. "How about you? We haven't had a sleepover in ages. We can have a *Price Is Right* marathon, and I'll make us the Johannsson Special."

"I can't tonight." I notice that she looks uncharacteristically shy. I narrow my eyes, attempting to parse out what's going on.

"Oh? And why is that?"

She bites her bottom lip and looks up at me through her lashes. "Because I'm going on a third date."

"Ali! Now who's the one holding out? How long has this been going on?"

"Not that long, I promise! Like, two weeks, tops?"

"Why didn't you tell me?"

"I didn't mean to keep it from you. It's just, you've kind of been going through something here."

Crossing the room, I wrap my arms around my friend, pulling her in closely for a hug.

"Ali, I promise you, no matter what is going on in my life, I will never be too busy for you. Please don't feel like you need to keep me in the dark about anything, ever. Okay?"

She smiles back at me. "Okay."

Once my friends leave, I slide onto my sofa and wrap myself in my white throw blanket. A sense of unease washes over me as my eyes drift around the room, suddenly aware of every dark, empty corner. What if someone cons their way into the building and gets into my apartment? I'm all alone here and completely defenseless.

My phone screen illuminates; relief floods through me as I peek at the screen and see Jake's name. It's as if he sensed my mood.

Miss me yet?

I smile as I type out a response.

Yes. It's too quiet in here without the sound of you singing the Golden Girls theme song.

A few seconds later, three dots appear, indicating that Jake is typing his response.

Then it's a good thing I'm standing right outside your door.

I leap off the sofa and yank my door open. Jake is leaning against the frame, a smirk stretched across his face.

"Couldn't stay away, could you?" I ask.

Jake shrugs. "I had a sneaking suspicion you needed me."

I press my face into his shirt, breathing in his warm, clean smell.

"I did."

S O?" JAKE VENTURES AN hour later, when we're laying in my bed, wrapped in each other's arms. "How was work today?"

I roll over to tuck my head into the crook of his shoulder, resting my cheek against him as I consider his question.

"Same as always," I admit. I tilt my head back to look at him.

"Do you ever feel like being a musician isn't what you thought it would be?"

"Only every day," he laughs. He wraps his arm around my shoulders, planting a trail of kisses up my collarbone. "Why do you ask? Is being a chef different than you thought it would be?"

"So different. I mean, I knew that I wasn't going to graduate culinary school and become an executive chef right away. But I didn't expect the day-to-day stuff to be so uninspiring."

"I know exactly how you feel," Jake agrees. "I thought being a musician would mean spending all day in the studio, writing music, jamming with other artists. No one tells you how much of your day is consumed by press junkets and ad campaigns."

I nuzzle deeper into his chest. It's crazy how similar our career paths have been, considering we're in completely different fields. When we first met, we were on the precipice of making our dreams come true, and now, we're grappling with the realities of them. The shared experience is one of the reasons we understand each other better than anyone else.

"Maybe working in a restaurant isn't right for you," Jake muses. "There's no shame in quitting and trying something new, you know. There are lots of other ways to explore your love of cooking."

My shoulders tense at the suggestion. Jake sees no problem with taking a leap of faith or trying something new without any type of backup plan. But not me. There's no way I would just quit, not when I've spent years working toward a goal. I just need to stick it out a little while longer. No one likes a new job right away . . . right?

Rolling over, I prop my chin on my hands, staring up at him.

"There are a few other things I wouldn't mind exploring."

19

"SO, I'VE BEEN THINKING it's time you guys met Jake." I look point-edly at Ali before adding, "Properly."

Chloe freezes, another scooped-out bagel hovering halfway to her mouth. Ali's response is predictably less elegant; she spits out her iced coffee, spraying droplets across the table.

"Fuck. Yes," she breathes, bringing a fist to her mouth. "I swear I never thought this day would come."

"I was thinking about having a dinner party on Sunday night since I'm off after brunch service." I dab at the wet spot on the table with a napkin. "It's been ages since I cooked for you guys."

"Well, I'm in. You know I'll never say no to your cooking," Chloe says, finally taking a small bite.

"This is so exciting! What are you going to make?" Ali props her chin on her hand.

"I'm not sure yet." I've been running menus through my head since I first came up with this idea in the shower last night. Should I go the Mediterranean route, falafel and mezze platters? I could marinate some feta with sundried tomatoes and steal fresh pita from the restaurant. Or maybe Indian flavors? I just found a new recipe for sweet potato curry that I've been dying to try.

"What's your gut telling you?" Chloe tucks a lock of golden

hair behind her ear. She's just gotten a fresh manicure, a steely-blue color that looks perfect against her skin.

My gut? Jake's face pops up in front of my eyes, and for the first time, I know exactly what my gut is telling me.

"My gut," I reply, a slow smile spreading across my face, "is telling me that you two are in for some Southern hospitality."

SOMETHING SMELLS AMAZING." JAKE walks into the living room, running a towel through his still-damp hair. He looks sexy as hell in a navy knit with the sleeves rolled up and dark jeans. Once again, I marvel at how right it feels to see him against the backdrop of the apartment. Like he's not a visitor at all, but a part of the foundation. "What are you making?"

"'What am I *not* making?' is the better question." I glance at my handwritten menu. "Let's see. Grilled salmon with Cajun aioli. Tomato and mozzarella caprese salad. Smashed potatoes with truffle oil. Orange and fennel braised greens. And . . ."

Walking over to the fridge, I retrieve a glass pitcher.

"Can I offer you some sweet tea?"

Jake's eyes go wide. "You didn't."

I grin as I pour him a glass. "Apparently the secret is making simple syrup on the stovetop." I hand it to him and watch with anticipation as he takes a sip. "Well . . . what's the consensus?"

Jake drains the cup and then smacks his lips together. "Holy cow. Are you trying to make me fall in love with you?"

Instantly, my cheeks flood with heat. My mouth drops open, but I can't get a single word past my lips. My skin is still burning when the door opens a moment later, and Ali and Chloe step inside.

"Hello, hello!" Ali crows. She's dressed in a black halter top and wide-leg, mustard-colored pants, her dark curls spiraling around her head. When she sees Jake, she pales before dropping into a small curtsy.

"You probably don't remember me, but I'm Ali," she says.

"Pleasure to meet you. I'm Jake."

Ali's eyes flood with gratitude as she realizes he's too polite to bring up their fateful first meeting or her cringeworthy text.

Jake smiles warmly. "Is it okay if I give you a hug? Since we're destined to be best friends and all?"

Ali nods numbly, looking like she might pass out. When his arms encircle her, she presses forward to sniff his hair.

"You'll have to excuse her. She's not used to humans." Chloe grips Ali by the elbow and pulls her away. She sticks out a hand toward Jake. "I'm Chloe." He grins at her and shakes it.

I carry a charcuterie board toward the table. "Can I get anyone some wine?"

"Oh, that reminds me!" Ali reaches into her bag and withdraws a bottle of Sancerre. She holds it out in front of her, wiggling it back and forth. "Look what I stole from work!"

A few minutes later, we're gathered around the kitchen table, tucking into the overfilled wooden board. Jake fiddles with Ali's wine bottle for a minute before realizing it's not the twist-off kind I normally keep in the apartment.

"Hey, Lex, do you have a wine opener?" he asks.

"Yep." I pull it from the kitchen drawer and toss it to Jake, who catches it deftly in one hand.

"Wow, nicely done." Chloe looks uncharacteristically impressed.

"Thanks. I've gotten a lot of practice in the past year. For some reason, people love throwing stuff onstage while I'm performing."

"What kind of stuff?" Ali smears brie and fig jam across a cracker.

"Flowers, water bottles. The occasional cell phone. A few bras here and there." His eyes sparkle with amusement. "One time someone threw a vibrator at me. Hit me smack in the middle of my forehead."

"No way! Which model?" Ali's eyes are wide.

Chloe twists her body toward her, exasperated. *"That's* your first question?"

Ali shrugs, popping a candied pecan in her mouth.

"And on that note." I raise the lid of my Dutch oven with a flourish, releasing an orange-scented steam. "Dinner is served."

UGH, I CAN'T EAT another bite. I literally do not have enough skin," Ali moans as she leans back in her chair, clutching her stomach. I glance around the table at the people I care about most, and soak up the endorphins. Seeing the pleasure in their faces after filling their bellies with something I made is by far the best part about cooking. It's what keeps me going, even when I'm exhausted and frustrated by the most challenging aspects.

"The talent in this one. Best meal of my life. You really outdid yourself, Lex." Jake's eyes are alight with pride as he slings an arm over my shoulder, fingers drifting through the ends of my hair. "Now, if you ladies will excuse me, I'm going to take out the trash, and then I'll get started on the dishes."

"Jake Taylor takes out the trash?" Ali whispers to Chloe.

Jake breaks into an easy laugh as he stands. "Happily. Have to earn my keep. I'm just grateful Lexi's tolerated me crashing with her for so long. I know being with me isn't always easy to deal with." He heads into the kitchen, pulling out the trash bag and knotting it.

"When you come back, we'll have dessert. I made a peach pie," I tell him.

Jake claps a hand over his heart before slinging the bag over his shoulder and heading out the front door.

Chloe turns to me, eyebrows raised. "You baked? You hate baking."

Ali flicks out her wrist as if to say, *Isn't it obvious?* "Duh, Chlo. She baked because she *loves* him." She lets out a dreamy sigh. "And clearly, it's mutual. I feel like I just had dinner in a Nicholas Sparks novel."

"He's breathed life back into you, Lex," Chloe agrees. "But I think you've saved him, too."

"What do you mean?" I ask.

"Nice guys like Jake, who are thrown into this industry where they're surrounded by piranhas, tend to get eaten alive. But you're a life raft, holding his head above water. You keep him from drowning."

I'm not quite sure what to say to that, so I stand up and begin collecting the plates.

"Can I get you guys anything? Tea? Coffee?"

"Just dessert for me." Ali smirks. "Cut me a big slice of that infatuation pie."

TONIGHT WAS INCREDIBLE. YOU are incredible." Jake's hands slip around my waist, pulling me against him after I place the last dish he dried back into the cabinet. I drape my arms around his neck.

"Thank you so much for doing this. It meant so much to be able to introduce you to Ali and Chloe."

"They were great. And of course I wanted to meet them. They're a part of who you are. And I want to know every part of you." He smiles, running his eyes over me. "Look at you. You're glowing."

"I'm just so happy. Making food for the people I love . . . it's just such a rush. I really should do it more often."

"Love, huh?" Jake's eyes are fiery as they bore into mine.

I open my mouth, and then close it again. Jake laughs as he pulls me toward him.

"Don't worry, I'm not going to make you say it. But you should know that just because I'm not saying it either, it doesn't mean I don't feel it."

We stand there for a moment, the air between us charged.

I break the silence first. "How about an episode of *Golden Girls* before bed?"

"Yes." He flashes that devastating, dimpled smile. "That sounds perfect."

T HE FOLLOWING WEEK, I call my dad after lunch service. I've been so busy that I hadn't returned his last two calls, and the guilt was starting to eat away at me. He picks up on the first ring.

"Lexi Loo!" he crows, his voice brimming with an extra decimal of excitement that immediately sends my guard up. My mind races with the possibilities as I wait for him to explain the source of it. Maybe he and Fran are expecting a baby of their own somehow? Or perhaps they're planning to move even farther away, maybe to live with Fran's parents in San Diego. But instead he simply says, "What's new with my baby girl?"

For a moment, I'm not sure how best to answer the question. What's new with me? Well, let's see. I'm now dating a celebrity who wrote a wildly popular song about me, and if the amount of time I spent listening to him murmur in his sleep this morning is any indication, I'm falling head over heels for him at a speed that's quite frankly alarming.

"Not much," I say in response. My dad lets out a low hum, and even over the phone, I can sense his disappointment.

"You know, I'm always here for you, Lex. You can talk to your old man." His words tug something loose inside me, and I'm suddenly itching to confess everything that's happened over the past few months. To gush about my too-big feelings for this boy who's torpedoed my quiet, tidy life, to ask for advice about the paparazzi who are only now starting to dissipate after stalking my building all week. Tears spring to my eyes as the part of me that longs to be his little girl again threatens to escape from where I normally keep it under lock and key. But nostalgia is quickly replaced by indignation as I remind myself that I wouldn't have to fill him in on anything if he hadn't abandoned me in the first place. My heart hardens again.

I can sense his anticipation on the other end of the line and wonder fleetingly if he knows about me and Jake. I'm hardly big news outside of social media gossip, and my dad, like most boomers, only has Facebook, which he seems to use exclusively for sharing memes with friends he hasn't seen since high school. I decide that if he brings up Jake, I won't deny it, but I can't bring myself to tell him outright. My relationship with Jake is precious, and my dad feels undeserving of that information after what he's put me through, though some part of me aches to tell him all the same. But as the silence drags on and he says nothing, I realize he's not going to ask.

"I know," I say finally. "Just another long week at work."

We make small talk for a few more minutes before hanging up, our mutual disappointment with the conversation palpable. I do my best to swallow it as I slip my phone back inside my bag, because the last thing I need is to show any sign of weakness in front of my coworkers. Rising from the pavement outside the service doors, I release a breath, square my shoulders, and head back into the kitchen.

JAKE'S SCHEDULED TO APPEAR on *The Tonight Show* the following week, and since his spot falls on a Monday, I'm able to attend. Though the show doesn't air until 11:30 P.M., filming starts at five, and when I arrive at the studio at four-thirty, the sidewalk outside Rockefeller Plaza is already a mob scene.

Despite Chloe's warnings, I am in no way prepared for the massive throng of fans who turned out to see Jake. There must be close to a hundred of them, mostly teenage girls, camped out on the sidewalk and toting handwritten signs. Though a few shoot me curious looks, like they recognize me but aren't sure from where, I manage to slip through the doors incognito and head back to Jake's dressing room.

I gasp when I step through the doorway. The dressing room is tiny, but stunningly decorated, and oozing old-world glamour. The cobalt-blue walls are decorated with eclectic gold frames, and there's a collection of vintage vinyl sitting beside a record player on the cherrywood desk. Lydia and Vinny are entrenched in the deep blue velvet couches, both predictably glued to their phones. And seated at the makeup table, haloed by the light of the dozen bulbs surrounding the mirror, is Jake.

"Hey, you," he says, grinning at me when our eyes meet in the mirror. Heat spikes through me, and once again, I wonder how I was able to resist that smile for as long as I did. The makeup artist steps aside and I squeeze through the narrow space to plant a quick kiss on Jake's cheek. I'm just backing away so the makeup artist can resume when I hear the buzzing of his phone on the table in front of him. We both glance down at the same time to see a name pop up on the screen: Madison St. James.

"Why is Madison texting you?" I ask, cringing at the unintended whine in my voice. Behind me, I feel Vinny stiffen. That got his attention.

"Just wishing me luck today. She did Fallon last week," he says. He shoots me a quick smile that doesn't quite reach his eyes, and the conversation ends abruptly as the makeup artist swoops back in place to finish the job. She's just swept another dusting of powder across Jake's face when an assistant pokes his head in the door and tells Jake it's time to head backstage.

Neither Lydia nor Vinny bother to acknowledge me after Jake leaves, so I sit down on the hard-backed makeup chair instead of joining them on the sofa. There's a monitor on the wall across from us, and I do my best to get comfortable as I settle in to watch the show.

After his opening monologue, Fallon calls out Jake's name, asking fans to welcome him to the stage. The cheers grow to a volume I haven't heard since my parents took me to a One Direction concert. Jake emerges from backstage, dressed in a black Gucci suit over a pale blue dress shirt. He looks good. Really good. He flashes a shy, crooked smile as he waves to the audience and shakes Jimmy's hand.

He also looks more nervous than usual, hands trembling ever so slightly as he unbuttons his suit jacket. Finally, he settles into a seat. For a person who's effervescent onstage, he seems so much less comfortable in this setting.

But when Fallon asks about his recent trip back home, Jake seems to relax. I can see the happy memories flash across his face as he explains the intricacies of deep frying a turkey.

"Tell me something. How do you avoid getting splashed with all that hot oil?" Fallon asks.

"Very carefully." Jake smirks. Jimmy throws his head back with laughter. But then he straightens and taps his cue cards on the desk. One look at his expression, and I know what's coming next.

"Speaking of food," he says. "Rumor has it that your first single, 'Blueberry,' was inspired by a real-life relationship with a chef."

Jake's smile dissolves. He clears his throat and stares at his shoes. "I mean . . . you know . . ." His voice trails off, and red splotches rise around his collar.

"Well, don't leave us hanging!" Jimmy leans closer and tucks his fists under his chin. "Are you two still an item? Are you off the market? Inquiring minds want to know."

Jake's brow glistens with sweat. His right knee bounces up and down. Panic bubbles in my veins. *Shit.* This is it. He's going to tell the world about me, right here on national television. My life as a private citizen is officially over.

Jake looks up at Jimmy. His lips part as if he's about to say something. And then, he grabs a coffee mug from the desk and buries his face inside it. He tilts his head back in an exaggerated gulp. The audience goes wild with laughter. Jimmy just shakes his head. He's not going to get anything from Jake, and he knows it.

"All right, all right," he says. "I can take a hint. Let's talk about your latest album, which hits shelves a week from tomorrow . . ."

That's it? I'm frozen in my chair. *He's not even going to acknowledge me?*

A million conflicting thoughts race through my mind. On the one hand, I'm grateful Jake's protecting my privacy. The little bit of attention I've already gotten is overwhelming enough, and the last thing I need is for him to add fuel to the fire. On the other hand, I hate that he's hiding our relationship. I've never felt about anyone the way I feel about him, and the secrecy makes me feel more like a mistress than a girlfriend.

And if I'm *really* being honest, I wanted to hear him gush, to see his eyes light up when he said my name. I wanted to know that he feels the same way about me, that I'm more than just some girl he wrote a song about.

I stand up abruptly, causing the wooden chair legs to scrape loudly against the floor.

"I'm, um . . . going to get some air," I hear myself say. Lydia makes a humming sound in acknowledgment, and I don't bother looking back at either of them before shoving through the dressing room doors and escaping the building as quickly as possible.

Numbly, I make my way back to my apartment, barely aware of the city around me, and ignoring the continuous buzzing of my cell phone. I'm still sulking when Jake gets home an hour later, face glistening with remnants of his stage makeup.

"There you are. I've been calling and calling you. Vinny said you left in the middle of taping, and I was worried you were sick or something." His voice is tight, and I can feel the tension radiating off his body. I shrug, not bothering to look away from the TV. I *do* feel sick to my stomach, but not in the way that Jake means.

"I'm fine. I just wanted to give you some space. I figured you wouldn't want to be seen coming out of NBC with me anyway."

Jake walks over to stand in front of me. He grabs the remote out of my hand and switches off the TV. His eyes narrow.

"So, you just left?"

My throat feels like it's filled with gravel. I'm not sure if I'm angry or just hurt, but either way, I'm too distraught to put my feelings into words. So instead of answering, I draw my knees to my chest and wrap my arms around them. Jake sits down beside me. He slips a finger under my chin and lifts it up until my eyes meet his.

"Lexi, what's going on?"

"Why didn't you say anything when Fallon asked if you were dating anyone? Are you embarrassed of me?"

"Of course not. It's nothing like that. It's just—" He lets out a long, labored sigh. "I'm trying to protect you."

My jaw clenches as a flicker of anger ignites in my chest. "That's how you protect me? By lying?"

"I didn't lie! I just didn't go on one of the most popular talk shows on television and tell the entire world about my private relationship."

"Lying by omission is still a lie, Jake. Why are you hiding me like I'm a bottle of Smirnoff on a band-camp bus?" I let out a bitter scoff. "Besides, it's not like people don't already know about us. It's all over the tabloids."

Jake shakes his head. "I'm not *hiding* you. I'm just trying to keep you safe. And I thought keeping you out of the spotlight was the best way to do that. I don't want the attention I get to cause you any more problems, like it did when I showed up at your work."

"I don't need you to protect me, Jake! I've been taking care of myself for a long time. I think I could survive a few paparazzi photos."

The truth is, I do understand where Jake is coming from. But my rational side can't seem to surmount the overwhelming waves of anger in order to talk through it. It isn't strong enough to topple the walls that are instinctively rising around my heart.

"Lexi, look at me."

Reluctantly, I drag my eyes away from the TV and meet Jake's gaze. His chocolate eyes are wide, his mouth set in a hard line.

"I get that you're upset, and rightfully so, but this is never going to work if you shut me out. You've gotta talk to me. I'm not going anywhere, not this time."

My jaw tightens at the reminder of our past. But at the same time, I feel the anger start to dissipate. Scary as it is, there's something comforting about being so seen, about having all your emotional armor stripped away.

"I understand why you did it," I say quietly. "And you're right; I don't want my life to be completely disrupted. Having the paparazzi linger outside the restaurant is bad enough. But I also don't want to feel like I'm someone's dirty little secret."

"I know," Jake sighs. "Lex, I'll never stop trying to take care of you. But we are partners, and what you want matters too. I'm not trying to hide you. I'm proud to be with you. So, if going public is what you want, then . . . okay."

"Really?"

"Really." He runs a hand through his hair. "I'm actually heading to LA for a few days next week. My team scheduled a couple of press junkets, plus I was invited to a film premiere." His eyes crinkle with amusement. "You know that new Pixar one, where the pets open a babysitting agency?"

"Sounds like fun." I sigh. "I've always wanted to go to LA."

Jake's expression turns hopeful. "So why don't you come with me?"

"You want me to go to a movie premiere with you? Like, as your date? In public?"

He nods. "Yeah. I still don't want to talk to the press about us, but an appearance together will confirm our relationship. And having you by my side would be a dream. Maybe I've been more concerned about this than I need to be." He tilts his head. "Think you could get off of work?"

A nagging sensation tugs at the back of my mind as I consider my limited amount of leave time, but I brush it away.

"Probably. I haven't taken any time off, other than that visit to Marietta. I guess it would be okay."

Jake grins. "This is going to be amazing. I can't wait to get you poolside in a bikini, a whiskey sour with two cherries in each hand." He buries his face into my neck, and I giggle as I wonder what on earth I'm going to tell Oren.

20

THIS IS GOING TO change everything. But there's no one I'd rather be here with."

The look Jake's giving me, a mix of adoration and protectiveness, makes my body feel like an overcooked noodle. That, plus the devastating sight of him in a slim-cut Tom Ford suit. His hair is pushed off his face with product, and his dimple looks deeper than ever.

Oren begrudgingly agreed when I requested the weekend off, but I'll be working every day next week to make up for it. Jake and I took a flight out on Friday afternoon and touched down in LAX at seven that evening.

Now we're sitting in a limo outside El Capitan Theatre, waiting for our turn to walk the red carpet. I wipe my increasingly clammy hands against the pleated skirt of the silk dress that Chloe lent me. With a pair of red strappy sandals from Nordstrom Rack and a blowout from Drybar, I barely recognized myself in the hotel room mirror. Who even am I without a sweaty top knot and pit-stained chef's jacket?

Jake's smile fades a decimal as he squeezes my hand. "The press will be out in full force tonight. This makes things between us official."

"Were they not already?"

"I just want you to be prepared. Especially for all the attention. Things are gonna be different after tonight."

"Are you suggesting it's too late to go home and call the whole thing off?"

He laughs as he leans forward to kiss me. "It's definitely too late." When he pulls back, his eyes are serious again. "And we're not calling anything off. Afraid you're stuck with me."

His expression is intense when he reaches up to cup my face.

"Seriously, thank you for coming tonight. You don't know what it means to me." He peeks out the window. The noise outside is already deafening. "Ready?"

I nod, but in truth, nothing could have prepared me for the onslaught of flashing cameras. I'm blinded the minute we step out of the car. Between the bright lights and the paparazzi screams, I can hardly remember where I am, let alone what I'm supposed to be doing. That is, until Jake's fingers slip through mine, pulling me forward.

"Jake! Look here! Jake, this way!"

It's then that I notice Jake isn't looking at the camera. He's turned backward, beaming at me, as though the hundreds of people surrounding us have disappeared, and I'm the only one he can see.

Jake guides me over to the movie's oversized poster. We pose in front of a cartoon dog sporting a vomit-splattered T-shirt and a diaper bag. Nerves running high, I straighten my back, doing my best to project confidence. Which is no easy task since I'm also trying to ignore the uncomfortable pinching around my toes.

"Jake, who are you with tonight?"

His face lights up as he stares at me. My stomach flip-flops as he smiles and finally says the long-awaited words.

"My girlfriend."

WHEN THE MOVIE ENDS, we head upstairs to the after party. Pushing through the crowd, I make my way through the throng of tall and glamorous superhumans. They might be looking for celebrities to schmooze with, but I'm on the hunt for something more important: a bathroom.

I'm washing my hands when a toilet flushes behind me. A gazelle-like brunette with exquisite cheekbones steps out of a stall, adjusting a gold sequined dress that barely reaches the tops of her thighs. When she starts washing her hands at the sink beside me, her eyes meet mine in the mirror and widen.

"Oh, you're *her*, aren't you? The 'Blueberry' girl."

Yup, that's me.

I nod, extending a hand. "I'm Lexi."

She looks vaguely familiar, but I can't quite place her. I study her flawless skin, wondering how she managed to erase her pores entirely.

"Olivia," she says as she shakes my hand. "I'm Liam Thompson's fiancée."

Of course, that's why I recognize her. Liam Thompson, the British boy bander turned actor, voiced the film's English bulldog character. She and Liam have been a fixture in the tabloids for years.

"How are you holding up? You must be feeling pretty overwhelmed." Her crisp London accent elicits a fresh wave of self-consciousness.

"Definitely overwhelmed. Short, too." Even in three-inch heels, I'm a full head shorter than her. And pretty much every other beautiful gentile here.

She laughs softly. "I remember the first time I went to a big event with Liam. I was taking photos of all the celebrities I saw and texting them to my friends." Her eyes soften at the memory before lasering in on me. "So, you're, like, a cook, right?"

I bristle a bit at the way she says the word "cook," like it's so pedestrian. Like I'm a member of the waitstaff.

"Uh, yeah. I work at a restaurant in New York."

Olivia pulls out a tube of lip gloss and begins carefully applying it in the mirror.

"Well, at least you won't have to do that much longer," she says with a wink.

Her words catch me so off guard that I just stand there, unable to formulate a response. *What the hell is that supposed to mean?* I guess I'm quiet for too long because she turns away from the mirror, her face apologetic.

"Oh, god. I'm sorry. I hope I didn't offend you! It's just that it's impossible to have a job like that when you're dating a celebrity. The only way to make it work is to travel with them. Especially when they go on tour. You can't really make that happen while holding down a nine-to-five, you know?"

My chest tightens as I fully absorb the impact of her words. I'd resigned myself to the idea of Jake traveling for events, but I had forgotten about touring. A few weeks here and there is one thing, but how will our relationship survive if we need to spend months at a time apart? I know firsthand how easily distance destroys a relationship. The way it erodes everything you once shared little by little, until you can hardly remember the way things once were. My relationship with my dad is a prime example.

"Ohmigod, your face! Here, have a Xanax," Olivia offers, flipping open a monogrammed pillbox and extending it toward me. When I shake my head to decline, she shrugs, popping a tiny white tablet into her mouth and swallowing it dry before dropping the case back into her purse.

"Anyway, I know how you feel," Olivia continues. "I was in my second year of law school when I met Liam. My parents were horrified when I dropped out to go on tour with him and the band. But, like, what was I going to do, let him spend nine months getting road head from a bunch of prepubescent groupies?"

My head spins as I try to process it all. "So, you just gave up your dream of becoming a lawyer? Don't you miss working?"

"Oh, trust me, honey, I work." Reaching into her bag again, she retrieves her cell phone and clicks open her Instagram page. My eyes widen as she scrolls through the images, all of which feature her rail-thin frame in various designer outfits. What's even more shocking is that she has 1.7 million followers.

"Being a brand ambassador isn't easy," she sighs. "But you can't beat the perks. I have to rent an extra storage unit to hold all the free clothes." She looks up at me, her eyes flashing with inspiration. "You should totally become a food influencer! You could be, like, a pre-scandal Chrissy Teigen! Jake's fans would eat it up." She tilts her head to the side thoughtfully. "Just remember: whatever you do, never, ever read the comments."

B Y THE TIME I leave the bathroom, I'm a mess. My hands are slick with sweat and my chest is tight. It takes me a few minutes to find Jake in the crowd. The air is dense with body heat, the deafening bass music pulsating through the speakers. I finally spot him in the back of the room, leaning against a metal beam and holding court with a group of women I don't recognize. Probably publicists or models or television stars. Who even knows? The one thing I do know is that none of them have been elbow deep in an industrial sink in the past thirty-six hours.

His face lights up when he sees me, then falls as he takes in my expression.

"What's wrong?" His voice is thick with concern. "Are you okay?"

The women he was talking to sulk off, whispering among themselves. One of them shoots me a look over her shoulder but I ignore her.

Well, I want to say. *I was just accosted in the bathroom by a stunningly beautiful Brit who basically told me it was pointless to pursue my career now that we're in a relationship.* But we're in public and there's no way I'm going to ruin our night by dumping my personal neuroses on him right now. Besides, the last thing I need is to give the roaming eyes in this room fresh gossip for their blogs.

"Everything's great," I say, taking a sip from the glass of champagne in his hand. "We can talk about it later. This is a party. Let's just have fun." I look up at Jake, forcing my lips into a smile, but his own mouth remains twisted downward.

"I can't have fun if I know you're upset," he says softly. "Please, just tell me what's going on."

I take a deep, steadying breath.

"Do you think I'm going to quit my job now that we're together?"

The wrinkle in Jake's forehead deepens.

"What? Where did you get that idea?"

I recount my bathroom conversation with Olivia. Jake's brow lowers as he listens. When I finish, he takes both of my hands in his, pressing his forehead against mine.

"Lexi, I would never, ever want you to quit being a chef. This is your dream. And I'm always going to support you, just like you support me."

Sulkily, I look down to avoid meeting his eyes.

"Yeah, but it's not like you're going to be staying in New York full-time. What happens when you need to travel? Or go on tour? Practically speaking, how is this going to work?"

Jake shifts from one foot to another, stalling for time, and with each passing moment, it's becoming increasingly clear that there is no good answer to my question.

"Look, we don't need to have it all figured out right now. But we'll make it work, okay? I'll be in New York as much as I can, and you can come to a show or two when your schedule allows. I won't give up on us. We'll find a way." His eyes dart to the dance floor before he turns back toward me, extending a hand. "In the meantime, would you do me the honor?"

With a resigned huff, I turn on my heel and begin weaving my way through the crowd toward the dance floor. A moment later, Jake's hand slips through mine, pulling me back toward him. He spins me around so that I'm facing him.

"Hey." His eyes search mine as he takes both of my hands in his. "Are we okay?"

I swallow and nod. "Yeah, I guess. Everything is just so uncertain, and I hate the way it makes me feel."

Jake nods glumly. "I know." He lifts my arms and loops them around his neck. Pressing a hand into the small of my back, he pulls me closer until our bodies are flushed together. "Come here."

The floor beneath us vibrates with bass music as his hands slide down to my lower back, the heat of his palms permeating the thin fabric of my dress. My breath hitches when he slides one hand beneath the hem, his fingertips brushing against my thigh.

"Let's get out of here." His breath is warm against my ear, and I can feel the baby hairs rise on my arms.

"Now?"

He pulls me closer to him, and I feel his hardness prod my belly. I close my eyes and breathe him in. The intoxicating mix of his clean scent is intermingled with sweat and hunger. The hand on my thigh continues to migrate north, and I intake a sharp breath when his fingertips brush against the damp fabric of my underwear.

"Yes, now," he murmurs against my earlobe.

"Yeah, okay. Call the car."

21

"YOU LOOKED STUNNING," CHLOE says when she calls me the following morning, just as I'm walking through the service doors at Olive & Pomegranate. I woke up this morning to a series of links she'd forwarded via text. *Elite Daily. Us Weekly. Page Six.* Every major media outlet covered the premiere.

"I mean, the way he's holding your hand, smiling back at you on the red carpet. Honestly, it's to die for. And the way you handled yourself was flawless."

"Yeah, you can hardly tell that I couldn't see a foot in front of me."

I suppress a yawn. We hopped on a red-eye after the party and didn't get back to the city until almost 5 A.M. I was too wound up to sleep once we made it back to the apartment, the excitement of the evening compounded by the fact that I'd made the regrettable decision to check my phone after plugging it into my portable charger on the cab ride home. The moment it sprung back to life, it began vibrating incessantly, alerting me that I had over a hundred new text messages. Everyone I've ever had in my phone—and some I hadn't—had reached out. Friends from camp, middle school classmates, my Bat Mitzvah tutor. People I hadn't heard from in years. All of whom suddenly seemed to have a renewed interest in me. Jake's words replayed in my head: *Things are going to change after tonight.*

The moment I step through the service doors, Oren calls my name. I poke my head into his office, and he gestures for me to step inside.

"Hope you're not planning to take any more time off, because our reservation list is completely booked up for the next three weeks."

"Oh, that's great." I pause. "That's great, right?"

He crosses his arms, leaning back in his chair. "Maybe. Guess it depends on how many of them show up. Quite a few of the Open-Table reservations include requests to be seated next to Jake Taylor." He raises an eyebrow. "Publicity is one thing, but teenage silliness is another. End of the day, we still have a business to run. You get what I'm saying?"

I nod, as I try to figure out what to say next.

"What are you going to do, Berman?" he asks after a minute, and I know he isn't just asking about the reservations.

Biting the inside of my cheek, I straighten my white coat. "I'm going to get started on my *mise.*"

M IA IS ALREADY SETTING up at our station when I arrive in the kitchen. She doesn't bother to look up as she violently slashes her way through a cucumber. Her shoulders are so tense they're practically touching her ears.

"Are you okay?" I ask tentatively as I begin to sharpen my own knives beside her.

"No," she mutters as she scoops the slices into a metal bowl. "Did you hear about Stefan?"

I shake my head and she huffs a sigh before continuing.

"He just gave notice. Got a job as an assistant sous chef at some place in the Village." She starts slicing faster, and a piece of cucumber flies off the cutting board, landing on the floor a few feet behind us. It's not clear if she doesn't notice or simply doesn't care.

"I told Oren that I want his job and the son of a bitch said it's not gonna happen. Apparently, I'm 'too green,' and I'm 'not ready.' The usual bullshit."

She drops her knife against her cutting board and turns to face me. Her eyes narrow as she crosses her arms across her chest.

"I've been working on garde-manger for two years now. I'm more than ready to move up to vegetables. The only reason he's refusing to give me the job is because I'm a woman. Among other things."

Guilt floods through me as I mentally fill in what she's not saying. That the other reason she can't leave the station is that I'm not ready to run it unsupervised. That maybe, if I spent more time in the kitchen and less at movie premieres, I would be better at my job, and she wouldn't have to pick up my slack.

When I fail to say anything, she rolls her eyes and starts slicing again.

"I'm so sorry, Mia," I finally say. "I know you must be frustrated. But you're going to get there soon. It's only fair."

Mia barks out a humorless laugh and shakes her head.

"You really don't get it, princess. Working in a restaurant isn't like whatever fancy private school you went to. You don't get a gold star just for showing up. Things aren't always fair."

She whirls around again, this time gesturing in Corbin's direction with her knife.

"See that dickhead over there? When I first started working here, I had your job and he was in my role. And every day for months, he found some way to put his hands on me. A slap on my ass every time I walked by, a grope in the basement storage room. Every. Day. Until one day, I finally had enough and stabbed him in the leg with a fork."

The corner of her mouth twitches into a proud smirk at the memory. Then, just as quickly, her frown returns.

"And guess what? Six months later, he moved up to vegetables. *Six months.* So, trust me when I say that nothing about this industry is fair when you're a woman. Especially a queer woman."

A ball of lead forms in the pit of my stomach. I've never really warmed to Corbin, but the thought of him putting his hands on Mia like that makes me want to hurl. Unfortunately, her story isn't surprising. I've heard plenty of rumors about sexual harassment in restaurant kitchens. Still, hearing horror stories about strangers is one thing. Seeing one play out in front of you is something else altogether. I take a breath, trying to arrange my thoughts into some semblance of order.

"Why didn't you report Corbin? Oren would have fired him."

Mia looks at me again. But this time, it's not anger in her eyes. It's pity.

"Oh, Lexi," she says. "What makes you think I didn't?"

J AKE'S ALBUM RELEASE CONCERT is the following Thursday at Radio City Music Hall. Thankfully it fell on my one night off, ahead of the three extra shifts I'm taking to make up for the LA trip. I don't even want to think about how exhausting it will be to work for ten days straight, but the past few days have been so busy that I've barely had time to worry about it.

When Jake and I arrive outside the theater, I'm as jubilant as a little kid taking their first trip to Disney. I probably look like a tourist, but I can't resist pulling out my phone to snap a photo of the iconic red and blue lettering.

As I'm aiming the camera for a second shot, Jake jumps in frame, throwing his arms out to the side and grinning maniacally.

"You almost forgot the most important part. The talent."

I roll my eyes but oblige him by snapping another few photos.

"I'm just grateful you've managed to stay so humble, despite your celebrity status."

"Send me that one," he says, pointing to the screen. "I want to get a framed copy for Jeffrey Taylor's desk."

When we step into the empty theater, Jake's backing band is already tuning their instruments onstage. The last time I was here was in the fourth grade, when my parents took me to see the *Radio City Christmas Spectacular.* For two weeks afterward, I practiced my high kicks so relentlessly that I nearly pulled a hamstring.

The space is as breathtaking as I remember. The orange arc above the stage looks like a sunset, and the rows of dark, empty seats make the theater look cavernous. Grabbing my hand, Jake leads me up the staircase to introduce me to everyone.

Unlike Jake with his clean-cut, Southern boy-next-door look, the rest of the band look like rock stars. The keyboardist, Tessa, is sporting a choppy mullet, with half a dozen earrings crawling up one earlobe. She's dressed in a ruffled white blouse with a black ribbon necktie and has a series of black tattoos scrawled across both hands. Jack, the lead guitarist, is wearing a flared velvet suit and has long, dark hair that hangs like a curtain over his face, parting down the middle to reveal an aquiline nose. Only Matt, the drummer, is unremarkable, with his head of blond curls, plain white tee, and blue jeans.

As Jake chats with the band, I look out into the audience. So, this is what it looks like from his point of view. Only half of the stage lights are on, but it's far brighter than I imagined. Will he even be able to see me watching from the crowd?

After some vocal warm-ups and a sound check, we head to Jake's dressing room so he can change. Adena, his stylist, is waiting for us, clutching an enormous Starbucks cup. She rolls her eyes when she sees me. I guess my Jack Sparrow comment has not been forgotten.

As she pulls items off hangers and hands them to Jake, I sink into the green leather couch against the wall and take out my cell phone to review the photos I took earlier. The one I snapped of the marquee before Jake jumped in front of it came out great, and after a moment of deliberation, I decide to upload it to Instagram. Chloe made it crystal clear I shouldn't post about Jake. I believe her exact words were: *I love you, but god help me, I will not hesitate to kill you.* I'd gotten similar instructions from Jake's PR team. But I'm too excited and proud to resist. Besides, it's just one photo and he's not even in it.

It's been ages since I last checked Instagram, and when I scroll to the icon, my body turns cold. Two hundred and thirty-five new notifications. *Holy shit.* Clicking it open, I see there are hundreds of comments underneath my photos and over a dozen DMs. I'd meant to set my Instagram to private, but I suddenly realize that in the chaos of last week, it completely slipped my mind. Chloe's going to be pissed. Her voice echoes in my head. "Whatever you do, never ever read the comments." But I can't help myself. And as I scroll through the dizzying array of missives from complete strangers, I instantly regret it.

> sriously who does this girl think she is?
> your not even that cute tho LOL
> so pathetic jake can do way better then some basic af bitch
> U R NOT EVEN A REAL CHEF LMFAO
> u guys relax it's just publicity stunt. #TeamMadison for lyfe!

Someone with the handle @REALJakeTaylorGF has commented on every one of my photos from the last three years with a single word: "fugly." Why is it that, regardless of their platform, internet trolls universally struggle with basic grammar and spelling? At least I can still laugh about that. *Sure, @jTforLyfe42, you might think I'm a diarrhea-faced bitch, but between the two of us, I'm the only one who can actually spell "diarrhea" correctly.*

Even so, shock must be written all over my face. When Jake steps back out in an unbuttoned black dress shirt over a white tee and black skinny jeans, he hurries toward me.

"Hey. What happened?"

I bite my bottom lip guiltily. "I read the comments."

"Oh, Lex." He sinks into the couch, pulling me into his lap. "I'm so sorry. Are you okay?"

Shrugging, I toss my phone back into my purse. "It doesn't matter. I'll set my profile to private. Or delete it." I've just opened the app to do so when the screen goes black, and I realize I completely forgot to charge my phone earlier. "Seriously, it's fine," I reassure him, lacing my fingers through his. "I'll take care of it later. Let's drop it, okay? Tonight is about you."

He doesn't look entirely convinced, but offers a half smile as he pulls me closer. His lips brush against mine gently, just as Kenneth, the makeup artist, sidles up beside us.

"All right, that's enough, lovebirds. It's time to get Pretty Boy into the makeup chair."

A NOTHER HOUR PASSES BEFORE Jake is scheduled to take the stage, and he's growing more restless by the second. He paces back and forth across the small dressing room, mumbling to himself, yanking his hands through his hair, circulating through the entire catalog of Jake Taylor Twitches I've come to know so well. Finally, he wanders over to the couch, plopping down with a heavy sigh. He picks up an orange from the fruit bowl on the coffee table, staring at it intently as if the peel holds the answer to the meaning of life. Then he sighs heavily and puts it back.

"What is it?" I ask, even though I know exactly what he's thinking.

He collapses against the back of the sofa and drags his palms over his face. From the corner, Kenneth cringes.

"I'm worried they're going to hate the album," he finally confesses. "What if I really am a one-hit wonder? What if this album bombs and I have to listen to my dad gloat about how he was right all along? I'm telling you, Lex, I don't think I have it in me."

I reach across his lap, taking both of his trembling hands in mine.

"You are not a failure," I say firmly. "You are the most talented person I know, and this new album is going to be great. Everyone is going to love it just as much as I do. Just as much as I . . ." Words begin to rise in my throat, words too scary to say out loud. I bite my bottom lip before they can escape. Fortunately, Jake seems too preoccupied to notice, and I quickly recalibrate.

"You know what my dad used to say?"

Jake drags his hands off his face to look at me.

"What?"

I lower my voice and do my best impression of dad's heavy New York accent.

"Never let the bastards get you down."

A beat passes, and then Jake bursts into laughter. He collapses against the back of the couch, clutching his stomach as he gasps for breath. I lean in, relieved to see him smile. But I also feel a twinge of guilt at the thought of my dad. Things have been so busy lately that I've missed our last two Friday calls.

Jake fixes his gaze on me again. Those penetrating brown eyes are looking right through me.

"You're the best," he says. "Seriously. I don't know what I would do without you."

I squeeze his hand. "You're not too bad yourself." Which is an understatement, to say the least. It's crazy how quickly my feelings for him have deepened over the past two months. How he's gone from being a charming weekend fling to the center of my entire world.

"Now come on," I say. "Let's go give the people what they came for."

T HE AFTER PARTY IS crowded and loud, the venue filled to the brim with all the usual suspects. Music execs. Influencers. Bravolebrities with tummy tea brands. Magenta lights flash over the dizzying chevron-print floor. Music floods the speakers. I'm scanning the room for Jake, whom I haven't seen since his performance ended an hour ago. Just then, a tuxedoed waiter materializes in front of me, holding out a silver hors d' oeuvres tray.

"Moroccan beef spring roll?"

"Absolutely."

I pick one off the tray and pop it in my mouth, pausing to appreciate the explosion of flavor and parse out the ingredients. Paprika. Cumin. Ground beef. I'll probably go with lamb if I try to recreate it.

I've just helped myself to a second one when I finally spot Jake across the room. He's leaning against a pole, deep in conversation with Vinny. For a moment, I study him, admiring the way his arm muscles flex as he runs a hand through his hair. Then he looks up, catching my eye. His face melts into an expression so full of affection that my skin tingles. I cross the room toward him.

"There you are."

He wraps an arm around my waist, leaning forward to kiss me. I press into him, nuzzling my nose against his neck. Vinny mumbles something about checking in with security about a Jared Kushner sighting, and excuses himself. Jake barely seems to notice.

"So?" he asks the moment we're alone. "Do you think it went well? I feel like it went well. The energy from the audience felt really strong." His face is flush with post-performance nerves, the words coming out a mile a minute. I place a hand on his arm, steadying him.

"You were incredible," I assure him. "Seriously, I'm so proud of you."

"He *was* incredible, wasn't he?" The saccharine tone ringing out from behind me is unmistakable, considering she's one of Spotify's top-streamed artists. Jake and I turn at the same time to see her: Madison St. James. Somehow, I'm not surprised that she's ten times more stunning in real life than in pictures. Long, thick waves of glossy red hair. Cornflower-blue eyes set against pale, creamy skin. Sexy, hourglass curves swathed in ice-blue fabric. Up until this moment, I'd felt downright glamorous in my dress. But as I watch Madison's lips brush against Jake's cheek, I feel like a middle-schooler who's crashed the senior prom.

"Madison . . . hi." Jake's voice comes out an octave higher than usual. I look up at him, confused by his sudden shift in tone. Madison steps closer, her crimson lips parting.

"I just wanted to extend my congratulations. You did *amazing* tonight, Jake. This album might be an even bigger hit than your first one," she drawls, batting her lashes. It's truly unfair that such insanely attractive people are allowed to walk the earth among us mere mortals. Especially when they look like a real-life version of Jessica Rabbit.

"Anyway, we *have* to get together!" she continues. "I'm dying to hear about your inspiration for the new record." She still hasn't even bothered looking in my direction. When she reaches out a perfectly manicured hand to squeeze Jake's bicep, it takes everything inside me not to slap it away.

"Oh, I've got my sources," Jake replies, pulling me closer toward him. It's only then that Madison notices the arm she isn't clutching is looped around my waist. Her energy shifts. For the first time since she began talking to Jake, she realizes I'm Somebody Who Matters. Tilting her head, she fixes her gaze on me, and a tight smile forms on her lips. It doesn't quite match the cool, appraising look in her eyes. I can only imagine the thoughts running through her mind. Chief among them: *Who is this short, lumpy pedestrian, and what on earth is she doing with Jake Taylor?* Which means she's either managed to avoid tabloid gossip about Jake or has elected to completely disregard it.

Matching her smile, I extend a hand.

"Lexi Berman." My voice miraculously sounds far more confident than I feel. "Jake's girlfriend."

Madison's eyebrows spring up as high as her Botox will allow. A surge of adrenaline shoots through me. *Yeah, that's right,* I want to say aloud.

Madison's eyes lock with mine. If it were possible to freeze someone with a frigid glare, I'd be an ice sculpture right about now. Then she flicks her gaze over Jake's shoulder, wiggling her fingers at someone in the distance.

"Well, I'd better go mingle," she purrs, once again focused solely on Jake. "But it was great to see you. Congrats again!" When she slides past in a cloud of perfume, her shoulder bumps hard against mine. Somehow, I don't think it was entirely accidental.

I watch uneasily as she floats through the crowd. When I turn back to Jake, my stomach is twisted in knots.

"You guys seem . . . friendly," I say, searching and ultimately failing to find the right word.

Jake shrugs. "She's looked out for me from the start. The press has been writing trash about her for years, and it was nice to talk to someone who's been through it all. She has a great perspective on everything."

"And you really never had feelings for her?"

Jake's told me before that nothing ever happened between the two of them, but right now, I need to hear him say it again. I can't shake Madison's jealous expression, or the possessive way she clutched his forearm. It may have meant nothing to Jake, but it's hard for me to believe Madison doesn't have any feelings for him.

"There's only one person in this room I've ever been interested in." His lips brush against my ear. "Come on, let's go home."

I'M QUIET DURING THE entire car ride, but my brain is racing. I try leaning back against the seat and closing my eyes, but the image of Jake and Madison together is burned into the back of my eyelids. The worst part is how insanely good they look together. She's the type of woman Jake belongs with, a fellow Beautiful Person. Not some line cook with a hot-oil burn on her wrist, a woman who goes back for seconds on appetizers. Someone who is decidedly not "fugly."

By the time we step through my apartment door, the wave of insecurity bubbling inside me has grown to a full-blown tsunami. I can tell by his worried glances that Jake senses the tension radiating through my pores.

He collapses on the sofa, knees spreading apart, and reaches out a hand to me. Lacing his fingers through mine, he brings me down to straddle his lap, resting his hands on my hips. He leans forward and makes an admirable effort at distraction. His lips graze my cheekbone, then slowly make their way down to my neck. But I can't keep my anxieties from spilling out.

"Are you sure it was okay to leave so early tonight? I feel like I've stolen you away from all your adoring fans."

"I've got all the adoring fans I need right here," he murmurs against my skin, slipping one hand beneath the hem of my dress.

"Not Madison St. James."

He pulls back, his eyes filling with caution.

"Madison is not the person I want to be with. You are," he says slowly.

I shrug, biting the inside of my cheek as I struggle to keep my expression neutral.

"Lexi, what is this really about?" His dark eyes flit over my face, and I feel too exposed. It's a level of vulnerability that I am in no way comfortable with. Drawing back, I cross my arms tightly across my chest.

"What are you even doing with someone like me, Jake? You belong with someone famous and glamorous. Someone who's actually in your league."

Jake sighs.

"I'm with you because I like you, Lexi. I like the way you make me feel like myself, and not just some celebrity people want to grab on to. You're funny and kind and real. You're driven and talented, not to mention insanely beautiful. I like forcing you to take risks and be spontaneous, because even though you fight me every step of the way, I know you secretly enjoy it." He adjusts his head, leveling his gaze so that he's looking straight into my eyes.

"I like the way you feel like home."

I feel like all the air has been sucked out of my lungs as I internalize his words.

"Look, I can't imagine that this is easy, dealing with all the things people say, or the stories in the tabloids. But I'm with you because I want to be with you, not Madison or anyone else. You can't let everyone else get into your head, or this is never going to work."

Taking my hands in his, he looks up at me through his lashes.

"Do you want to be with me?"

I nod. Of course I do. As much as it terrifies me, I can no longer imagine a reality that Jake isn't a part of.

He gives me a small smile. "Then that's the only thing that matters. You and me. No one else, okay?"

"You're right." I lean forward, brushing my lips against his. "I'm sorry. I didn't mean to put a damper on your night."

"You didn't put a damper on anything." He leans back, his eyes boring into mine. "Lexi, the complete opposite is true. Having you there makes it mean so much more."

I wrap my arms around his neck and draw him toward me as his lips mold to mine. He pulls back, our eyes never breaking contact as he lifts my dress over my head and drops it over the edge of the sofa. His eyes widen as they roam over the lacy pink bra that Chloe snuck into the shopping bag when she delivered my loaner dress. Reaching behind my back, he unclasps it, then slides the straps down my bare shoulders. His hands are warm as he reaches around my breasts, kneading them gently with calloused fingertips.

I move my hands into his lap to unbutton his pants, and he helps me tug them down to his knees, along with his boxers. I stand up to step out of my matching underwear, and he unbuttons his shirt, discarding it beside my dress.

His eyes never leave my face as he presses a hand into the small of my back, lowering me into his lap.

"Come closer," he whispers.

I gasp when he enters me, and I rest one hand against his chest to hold my weight as we begin to move together. Our breathing grows heavier, and I watch as beads of perspiration form around his hairline. Jake leans forward, pressing his forehead against mine.

"Please don't give up on me," he whispers, his eyes pleading, his words thick with emotion. "You're the one thing in my life I'm sure of. I don't know what I'd do if I lost you."

My breath catches in my throat, and I nod once, unable to form words. Suddenly hot under his penetrating gaze, I break eye contact, sliding my lips over his neck to taste his salty skin. He groans and shifts his hips as we begin to unravel each other. When we finish together, Jake collapses back against the cushions, and I fall against his chest, our bodies a tangle of limbs and jagged breath. I press my cheek against his slick skin, my body rising and falling against his until I can tell he's drifted off to sleep. But sleep eludes as I lay awake in the darkness, thinking about what he said to me, and not knowing what's worse: that I can never bear to leave him, or that there's no way we can ever last.

22

THERE'S ONLY SO MUCH coffee can do when a person is running on three hours of sleep, and even after chugging an entire thermos during my commute, I can barely keep my eyes open the following morning. My limbs feel like they're filled with cement, heavy and dragging. Judging by the looks I'm receiving from the rest of the team, it's possible that I'm moving even slower than I think I am.

Even the ticket orders seem too loud today, the roll of paper exploding through the top of the printer with an offensive screeching sound. Squinting, I peer down at the newest ticket. Two orders of tabbouleh salad should be easy enough; that is, until I realize I have no idea where I've put the lemon vinaigrette. Panic grips me as I run my hand across the sides of the dressing bottles, frantically checking the labels in an attempt to locate it. I've been on this station long enough that I should have committed the position of each item to muscle memory, but somehow, I just can't get any of it to stick.

I'm about to ask Mia to grab the vinaigrette for me when I remember she's no longer at my station. After a joint plea session, Oren finally agreed to let me work unsupervised, and this morning, she's working at the hot apps station on the other side of the kitchen. The irony is almost too cruel; things are finally going right, but I'm too exhausted and overwhelmed to appreciate it.

"Where is my goddamn tabbouleh?" Chef's voice cuts through my thoughts, and looking down, I realize I still haven't finished the two bowls in front of me. Panic rising, I finally locate the vinaigrette and quickly coat each dish before shoving them onto the pass.

"What's your deal today, Berman?" Corbin's terse voice echoes from across the kitchen.

"Didn't you hear? She was out at her boyfriend's concert last night." Ethan's eyes shoot over to me from his station, and the look of naked hurt in his expression sends a fresh wave of emotion pulsing through my veins.

"Yeah? Well, I don't care who she's screwing," Corbin growls. "If she doesn't get first courses out faster, we're all fucked."

I slam my hands down on the countertop as frustration explodes out of me like hot lava.

"You think you can do better? Why don't you come over here and do it yourself?"

A series of low "oohs" erupts through the team.

"Yes! There it is!" Mia crosses the room to give me a triumphant fist bump. "I knew you had it in you."

Corbin barks out a humorless laugh.

"Nice try, sweetheart. But there's no way in hell you could ever get me to go back to garde." His words make me physically recoil, and I know the reason they cut so deeply is that they're true: there isn't a chef in the kitchen who wants to be in my position right now. Including me.

"Screw you, Corbin." Bitterly, I tear off the two tickets that have just emerged from the printer. It's nice to finally have Mia's approval, but I'm too upset to take any pleasure in her camaraderie. One way or another, someone needs to work garde-manger, and if I fail, she's the one who will end up back here. I can't let that happen, not when she's finally moved up. Corbin is right; I need to get it together, for everyone's sake.

The adrenaline of the fast-paced kitchen is usually enough to get me moving, but today, nothing seems to be doing the trick. I'm so sluggish that I can't keep my station in order—alarmingly, it looks like a lettuce-and-tomato-filled bomb exploded—and I reflect ruefully on how I cited my organizational skills as one of my greatest assets during my interview. *What happened to me?* I wonder, prompting a voice in the back of my mind to reply, *It's not a what, but a who.*

BERMAN? GET IN HERE." I've just packed up when Oren calls me from his office. Poking my head through the doorway, I see him pinching a slip of yellow paper between his fingers. My most recent request-for-leave form.

"What's this?"

"I need next Sunday off so I can go with Jake to the VMAs. Last year they were at Barclays Center, which would have been *so* much easier. At first I thought I could fly out after brunch service, but I figure with the time difference, I—"

"Sorry, Berman, but it's not gonna happen. You've used up all your leave time," he interjects.

"I . . . *all* of it?" Panic washes over me. *That's not possible, is it?*

Oren nods, confirming it.

"But . . . it's the VMAs. He's nominated in two categories."

Oren picks up the half-wrapped bagel sitting on the corner of his desk and takes a large bite.

"And that's very exciting for him. But *you* still have a job, and I've been as lenient as I can. In three months, you've already used up a whole year's worth of leave. You've been out way more than any other member of the team. And don't think they haven't noticed either."

Anxious thoughts storm my brain. Have the other team members really been discussing my time off? I hate the idea that the staff is questioning my work ethic.

I spend the next hour contemplating how I'm going to tell Jake I can't go to LA with him, and the longer I mull it over, the angrier I become. I'm not sure what bothers me most: the fact I can't be there for him; that being a chef means I never have time to do anything but work; or that I'm in this position at all, forced to choose between a relationship and my career.

It's times like this when I desperately wish I could talk things out with my mother. I try to imagine what advice she'd give right now. Knowing her, she'd probably remind me about the importance of commitment.

When I was nine, I begged her to let me sign up for ballet lessons. I loved every minute of it, until I realized Katie Steinberg's birthday party at Dylan's Candy Bar was scheduled for the same time as my Saturday class and begged her to let me skip a week.

"But Mom! Everyone will be there but me!" I'd pleaded when she refused.

She was firm, though, shaking her head with her arms across her chest.

"You made a commitment, and you're going to stick to it."

At the time, I was furious, but the lesson stuck with me ever since. Following through on commitments is firmly rooted in my sense of work ethic; I'm not a quitter and I never have been. Deep down, I know exactly what my mom would have advised. What I'm less sure about is what she would have thought of Jake. I can't help but wonder if she wouldn't have adjusted her rules for him.

"What's your deal today?" Mia looks me up and down curiously. "Did the Lady Killer dump you or something?"

"Uh, no."

Grabbing a knife, I start working on my potato galettes. At this point, I have them down to a science, and can prepare them to

Chef's ideal level of crispness with my eyes closed. I'm grateful for the distraction, but I'm not interested in talking about this with Mia, regardless of how much our relationship has improved lately.

Mia shrugs her shoulders when I fail to elaborate.

"Well, you can take your bad mood out on the dishes. Luis's out with the flu so we're understaffed over there. And guess who's next on the totem pole?"

Ugh. I was really hoping to get out of here early. Jake and I need to talk about the VMAs. But now there's not a chance in hell I'll be out of here before midnight.

Sure enough, it's quarter to one in the morning when I finally stumble through my front door, half asleep and reeking of dish soap, my hands red and raw. I expect Jake to be passed out, but he's sitting on the sofa, nursing a bottle of beer when I walk through the door.

"Hey," he says, his voice full of enthusiasm. "How was your day?"

I slip off my clogs and place them neatly by the door. My legs are aching, my temples throbbing. The last thing I feel like doing right now is having this conversation.

Jake soldiers on, oblivious to my dark mood. "You're home later than usual. Did everyone want to go out for a celebratory drink?"

"Our senior dishwasher was out, so I had to stay late to wash dishes. Oh, and Oren isn't letting me take any more days off, because I've used up my leave time already, so I can't go with you to LA. And I'm exhausted. So, if you'll excuse me, I'm going to jump in the shower."

I'm too upset to even look at Jake, but as soon as I step into the bathroom, I can hear his footsteps behind me.

"Wait, are you serious? You're really not coming to the show?"

I reach over to the tub and twist the handle upward, turning on the water. With a sigh, I lean back against the sink, crossing my arms.

"Yes, Jake, I'm really not coming."

Jake's brow furrows. "Can't you switch around your schedule with someone? I know it's inconvenient, but this is a big deal."

"Well, I hate to break it to you, but in the real world, work doesn't just stop for the VMAs." My voice is harsher than I had intended; I can tell I'm on the verge of pushing too far, but I can't seem to control the anger bubbling up inside me.

"Don't you get it?" I continue. "My life isn't like yours. People don't just bend over backwards to accommodate me every time I make a request. Or have you already forgotten how Normal Humans live?"

Jake's expression falls. "Is that really what you think of me?" he asks softly.

My chest tightens as I absorb the hurt in his tone. This is exactly why I didn't want to have this conversation at 1 A.M. Desperate to end this exchange before I say anything else I'll regret, I step into the shower. But I've barely wet my hair when the curtain pulls back and Jake steps inside.

"Geez, have you ever heard of privacy?"

"We aren't finished talking yet. You don't just get to avoid me every time a topic of conversation gets uncomfortable." Jake's mouth is set in a hard line. Droplets of water run down the tips of his hair, getting caught on the tips of his eyelashes. His face softens. "I'm sorry. I shouldn't have pushed you to take off work. I just hate the idea of being there without you."

I close my eyes, letting the hot water run over me. "I'm sorry too. But you know how much I want to be there, right? I would never miss it if I had the choice."

Jake nods. His eyes shift from my face down the length of my body, carefully watching my every movement as I pick up the soap bar and begin scrubbing the kitchen smells from my skin. His breathing hitches slightly, and I can sense his frustration beginning to melt away.

"Here, let me help you." He takes the soap from my hands,

rubbing it between his own to form a lather. Stepping behind me, he places his hands on my shoulders, massaging them into the tight muscles.

"That feels good," I sigh as he kneads gently, my muscles loosening beneath his calloused fingertips. My body relaxes as he combs shampoo through my hair, and I allow my mind to go blank, all thoughts of dirty dishes and leave slips disappearing down the drain. He presses a soft kiss to the shell of my ear as his fingertips skim across my shoulders, drawing goosebumps even under the heat of the water. When I turn to face him, he presses his hands against the tile wall behind me, caging me in. His eyelashes lower to half-mast as he drinks me in, gaze locked intensely on mine, and I drape my arms around his neck, fingers drifting through his damp hair. My breathing grows labored as we stare at each other, until I can't take it any longer, and I rise onto my tiptoes to meet his mouth with mine.

A low rumble in Jake's throat sends a spark through me. I pull him closer, deepening the kiss, and soon I feel myself melting into him the way that I always do, the world around us fading like chalk illustrations in a rainstorm. When he finally pulls away, his expression is content and dreamy, a mirror to my own internal state. His thumb skates across my cheekbone, and the tender way he's staring down at me robs the air from my lungs.

"Come on," he says huskily. "Let's get you to bed."

But by the time he dries me off gently with a towel and tucks me beneath the sheets fifteen minutes later, I feel unsettled again. And deep down, I know things are only going to get worse from here.

JAKE FLIES BACK TO New York the Monday after the VMAs. He lost both awards. When his black Suburban arrives outside my apartment shortly after 6 P.M., I open the car door and slip into the back seat beside him.

"Hey." He leans forward to kiss me. His leather bracelets brush my cheek as he cups my chin. Then he slinks back into his seat, staring straight ahead. I struggle to read his vacant expression.

"Sorry about your loss. You were robbed, obviously." I offer a small smile, desperate to break the uncomfortable silence. Our schedules have been so busy that we've barely spoken since he left for Los Angeles two days ago, and the tension is palpable. I reach up to chew my nail but stop midair, twisting my hands together in my lap instead.

Jake's voice is flat, his eyes in his lap. "I don't care about the awards. I just wish you had been there."

"You know I wanted to be, Jake." The rest of the statement is left unspoken, but it's still there, wedged between us.

He sighs. His face softens as he reaches for my hand. "Yeah, I know."

I give his fingers a tight squeeze. "I'll be there next time."

He attempts a smile, but the empty words hang in the air, taunting us in silence. Because the truth is, we both know I can't make that promise.

IT'S BEEN AGES SINCE I last dined at Mr Chow, Tribeca's glamorous if wildly overpriced Chinese restaurant, but the place is exactly as I remember it. Crisp white tablecloths, glossy surfaces, oversized floral arrangements. Not the best place to avoid being photographed, but I wanted to take Jake somewhere nice to make up for missing the VMAs. To celebrate his nomination, even if he lost this time.

The maître d' is escorting us to our table when I hear Jake's name. A hand shoots out from the booth beside us, snaking itself around his wrist. My eyes follow it up a long, pale arm, which is attached to a woman with a head of crimson waves and a toothy smile. Madison St. James. Of fucking course.

"Jake!" she squeals. "I didn't realize you were also flying into New York today! We could have shared a plane!"

A hot spike of jealousy pulses through me as I watch her ogle my boyfriend with naked adoration. I still don't understand how Jake can't see it; Madison's lashes are practically curling as she stares up at him.

"How insane was Shawn's after party? I think I'm still a little drunk!"

Jake smiles politely, extracting his hand. "Yeah, it was a good time. He's got quite a house."

Madison is still beaming at Jake like he is the actual sun. I can't stop staring at her teeth. She's got to have more than the average person. Maybe they're implants. I make a mental note to bring it up with Ali. If anyone will know, it's her.

"How long are you in town? Are you back at The Pierre?"

"Technically. Although I'm still crashing with this one half the time." Jake grins at me and Madison's smile slips momentarily as her gaze flicks toward me. Her cornflower-blue eyes run up and down my dress, a floaty, tunic-style number from Anthropologie that felt ethereal when I put it on but is now making me feel decidedly like what Vinny would call "a regular."

She presses her lips together in a tight smile, extending a bony hand toward me.

"Oh, right," she says. "We've met before. You're . . ."

"Lexi. My girlfriend," Jake supplies helpfully. We exchange a limp handshake that possesses all the warmth of a meat locker. After some parting words, Jake presses a hand into the small of my back.

"We won't keep you. Enjoy your dinner," he says, as he guides us away from her table.

Jake and I spend the next two hours lingering over a feast of chicken satay, pot stickers, and the famous Mr Chow's noodles, our ankles interlocked under the table. I do my best to focus on the incredible food, and Jake, and expel all thoughts of his and Madison's wild after-party adventures.

He fills me in on his newly updated schedule. The remainder of the year will be dedicated to promoting his sophomore album, which means press junkets, a handful of small venue concerts, and a guest spot on *Dick Clark's New Year's Rockin' Eve with Ryan Seacrest* in Times Square. I can't help but beam with excitement at the last part.

As a kid, I begged my parents every year to take me to see the ball drop, and every year they refused. (*Let the tourists venture into the belly of the beast!* my mother would say.) I finally went with friends as a junior in high school. That night, we learned the hard way that New Year's Eve attendees are penned into Times Square like cattle for seven hours, with no access to a bathroom. Still, it's a New York tradition, and I'm excited he'll get to be part of it. Then, he drops the bombshell: on New Year's Day, he'll be leaving for a ten-month tour across five continents to promote his new album.

"*Ten months? You can't be serious.*"

I knew Jake wasn't going to be staying in New York after December, but I figured he'd only be gone for a few weeks at a time. I never anticipated a ten-month tour. It hasn't been that long since he returned from the last one. The pit in my stomach swells as Oren's words echo in my brain. *In three months, you've used a year's worth of leave time.* Without any time off, when will I ever see him?

"I know it's a really long time," Jake acknowledges. He takes a deep breath, reaching across the table to take my hand in his. "And I know I'm taking a shot in the dark here, but I was hoping you'd consider going with me." He seems to hold his breath as he studies my face, gauging my reaction.

"On tour? For ten months?" I don't bother trying to mask the exasperation in my voice. "How could I do that? What about my job?"

Jake stares down at his plate forlornly. "I know you have a

career of your own, and I have no right to ask you to give anything up for me. But it's a long time to be apart, and I had to at least try."

Half a dozen people stop by our table over the course of the evening, asking for autographs or photos with Jake. He graciously obliges, but he looks tired, worn-out, like a small piece of him leaves his body with every flash of the camera. After we settle the bill, we decide to walk for a bit before heading back to my apartment.

He's silent as we stroll through the streets, our arms linked, his eyes roving over the storefronts.

"You know, I could always take a break," he says so softly that I almost don't hear him. "Just a short one. Postpone the tour, take a few months off."

I stop in my tracks, dragging him back toward me. "What do you mean?"

"I don't know." He takes a shaky breath. "Let's face it, it's just been a nonstop whirlwind for the past two years, and I haven't really taken a beat." He shoots me a sideways glance. "Plus, it would give me some more time to spend with you."

Guilt floods my body as I study Jake's face. Could I live with myself if he gave up everything he's worked for to be with me? We're both quiet for a moment, considering it.

"Does performing still make you happy?"

Jake intakes a breath, studying his shoes. He nods.

"Then you don't quit. You never give up if your dream is still what fills you."

He turns to look at me, the side of his mouth curling upward in that way that still makes my heart flutter every time.

"You're pretty cool, you know that?"

I shrug, smiling. "So I've been told. But please, do continue to list my best qualities."

He wraps an arm around me, nuzzling his face into my neck.

"Hmm, let's see: you're smart, and funny, and beautiful. Amazing cook. Definitely a better-than-average kisser."

He stops right there, in the middle of the street, pulling me in close. But just as he's about to press his lips to mine, I feel his body spasm, and he erupts into a loud, wet sneeze.

"Ugh, you beast!" I scream, shoving him away from me in mock repulsion. Jake laughs, reaching his hand out for me, but I swat him away. "Seriously, stay away from me. I'm not prepared for this. The forecast didn't indicate that I needed to pack an umbrella."

"Baby, I'm sorry! What's it going to take to make it up to you?"

I cross my arms, pretending to mull it over for a second. "Take me to Big Gay Ice Cream and buy me a cone."

"You got it. I assume you'll be having your namesake?"

I giggle. The quirky ice cream shop sells a cone called "The Dorothy," which consists of vanilla ice cream, dulce de leche, and Nilla wafers.

"Nope. I'll be having *your* namesake: the Salty Pimp." Jake reaches a hand around my waist, tickling me as I shriek. I'm so wrapped up in him that I don't even notice the flash of the camera from across the street.

23

"HAVE YOU SEEN THIS?"

When I burst through the door of Jake's suite at The Pierre, I'm clutching this week's issue of *Us Weekly* so tightly that the ink is smearing right onto my sweat-soaked palms. As much as I hate to admit it, I'm finally starting to appreciate the warnings Chloe and Jake gave me about how easily the media twists reality. The paparazzi photo on the cover caught Jake mid-sneeze, and with his scrunched face and open mouth, it really does look like he's screaming at me.

Jake's head pops up as he looks at me from across the room. He's seated at a table with Vinny and Lydia, his publicist, and another man in a charcoal suit I don't recognize. I freeze mid-step, embarrassment flooding my cheeks. It never occurred to me that Jake wasn't in here alone.

From his seat at the marble table, Vinny rolls his eyes. But it also looks like he's . . . smirking? Before I can read any further into it, Jake rises from his chair and crosses the room to pull me into a tight hug. I press my face into his shirt, some of the tension in my shoulders immediately dissolving as I inhale his comforting smell.

"Hey, you," he says, and it doesn't escape my attention that he's ignoring the magazine in my hand. He hooks his index finger under my chin and plants a soft kiss on my lips. "We were just working on the tour schedule."

"Oh, right." In the heat of the article scandal, I had (perhaps willfully) forgotten all about the tour. The truth is, I've spent the past week dedicating as little thought as possible to Jake's upcoming departure, finding ways to change the subject every time he brings it up.

His eyes drop back down to the table. "And, uh . . . there's something else I need to tell you."

Before he can continue, the other man at the table rises, buttoning his suit jacket before extending a hand toward me.

"Rudy Silverman, Madison St. James's manager. It's a pleasure to meet you, Lucy."

"It's Lexi, actually." *Madison St. James's manager?* What's he doing here? I turn toward Jake, my brow furrowing in confusion.

Jake clears his throat. When he speaks again, his voice is calm, but the two tiny pops of color in his cheeks betray him.

"Lady Gaga is hosting a benefit concert at Madison Square Garden next month to raise money for her Born This Way Foundation. She's having a few artists do guest performances—"

"—and we thought, what could be better than two of the hottest acts in music performing a duet? The fans will go ballistic to see Jake Taylor and Madison St. James onstage together. I mean, think of the buzz it will generate, especially with both of their upcoming tours!" Rudy is practically salivating as he cuts Jake off mid-sentence.

"Of course, the most important thing is the foundation," Jake adds quickly. "This type of fundraising could help so many kids in need."

"It's genius. Remember how people reacted to Lady Gaga and Bradley Cooper's Oscar performance?" Vinny is smiling, but when his eyes meet mine, there's a hard glint behind them that sends a shiver down my spine. As a matter of fact, I remember that

Oscar duet very clearly. Especially the part where Gaga and Bradley ended things with their significant others shortly thereafter. A pit of unease forms in my stomach.

Jake stiffens beside me. He clears his throat, turning to address the table.

"Anyway, I think we're good for today, right?"

I peek over his shoulder and it's clear from everyone's confused expressions that this is news to them.

"Okay. I'm sure you two have some things to talk about." Vinny's expression is smug as he stands up. Lydia is the only one who looks vaguely uncomfortable. Her eyes flit over to mine as she shoots me a quick, sympathetic smile. Nevertheless, the three of them pack up without argument, and a few minutes later, we're alone in the suite.

I make my way over to the window, fingering the sheer, elegant curtain and admiring the way it gently diffuses the outside light. A moment later, Jake comes up behind me. His lips press into the curve of my ear as his arm slides around my waist, pulling me against him. I feel his fingers run across the bottom of my shirt and intake a sharp breath when they slip underneath the fabric to graze my skin.

"There's my Salty Pimp," he breathes into my ear, and I can feel his lips curving into a smile. Turning around to face him, I wrap my arms around his neck.

"So . . . a duet with Madison St. James?"

Jake shrugs. "Sure. It makes sense, logistically speaking. We're both wrapping up new albums and will be going on tour around the same time. The label figured having us perform together would generate a lot of excitement with our fans. It'll be good for record sales."

My eyebrows knit as I consider this. Something about it isn't sitting right.

"Don't you find it a little bit suspicious that Vinny is once again using Madison to get you press?"

Jake's forehead furrows as something dark passes across his face. Then he blinks and it's gone.

"Nah, he wouldn't try that again. He knows how angry I was the last time he pulled that. Besides, this is just one show. Not a huge deal." He brushes his nose against my neck. "Now come on, I haven't seen you in two days, and I've missed you like crazy."

He takes me by the hand and leads me over to the sofa, pulling me into his lap. Reaching my hands under his plain white tee, I run my hands over his soft skin, the muscles of his stomach rippling beneath my fingers. Jake stares at me, his eyes darkening as I lean in to mold my lips to his. His tongue runs over my bottom lip as he slides one hand under my shirt to unhook my bra.

But I can't concentrate. Excerpts from the *Us Weekly* article are playing on an endless loop through my brain, refusing to be banished no matter how much I try to push them away. *Have the pressures of fame caught up to the kitchen hand so soon? Or is she just upset after seeing the steamy photos of Jake and Madison St. James at Shawn Mendes's Billboard Awards after party?* A comment from Instagram breaks through: *"Srsly who does this girl think she is?"*

I thrust my hands against Jake's chest to push myself off his lap and into a standing position.

"What is it?" he asks, his voice still husky with lust.

"I . . . I don't know," I admit. "It's just . . . you're going to be leaving on tour soon, and then when will we see each other? I mean, let's face it, it's not like I'll be getting any time off for the foreseeable future."

Jake tilts his head, his brow wrinkling, but I push on.

"And I know you want me to see you as more than just a celebrity, but some days it's harder to ignore the fact that you are one. To me, you're just Jake, but to the world, you're Jake Taylor, the musician. You don't belong with someone like me. You should be with someone from your own world."

Jake's expression darkens.

"What are you saying? You don't want to be with me?"

"I'm saying that I don't understand how this is going to work. It's not like you live here full-time."

His jaw tightens, his voice terse. "I've been upfront with you from the beginning about the realities of my life."

"I know that. But come on, Jake, let's be realistic. We live completely different lives. You're a rock star—"

"We're both chasing our dreams! How is that so different?" He steps back toward me, bringing his thumbs to rest softly on either side of my cheekbones and tilting my face toward him. My heart flutters as his chocolate eyes melt into mine.

"I'm not going into this with blinders on. I know it won't always be easy. In fact, it's going to take a lot of work. There will be bumps in the road, and we'll probably get pissed off at each other sometimes. But you and I found our way back to each other for a reason, and I'm not about to let you go again. Please, Lexi . . . don't push me away."

I let out a shaky exhale as I tuck my head under his chin and wrap my arms around his back. As I stand there, my cheek pressed against his chest, a small part of me wonders what I'm doing. Why do I keep trying to push him away when being apart from him is the last thing I want? Maybe it's because it's growing harder and harder to ignore the fact that a few months from now, it won't matter either way. He'll be leaving all on his own.

24

JAKE LEAVES THE FOLLOWING week to kick off his press tour with a handful of appearances and concerts across the country. For the next three weeks, we barely see each other as he jets from San Francisco to Los Angeles, and then to Boston and Nashville. Despite my efforts to stay as busy as possible, it's been harder to cope than I expected. I can't help but feel a chasm growing between us in his absence, especially as the tabloid rumors about our alleged breakup have continued to swirl. I hate being apart from him all the time, wondering what he's doing and who he's with.

But now, he's finally home, having touched down in New York earlier this morning. The concert is only two days away, so Jake will spend the next forty-eight hours tied up in rehearsals. He's invited me to join him for a working lunch with Vinny, Madison, and her manager this afternoon, and I've missed him too much to turn him down, despite how I feel about the other attendees.

I turned down Jake's offer to send a car, figuring the train would be just as fast and a lot less flashy. What I hadn't counted on was construction delays, which put me twenty-five minutes behind schedule. By the time I burst through the doors at Estiatorio Milos, my carefully blown-out hair is both flat and staticky, and my cheeks are wet with windblown tears from running from the Thirty-Fourth

Street station. I swipe my hands across my face, attempting to repair the damage as the hostess leads me through rows of tables covered in crisp white tablecloths. Finally, I spot everyone seated at a table in the corner. Jake's back is to me, and I realize with a sinking feeling that the only remaining empty seat is next to Madison.

Naturally, she looks immaculate, her flawless red waves and perfectly applied makeup a testament to the fact that she has a driver and therefore never needs to run anywhere. Her blue eyes widen as she takes in my disheveled appearance, but before she can react, Jake turns around, his face lighting up.

"There she is."

Jake stands and wraps his arms around me. A wave of contentment rolls over me as I press my face into the soft fabric of his black sweater, breathing in his familiar, clean smell.

"We were just talking about you," Jake says, his eyes never leaving mine as I begrudgingly slide into the plush white banquette beside Madison.

"Yup. Jake was telling us all about how you work in a restaurant kitchen." The corners of Madison's mouth turn up in amusement as she swivels her head toward me.

I know exactly where she's going with this; her sweet, breathy voice barely disguises her condescending tone. But there's not a chance in hell I'm going to give her the satisfaction of knowing she's gotten to me.

"That's right," I say, plastering on an equally fake smile.

"How interesting. Now, what do you do on, like, a daily basis? Does everyone take turns washing dishes or is that, like, a special position?"

"Lexi is an unbelievable chef," Jake cuts in before I can abandon all prior thoughts of playing it cool and instead drag Madison into the kitchen by her hair. Shoving her face into a sink full of dirty dishes would teach her exactly how well I can handle a wash.

"She's incredibly talented," he continues. "And she's going to own her own restaurant one day. I just hope I'll be lucky enough to score an invite to the opening." He winks at me and my stomach flip-flops.

"Ooooh. So, you're, like, the head chef?"

"Um, no. I've only been working at the restaurant for a year now. It takes a while to work your way up to those positions." I open my mouth to elaborate, then shut it again. What's the point of explaining my career trajectory to these people? No one at this table besides Jake gives a shit what I do.

"Wow, that's, like . . . *so* brave. I don't know if I have the patience to wait that long for success." Madison turns to Jake. "We aren't behind-the-scenes people, are we, Jake? We get fulfillment from audiences cheering us on, screaming our name. That's why the two of us get along so well." She places one hand over Jake's and peers up at him through her fake lashes. My own hands curl into fists in my lap.

"I think this performance is going to be huge for both of your careers," Vinny says. He claps a hand on Jake's shoulder and looks back and forth between him and Madison. It feels like he's making a point to ignore me. A hollow feeling swells in my stomach as I consider the fact that he'd probably prefer it if I weren't here at all.

Jake's face breaks into a grin. "Yeah, it's going to be great."

I'm not sure what irritates me more; the fact that Jake and Madison are going to be onstage together, or the fact that Jake seems genuinely excited about it. The way she's acting like she and Jake are some dynamic duo is getting more insufferable by the minute. Part of me wants to grab Jake by the collar, kiss him in front of everyone, and make it clear exactly who he belongs to.

I take a deep breath then release it slowly, carefully arranging my face into an expression of nonchalance. Reaching into my bag, I click on my phone to check the time. This can't go on too much longer, right?

My screen illuminates and a new text from Ali pops open.

Tried to find the vid of someone throwing a vibrator at Jake and found THIS!!!

There's a link attached, and when I click on it, it opens to an Etsy listing for a vibrator with Jake's face on it.

Before I can respond another three dots appear.

FWIW it has 10 vibration speeds and is waterproof. Wonder if it's better than my Pete Davidson one??

Shaking my head, I shove the phone back into my purse without responding. The conversation at the table has turned to industry talk. Madison is gazing at Jake with blatant adoration as he postulates about artists' rights to retain ownership of their masters.

Once again, it's hard not to notice how right they look together. Two gorgeous celebrities with similar goals and career paths. They inhabit the same world and know all the same people. They make more sense as a couple than Jake and I ever would.

At the end of the day, what do he and I really have in common? His star is just going to continue to rise, and the more famous he gets, the less it will make sense to keep hanging around someone like me. Even if he wants to stay together, hanging around New York instead of touring would only stunt his career. I can't help but feel like I'd be holding him back.

When we arrive at Madison Square Garden thirty minutes later, Jake's backing band is already onstage. He's scheduled to perform "Blueberry" before Madison joins him onstage for their cover of Ed Sheeran's "Perfect," so when he heads up the stairs to warm up with them, I follow Vinny and Madison to the pit. Once we've found a spot in front of the stage, Vinny's phone rings, and he wanders off to take the call just as an assistant wearing a black jumpsuit and a headset appears in front of us.

"Hi! Can I get you anything?" she asks, her voice wobbly. Her eyes are wide as she stares at Madison. "Coffee? A bagel?"

"A bagel? You're *hilarious!*" Madison emits a high-pitched giggle as the assistant's face goes crimson. "I'll take hot water with lemon," she instructs, before tossing the poor girl the fakest smile I've ever seen. "Thanks, sweetie!"

"And, uh, I'll take a coffee, please," I say, but the assistant seems not to hear me. Her eyes are fixated on her shoes as she scampers off.

"Oh my god." Madison shakes her head incredulously. "Can you believe there are still people who eat *carbs*?"

I shift uncomfortably, unsure how to reply, when I'm mercifully saved by the sound of Jake's breathy voice through the microphone. Glancing up, I can't help but smile as our eyes meet and he winks at me before breaking into the opening lyrics of "Blueberry."

"You guys are super cute together. I can see why he likes you." The overbearing scent of Madison's floral perfume invades my nostrils as she sidles up beside me.

"Thanks," I reply, my eyes still fixed on Jake. He runs a hand through his hair, his eyes fluttering shut over a breathy note. His voice is my favorite sound in the entire world. It takes everything in me not to sigh like a smitten schoolgirl.

"And, honestly, you shouldn't feel bad about being his muse."

That gets my attention. It's that word again. "Muse." I whip my head around to face her.

"What do you mean?"

Madison gives me a sphinxlike smile.

"That's why you guys got back together, right?" She waves a hand in Jake's direction. "I mean, let's face it, he's basically a one-hit wonder. You inspired the song that catapulted him to stardom. Why else would he come find you when he got back to New York?"

The air whooshes from my lungs as my brain turns over her words. There's no way Jake would ever do something like that. Our relationship isn't just fodder for his music career. Still, I can't ignore the lump rising in my throat. An uninvited thought shoves itself forward. *It's not like you never thought about this before.* After all, he did show up to my apartment right before he started recording his second album. And he's been inspired to write again since he's been back. Did he have an ulterior motive for ringing my doorbell that night?

Madison tilts her head, regarding me with faux sympathy.

"Oh my god, sweetie. You can't really be that naïve, can you? It's just what artists like Jake and I do. Half the men I date are for material. It keeps the well fresh."

She pauses, holding my gaze, and the cold smile she gives me sends a shiver down my spine.

"Woman to woman, I hope you realize this thing between you guys isn't going to last. Celebrities never stay with the people they dated before they were famous. It just doesn't work. And I'd hate to see you get your heart broken because you're too blinded by infatuation to see reality."

Before I can respond, the assistant returns, her hands trembling slightly as she hands Madison a piping white mug. Madison accepts it without even looking at her, then extends it toward me.

"Here, why don't you take this? You're looking a little pale."

Wordlessly, I accept the mug as Madison rests a hand on my shoulder. "I hope you don't take it too hard when he moves on to someone in his own league. But just think: you'll have a great story to tell your grandchildren." With that, she spins on her red-soled heels and heads toward the stage doors, leaving me standing there, heart hammering, my fingers burning beneath the white porcelain.

J AKE IS SO BUSY with rehearsals that I barely see him for the next two days. When my doorbell rings on Saturday afternoon, I can hardly contain my excitement to see him as I yank open the door. But instead of Jake standing on the other side, I'm greeted by a uniformed courier, who looks slightly alarmed by my enthusiasm for his arrival.

He glances down at the electronic pad in his hand. "Alexa Berman?"

When I nod, the courier wheels an enormous black box tied with ivory ribbon into the center of the living room. Before I can ask any further questions, he thrusts the tablet forward, gesturing for me to sign. I've barely finished scrawling my signature before he drags the squeaking dolly back out into the hallway, pulling the door shut behind him.

The word "Prada" is written in silver letters on the right side of the box, and my first thought is that there must be some sort of mistake. Curious, I check the card on the side of the box and spot my name. Somehow, it seems this really is for me. Tugging the envelope loose, I open it up. The message inside says, "Wear me tonight."

Apprehensively, I tug one end of the ribbon to unravel the oversized bow and slide it off the box. I lift off the top and carefully remove a layer of tissue paper to reveal a shimmering, V-necked emerald dress with cascading ruffles and a pair of gold heeled sandals. Gingerly, I lift it up and hold it against myself. It is, without a doubt, the most beautiful dress I have ever seen.

Grabbing my phone, I shoot Jake a text.

Hi! Where are you? And also, this dress???

Jake responds a few minutes later.

Glad you like it. Stuck in rehearsals the rest of the day but I can't wait to see you in it tonight.

A flutter of excitement ripples through my chest as I look at the dress again. It's a bit much for a concert, but it sure as hell beats the black jumpsuit Ali helped me choose from the clearance rack at Bloomingdale's last week. I snap a quick picture and text it to both Ali and Chloe. Chloe writes back first, which makes sense since her phone is in her hand 90 percent of the time.

Love it! Make sure you have a strapless bra ;-) And remember the poses I taught you.

When Ali responds twenty minutes later with a series of gifs
ranging from Lauren Conrad mouthing "Whoa!" to Jonah Hill
holding his cheeks and screaming, I can't help but laugh. Maybe
I'm overthinking things; maybe all my worries have been for nothing. I'm so excited as I slip into my bedroom to get dressed that I
almost let myself believe it.

THE ROAR OF THE crowd is deafening as the stage lights go up to
reveal Jake's dimpled grin. Even from a distance, it's impossible
not to feel his electrifying magnetism. When the drummer slams
down his sticks, Jake throws back his head, showcasing his square
jawline and breaking straight into "Dorothy." Watching him perform never gets old; it's incredible to observe his particular brand
of magic, the way the air around him pulses with excitement as he
absorbs the crowd's energy. By the time he finishes the first song
with a deep bow and a blown kiss, a sheen of sweat dampening the
chestnut hairs around his forehead, he's got the audience in the
palm of his hand.

He takes a sip from a water bottle, then leans into the mic.

"How y'all doing tonight?" They scream in response. "I'm going to have a friend join me for my next song. You may have heard
of her. Please welcome to the stage, Madison St. James!"

The crowd goes wilder than ever when Madison sashays her
way out from the wings. She's wearing a long white gown adorned
with pale pink rosettes, long hair hanging halfway down her back.
As much as I hate to admit it, she looks breathtaking.

The girl seated next to me in the front row, who can't be a day
older than sixteen, screams as she holds up her cell phone to film
the performance.

"Ohmigod, I literally can't deal with how cute they are. They are the hottest couple I've ever seen!" she squeals to the friend standing next to her.

I'm just about to correct her when the music starts, redirecting my attention back to the stage. Confusion washes over me as I hear the opening notes of "Blueberry." *Wait . . . weren't they supposed to perform a duet of "Perfect"?*

Jake and Madison turn to face one another, their gazes locked. She slips a hand into his and bends toward him. A hot, sour feeling blossoms through my chest as realization dawns on me: they're about to perform *my* song. The song Jake wrote about me. It's bad enough that the whole world thinks they're in love. Now she's hijacking this too? I feel like I'm being replaced entirely. Like I never existed at all. *Just like Dad replaced Mom,* a nagging voice in my head whispers.

I don't even notice the song has ended until the audience leaps to their feet for a standing ovation. Slowly, I stand to join them, clapping gingerly.

I take a deep breath, attempting to reassure myself. Jake and Madison's onstage chemistry is just that . . . onstage. They're just two performers doing their jobs. As for the song? There's got to be a reasonable explanation. I need to get backstage to see Jake. Everything will be okay again as soon as we're together.

I elbow my way through the small crowd congregating in front of the stage doors, coming to a halt in front of two stern bodyguards who look like they were imported straight from Buckingham Palace. When I hold up my backstage pass, they grunt and step to the side.

The blue-and-white hallway beneath the stage is narrow and even more crowded than the densely packed theater, the walls vibrating with the hum of the bass music up above. I jostle my way through the throng, shimmying past a sweat-soaked bass player and a group of gazelle-like models taking long drags from their cigarettes. Somewhere up ahead, a camera flashes. I dip my head, doing my best to avoid being photographed as I scan the crowd for a familiar face. Finally, I spot Vinny's dark head at the end of the hall, standing outside one of the dressing room doors. A quick glance confirms I'm in the right place when I spy a sheet of paper with Jake's name on it taped to the wall.

"Hey!"

Vinny looks up from his phone, startled. He shifts uncomfortably, his eyes darting back and forth between me and the closed door. A long moment stretches out between us.

"Is he in there?" I finally ask.

Vinny nods, his expression inscrutable.

"Uh, yeah, but he's busy. He should be out soon," he replies carefully.

"Oh, come on. It's just me," I reply, cringing at the hint of desperation in my voice. Sliding past him, I twist the brass door-knob, pushing my way through the threshold. The dressing room is shabbier than I expected, with dim overhead lighting and a grimy carpet.

Jake's standing across the room with his back to me. I expect him to turn at the sound of the door opening, but the creak must get swallowed by the music above us. His white T-shirt is molded to his body with sweat, highlighting the muscles in his back. He's facing a woman with long, red waves, who reaches forward to press a hand against his chest. *No, it can't be.*

"You were so great tonight. I told you the crowd would love us together," she murmurs.

"Listen, I really should—" But before he can finish, she closes her mouth over his.

I don't even realize I've made a sound until Jake whips around to face me, his eyes wide with surprise. Madison St. James's heavily made-up face peeks out from behind him, her mouth twisted into a self-satisfied smirk. Bile rushes to my throat.

"Lexi." Jake's voice is barely a whisper as he takes a step toward me; subconsciously, I take one step back.

My eyes dart back and forth between the two of them, every neurosis I've experienced over the past few months pushing its way through my brain at once. Jake's lips part, but it's Madison who speaks first. My blood turns cold as she wraps long, possessive fingers around his arm.

"I was just congratulating Jake on his performance. I think everyone will be talking about tonight's show for a long, long time." Her voice drips with smugness as she stares at me triumphantly.

I turn to Jake, waiting for an explanation, but he's frozen. My heartbeat thumps against my rib cage like a snare drum.

"Fuck you, Jake." Turning on my heel, I shove past Vinny, who's lingering in the doorway, and race down the hall.

"Lexi, wait!" Jake's desperate voice stretches out from behind me, but I don't stop. I barrel past the musicians and the models and their cigarettes and their stupid skyscraper legs. I keep running through the darkened theater, ignoring the protests of disgruntled audience members, never slowing down until I finally reach the street.

Breathless, I bend forward, hands on my knees as I gasp for breath.

"Lexi, please."

I twist my body to look at Jake, his pained expression blurred by my tears.

"What the hell was that?" I cringe at the sound of my voice, ragged and bordering on hysteria.

"It's not what it looked like. I promise. God, that sounds so cliché, but it's true."

"Really? Because from where I was standing, it looked like Madison St. James had her tongue down your throat."

"Fuck, I know. I swear, I don't know what she was thinking." Jake yanks an exasperated hand through his hair, tugging at it even harder than usual. "I have no idea why she kissed me. But I promise you, there's nothing going on between us. I was just as surprised as you were."

"There's nothing going on between you? You mean tonight, when I had to watch you two practically fornicate onstage? Or do you mean while you were having rooftop champagne together in LA? Or maybe nothing happened some other night when I wasn't around?"

The look of naked hurt etched across Jake's face threatens to crack my heart in half.

"You know I would never do something like that," he says, his voice thick. I can't bear to look at him, so I stare at the ground as I give a slow, resolute shake of my head.

"Face it, Jake. We exist in completely different worlds. Our lives just don't fit together, and they never will. We should end this now, before we hurt each other more than we already have."

Jake takes a step toward me and I can feel the pain radiating from his body.

"I know what you're doing," he says softly. "You're scared and you're trying to push me away. But you're wrong. We're supposed to be together."

A fresh wave of tears floods my vision, and I wipe them away angrily with the back of my hand. Jake takes another step forward, closing the space between us. His hands reach out to cradle my cheeks.

"You are everything to me, Lexi. I *need* you. And I know you need me too."

It's the word "need" that shakes something loose inside me. Pulling his hands off my face, I take a step back, and when I speak again, my voice is cold.

"Haven't you already gotten everything you need from me? You used me for a song, and it got you the career you've always dreamed of. And I'm proud of you, I really am. But I'm also not going to stick around like some idiot until the day you decide we've outgrown each other and it's time to move on to bigger and brighter things."

Jake's entire body seems to collapse upon itself. "That couldn't be further from the truth," he says, his voice ragged. "Lexi, please. You have to know that."

I take a fortifying breath to push past the wedge lodged in my throat. If I'm not careful, I'm going to relent, and I can't let that happen, not before I finish what needs to be done. Taking a breath, I summon the lingering strength I have, mustering the courage to finish this.

"What I *know* is that my life was going exactly the way I wanted before you showed up and torpedoed everything. You make everything about you and expect me to drop everything and go wherever you need me. And I can't do it anymore. I can't let you ruin everything I've worked so hard for."

Jake's eyes narrow, the hurt in his features transforming into anger. Exasperated, he throws his hands up in the air.

"Your *life*? What life? You spend all your time slaving away at a job you hate, and then you go home to an apartment that's a shrine to the past! I'm right here, right now, and I'm not going to let you cut me out of your life just because you're afraid of getting hurt. I'm not going to let you erase me the way you erased your dad."

His voice cracks at the end and it makes my tears fall harder than ever. But now they've turned hot, boiling up with newfound rage.

"Take that back," I say through gritted teeth, my voice quavering.

Jake shakes his head, crossing his arms across his chest.

"You think I ruined your life? Well, let me tell you what I think. I think you've spent years hanging on to this idea of who you're supposed to be, and you want someone to blame for the fact that things aren't going according to the grand life plan you've envisioned for yourself. But the problem isn't me, Lex. It's you. Because the truth is, you aren't that person anymore. You haven't been for a long time."

Fury buzzes in my ears, my chest rising and falling rapidly. The worst thing of all is that through my anger, a small part of me knows what he's saying is true. Even so, I can't do this anymore. Everyone told me that a relationship with Jake would be impossible, and they were right. This is just too hard, too complicated. I need my life to go back to the way it was before he came barreling through it.

"Well, maybe I'm not the person you think I am," I whisper. "But I'm not the only one who's changed, Jake. You're a completely different person than the guy who sang me showtunes in a bar. You've gotten swept up by this world, and I barely even recognize the person you've become. So let's stop pretending this was ever going to work, and call it what it really is. Over."

Through the blur of tears, I see Jake's face fall, but I tear my gaze away. If I stand there for one more minute, I'm going to lose my nerve, so I pivot on my heel, and start walking toward the train station.

"Lexi, wait." Jake's voice trails from behind me, but this time, he doesn't run after me, and I know that it's finally, truly over, and that he'll never be running after me again.

I T'S NEARLY MIDNIGHT WHEN I stumble into my dark apartment. I kick off my shoes, not even bothering to line them up on the mat. The first thing that catches my eye when I flick on the light switch is the framed photo on my entryway table: me, Jake, and Éponine, our arms wrapped around each other as we posed backstage at Les Mis. I'd stopped crying by the time I crawled into the back of my Uber, my tears hardened to cold anger, and now that anger has risen to the surface, threatening to swallow me whole.

Picking up the frame, I hurl it against the wall, reveling in the satisfying crunch of the glass shattering into pieces.

Shuffling to the bathroom, I turn on the bathtub faucet, sinking to my knees as the hot water streams into the tub. I lay my cheek against the cool porcelain tile, listening to the steady hum for several minutes as I wait for the bath to fill. When it's still empty a few minutes later, I realize I never bothered to push down the drain. The revelation brings a fresh flood of tears as I twist off the faucet and curl up in the fetal position on the bathmat.

I'm not sure how long I lay there, my body wracked with sobs, before I finally manage to drag myself up off the floor. When I catch a glimpse of my reflection in the mirror, I hardly recognize the face staring back at me. The combination of limp hair, swollen eyes, and ribbons of black mascara makes me look like a character from a horror movie. I pull the gorgeous dress over my head, leaving it in a puddle on the bathroom floor, and walk into my room.

When I yank open my drawer, the white Hanes undershirt on top is Jake's. Crumbling it in my hand, I think about tossing it into the trash, but ultimately shove it back inside and pull out an old NYU tee. I slide into bed, expecting to spend the rest of the night lying awake. But within minutes, I fall into a deep, dreamless slumber.

MY EYES ARE BURNING as I squint at the cutting board in front of me. My face is still puffy from crying last night, but I couldn't muster the energy to put on any makeup this morning. Mia shot me an alarmed glance when I arrived at work, but graciously chose not to say anything. Even Corbin is quiet, neglecting to comment on the fact that I've been moving at a sloth's pace for the past hour.

"Berman." I look up to see Oren standing in his office door. He's staring hard at me, his expression unreadable. "Chef wants to see you in his office."

My stomach drops to the floor. Blowing out an exhale, I lay down my knife and follow Oren to the office.

When I step through the doorway, I see Chef seated at his desk. He glances up at me over his reading glasses as Oren plops onto a chair, crossing his arms across his chest and staring at an invisible spot on the floor.

"Shut the door," Chef says. With mounting dread, I pull the handle shut and slowly approach the desk. Chef leans back in his chair.

"A kitchen staff is a team," he says quietly. "And a team can only succeed if every member pulls their weight. You've only been here a year, yet you've called out more than any other team member. And when you are here, you're slow and inefficient, leaving everyone to pick up your slack."

A torrent of panic whips through me. This can't be happening.

"I know I've made mistakes, and I truly apologize," I say imploringly. "My behavior has been unprofessional and damaging to the team. But I've made some changes to my life, and I promise, things are going to be different from here on out."

Chef's eyes bore into mine, and I know what's coming next before the words even leave his mouth.

"This isn't working out. We're going to have to let you go."

His words hit me with the force of a train. All the years of hard work and training, gone in an instant. I expect to start crying, but the release of tears never comes. Instead, I feel a hollow numbness mixed with something else. Something that feels suspiciously like relief.

Oren finally drags his eyes off the ground, his expression apologetic.

"I'm sorry, Berman," he says softly. "I tried to warn you: relationships and chef life just don't mix."

He's right, of course, but it's a lesson I learned too late.

"I want to thank you both for the opportunity, for taking a

chance on me." I extend my hand forward and Oren's mouth lifts in the corner as he shakes it.

"Good luck, kid," he says. On the way out the back door, I peek my head into the kitchen. The only person who looks up from their station is Ethan. I can tell by the look on his face that he knows I've been let go, and though he's still hurt, his face is sympathetic. He gives me a brisk nod and I lift my hand in a wave before slipping out through the service doors.

Dark clouds shroud the sky as I step outside. The door slams shut behind me, causing an unexpected gust of cold air that knocks the hard truth into me: for the first time in my life, I have no plan. I think about heading over to The Carlyle to see Ali, but then, as though through divine intervention, my phone buzzes in my handbag. When I see the name flash across the screen, I realize exactly where I need to be.

"Hey, Dad," I say.

25

THE FIRST THING I notice when I step through the automated doors of the Fort Lauderdale airport is the crushingly oppressive heat. Back in New York, the October air has begun to turn crisp. Down here, it feels like I've walked straight into Hadestown.

My armpits dampen instantly as I drag my rolling suitcase down the sidewalk. The minute I see my dad's white Lexus swing around the traffic circle, my heart swells, and I know it's not just from the thought of air-conditioning.

When I climb into the car, Bruce Springsteen is blasting through the speakers. Two Venti-sized Starbucks cups are jammed into the cupholders. Dad leans across the console and hugs me tight.

"Hey, Loo."

My eyes tear up instantly at the sound of my childhood nickname. Before they can spill over, I press my face into his shirt and breathe in his smell, a mix of spearmint mouthwash and cigars. He smells like home. Despite my best efforts, a few tears escape, dampening the front of his shirt. He must notice, because when he pulls back, his clear blue eyes, a mirror image of my own, are filled with concern.

"Everything okay?" He runs his hand over my arm, and I nod, wiping my eyes with my knuckles.

"I'm fine. Just hot, that's all," I say. I turn my head to gaze out the window so I don't have to look at him, because I know without a shadow of a doubt that one look at his worried expression will push me over the edge.

Dad makes a small noise to indicate he's not convinced but decides not to push it. He carefully shifts the car into drive and weaves through the traffic circle, cursing under his breath as a car pulls out unexpectedly in front of him. I can't help but smile at the juxtaposition of his heavy New York accent against the South Florida backdrop. Tension radiates off him as he maneuvers his way out. Even after years of living here, he's still a New Yorker who isn't quite comfortable behind the wheel of a car.

"So," he ventures once we're out on the highway. "Any special reason you decided to come visit your old dad?"

"I missed you. It's been too long," I reply, staring out the window at the flat, dry landscape.

"I missed you too," Dad murmurs, and then turns his attention back to the road. He's always been this way, quieter than Mom, more willing to listen than to be the first one to talk. Usually his technique works, and I feel compelled to fill gaps in conversation, confessing whatever's on my mind. But right now, it's all packed too tightly inside me to unravel. We spend the rest of the thirty-minute drive in comfortable silence, listening to the Boss as I keep my eyes peeled for rogue alligators.

When we pull into the driveway, the late afternoon sun is casting long shadows over the house's pale stucco exterior. I climb out of the car and start up the porch steps as Dad grabs my suitcase out of the trunk. Pushing my way through the front door, I flick on the lights, glancing around the entryway. Everything is largely unchanged since the last time I was here three years ago; it's all peach walls, peach upholstery, and peach decorative vases. Fran truly has the design aesthetic of a mid-90s grandma. Dad comes in behind me, propping my suitcase by the front door and heading into the kitchen.

"Fran is at Panera playing mah-jongg. It's just us," he says. He pulls out a kitchen chair, gesturing for me to sit. Removing his phone from his back pocket, he holds it up questioningly. "Should I call for Chinese?"

I nod happily. It's my favorite type of comfort food, what we always ordered when I felt down as a kid, and a wave of tranquility washes over me. Jake's mom's voice echoes in my head. *Food is love.*

After placing an order, he slides into the kitchen chair across from me, resting his elbows on the table and leaning forward to stare straight into my eyes. It's his no-nonsense lawyer pose, the one he reserved for stern talks when I broke curfew or got a bad grade on a math test.

"All right, enough beating around the bush. I know all about you and that crooner, Jake something or another. I read the tabloids. I know what's going on in the world."

"Oh yeah? Since when do you read tabloids?" Despite the heaviness pressing down on my chest, I can't help but laugh.

Dad throws up his hands in a gesture of exasperation. "Okay, fine, Fran reads them. And I'm pretty sure she's got a thing for your man, by the way, but we can table that one for now."

He gives me a pointed look. "But it's just the two of us here, Loo. Tell me what's going on, and we'll figure something out. Unless, of course, this Casanova hurt my little girl, in which case I will punch his lights out. I mean it. I don't care how famous he is."

The entire story tumbles out of me—how Jake and I first met and how he came back into my life so unexpectedly. How I tried and failed to balance my work schedule and Jake's engagements, and how miserable I felt when I couldn't be there with him. And how, despite my best efforts to juggle it all, I still lost everything. I still got fired from the restaurant. And Jake. *Jake*. It hurts too much to even think about a future without him.

The food arrives and Dad unpacks everything from the soggy brown paper bag, handing me a carton of General Tso's chicken.

My stomach grumbles with anticipation. After all these years, it's still my favorite.

"The worst part is knowing that I let Mom down," I say miserably, as I close my chopsticks around a piece of chicken.

Dad pauses, a hand clutching an egg roll hovering halfway between the paper wrapper and his mouth. "What do you mean?"

"She always said she wished she could have seen me become a Michelin-star chef, that she could have eaten in one of my restaurants. I tried so hard to make it happen, and I just failed." A treacherous tear slides down my cheek and I press it away with my thumb.

"Oh, honey." Dad reaches out to rub my forearm. The kitchen light bounces off the thick gold watch band encircling his hairy wrist. "Mommy was always proud of you. You know that, right? But it wasn't because of your cooking career. It was because of who you are. The loving, caring person you have always been."

I sniffle. "You don't think she'd be disappointed?"

He shakes his head. "Of course not. She didn't care about you becoming a chef in a big restaurant. Not unless that's what you wanted. Cooking isn't about achievement. It's about comfort and taking care of others. That's why you started doing it in the first place, right? To take care of Mommy when she was sick. Food is your love language."

I tilt my head, staring at him in disbelief. "My love language? Who are you?"

Dad barks out a laugh. "Fran might have made me take a couple of those *Cosmopolitan* quizzes." He shakes his head, smiling ruefully. "But really, Loo. The only thing your mom really wanted was for you to be happy. To love and to be loved." He looks across the table, locking his eyes with mine. "Which begs the question. Are you happy?"

Instead of answering, I pick up another piece of chicken and chew it carefully. I might not be ready to admit it out loud, but deep down, I know I haven't been happy for a while now. I thought being a chef was what I wanted, what I needed to do with my life. But it never satisfied my need to nurture, to create. Those urges have been lying dormant inside me and neglecting them has taken its toll.

"Listen, I don't know what happened between you two, but I saw some of those magazine photos, and I've never seen you look happier. Even an old schmuck like me can see how you felt about each other."

"Yeah, well, not all love stories last forever," I mutter. Love. A word I never even managed to say to Jake. Do I love him? But I know the answer to that one without a moment's hesitation. I've known for a long time.

The realization sends a spark through me, igniting the flame of anger that's been slowly simmering for years. And suddenly, it's boiled to the surface.

"Besides, you're hardly qualified to give me a lecture on forever romances. You spent half of your life with Mom, and you don't even seem to care that she's gone."

My face flushes with heat the moment I spit out the angry words. For so long, I've pushed my resentment down, locking it away somewhere deep inside me. But now the dam has burst open, my fury flooding loose.

"You gave up on us, Dad! On both of us. You just packed up and left. You replaced her so fast, it was like she never even mattered. Like neither of us did."

I stare at my feet, too angry to look at him. A long moment passes.

"You're right, Loo," he finally says, quietly. "I did abandon you. It's my greatest regret. I know it's why you've kept me at arm's length all these years. And I know that I probably deserve it. Believe me, I would do anything to take it back."

He lets out a shaky breath.

"But you're wrong about one thing. I could never replace your mother. She was my whole world. When she died, I couldn't even remember how to breathe. And I didn't know how to be alone. The hole she left behind was too big. I needed someone to fill it and to do it fast, because if not, I would have drowned. The problem wasn't that I didn't love her. It was that I loved her so much I didn't know how to live without her."

I finally manage to drag my eyes off the ground and take in his crumbled form. His eyes are shining, and I realize it's only the second time in my life I've seen my dad cry. Immediately, the walls that I've built up inside me come crashing down. For so long, I've felt like I mourned my mom alone, while my dad picked up and moved on with his life. Now I can see that we were both drowning in our grief. We just did it in our own ways.

Rising from my chair, I fling my arms around his neck, burying my face in his chest. For a moment, he seems startled. Then his arms tighten around me, drawing me close. We stay like that for a long time, and I feel like a little girl again as he comforts me, stroking my hair.

Just then, I hear the creak of a door opening. Turning, I see Fran standing in the doorway, car keys clutched tightly in her French-manicured hand. She glances back and forth quickly between me and my dad, her expression uncertain.

"I hope I'm not interrupting," she says quickly. "I just wanted to see Lexi before she turned in for the night." She gives me a cautious smile and for the first time, I see Fran in a new light. She'd wanted kids with her first husband, but wasn't able to have them, and I think she's always hoped she could be a proxy mother figure to me. But I've steadfastly kept my distance, shooting her down every time she's offered to spend time with me. Yet no matter how badly I've treated her, or how often I've rebuffed her attempts to forge a relationship, she's never given up on me. She's never stopped trying. It wasn't until this moment that I realized how lucky I am to have so many people in my life with unwavering faith in me.

"Hi, Fran," I say, offering her a small smile. "I was thinking . . . maybe we could get a manicure tomorrow?"

Fran's face lights up. "Oh, Lexi," she says, and her entire body softens. "I would love that."

That night, I sleep in the guest bedroom that Dad and Fran have always kept for me, despite how infrequently I visit. After changing into a T-shirt and boxer shorts, I slip into the double bed, pulling the pink quilt up to my chin and doing my best to ignore the humidity that creeps through the window despite the eternally running AC.

When I close my eyes, Dad's words echo in my head. *It's not about achievement, it's about comfort. Food is your love language.*

And just like that, inspiration strikes.

26

TWO MONTHS LATER

DAMN IT, I'VE LOST the edge of the tape again. Biting my bottom lip in concentration, I slide the edge of my thumbnail beneath the sticky surface. I'm cross-legged on my bedroom floor, surrounded by cardboard boxes as I pack up the last of my mother's clothes to give to charity.

When I first moved into my parents' bedroom a few years ago, I took her clothes from their closet and stuffed them into my much smaller one. Back then, getting rid of her things felt like a betrayal. Like I was letting her go. But now, the timing feels right. I find the edge and lift the sticky film, then use it to close another box.

In the end, I kept three things: her wedding dress, her treasured leather briefcase, and her favorite blue sweater, the one she wore on repeat toward the end, when she was skin and bones, and almost always cold. I run my thumb over the cotton, pilled from so many washes, and press it to my nose. Time has erased any lingering trace of her smell, but the familiar fabric is still comforting.

As much as Jake's words hurt, I couldn't ignore the kernel of truth buried within them. I have unintentionally made the apartment a shrine to my lost family. It's time to let go of the life I once had and make a home of my own.

So, with Dad's blessing, I listed the apartment. Given its amenities and prime location, it sold within a week, and I used the profits to pay off the rest of my student debts in full, with plenty left over for my next venture. In four days, I'll be moving in with Chloe until my one-bedroom rental in Cobble Hill is ready in February.

My buzzing doorbell startles me, and Jake's face flashes briefly through my mind. I brush the thought away. I don't let myself think about him, not anymore.

In the days following our breakup, he called and texted every day, filling my voicemail box with messages. I deleted each one without listening and erased all the old ones, so I wouldn't be tempted to torture myself. He didn't give up, of course. My phone buzzed for four days straight, until finally, I blocked his number and deleted his contact info. It's what we needed: a clean break.

Even so, I couldn't bring myself to erase my photos of him. What we shared might be over, but I can't pretend it never happened.

The doorbell rings again. I drop the sweater onto the bed and head down the hallway. When I pull the door open, I feel only the faintest tinge of disappointment to see a different familiar face on the other side.

"Hey, thanks for coming." I step aside to let Mia in. Her eyes widen as they drift around the living room, which is covered floor to ceiling in moving boxes. She pauses when she spots a lone unpacked object on my bookshelf.

"What's with the mallard?"

"Oh, that. I haven't quite decided what to do with it yet."

She stares at me for a long moment, then steps into the kitchen and surveys the messy countertop.

"Looks like you've been busy," she says. It's the first time I've ever heard her sound impressed.

"Yeah, I've been recipe testing at all hours." I head into the kitchen and grab my notebook from the cluttered countertop. "But I think I've settled on at least three dishes."

Once the sting of losing my job at Olive & Pomegranate wore off, I spent some time thinking about what I wanted to do next. Getting fired was a setback, but it didn't have to ruin my plans entirely. I could have updated my résumé and started looking for a new restaurant job. I could have spent the next ten years pursuing my dream, working my way up the food chain until an executive chef position opened.

But the more I thought about it, the more I dreaded filling out applications. Because as hard as it was to admit to myself, Jake was right. My dreams have changed. Yes, I love cooking. But it's never really been just about the food. It's about taking care of people. And that's when it all clicked into place.

A La Heart will be a gift service that allows customers to send comfort-food care packages to loved ones. During my flight home from Florida, I sketched out my preliminary business plan on a drink napkin. Selling the apartment took care of seed money for startup costs, and Chloe volunteered to help with marketing. But when Mia texted me a few days ago to say she'd quit her job at the restaurant, I knew bringing her on as my business partner was the final piece of the puzzle.

We're starting off with three boxes: Flu Fighters, stocked with the matzah ball soup recipe I finally mastered; Comfort Food Rx, containing bite-sized portions of the Johannsson Special; and Tastes Like Home, which includes an individual portion of Southern macaroni and cheese casserole.

Mia shoves my notebook aside to set down the small blue cooler she's been carrying. She extracts a small, square Tupperware and pops off the lid with a flourish.

"My mother's famous empanadas," she says, her chest puffing with pride.

I dig in with a fork, closing my eyes as my tongue rolls over a bite of savory beef and crispy dough.

"These are incredible," I declare, and Mia beams. "Which box are you thinking? Tastes Like Home?"

"What if we added one more?" She looks at me carefully. "The Mom Box."

Emotion beats against my rib cage like a set of butterfly wings. I bite my bottom lip, blinking back tears.

"It's perfect," I finally manage.

Mia tilts her head and gives me a searching look.

"So," she says, and I can tell by her shift in tone we're about to enter a less comfortable territory of conversation. "How have you been?"

"Fine," I reply, probably too quickly. "Really, I'm okay."

Mia nods but doesn't say anything. I ramble on, filling the silence.

"I mean, am I grateful I've been too busy with A La Heart to check social media or go to the grocery store and hear one of Jake's songs blasting through the speakers? Of course. But I'm fine. Really. I made the right decision. This is all for the best."

She nods slowly, graciously choosing not to point out how many times I used the word "fine" in under a minute. I let out a relieved breath. *Maybe she'll let this go,* I think. But I'm not that lucky.

"Do you still have feelings for him?"

My chest tightens. "Yeah, of course. I probably always will."

Mia shoots me a look of utter exasperation.

"What?" I ask.

"Then what is the issue? Why aren't you with him?"

"Because feelings aren't enough!" I didn't mean to yell, but being Mia, she doesn't even flinch. She just continues staring me down with eyes that say, *You might just be the biggest idiot in the history of idiots.*

"It was never going to work out," I go on. "He belongs in his world, and I belong in mine. We're like Romeo and Juliet, except I'm not as hot as Claire Danes and he's way hotter than Leo, and we don't have a Baz Luhrmann soundtrack. I'm just cutting my losses so I don't end up with a dagger in my chest."

Mia purses her lips. "Hmm."

"What is 'hmm'?"

"Well, if it was all so inevitable, I guess you won't be at all interested in this." She reaches into her backpack and withdraws a rolled-up magazine. She drops it on the countertop, its glossy surface reflecting the overhead lights.

"What's this?" I ask timidly.

She shrugs. "Just something that caught my eye at the bodega this morning." She straightens, readjusting her backpack straps. "I'm heading out. See you tomorrow?"

I nod wordlessly as she navigates the maze of brown boxes to find her way back to the door. It's only when I hear it shut behind her that I bring myself to look at the cover.

Half a dozen famous faces are splattered across the page, but I immediately zero in on a familiar pair of milk-chocolate eyes. The photo is of him and Madison onstage, with a rip down the middle. "Jake and Madison: It's Over!" the caption screams.

I shouldn't do it. I know I shouldn't. I've come so far and reading this will only set me back. Without bothering to open it, I toss the magazine into my recycling bin. I feel a mixture of pride and contentment at my own restraint.

There, it's done. This was exactly the closure I needed.

With a renewed sense of lightness, I begin straightening up. I'm just getting ready to wipe down the counters when the doorbell rings again.

"Coming!" I call, weaving through the path of boxes. Mia must have forgotten something.

But when I pull the door open, it's not Mia's sardonic expression staring back at me. Instead, it's an annoyingly perfect one, framed by a thick fringe of false lashes and crimson hair. Standing on the other side of my door, dressed incredibly inappropriately for the December weather in a floral-print dress and studded white booties, is none other than Madison St. James.

"What the hell are *you* doing here?" I ask icily.

Madison rolls her heavily made-up eyes. "I came to talk to you. Obviously."

"How do you even know where I live?" *And why,* I wonder to myself, *did Lionel let her up here without buzzing?* Honestly, I could really do without his editorializing.

Madison tosses her hair over one shoulder and huffs out an impatient sigh, like she can't believe I'm wasting her time with such a ridiculous question.

I lift my chin. "You know what? I think I'll pass." I try to swing the door shut, but Madison extends her arm, pressing her palm against it.

"Lexi, please."

Now it's my turn to sigh. I wish I had the willpower to slam the door in her face. But at this point, curiosity has gotten the best of me.

"Fine." I open the door just wide enough for her to slip through. "You have five minutes."

Madison slips past me. Her expression curdles with distaste as she surveys the stacks of moving boxes. "Charming little place you've got here."

"What do you want, Madison?"

"Can I sit?" When I glare at her instead of answering, she struts over to my sofa. She perches right on the edge, putting as little of her body as possible on the cushion, like she's worried about contracting a communal disease from my furniture. Her fingers tighten around the handle of her pink Celine bag as if drawing strength from its designer properties.

"Look," she says. "I came here to apologize for what went down between me and Jake. It was very uncool of me to pull a Baroness Schraeder on you."

I blink at her. "Excuse me?"

She rolls her eyes impatiently. "You know. Trying to gaslight you into breaking up with the man we both love." For a long moment, I stare at her disbelievingly, and it occurs to me that under a different set of circumstances, I might actually like this woman.

Madison stares back at me through her lash extensions, and for once, her expression is devoid of confidence, filled instead with genuine remorse.

"What I did was wrong. I never should have kissed him."

"You got that right." I gesture toward the door. "Well, you've done your due diligence. Now you can head off to goat yoga with a clear conscience. Goodbye, Madison."

"Will you stop being so stubborn and listen?" Madison's voice, now devoid of all pretenses, rises an octave. "It's not what you think. I only kissed him because I thought that's what he wanted."

My eyes narrow. "Why on earth would you think that?"

Madison's gaze shifts to her lap as she twists a finger around one long, red lock. When she speaks again, her voice is softer.

"Because that's what Vinny told me."

"He . . . what?"

"I'm not even sure why I believed him. Anyone with half a brain cell can see Jake only has eyes for you. I guess . . . well, I guess I *wanted* to believe it. Because I was maybe, kinda, you know, like . . . jealous."

I scrunch my forehead, trying to make sense of what she's telling me. "What are you talking about?"

Madison rolls her eyes again. "Look, *clearly* I don't have any trouble finding men. I've made a whole career writing songs about them. Songs that happen to be masterful, award-winning works of art that Billboard once described as 'permanently embedded in the cultural lexicon.'" One corner of her mouth ticks upward and I can practically see her mind's eye taking inventory of her Grammy collection. Then she blinks a few times and straightens in her seat.

"But Jake is not like other guys. Especially not the ones in the industry. He doesn't have a list of acceptable color schemes for his dressing rooms. He'd never contractually banned an employee from making eye contact or refused to go into a recording studio before its aura was cleansed. Once, when we were on tour, he stopped the show mid-song because a little girl in the front row was covering her ears and he was worried the music was too loud for her! Who does that?! Do you know who the first person on his speed dial is? His *mom*. I mean, *god*! I'd kill to be with someone as pure as him."

She levels her gaze at me. "I've had this body since I was twelve years old, which means I've been getting attention from men since middle school. Never once have they ever seen me for anything besides princess hair and a great set of tits. Once I got famous, I was also a meal ticket and a magnet for spotlight hunters. Even my ex, Oliver, was only interested in me when the cameras were around." Her mouth turns downward. "But Jake is different. He was the first guy who ever treated me like a person, like he really saw me. And I so desperately wanted to be with someone like that, even though he was already taken, because he's one of the best people I've ever met. And *you* would be a complete moron to let him go."

I cross my arms. "Yeah? Well, it's a little late for that."

Madison continues as if she hasn't heard me. "I was so enamored by him that I let myself get completely blinded to what was happening right in front of me. After so many years in the business, I'm kind of embarrassed I didn't realize sooner that Vinny was playing us. Not only was he lying to me about Jake, but he was also tipping off the paparazzi whenever he knew we'd be in the same place. He even hired a photographer to follow us around Shawn Mendes's party so the press could get a photo of us together. I guess he figured rekindling rumors about our relationship would drum up publicity for the concert and Jake's new album. He knew Jake would never go for it, so he did it behind his back. But obviously, that backfired spectacularly."

"What do you mean?"

Madison squints at me. "Once I figured out what Vinny was up to, I told Jake everything. He fired Vinny on the spot. Didn't he tell you?"

"No. I haven't been taking his calls."

She nods, pursing her meticulously painted red lips. "Hmm."

"What is 'hmm'?"

"I haven't seen Jake in weeks. No one has. I heard he's been holed up in his hotel room. Now I know why." She shakes her head slowly. "For reasons I'll never understand, that boy is head over heels in love with you." Her tone is as condescending as ever, but there's a tiny smile playing in the corner of her lips. "Anyway, I thought you should know the truth. Because if someone as amazing as Jake Taylor likes you, you must be a pretty decent human being, too."

Madison stands up, brushing an invisible speck of dust off her dress.

"Well." She sniffs. "I'd better get going. My driver is parked out front, and that bootleg bodyguard you call a doorman threatened to call the police if I wasn't back downstairs in ten minutes."

Despite the hurricane of emotions barreling through my chest, I can't help but smile. Lionel truly is one of a kind.

Madison slips on a pair of dark sunglasses and makes an exaggerated display of sashaying through the boxes. After stepping through the doorway, she turns back to look at me.

"Just think about what I said, okay?"

Then she pulls the door shut, leaving me behind in a cloud of perfume to sort through a jumble of feelings growing more complicated by the minute.

Well. There goes my fucking closure.

27

ONE OF THE THINGS I was most looking forward to as a career chef was never needing to make New Year's Eve plans again. It's my least favorite holiday, one that's laden with entirely too much pressure and an expectation to stay up way later than I prefer to. If I were still gainfully employed, I would have had a perfect excuse to get out of plans: Olive & Pomegranate is famous for their New Year's Eve parties, which feature a four-course dinner menu, a live countdown, and even a champagne toast. Unfortunately, I now have no excuse to turn down Chloe's invitation to her friend Luca's New Year's Eve party. Luckily, I've convinced Mia to come with me, on the promise of free booze.

It's nearly quarter to ten when we arrive at Luca's Chelsea apartment. Mia's dressed in her usual jeans and leather jacket, and I'm wearing the same thigh-skimming black dress I pull out of my closet every New Year's Eve. Ali hasn't arrived yet, so I'm relieved when Chloe, the only other person I'll know here, is waiting for me by the door when I arrive. She looks as stunning as always, wearing a silver sequin wrap dress paired with delicate strappy heels, and clutching a vodka soda in her manicured hand.

"Hey, babe," she says, leaning in for a cheek kiss. "I'm so glad you came. And look, you got a manicure!" She lifts my right hand in hers to study the glossy red polish. My heart swells with a mix of emotions as I follow her gaze. I nearly lost my nerve the first time I stepped through Diva Darlings' glass doors, the smell of acetone immediately flooding my chest with memories of my mom. But as the weeks have gone on, being there has made me feel closer to her; best of all, my weekly appointments have helped me kick my nail-biting habit once and for all.

"Chloe, this is Mia. Mia, Chloe."

Chloe shifts her attention to Mia. Her eyes widen, and her cheeks flush pink. "I'm sorry. *You're* Mia?"

Mia smirks, her eyes taking a leisurely perusal of Chloe's dress. "In the flesh, baby."

The two of them stare at each other for a few moments before I clear my throat.

"Oh, right." Chloe's voice is uncharacteristically flustered. "Come in, I'll introduce you to everyone."

Mia excuses herself to get a drink while Chloe links her arm through mine and swings me around the room, occasionally peeking over her shoulder to sneak covert glances at Mia. She introduces me to our host, Luca, who I learn is a PR assistant at Tory Burch.

Luca's mouth droops into a frown as he looks me up and down.

"Honey, I didn't think it was possible, but your outfit is suffering from depression," he declares.

"Babe! Remember what I told you? We're not discussing Lexi's outfit or her sadness this evening, because this is a *happy* occasion, and she has just been through a rough time, remember?" Chloe's voice is imploring at the end, and Luca's face changes as he registers that I'm *that* sad friend. Straightening, he attempts to recalibrate, his eyes blinking rapidly behind his clear Warby Parker frames.

"Oh, right. Of course!" he says. "Let me get you a glass of champagne." For the next half an hour, I try my best to socialize, but it's hard to summon the energy. Mia and Chloe are chatting animatedly by the bar, and I don't know anyone else here. By ten thirty,

I'm slouched in the corner of Luca's black leather sofa, taking hearty swallows from the bottle of tequila I grabbed off the bar and engaging in a stare-down with his creepy, hairless chihuahua.

One of the other guests, a tall guy with a thick, auburn beard and a man bun, darts in front of the sofa, grabbing the remote off the coffee table and shouting something about not wanting to miss Olivia Rodrigo's performance on *New Year's Rockin' Eve*. When the image of Times Square fills the screen a few seconds later, my heart skips a beat. I try and reassure myself that I probably missed Jake's performance—after all, the show started two hours ago—but then the camera pans back to the stage, and there he is, sandwiched between Seacrest and his cohost, Trixie, the star of some new Freeform show about vampire sorority girls.

Seacrest is, of course, beaming. "Welcome back to *New Year's Rockin' Eve!*" he declares, as Trixie bounces up and down, blowing on her gloved hands and rubbing them together. "We're coming to you live from Times Square, where we're joined by one of this year's hottest musical sensations, Jake Taylor!"

It's been two months since I've seen Jake, and the very first thing I notice is how sad his eyes look. It's a detail that's probably imperceptible to anyone else—in his skinny dark jeans, white tee, and brown leather jacket, he's a portrait of the perfect pop-rock star. He's smiling, but it's his polite TV smile, the one that doesn't reach his eyes. Nothing more than a mask. His dimple lies dormant in his cheek and his chocolate-brown eyes are flat, with no trace of their usual luster. He's doing his best to hold it together for the cameras, but I see right through the act. I feel a sharp pang of sympathy and hate myself for it.

Seacrest is bundled up in a black coat, plaid scarf, and earmuffs, but Jake's only protection against the chill is a navy beanie and gloves. Poor Jake. He hates the cold. If it were up to him, he'd be up onstage wrapped in a down comforter. The man just isn't built for New York weather.

"So, Jake. It's been an epic year for you, man. We're all looking forward to hearing you sing for us tonight."

Jake's smile evaporates. He drops his gaze to the ground, nodding.

"Yeah," he replies tersely.

A long, uncomfortable beat stretches between them, and Seacrest clears his throat awkwardly. "Well folks, we're going to take a quick commercial break, but stay tuned, because when we come back, Jake Taylor will be performing live!"

"Hey!" Ali's familiar voice cuts through the crowd, her petite body shuffling through the throng of bodies. "Somebody turn that off! We've got a woman with a broken heart over here! What are you trying to do, give her a stroke?" She grabs the remote and clicks off the TV, an action that's met by an angry murmur from the crowd.

Man Bun picks up the remote and glares at us as he clicks the TV back on.

"I *said* I want to hear Olivia," he says through gritted teeth.

Ali shoots me a helpless look, but I wave her off.

"I'm fine!" I say, somewhat surprised when I hear myself slurring. I guess I drank more tequila than I thought. "Totally and completely fine."

She raises one eyebrow skeptically. "Are you sure about that? Because from where I'm standing, you look like Dr. Evil." Her eyes shift downward. The chihuahua has found its way into my lap. Even worse, it seems I have unconsciously begun stroking it.

I shrug, then take another swig. "You, of all people, shouldn't be judgmental about my new boyfriend."

"Rude, yet merited." Ali takes the tequila bottle out of my hand, placing it down on the sofa table, and sits down beside me. "Listen, if you're seriously going to watch this, then I'm going to be right here by your side."

"Us too." Chloe and Mia materialize in front of us. Mia's holding a beer and Chloe's clutching two glasses of champagne. She hands one to Ali and then sits down on my other side, slipping a hand through mine.

"You are not alone, okay? I promise you; you will never be alone."

A second later, the commercial break has ended, and Seacrest's face fills the screen again.

"Welcome back, everyone! We're live at Times Square for *New Year's Rockin' Eve!*" The crowd explodes in applause. "Ladies and gentlemen, here to perform his smash hit, 'Blueberry,' the one and only Jake Taylor!"

The camera pans to Jake, who is standing behind a microphone. He takes a step closer, wrapping his fingers around the base, and I inhale sharply as I brace myself to hear his voice. I think I fell in love with Jake the very first time I heard him sing, and despite everything that's happened between us, my feelings for him haven't faded a decimal. I know perfectly well that no matter how hard I try to convince myself that things are over between us, my body will betray the lie the moment I hear him sing the words he wrote for me. I straighten my shoulders and blow out an exhale, resigning myself to my fate. But before his band can start playing, Jake presses his lips to the microphone and clears his throat.

"Actually, there's been a slight change in plans." He's staring directly into the camera and somehow, it feels like he's looking right at me. A shiver runs down my spine.

"I recently lost someone incredibly important to me. The world may know her as the girl in the love song, but man, she's so much more than that. She's brilliant, and cool, and funny. An insanely talented chef. Basically the most amazing person I've ever met. She knew me before all of this"—he sweeps out an arm, gesturing to the crowd—"when I was just a nobody in a dive bar, and no matter how much my life changed, she never looked at me any differently. The truth is, she saved me. When I was at my lowest point, she took me by the hand and pulled me out of the darkness. She reminded me of the person I really am, even when I couldn't see it for myself."

The crowd has gone completely silent, hanging on to his every word. Hundreds of audience members are holding up their phones to record his speech.

Jake continues, his voice growing firmer, more resolute. "I've made so many mistakes. I've done things I'm not proud of, and forgotten about what really matters. I forgot why I fell in love with music in the first place. Worst of all, I neglected the people who matter most. I didn't appreciate her enough, not until it was too late. But that ends now. I'm making some changes in my life, and I'm prepared to spend the rest of my days trying to become the man she deserves.

"So tonight, I'm going to play a different song. A far more important one. Because the truth is, none of my songs, especially 'Blueberry,' would have been possible without this one."

He turns and nods to the drummer, who rests his sticks down. Suddenly, it's clear that there will be no backing band.

The audience grows quiet. After a beat, Jake runs his thumb over the guitar strings. When the familiar chords waft through the TV screen, an invisible hand tightens around my heart.

"Isn't this that song from *The Music Man*? 'Till There Was You'?" Man Bun asks no one in particular, and someone murmurs in agreement.

Beside me, I hear Ali take a sharp breath, but I can't tear my eyes away from Jake. I feel exactly like the first time I heard him sing—completely under his spell. Listening to him feels oddly nostalgic; for the first time in a long time, I feel like I'm home.

After he delivers the final note, he reaches up, brushing a tear from his eye with the heel of his hand. The audience is quiet at first, then slowly breaks into scattered applause. The camera pans back to Seacrest, who clears his throat nervously.

"Wow, that was . . . um . . ."

"That was *heartbreaking,*" Trixie finishes for him. She's dabbing the corners of her eyes with one gloved finger, careful not to smudge her winged eyeliner. Ryan opens his mouth like he's about to correct her, but then closes it, nodding in concession.

"We're going to take a quick break, but when we come back, Olivia Rodrigo will take the stage! Stay tuned and, uh . . . maybe call your ex."

Even when the program switches to a commercial, I can't tear my eyes from the screen. I don't even realize I'm crying until I feel the warm wetness of a tear slip down the side of my cheek. Jolted back into reality, I realize the entire room has gone silent, save for the quiet whimpering of Man Bun.

"Did I . . . did I make a mistake?" I ask quietly to no one in particular. Chloe shifts her body beside me but doesn't respond. Man Bun mutters something under his breath, then takes a sip of his beer. Even Ali is quiet for once. It's Mia who finally speaks up.

"Yeah, dude! You made a *huge* mistake!"

"Mia!" Chloe chides her.

"What? We're all thinking it!"

I bury my face in my hands. "Oh my god, what have I done? I need to talk to him." I yank my phone out of my purse and click on my home screen. Just then, a panicky realization pops into the forefront of my mind.

"*Shit,* I deleted his number. And he's leaving tomorrow for his tour!" I stare down at my phone helplessly as I try to work out what to do next. But only one solution comes to mind. I stare at my two best friends imploringly.

"You guys . . . we have to go over there."

Chloe arches an expertly penciled eyebrow. "Over *where*? I know you don't mean over to Times Square."

When I stare back at her in silent confirmation, she shakes her head resolutely. "No, absolutely not. There is no way in hell I'm going to Times Square on New Year's Eve."

"*Please.* I can't do this by myself." I flick my eyes back and forth between Ali and Chloe, knowing perfectly well which one of them will crack first. And I'm not disappointed.

"You heard her; let's do this!" Ali claps her hands together as Chloe groans. Ali laughs, nudging Chloe with her elbow. "Come on, Chlo: You really want to be the person who stands in the way of true love?"

"Fine," she concedes. "But we need a plan. How exactly are we going to get there? The trains are a mess and there's no way in hell we'll be able to get a cab this close to midnight."

"We need someone to drive us," Mia says. She wrinkles her forehead. "Do you guys know anyone in the city who has a car?"

A beat passes and then Chloe lets out a low groan. "As a matter of fact," she says, "I do."

28

TWENTY MINUTES LATER, THE four of us are huddled together beneath the awning outside of my apartment, our breath clumping together to form a white mist in the cold night air. I'm beyond jittery, my earlier drunkenness now replaced by restless energy as I bounce up and down on the balls of my feet. I'm about to ask Chloe about her mysterious ride for a third time in under five minutes when I hear a cacophonous rumble approaching. A moment later, a neon-yellow Hummer H2 barrels up the street toward us.

"Jesus Christ," Mia mumbles under her breath. "What kind of asshat drives a Hummer in New York City?"

Chloe lets out a resigned sigh. "That," she replies, "would be our asshat."

The truck slows to a stop. The window rolls down and the overwhelming stench of AXE body spray seeps out. The spiky blond hair that follows confirms the worst-case scenario has come to fruition. Briefly, I consider how dangerous it would be to hop into a complete stranger's car and ask for a ride instead. Sure, the evening might end with my dismembered body parts scattered across the Hudson River. But on the other hand . . .

"Hey, ladies," Chad says, and then he literally *winks* at us. "Heard there were three damsels seeking a knight in shining armor."

Chloe groans. "If that were the case, I definitely called the wrong number."

Chad flashes his irritatingly attractive dimples and jerks back his thumb, gesturing for us to climb in.

"Who's the Lifetime movie villain?" Mia asks as she slides into the back seat beside me.

Chad reaches into the back seat and extends a hand. "Chad Campbell. Part-time bachelor, part-time DJ, and full-time engineer of the female orgasm."

"What the hell is wrong with you?" Chloe asks him as she clips her seat belt. "You're on a probationary license, and you're cruising around New York City in the world's most ostentatious automobile? Is your masculinity really that fragile?"

Chad opens his mouth, but she holds up a hand before he can respond.

"You know what? I don't have time to unpack this with you right now. We need to get to Times Square."

Ali pokes her head into the front seat. "For what it's worth, Chad, I think it was completely unfair for Distractify to rank you the third worst bachelor of all time. Clayton Marsh was number five and he literally *vomited* on Emily H. during the final rose ceremony."

"Thank you!" Chad punches a fist through the air and grins at Chloe victoriously.

She rolls her eyes. "Yeah, you're basically our generation's Clark Gable. Can we go now?"

"How about some driving music? You ladies want to hear my new set list?"

"Absolutely fucking not, Chad," Chloe says, swatting his hand away from the speaker. Chad shrugs. Then he throws the car into drive and we're off, weaving our way through the dark streets.

"Take a right here at West Thirty-Second," Chloe says, holding up her phone. "Waze is saying we should take Sixth Avenue toward

Bryant Park." We make our way down Seventh Avenue until the car slows and then comes to a complete stop.

"Uh-oh," Chad says.

"What? What's going on?" I ask, craning my neck to peer through the front windshield.

Chad squints. "There are parked cars on either side of the street, and I don't think I can get through. It's too tight for me to fit." He barks out a laugh. "Ha! That's the second time I've said that to a woman tonight."

Chloe pinches the bridge of her nose. "You are literally the worst human being on the planet."

Heart thumping, I glance at the dashboard clock.

"It's already 11:27. We're never going to make it!" My thumb reflexively slides toward my mouth, but I lower it before my nail can find its way inside.

No more nail biting, I remind myself. My nerves find other ways to escape my body, however; my knees are bouncing so vigorously that Ali leans over to put a hand on my shoulder.

"You need to calm down," she says. "Seriously, you're making me nervous."

I bite down on my lip. "How far away are we?"

Chloe peers down at her phone again, brow furrowing. "About ten blocks."

I take a deep breath. Decision made, I unclip my seat belt.

"All right. I'm going to make a run for it."

"Are you serious?" Mia's eyebrows shoot up, but I've already opened the door.

"It's the only way I'm going to get there in time. You guys coming?"

Chloe looks down at her strappy high heels and sighs. "My brand new Aquazzuras," she says mournfully. "They're going to be completely destroyed."

"And that's why I never wear high heels," Ali says, lifting one foot to show off her Air Force 1 sneakers. "You never know when you're going to be chasing a celebrity through New York City!"

"Well, guess I'm off to Shia LaBeouf's party," Chad says, revving his engine.

"You're still banned from the Rainbow Room, Chad," Chloe reminds him. "For god's sake, do humanity a favor and spend the rest of your night alone in a hotel room." She steps out of the car, but before she closes the door behind her, she ducks her head back in and lets out a begrudging sigh. "Thanks for coming through for us tonight," she tells him. "You did good."

Chad positively beams at her as he scrubs a hand through his hair. "Anything for you, Chlo-money. And listen, if you're free later, maybe we can—"

Chloe holds up a hand to stop him. "Still gay, Chad. And still not interested in your offer to be 'the stallion who flips me.' And for the love of god, don't even *think* of calling me before Monday."

And with that, we throw open the doors of Chad's car and spill out into the street.

We race down the busy sidewalks, shoving past hollering tourists and drunk teenagers and an off-brand Elmo who reeks of bourbon until we come to a halt in front of an enormous crowd. The entire street is blocked off by wooden barricades, guarded by a dozen police officers on horses.

"Now what? How are we going to get through?" I pant, my chest heaving with exertion.

"Let me handle this," Chloe says, squaring her shoulders. We shove our way through the crowd until we're standing in front of two policemen.

"Excuse me, Officers," Chloe says, putting on her most professional, boss-bitch voice. "My friend needs to talk to her boyfriend, Jake Taylor. He's performing at the *Rockin' New Year's Eve* show. Can you kindly let us through?"

The officers look at each other for a moment before throwing their heads back in laughter.

"Lady, do you have any idea how many girls have told me they're Jake Taylor's girlfriend tonight?" one of them guffaws.

"Yeah, but Lexi really *is* his girlfriend," Chloe counters, taking me by the shoulder and shoving me forward a bit. It's clear by the edge in her voice that she's losing patience, and probably also circulation in her feet.

One of the officers, who is inexplicably wearing sunglasses at night, lifts one corner of his mustachioed mouth in amusement.

"Well, riddle me this: If you're Jake Taylor's girlfriend, then why aren't you at the show *with* him?"

"Because"—Ali steps forward to stand in front of us—"they broke up! Which was a huge mistake, *obviously,* completely perpetuated by unfair pressures of celebrity and social media. I mean, honestly, how do you not recognize her? Do you not follow E! News?!"

Sunglasses lowers his shades to look at me. "Wait a second. Are you the girl from that photo at the ice cream shop?"

His partner claps his hands together and then points at me. "Yes! I told my wife, they ain't having no fight! That dude is just sneezing!"

"Exactly!" Ali agrees. "See, you understand. The media just twists everything, you know?"

Sunglasses nods his head. "Okay, lady, I'll let you through, but I can't let all of you in. Just three."

Mia nods. "This is where I leave you guys." She turns to Chloe, then grabs her by the waist, dipping her backward and smashing their lips together. When Chloe rights herself a minute later, her face is flushed.

"Right, then. Shall we?"

Nodding, I turn back to Ali. "You ready?"

Ali nods. Chloe straightens her shoulders and lifts her chin resolutely.

"Let's do this." For a moment, I stand there, staring at my two best friends in the world. There's a new trio of Musketeers now, and there's not a chance I'll ever let them go.

The officers pull the barricade aside and we slip through, weaving our way through the crowd. The music is growing louder, the streets filled with the sound of whistles and the flash of multicolored lights. A huge billboard advertising JLo Beauty blinks above us. Up ahead, I can hear the bass music of the current musical act pumping through the speakers.

Then, I spot the ball, its illuminated star pattern twinkling against the night sky. I stop in my tracks and stand there for a moment, staring up at it. As a kid growing up in New York City, all I ever wanted was to see the New Year's Eve ball. Somehow, it seems fitting that it's Jake who finally made this dream a reality.

Chloe's hand slips through the crook of my elbow, shaking me from my daydream.

"Come on, we need to move," she says urgently. She hooks her other arm through Ali's, then pulls us through the crowd, shoving past the North Face–clad bodies, until somehow, we make our way to the very front of the barricade.

We're standing to the right of the stage. Ryan is in the center, surrounded by the evening's performers. My heart catches in my throat as I spot Jake. He's staring listlessly into the crowd, looking more morose than ever. I scream his name, but it gets drowned out by the surrounding noise.

"We've got about five minutes left until the new year!" Ryan cries gleefully into his handheld mike. "Let's head down to Trixie. Trixie, what's going on with you?"

On the huge screen behind Ryan's head, I see Trixie standing in the crowd, surrounded by a group of vaguely familiar-looking men.

"I've got the Backstreet Boys here with me!" Trixie squeals, gesturing excitedly toward the band as if she has any idea who they are. She turns to Brian, who looks slightly startled when she shoves the microphone in his face. "Do you want to give anyone a special shout-out before the ball drops?" Behind him, a group of teenage girls are jumping up and down, holding handwritten signs that say, "We love you, Jake Taylor!"

"That's it!" Ali hisses. "We need to get behind Trixie so we're on camera. It's the only way Jake's going to be able to see you." Together, we shift through the crowd again, shoving up against the teens with the signs.

"Hey, watch it! This is our spot!" one of them huffs as Chloe tries to elbow her way past them.

Chloe whips out her clutch and opens her wallet.

"How about this? I'll give you a hundred for your spots," she says, holding up a few crisp twenties.

One of the girls cackles. "A hundred dollars? My friends are making three times that much to babysit tonight! I don't think so."

I step forward, pulling out my phone. "I used to date Jake Taylor," I say. "And if you give us your spots, I will give you his cell phone number." The shortest of the girls raises her eyebrows skeptically. Between her dark curls and sassy attitude, it's like going head-to-head with a miniature Ali.

"Oh yeah?" she scoffs. "Prove it."

I click open my phone and pull up a photo of me and Jake at the karaoke bar in Atlanta. All four of their mouths drop open.

Little Ali nods eagerly. "Uh, *deal*," she says. She holds out her phone and I punch in a number before handing it back to her. The girls giggle as they scurry off into the crowd.

"Wait a second," Chloe says, her face a mask of confusion. "I thought you deleted Jake's number?"

I shoot her a tiny smile. "I did. I gave them Vinny's."

Chloe stares at me for a long second, a slow grin spreading across her face. "I have never been prouder of you," she says with admiration. She wraps an arm around my shoulder as Seacrest's voice blasts through the speakers, shattering the moment.

"Twenty seconds left!" he screeches. "The ball is nearly twelve thousand pounds and look at that beautiful sight! Four hundred seventy-two feet above the street. Two thousand six hundred eighty-eight Waterford crystals make up that ball."

The clock above his head keeps ticking. *Fifteen, fourteen, thirteen.* I crane my neck, still trying to make eye contact with Jake, but it's no use—he's too far away. I scream his name until my voice is hoarse, but I can barely hear myself over the deafening roar of the crowd.

"Grab someone you love, because it's almost time for that New Year's kiss!" Seacrest squeals. Ali and Chloe each slip an ice-cold hand through mine, and Chloe gives me a reassuring squeeze. With each passing second, I feel any lingering sense of hope drain from my body. I'm almost out of time; once this night ends, Jake will be gone, and I'll have lost my chance forever.

"THREE . . . TWO . . . ONE . . . HAPPY NEW YEAR!"

Confetti rains down on us as the crowd explodes into cheers. Fireworks shoot through the air as "Auld Lang Syne" blasts through the speakers. Everyone around me is hugging and kissing but I'm frozen in place, my eyes never leaving Jake. The other guests onstage hug him, and he gives them all a limp smile, sending a halfhearted wave to the crowd. My heart sinks. It's over. I've lost my chance.

The camera pans through the crowd. Images of couples kissing are broadcast around us as the music transitions to Frank Sinatra's "New York, New York."

And then, it happens.

The camera returns to Trixie. I see myself behind her on the big screen. My eyes are red, and my face is streaked with tears. It's a less than ideal look. Jake has just pulled back from hugging Fergie when his head turns toward the screen behind him. He freezes in place. His shoulders go rigid. He sees me.

He whips his head around, narrowing his eyes as he scans the crowd. Just then, the teenage girl gang swoops in front of me. Little Ali has her hands on her hips, her eyes narrowed.

"We called the number you gave us, and some jerk named Vinny answered," she sneers. "How stupid do you think we are?"

I'm contemplating the best way to answer this when Seacrest's voice erupts through the speakers. It's the first time I've ever heard him sound anything other than cool, calm, and collected.

"Hey, man, what are you doing?" I look up and see Jake beside him, trying to wrestle the microphone from his grip. Seacrest holds on tight, his brow wrinkled in confusion. The pom-pom on his cap jiggles as Jake shakes his arm. Undeterred, Jake presses his lips to the mic.

"Lexi!" Everyone around me freezes. I take this opportunity to shove past the teens and lean my body over the fence.

"Jake!" But the roar of the crowd drowns out my voice. I twist my head around frantically, looking for a way to get higher. Then suddenly, a microphone appears in front of my face. Turning, I see Trixie's face beaming at me. She nods encouragingly. I take a deep breath before shouting into it.

"Jake!"

Our eyes meet, and Jake's face lights up like the sun. Shoving Seacrest out of the way, he leaps from the stage. At first, everyone is confused. Fans scream and surge toward him, grabbing at his clothes. But then, the cameras zoom in on me, and people register what's happening. The crowd parts like the Red Sea to let him through, and he jogs across the gravel, never breaking eye contact.

Then, finally, he's standing right in front of me. His chest is heaving as he grips the metal barricade. The tip of his nose is pink, and a cold mist escapes through his lips.

"Hey."

"Hey."

We stand there for a long moment, drinking each other in. Then, we break into nervous laughter when we both attempt to speak at the same time.

"Jake, I—" I start, just as Jake blurts out, "I'm an idiot."

"Oh, sorry," we say in unison.

"You go first," I offer as Jake blurts again, "You talk. I'll listen."

A beat passes, and neither of us says a word. Then Jake leans forward, taking my cheeks in his gloved hands.

"I'm so sorry, Lexi. I never should have said those things about your life and your family. It was completely out of line. And you were right all along. Vinny was playing me. He even changed our duet at the last minute just for press, and I . . . *god,* I just missed you so much."

I cover my hands with his.

"I'm sorry too," I say. "I can't even explain how much I missed you. I don't know why I ever doubted you. I was just scared, and I got in my own head."

Jake tucks a strand of hair behind my ear. "I never should have asked you to go on tour with me. I know how important your job is, and I promise, from now on, I'm going to do what I can to accommodate *your* schedule."

"Well, as it turns out, I'm no longer working at the restaurant," I say. "So, I guess I'm wondering . . . is there any chance the offer to join you on tour is still open?"

A funny look passes over Jake's face, and he shakes his head.

"Unfortunately, that offer is closed, because the tour has been postponed. I wasn't ready to leave New York. Or you. So as of next month, if you want to see me, it'll have to be at the Imperial Theater, where I'll be performing a twelve-week stint as Marius in *Les Misérables.*"

"Seriously?" I squeal.

Jake nods. "Yes, seriously. Looks like you're going to be getting more than your fill of Broadway shows." He leans closer, his chocolate eyes melting. "Now do I get to kiss you or what?"

"I suppose that seems fitting."

Jake grins as he slips his hands under the barricade, attempting to move it out of the way, when I put out a hand to stop him.

"Hey, what are you doing?" I glance around nervously. "You can't just move that."

Jake's chest ripples with laughter. "Man, even after all this time, you're still such a rule follower."

"Yes, I am. But you like me anyway."

Jake's expression grows serious as he shakes his head.

"No, I don't like you. I love you, Alexa Danielle Berman." And with that, he leaps over the barricade, closing the space between us. When he presses his lips against mine, his kiss is filled with so much longing and relief and sheer happiness that it takes my breath away.

Somewhere in the distance, I hear a loud cheer from the crowd and sense the flashing of cameras. When we finally break apart, his eyes lock with mine.

"I mean it. I love you," he breathes. "You've always been more than a muse to me. You are everything, and I'm never going to take you for granted again."

"I love you, too." He kisses me again, and I melt into his arms. The world behind us fades into the background as Ryan Seacrest's voice echoes through the speakers.

Jake wraps an arm around me as we turn back toward the stage. The Backstreet Boys have made their way up there, their arms draped around one another, kicking out their legs as they dance to Frank Sinatra. And is that . . . Ali in the middle?

I spot Jake and myself on the screen behind them, a video of our kiss playing on a continuous loop. The press is going to have a field day with this one, but for once, I couldn't care less.

"There's nothing quite like live TV, am I right, folks?" Seacrest says, flashing a dazzling smile at the camera. "Except love, and fireworks, and maybe New York City. It's magic every year, and something tells me this year is going to be the best one yet. Happy New Year, America! Don't change that channel. We'll be right back."

Acknowledgments

It's wild to be writing acknowledgments for *Till There Was You*. I'm still pinching myself that a story I conceived while folding laundry during COVID lockdown is now a real book in the hands of readers.

It takes a village to raise a child, and the same is true of book babies. Publishing *Till There Was You* wouldn't have been possible without the help of so many people, all of whom have my eternal gratitude.

First and foremost, I want to thank my incredible agent, Melissa Edwards, who pulled my manuscript out of the slush pile and enjoyed it enough to miss *RuPaul's Drag Race*. None of this would have been possible without you, and I'm so appreciative of your tireless support. I'm grateful to my phenomenal editor, Sallie Lotz, who shaped this book into its best possible self and shepherded me through the publication process. Most importantly, she cracked Jake's reason for ghosting, a plot point that plagued me for countless drafts. I can't wait to write another book together!

I want to extend my gratitude to everyone on the St. Martin's team, including my copyeditor, Sara Thwaite; my publicist, Meghan Harrington; my marketing team, Kejana Ayala and Brant Janeway; and everyone else who had a hand in the production process. A special thanks to Olga Grlic for designing the cover of my dreams, and Petra Braun for illustrating it.

Jane Driver was the first person to ever read pages of *Till There Was You*. Her thoughtful feedback and careful line edits are an inextricable part of this story, and I hear her voice in my head every time I read it. I feel incredibly lucky to have befriended someone so talented.

The first draft of *Till There Was You* was composed in Jennifer Close's Catapult workshop. Jennifer, I'm incredibly thankful for your continuous support and guidance. Having your blurb on the front cover is truly a full-circle moment. Thank you to my workshop buddies: Georgia Silverman, George Gao, and Jennifer Ku. In an incredible stroke of luck, this workshop introduced me to my CPs, who have become two of my closest friends. Ellie McDonough and Haylie Swenson, you are my MVPs. Words cannot express my gratitude to you both for reading a million drafts, editing my query letters, and supporting me through every step of publication. I never want to write a book without you. Thank you, thank you, thank you.

I've never worked in a restaurant or cooked outside of my own home, but Chef Kelly English patiently answered all my questions about chef life, culinary school, and working in professional kitchens. I'm also indebted to Leah Konen, whose terrific developmental edits made this book much stronger.

Ambriel McIntyre helped me infuse emotion into this story when my cold Aquarius heart struggled to do so. You're such a great friend and I am incredibly fortunate to have you in my life. My *Frazzled* coeditor, Andrew Knott, not only proofread multiple drafts but also makes me laugh every day. Thanks for always saying exactly the right thing. A special thank-you to Craig Mutzman for inspiring Lexi's backstory.

Many (many) people were early readers of *Till There Was You*. Thank you to Lauren Ablondi-Olivo, Bobbie Armstrong, Elana Klein,

ACKNOWLEDGMENTS 307

Jenna Lowy Becker, Sarah T. Dubb, Blair Hurley, Lauren Spinabelli, and Sarah Adler. I want to give a special shout-out to Gracie Beaver-Kairis, who gave critical feedback and graciously obliged every time I texted, "How can I make this joke funnier?" All your feedback made this book what it is today.

Writing became a life raft for me during COVID, and I am beyond grateful for the incredible community of writers I met online before Elon broke Twitter. I can't list you all here, but I am grateful for your friendship. You inspire me daily.

I'm blessed to have an incredibly strong support system. The Real Housewives of Harrisburg are the best group of friends a girl could ask for. A special thanks to Emily Halper and Jackie Rubin, who made me feel so special during every publication milestone. Emily, your suggestion to have Madison and Jake do a concert together changed everything. Jessica Katz, your enthusiasm means the world to me. #TeamMelissa, you guys are the best, and I'd be lost without you! I'm grateful for my whole family, especially my mom. If you didn't keep asking me, "When are you going to write that book already?" I might never have done it. Jewish guilt is a powerful motivator. And I'm forever indebted to my two gorgeous babies, Jordana and Ezra, who make me want to be the best version of myself.

Finally, I want to thank my husband, Avi, my tireless champion and most loyal fan. Thank you for being the best proofreader, for doing everything in your power to help me succeed, for taking me to see Harry Styles in concert (twice!), and most importantly, for lending your dimple to Jake. You are my best friend and I love you more than anything.

Leslie Gilbert Photography

LINDSAY HAMEROFF is a writer, humorist, and former English teacher raised in Baltimore, Maryland, and based in Harrisburg, Pennsylvania. Her writing has been featured in *McSweeney's Internet Tendency, The Belladonna, Weekly Humorist,* and other outlets. She also coedits *Frazzled,* a parenting humor site. *Till There Was You* is her first novel.